Next to Life Itself

To whoever
Hope to run into
you again

a novel by

John Wilsterman

John Wilsterman

Wave Writer Publications, LLC
john@johnwilsterman.com

John Wilsterman

Next to Life Itself

Published by Wave Writer Publications, LLC
Townsend, GA 31331
www.johnwilsterman.com

Printed in the United States of America

Dedicated to millions of women who have battled breast cancer, their devoted families and the medical community who tirelessly wage war against this deadly disease. These are our heroes.

John Wilsterman

Next to Life Itself

Part One
Chapter 1

Podunk isn't really in Iowa.

Neglected by interstates or railroads, Podunk had just a two lane ribbon of asphalt in and out, one blinking light intersection and a few buildings, a bank, grocery, hardware store and pharmacy. A lonely bus station and a good auto mechanic assured no one really got stuck there. You go elsewhere if you need anything. Nobody goes to Podunk except to get lost.

"Podunk" means small, remote and unimportant. The name itself might attract attention so the town wasn't really called that, which made it ideal for WITSEC, the Federal Witness Protection Program.

WITSEC knew how to hide people, but they outdid themselves concealing the first great villain of the twenty-first century, the architect of the biggest stock swindle of the new millennium, the genius behind the so-called, "Hole In The Wall Street Gang," a man once known as Wylie Schram, the disgraced CFO of the fallen oil conglomerate InCorps, now buried in profound obscurity under his new name of Daniel Conklin.

WITSEC had faked everything about him. They gave him fake credentials to go with a faked past. They altered his face so he looked like a poorly rendered police sketch from an unreliable witness. They plunked him in a community where he was a stranger to work at a profession for which he was not qualified. They tied his federal leash so short he could hardly flush his toilet without incrementing a tally on a bureaucrat's computer in Washington.

Four years ago Wylie Schram died in a horrible automobile accident. The nightly news showed the photos of the twisted wreck, graphic enough to convince skeptics and conspiracy theorists. Wylie Schram died and Americans were cheated out of the media lynch-mob his trial could have been. His closed casket slid quietly into the ground and in a few weeks America stopped talking about him.

Even more quietly, the feds launched the newly minted Daniel Conklin in the small town that wasn't in Iowa. And although it wasn't called "Podunk" either, the place qualified for its namesake. The town's street names ended at Third Avenue and C Street where the landscape resumed its monotonous farms, pastures and prairies.

Daniel Conklin's house stood across the road from a cow pen holding a few head of sullen Black Angus. The feds bought the house cheap, not to save taxpayers' money but because cheap attracted no attention. WITSEC made him a pharmacist's assistant, a job where he could fill bottles with drugs only under the supervision of a licensed pharmacist. The town's real pharmacist owned the drug store. Federal agents pretending to be rehabilitation therapists had persuaded the pharmacist to take Conklin on as a project, a man recovering from a severe accident who needed a low-stress job in a quiet place. The town, the pharmacy and the job fit WITSEC's criteria, and no one there knew the United States Department of Justice was involved.

Dan Conklin played his part to perfection. The Feds gave him an app for his smart-phone enabling him to serve as a short-study pill counter. Hiring Conklin made the drug the largest enterprise in town.

Daniel Conklin had been warned by his WITSEC handlers not to get close to anyone. Friends could be nosey and they talked. Information could get back to the gangsters looking for him. The folks in town talked about the "new guy" in clichés. "He likes to keep to himself." "He's the quiet type," and the one that could have passed as the town's motto, "To each his own."

Having exchanged hard time in a penitentiary for a different sort of prison, Daniel Conklin settled into a tolerable existence. But he lived under a threat that one day the thugs looking for him would step around the corner and put a bullet in his head. Or worse.

Uneventful days turned into months and then years. If he had expected a quarterly WITSEC newsletter or monthly statement from the feds, he didn't get them. His disappearance seemed complete. Even phone solicitors couldn't find him.

The newness of his new life dissipated and he settled into an existence where little changed. Every day he shaved and showered and ate something from the microwave. He would walk to work because the half mile up the slight hill was all the exercise he'd get.

Because it was his nature, Daniel Conklin devoted his days at the pharmacy making subtle improvements to the business. He easily mastered the cash register and the store's computer. He installed much needed upgrades to the pharmacy's software. He connected the store's data to the state medical record system. And without anyone taking much notice, he revolutionized the drug store into the town's first twenty-first century business. In fact the pharmacist had noted the improvements and tried to thank the rehab therapists who had recommend this exceptional employee, but he couldn't find them. Conklin's recommenders had been federal agents and were now assigned to other projects.

Daniel Conklin would stroll home after work, enduring the baleful gaze of the cows at the end of Third Avenue. He'd drink beer, eat more microwave food and watch TV until his eyelids drooped.

The memory of being one of the most powerful financiers in the world receded, as did the memories of barking orders at his staff, pulling all-nighters studying financial data, filling notebooks with strategies, monitoring worldwide markets, and shifting millions of dollars around the globe. Gone were the meetings, the negotiations, the handshakes and deals. Wylie Schram's unique talent of generating huge piles of money to feed a cash-hungry enterprise had vanished like his old identity.

And had been replaced with an acute form of loneliness.

Sitting in his threadbare recliner, empty beer cans at his feet and a half-eaten TV dinner at his elbow. A muted television flashed something he didn't watch. Thoughts of Denise beat through his head like the unrelenting drip of a leaky faucet. Threads of a guilty conscience twined through the lattice of lies and logic that led him to his current circumstance and deprived him of her.

He had loved Denise deeply. He had devastated her with his crimes, the disgrace the world heaped upon him, and the ultimate falsehood about his death.

An innocent woman, this woman he loved. And she had returned his love with passion and loyalty, even after his arrest. She probably still loved him, or at least the memory of him. Denise had known the real Wylie Schram. She knew him intimately… or thought she did.

The beer from the empty cans could not dull his pangs of guilt. Denise had given herself to him and he had deceived her. He hadn't trusted her with the secrets of his crimes. He let her believe he died in that car crash. To save his own worthless neck, he had to keep the truth from her that he still lived.

On the nights when his dream came, it was always the same: Denise still loved him, forgave him, and wanted to know why he waited so long. His subconscious brought the memory of how warm she felt, how she smelled and tasted, the way her body energized his. The memory made the thought of another woman seem like sacrilege, and he awoke at the cruelest hours of the morning, heart pounding, sweat soaking his sheets and tears his pillow.

In the sobering light of another day he knew he lacked the courage to tell her he still lived, or to let her see what he had chosen over their life together.

Each day a single temptation tormented him. Wasn't it possible for her to steal away and join him, here in the little town that wasn't in Iowa? Had WITSEC boxed him in too tight, and was the danger that great?

Four years after he arrived in the little town, his loneliness reached a sort of critical mass. Conklin spent another painful night struggling with a desire to reach out to Denise. The difference between this night and all the nights preceding it was that it ended with a plan.

On his lunch hour he visited the local public library and used his computer savvy to hack into the library's computer. He looked through their catalog for likely titles and found two that suited his purpose, "Love Lives On" by Louis Legrand and "Looking for a Godly Man" by Keith Mitchell.

He created an entry in the library's database showing that Denise had borrowed these books, and failed to return them by the due date. The library's computer sent a request to their processing service in a city hundreds of miles away, a place with railroads and freeways.

Denise was mailed an overdue library notice about books she never borrowed, from a library in a town she didn't know existed.

A day later, Conklin snuck back into the library and erased all evidence of his intrusion. If the Justice Department ever discovered what he had done, they would have grabbed him up and relocated him under a new identity. But days passed and then a week and then two weeks with no response. Either she hadn't received the overdue library note or she hadn't deciphered its message.

Or so he thought.

On the fifteenth day Daniel Conklin made an ordinary trip to his mailbox, and there was the letter he had longed for and dreaded. Out of habit he looked up and down the street to see if anyone was watching. Then shrugging off his paranoia, he took the letter inside to read it at his kitchen table.

A minute later he knew he had to call Bentley.

Bentley oversaw many duties for the Justice Department, which included the federal witness protection program. Because Wylie Schram was such a high profile criminal, Bentley had handled his disappearance personally. He alone knew who Daniel Conklin really was and where he was.

Conklin's call was answered immediately.

A mechanical voice said, "Leave a message." Conklin left his message.

The following morning his cell phone showed a reply waited for him. The same mechanical voice said, "Go to work as usual. We will contact you with further instructions."

He didn't know it then, but it would be his last day in the little town that wasn't in Iowa and his last day in WITSEC.

Chapter 2

Through a meandering but reliable process the library's computer sent a letter to a woman in New Jersey over a thousand miles away. The library's mailing service printed the envelope with library's return address, the woman's address and a "Postage Paid" stamp, but divulged nothing of its contents. The delivery of the letter prompted a popup to appear on the computer screen of a high ranking Department of Justice official known as Bentley.

Bentley saw the popup immediately and clicked on it. Apparently the woman in New Jersey had received a letter sent from the town where he had squirreled away his most prized protected witness. The letter had been delivered to the mailbox of Denise Oliver, someone who was not in the witness protection program but who nonetheless had been under mild surveillance for the last four years because of her connection to someone who was.

Bentley groped for the right term.

She was the "significant other" of his most brilliant success, the star of his career in a career of many stars, a witness hidden so deep that only he and the deputy attorney general knew the whereabouts and the true identity of the infamous and despised Wylie Schram.

Denise Oliver had not been married to but had been the girlfriend of Wylie Schram, who now went under the name of Daniel Conklin.

For the last four years Bentley's surveillance teams had cataloged the generalities of Denise Oliver's life: her mail, her phone calls, her bank accounts, credit cards, and tax returns. No one analyzed the data in Denise Oliver's file. It was there only on the possibility she might someday be important enough to require further scrutiny, such as if Wylie Schram tried to contact her or if those looking for him would use her to get to him. Bentley believed in being prepared for that contingency.

Protected witnesses were supposed to hide from their past, but sometimes loneliness made them disregard the rules they had been ordered to live by. They often tried to reconnect with someone from their previous life.

Bentley looked for references to the letter but nowhere saw its contents. It annoyed him that something he wanted hadn't been made readily available. If it rated a popup, didn't it rate a little extra legwork? He knew he worked his team hard, but did he have to spell everything out for them?

Bentley strongly believed in Americans' right to privacy. However, if it interfered with his objectives, such rights could be overlooked. Bentley sent a snide email to his aide asking him, if it wasn't too much trouble, would he please obtain the contents of the letter.

Within a couple of hours Bentley had photos of the overdue library note. His operative had entered Denise Oliver's home using a key they kept for that purpose. Without disturbing anything else in the house he had spread out the letter's single page on the woman's kitchen table and took several photos.

The letter from the library appeared to be a standard computer-generated overdue notice, listing the unreturned titles and the total fine to date. "Love Lives On" by Louis Legrand and "Looking for a Godly Man" by Keith Mitchell. Bentley may not have known much about Denise, but he did know Daniel Conklin, aka Wylie Schram. The subterfuge brought a smile to his face.

"Daniel, aren't you the clever one."

It was a clear attempt by his witness to communicate with someone from his past, which was strictly forbidden. He'd have to come down hard on Conklin. After being a perfect witness for four years!

Bentley knew Denise Oliver had not heard from her boyfriend in all that time and didn't expect to because she thought he had died in a car crash. Now she gets this overdue library note from a place she never heard of. With those specific titles, she didn't have to be a genius to conclude the note might be a coded message.

Bentley thought about the car crash his crew had staged four years ago. Every faked detail had been arranged for plausibility. Wylie Schram's death had been instantaneous. The body had registered high alcohol content. No one had been asked to view the mangled corps on a morgue table. Schram had no close family. In addition to the crowd of morbid spectators and a phalanx of news reporters, Schram's stark funeral service had drawn only Denise.

Bentley could imagine her sitting at her kitchen clutching the overdue notice from the library in the town that wasn't in Iowa, and asking the question, "Does this mean what I think it means?"

This time Bentley agent's had been more thorough. Apparently Denise Oliver's trash held several unsatisfactory handwritten notes, which she had discarded. A link on Bentley's computer screen pointed to more photos, which were taken of the crumpled up notes after his agent had retrieved them from her trash. His agent also provided typed transcripts of her notes.

It became obvious to Bentley that Denise now knew what had been unknown to her for the last four years. Wylie Schram hadn't died in that car crash. Somehow he had been in hiding all that time. From the news stories about Russian mobsters, she probably understood why he had to hide to protect his life. Perhaps she concluded that he might be in witness protection.

Bentley was good at paralleling the thought process of others. Although Denise Oliver had been innocent and ignorant of Wylie Schram's crimes, it became obvious to the whole world when he'd been arrested and indicted. She might understand his life would be in danger if he were found.

But peoples' lives can be complicated. The reappearance of an old boyfriend might not be welcome if she had a new boyfriend. Bently scanned Denise's file for new relationships. He discovered there had been no new boyfriend.

So Denise, after rejoicing in discovering that her lover hadn't died in a car crash, had soul-searched about contacting him. Apparently she had started several letters, found them unsatisfactory and crumpled the sheets of paper into her trash.

Denise now knew that her old boyfriend still lived. She worked at an actuarial firm with massive databases so she also had the means to find his real address. And his new name. This posed a huge threat to Bentley's carefully laid plans.

Bentley read the aborted messages from photos of her crumpled and flattened notes. They all expressed the expected sentiments: what a shock it was to discover him alive, how much she missed him, and at that point her communication skills had bogged down. Denise did not suggest that they try to meet. She did not express that she would love to see him. One of the letters contained a half sentence, "Maybe it's best we…" Bentley's forehead wrinkled. What, that we don't meet or try to see each other? Because of the danger to him or was she trying to protect her own emotional wellbeing?

Bentley scanned the list of other mail she had been receiving: magazines, bills, junk mail and parcels from a mail-order pharmaceutical company. He frowned when he could not find a list of what prescription drugs she took. He fired off another rebuke to the team leader for lack of diligence, knowing he'd have the list in twenty minutes.

He then looked at the rest of Denise Oliver's surveillance file. A picture taken over four years ago showed an attractive, professional-looking woman smiling up at Wylie Schram. Wylie stared straight into the camera looking bored and cool at the same time. His right arm encircled her slim waist protectively while she beamed at him in profile.

Bentley checked the file for more recent photographs of Denise Oliver. He had her passport photo, a picture as unremarkable as anyone's but it was an older photo and there was no evidence she had ever used it. Since she was only under mild surveillance, there had been no reason for his team to take more photos of Denise Oliver. In all those four years, the only significant event in her life that interested WITSEC had been Wylie Schram's coded note.

But now Denise Oliver knew that she should be "Looking for a Godly Man" and that her "Love Lives On." Instead of making phone calls, writing a joyous response or packing a bag and setting out for the hard to find little town which was not in Iowa, Denise had spent a tortuous day trying to compose those aborted letters. It was obvious to Bentley she had something else to tell her Wylie.

Bentley ordered a complete analysis of Denise's recent activity, her internet access, her daily movements and a couple of recent photos, and specifically what drugs she had received from the pharmaceutical company. By the end of the day he had his answers.

The new photos told nearly the entire story which her medical records, now in Bentley's hands, completely supported. The healthy smiling woman from the photo four years ago had become a horrible caricature of herself. His agent's long distance telephoto lens captured a figure wrapped in a bathrobe, bent over, staring out her front window, her face drawn, her eyes dulled. The medical records brought tears to Bentley's eyes, but he smiled slightly, not at the poor woman's wretched condition, but because understanding her situation gave him powerful leverage over Wylie Schram, leverage Bentley would gladly use to obtain the bigger prize.

Chapter 3

Someone else had noticed.

Wylie Schram had stolen from him one and a half billion dollars.

Bogdan Ivanovich Vladoseev had never accepted the story that the former CFO of InCorps had died in a car crash.

It was just too much money.

Vladoseev knew his obsession with Wylie Schram and the money was irrational. He already had more money than he could spend in ten lifetimes.

He could afford to place a watch on Denise Oliver, which he did for four years, and he would have continued to search for Schram until he spent his final ruble. Even at today's outrageous exchange rates.

Four years of patient surveillance was difficult, especially under the noses of US federal agents, but it paid off. Suddenly so much activity! The feds were easy to spot because they rode around in big black SUV's, parked in plain sight. They favored Dunkin Donut coffee because of the donuts. His men could spot a federal agent from two kilometers. White cups with orange and pink lettering. Easy to spot. Easy to elude, especially when they were clueless about who else is watching.

When the feds upped their activity around Denise Oliver, Vladoseev's men rang their boss's bell immediately.

The feds had left this poor woman alone for four years, and now they break into her house and take long distance photos of her. All this flurry of G-men around Denise Oliver confirmed Vladoseev's four year old conspiracy theory.

Because Vladoseev's men were better paid and more dedicated, he had known of her cancer long before the feds did. Vladoseev even worried she would die before she could lure the wily Wylie Schram out of hiding.

Vladoseev smiled at his own mental play on words. English was almost as rich a language as his native Russian. As a boy back in Russia, he had watched American cartoons and his favorite was the Road Runner with the hapless Wile E. Coyote. "Beep! Beep!" needed no translation.

Now suddenly the feds are all over Denise Oliver. Vladoseev's heavy face creased into another smile.

His time for patience had passed. Now it was time to strike.

The wily Wylie had been a brilliant executive of InCorps but his antics had brought the company down. The heat from RICO investigators burned all who were involved. The Department of Justice had squeezed Wylie

Schram for his testimony that eventually steered the investigation toward Vladoseev himself. Only the skillful maneuvers of his lawyers had kept indictments from landing in his lap. Wylie Schram was due a whole lot of Vladoseev's kind of payback.

But Vladoseev wanted more than revenge. He wanted to recover what Schram had taken from him. It was an astronomically large amount of money. The number reverberated around in Vladoseev's head like an unsecured cannonball on the deck of a ship: one billion, four hundred ninety-seven million, seven hundred sixty-eight thousand, and four hundred and thirty-three dollars. And some change.

They could keep the change. Why be greedy?

Bogdan Ivanovich Vladoseev's reputation was also at stake. Nobody took his money. Nobody testified against him and lived. That bastard Schram had squealed on his own boss, Ray Suffield, and sent him to prison. He didn't say quite enough to send Vladoseev to jail, but still he had managed to steal and hide a billion and a half dollars, a sum Vladoseev's own experts declared was too large to hide. Vladoseev had invested millions of his own money with Schram and Suffield. Vladoseev felt the billion and a half was what those *ublyudki* owed him.

Vladoseev ran his empire from one of the smaller ballrooms of the Barclay Hotel on East 48th Street in Manhattan, which he had set up as an office and decorated in Czarist splendor with huge mirrors framed in gold lining all four walls. He chose one of the smaller ballrooms because the hotel's customers rented ballrooms, which brought in revenue. Why shouldn't he turn a buck?

Born in the wrong country, Vladoseev's natural talent didn't get much love from the former Soviet Union. They didn't appreciate entrepreneurs. His family had not been politically connected, which had doomed Bogdan Ivanovich to a miserable life in the factories or more likely, due to his nature, condemned him to the risky life of a black marketer. Unauthorized capitalism in the USSR brought you a one way train ride to the gulags if the government caught you or a bullet in a dark alley from the competition. When he could Vladoseev had bolted to a place where his ability and ruthlessness could be appreciated. Expecting America to be a wonderland of free enterprise, he found the business environment here to be nearly as stifling as post-Soviet Russia. Americans had more regulations than... the Russian proverb came to him, *osennikh drozdy,* autumn blackbirds. So to succeed in America you had to keep a low profile, hire an army of lawyers and use a strong arm when necessary.

All he wanted was to make a buck, live like a king and make more. And the decades since he had come to America had been very good to him. But here most of his business ventures were considered criminal by the *neprosveshchennyy*, and he lived under constant threat from federal, state and local police.

Fortunately he had a capable ally in one of his countrymen, his old friend Nicolay Karolovsky, a former security specialist for the Russian FSB, the agency that had derived from the Soviet KGB. Karolovsky managed the surveillance project on Denise Oliver and had prepared the report Vladoseev had just finished reading.

Vladoseev looked up from the report. His lieutenant slouched nearby in a gilded chair. Technically they were both in the same room, the ballroom turned office, but because the room was so large, Karolovsky sat nearly thirty feet away with a giant Kazakhstan rug stretched out between them.

Not wanting to shout, Vladoseev motioned him nearer. Karolovsky stood and took another chair nearer his boss's ornate desk.

"Four years and they leave her alone. Now they break into her house and take telephoto pictures of her."

"I think she received a letter." Karolovsky said. Everyone who worked for Vladoseev spoke English, but Karolovsky's accent still harkened to his native Hrodna. "From you know who."

"Schram?"

"Who else? The woman has no life. She used to go to work every day but now she spends all her days indoors. She no longer goes to work. She used to go to the clinic every Tuesday, but stopped going. Suddenly the feds are entering her house. Our man saw flashes, like he was using a camera flash. You can see it even across the street. Sometimes those guys aren't very careful."

"Pictures of what?"

"Our guy stayed in the car like he's supposed to, but he used his binoculars. He thinks they were taking pictures of something on her kitchen table."

"Not her breakfast?"

"The feds went through her trash and spread it out on the table. Took pictures of it. Put everything back the way it was and left."

Vladoseev points to the report. "Then a day later, we see someone taking pictures of her through her living room window with a big lens."

Karolovsky nods. "Our man is in different car every day. Parks in different spot so nobody notices."

After four years of constant surveillance, Vladoseev had built up a fleet of suitable nondescript cars from which his men could watch. The federal agents never noticed a pattern, which lowered the chances their man would be spotted.

"All this activity means something. You think a letter came from Schram."

Karolovsky nodded. "Let's say she gets a letter from Schram, who is supposed to be dead, but you never believed it, boss. We know Schram didn't phone her. We got her phone records and the Feds do too. She only gets a few phone calls a month. We know where they all come from, mostly related to her condition, like from the clinics, insurance and Medco. Now the feds go through her trash and take pictures inside her house. The feds got all excited about something. What else besides Wiley Schram?"

Vladoseev rose from his big leather chair. The ballroom had no windows but the gilded mirrors on the walls made it look like the room had a view. He studied his reflection in one of them.

"Until her cancer came along, the only thing in her life was Schram. The only reason the feds care about her at all has to do with Schram. Now she gets all this attention, which confirms to me he is still alive. Schram is trying to, how you say, 'Reach out' to her. So why doesn't he send her an email?"

Karolovsky shook his head. "The feds read her email too. If he is in witness protection they would slice and dice every email she gets. She works only from home now. She used her home computer a lot this week. We can hack into it, but her firm is an actuarial company. They use lots of security and encrypt everything, so we can't really see what she's looking at, but I think the feds can."

Vladoseev snorted. "But they already know where he is."

"Schram would be clever with his message to her. If he sends a letter he would code it to look like something else hoping the Feds won't catch on. But they do catch on. Perhaps Schram did not know the feds would still be watching her. He certainly wouldn't know we were watching her. We don't want to risk our guy getting caught so we can't do what the feds do, like break into her house. The Feds will put many cameras and watchers on her. This poor woman will have cameras in her toilette. Perhaps we should pull our guy off before they spot him."

Vladoseev shook his head. "It's the only link we have to Schram. Our guy is good isn't he? He's careful?"

19

"Yes, but with all the government agents..."

"They're not looking for us. They will be focused only on her. My guess is she figured out where he is now. She needed to know he is alive and a small clue where to look. If it's too obvious, witness protection program is all over him not her. The game they are playing is they're trying to leave him where he is and see if the situation between these two escalates."

Karolovsky frowned. "We must be careful, Bogdan Ivanovich. So far the Feds don't know we're watching her. If she makes a call we'll know where. But what if she finds where he is and sends a letter? How do we intercept her mail?"

Vladoseev smiled, "We do it like that movie."

"What movie?"

"With Lana Turner and John Garfield, *The Postman Always Rings Twice.*"

"Never heard of it."

"Old fashioned American detective novel. They made it into a movie and then remade it twenty-five years later. Typically the first version is better, but Americans like to push tried and true concepts. Everyone is already familiar and it's easier to promote. That's what we'll do. We push a tried and true concept only in a new light."

Karolovsky lowereded his eyebrows. "Boss, when you get these ideas in your head… sometimes you don't explain them too good."

"Use your imagination, Kolya. Now that she has a clue about lover boy, Denise will find his address by looking through her databases. She will discover the little *derevnya* they hid him in. She'll appreciate the need for secrecy so she won't call him. She'll put her reply to him in her own mailbox, mixed in with her bill payments, to hide her little love note from the feds.

"The day she posts that letter, the postman will come to Denise Oliver's mailbox twice."

20

Chapter 4

With each passing day, the woman in the house seemed to step closer to her grave.

Vladoseev's surveillance team parked within eyeshot of Denise Oliver's house. Their watcher arrived around sunup every morning and was relieved every three hours. At night they drove around the neighborhood at random intervals, driving right past the federal surveillance teams who had grown bored with the sparse and uninteresting traffic.

Karolovsky had given them new, very critical orders. If Denise puts anything into her mailbox, the watcher was to call immediately.

A week passed and she hardly made an appearance. Occasionally Vladoseev's man saw fleeting movement within the house, but Denise hadn't gone to the clinic again and came outside only to get what few scraps of mail the postman delivered. The watcher recorded the times when her door would open. Several seconds after the door opened a hunched figure would make halting steps down the porch step, inch along the sidewalk, one foot after the other, clutching her sweater close to her throat as if the wind would blow it away. She would open the mailbox door and retrieve her mail, then slowly return to the house.

She put nothing in the mailbox.

Getting a US Postal Service truck had been easy. His agents bought an actual US Postal Service truck at an out-of-state auction. They loaded it on a flatbed and hauled it to one of their chop shops. They removed all the nicks and dents and repainted it to look new. Then they ran it through potholes and mud puddles to make it look used again.

The call from their watcher came a few days later.

Denise had not made an appearance in several days. When her front door opened Karolovsky's spy nearly choked on his bagel. The hunched figure came creeping out of the door. With rising excitement, Karolovsky's man noted that she held a single envelope in her thin hand. The effort to open the mailbox door seem to exhaust her. She had to stop and rest. She finally got the door open and removed her accumulated mail. Then she placed the envelope inside. Another effort was required to raise the orange flag on the side of the mailbox. Karolovsky's agent nearly jumped out of his car to help her.

He made the call. It was time for Karolovsky to make a move.

Nicolay Karolovsky detested uniforms. Dressing up like a postman didn't suit his sense of style at all, but driving the postal truck with the steering wheel on the wrong side of the cab was the kind of challenge he liked. He also liked the tingling sensation that came from trying to sneak something out from under the noses of US federal agents.

Karolovsky knew the neighborhood well, all squared blocks with five or six houses on each side, sparse trees, power poles bordered the street. It was an easy neighborhood for surveillance. Denise Oliver's street had little pedestrian traffic, just a few people rushing in straight lines paying hardly any attention to anything. He knew where all the federal agents were parked. The feds' routine varied little from day to day. When the feds saw a car coming down the street, they chatted up the event on their radio. "Blue Toyota heading east on Pelletier. At the stop sign. Turning south. Looks like the blonde who works at the Starbucks."

"Hey, number four. It's your turn to get coffee, only the Dunkin Donuts is closer." The mild excitement subsided and they waited for the next event.

Karolovsky approached in the fake mail truck. He knew the precise moment when he came into view of the first federal agent, and that's when he began opening mailboxes. Karolovsky made a show of reaching inside and closing up the box. Then he'd move on to the next one. He wore buff colored latex gloves to avoid leaving fingerprints. He listened to the agent's chatter on his own radio which was tuned to the fed's frequency. The ever-diligent federal agents discussed his arrival on the scene.

"Here comes the US Postal Service, a little early today."

"Neither rain, nor sleet nor gloom of night…"

"Right. That's why it takes two weeks to mail a letter across town."

"I'll swap jobs with him. Better benefits and he actually gets to do something."

By the time he reached Denise Oliver's mailbox, Karolovsky's heart was pounding. He forced himself to slouch like a job-weary postal worker. He pretended to go through stacks of mail sitting in bins on his left, all of it fake of course. Vladoseev's planning was meticulous. If Karolovsky felt any threat from the watching federal agents he was to gun the truck's engine and speed out of there. His watcher at the end of the street would move to block any pursuit. They had placed several more men in vehicles along the escape route, with orders to get in the way if the federals gave chase. Once he got clear, Karolovsky would then abandon the postal truck and make it on foot to a public place, change clothes in a men's room and disappear somewhere for a while. It was a good enough contingency, but he hoped that they never had to use it.

He opened her mailbox. There was a single envelope on the flat bottom of the mailbox. Karolovsky fetched it out. His hammering heart hammered even more when he saw address written in shaky script. The address read, "Daniel Conklin, 725 C Street, Warhego, NE 69023" Karolovsky photographed it with his cell phone and sent the photo to Vladoseev. He then returned the letter to the mailbox. He drove to the next mailbox and repeated his pantomime. By the time he opened the third mailbox his heart had slowed to near-normal. He rounded a corner and was out of sight of the federal agents. He took out his cell phone again and texted the address to Vladoseev. Nicolay Karolovsky turned away from the neighborhood in Elizabeth, New Jersey and got on the turnpike to return to Manhattan.

An hour later, to the surprise of the federal agents watching Denise Oliver's house, a second postman came that morning. The arrival of a second postman did raise the alarm and the federal agents aggressively pounced on the frightened postal worker. After confiscating Denise's letter, the feds sat the postal worker in the back of the van, interrogated him and, when a supervisor back at headquarters realized what had happened, let the postman go.

Bentley issued orders to put the letter on a federal jet and fly it to an airport near Warhego, Nebraska. There they couriered it to the local post office, unintentionally setting a world record for speedy delivery of any letter from New Jersey to the little town.

Chapter 5

Karolovsky drove directly to the Barclay Hotel in Manhattan. He left the mail truck in an alley a few blocks away. US Mail trucks were seen parked in alleys everywhere in the city. One of their men would retrieve it later.

When he reached the office he could sense his boss' excitement.

"Kolya, you have done a great job! He is now called Daniel Conklin and lives in Warhego, Nebraska. Here it is on the map." Vladoseev pointed to a computer screen which displayed Google Maps.

Karolovsky peered over his boss's shoulder. "Where in hell is Warhego?"

"In Nebraska. That's 'War he go,'" Vladoseev chuckled.

"Funny, Boss. You sound like Gomer Pyle."

"Go to Denver. Rent a car. Go stuff *ublyduka* in the trunk and drive him back here."

"Boss, we should move carefully, here. The feds have the letter. They'll be watching his mailbox now in, uh, Warhego. To catch us, uh, I mean me."

Vladoseev seemed to consider this.

"Don't wait. Get out there before they move him. This is a hot trail. We can't let him get away! If I were the feds, I'd stuff him in a trunk and drive like hell."

Unfortunately Karolovsky's flight to Denver didn't leave until eight in the morning.

In Denver he rented a car and used the GPS function of his smart phone, which told him to head east on I-76. He arrived in Warhego in the afternoon and drove around the tiny town at least four times. He saw no one, not even a pedestrian. He drove past the house on C Street several times. The house seemed as empty as the town. If there were federals around he didn't spot them.

He went up and knocked on the door. No response.

Karolovsky called Vladoseev.

"Is he gone?" The anxiety in Vladoseev's voice was obvious.

"Nobody home, but he may be at work. His car is parked in the driveway. And I guess we don't know where he works."

"If you can find out, fine. Otherwise wait for him to come home."

"Thanks, Boss. I can go door to door. There aren't too many houses here. This place is really for the *krest'yane*."

"Be careful, Koyla. The *krest'yane* may be suspicious of strangers."
"No problem, I'll be Mister Friendly."
Karolovsky knew wasn't dressed like a local. He wore slacks, a shirt and jacket that looked like a stolen costume from a "Twilight" movie. No one answered his knock at the house next door so he went to the house on the other side of Schram's house. No one answered there either. He walked back to his car and stood with his hands on his hips staring at Schram's front door.
"You looking for Dan?"
The voice surprised Karolovsky. He spun around to find where it came from. Across the street was what looked like a cattle pen. A man dressed in worn, muddy boots, faded jeans and work shirt stood on the other side of a barbed wire fence. A heavily soiled and crumpled straw hat shaded his eyes.
Karolovsky walked across the street and faced the man who managed to look comfortable standing ankle deep in cow manure.
Karolovsky smiled. "I just drove out from Denver." He stuck out his hand. The cowboy seemed unsure whether to take the hand or not, since his gloves were also covered with cow manure.
Karolovsky kept smiling with his hand out. "Dan's family has some insurance business to take care of. Paperwork... I need to get some signatures and get back tonight right away."
The cowboy tilted his head as if to get a better look. Slowly he took off a rawhide glove. "What'd you say your name was?"
"Samuel Bernstein. They call me Sam." Karolovsky had to use his best American to charm this cowboy, and he knew didn't look Jewish. He was a tall, skinny Russian with red hair and pale blue eyes, but the moniker had worked before.
The cowboy grinned and stuck his hand across the barbwire fence. The two men shook, briefly contesting for the strongest grip.
"Didn't know he had any family. He don't talk much," the cowboy said as if he spoke for the whole town. "But you're likely to find him up at the drugstore."
"Which one?" Karolovsky asked.
"Aint but one. Just climb that hill. Half a mile on the left."
Karolovsky worked that out in his head. Eight hundred meters, an easy, ten minute walk.
He thanked the man and drove his rental car north. He easily found the drugstore and parked across the street at the hardware store, the only place

25

with a parking lot large enough for more than a few cars. Or trucks. His rental looked conspicuous among all the dusty pickups. He parked between two of them and watched the store across the street.

No one came or went. He called Vladoseev.

"You want me to go in? They might have security cameras."

"Which franchise is it? CVS or Walgreens?"

"No, Boss. This is just somebody's drugstore."

"They might not have security cameras. Everyone knows everyone. Low crime."

"Okay, I'll risk it."

Karolovsky got out of the car, removed his jacket and rolled up his sleeves. He approached the drugstore looking for outside surveillance. He knew such cameras could be almost invisible but people in this town probably were less circumspect. Even inside he didn't see any cameras, but he kept his head turning anyway. The place seemed empty except for a bored, pimple-faced youth slouching behind the cash register counter. Karolovsky had never met Wylie Schram but knew from photos what he used to look like. But surely the feds would have altered his face.

It was close to quitting time from the look of the cashier's body language. He shifted his weight to a new slump and gave Karolovsky a perfunctory, "Can I help you?"

Karolovsky took a gamble. "Is Dan here?"

The pimple-faced cashier pointed to the back of the store. "He's in the pharmacy."

Karolovsky's heart began pounding. He walked slowly toward the back of the store. It wasn't a long walk. Behind a pharmacy counter he saw a man who looked around forty and did not resemble Wylie Schram but had similar height and build. The man's hair was dark, not sandy brown. The nose didn't match the photos. The other changes were subtle, but still he didn't look like Wylie Schram.

"Dan?"

The man looked up from notes spread on the counter. He didn't say anything but something crossed his face. An expression, a thought, a question.

Karolovsky sped up and was nearly at the counter when the man turned toward a door and said very rapidly, "Excuse me. I'll be with you in a minute." In an instant he slipped through a rear door. The door closed behind him and there was a loud click.

Karolovsky spotted a security camera mounted high on the wall and froze in mid stride. The camera's lens was pointed right at him. He turned his head away and hurried over to the door. He tried the handle. Locked. It was a stout steel door in a steel frame, with a key operated deadbolt, not something he could quickly pick or bust down.

Karolovsky left the drugstore and headed around to the back of the store. The back entrance was also locked. The rear parking lot was empty. Karolovsky returned to his rental car across the street and called Vladoseev. He gave a brief update.

"Are you sure it's him?" Karolovsky could hear the eager tone in Vladoseev's voice. After four years, Schram was so close!

"It's him alright. He made me, boss, like he knew who I was. He ran for the back room. He locked the door and I'm sure he's calling the police or sheriff or whatever they have here. Wyatt Earp will come riding in six guns blazing."

"I don't think he'll call the police. Watch the place, but stay on the line. Who cares about minutes?"

The two Russians waited in silence, one in New York City and the other in Warhego, Nebraska. Fortunately Warhego had almost no traffic or pedestrians, so no one noticed him and no one asked him what he was doing in Warhego. Thirty minutes passed, then an hour. The drugstore front door opened and the pimply faced cashier left like he didn't have a care in the world. He seemed to have forgotten the tall stranger who had invaded the tiny town.

****

In the back room of the drug store, Daniel Conklin's hands shook when he pulled out his cell phone. The owner had taken the afternoon off and left Dan and the cashier to run the store. They had had almost no customers. Then the tall man had come in near closing time. It took Conklin a second to realize he didn't know this man, but it seemed like the man knew him. His instincts had kicked in and he ran for the back room and locked himself in.

Both the door to the pharmacy store room and the back of the store were heavy steel doors with dead-bolts. Crime was almost unheard of in Warhego but the pharmacist didn't want teenagers even thinking about breaking in. Conklin thought briefly of calling the police but rejected the idea. He knew that the man had come here looking for him. He didn't want anyone in this town to get hurt.

27

Instead, he called Bentley's number again. This time someone answered. Dan Conklin briefly explained the situation.

"Mr. Conklin, we have reason to believe you've been compromised. Our plan is to get you out of there as soon as possible. You are about to receive a FedEx delivery. The driver will ring your phone number and knock twice on the back door. You will open for him. Once inside, change clothes with the driver and drive the truck to McCook. Do you know where that is?"

"Yes, east on Highway 34, about an hour away."

"Excellent. When you get to McCook, call again. We'll have more instructions."

The line went dead. An hour passed. His phone rang and the sudden knock on the door startled Conklin enough to jolt him awake.

****

Karolovsky had slept little last night and this day had been full of excitement. He fought off sleep even though it wasn't late by local time.

Every few moments, Vladoseev voice came through the open cell phone connection.

"Anything?"

"Nothing, Boss."

"It's been an hour. You are absolutely certain it was the cashier who left, not Schram?"

"Yes, Boss. Schram's still in there. Nobody has gone in or out. Wait, here comes a truck." The fading light made identification difficult until the truck turned broadside in the drugstore parking lot. "FedEx Ground. Looks like a delivery."

"Just a delivery, then."

Karolovsky said, "Boss this may be our only chance. He's going to open that door for FexEx."

"Maybe we should wait until things quiet down. You go charging in there, he will call the cops. Why not try to get him when they open up in the morning?"

"You mean, I spend the night in the car?"

"Looks like it, old friend."

The lights in the drug store had gone out, matching Karolovsky's mood. He closed the cell phone with Vladoseev. Ignoring Vladoseev's advice, Karolovsky exited the car and walked around back of the drug

28

store. The FedEx truck parked right up against the back door. A man in a uniform and logoed cap exited the truck with an envelope, knocked on the door and the door opened a crack.

Karolovsky thought of rushing and overcoming them both in the back room. Then he'd take Schram prisoner and drive all the way to New York City with him in the trunk. But almost immediately the door opened wide and the FedEx man went inside. The steel door quickly closed. Karolovsky looked at his watch. Fifteen minutes later, the FedEx driver came out carrying his handheld device drove off. The truck pulled away and disappeared around a corner.

Karolovsky walked to the back door of the pharmacy and tried the door handle. Locked. He walked back to his rental car and settled in for a long night.

Post-sunset, darkness quickly descended upon the town of Warhego. There were no streetlights, and it looked like every house in town had drawn their blinds leaving not even enough light to draw moths.

By morning, the two Russians realized Wylie Schram had given them the slip.

Chapter 6

It was another town that didn't matter, so the name was irrelevant. A straight, two-lane highway ran between nondescript and mostly abandoned buildings. The town's businesses had died one at a time, but somehow the diner had resisted the demise. The diner's storefront window once held hand painted letters but the ravages of grit and wind left only 'DINE' and 'FOOD.'

Recovering from the effects of a long bus ride, Daniel Conklin crossed the road on stiffened legs and entered the restaurant.

The diner was prototypical: counter on the right, booths lining the left wall, with a wide, checkerboard vinyl floor in between. A bell on the door announced his arrival. All the diner's patrons, mostly withered men in dusty cowboy clothes, turned to look him over. Four years in hiding made Conklin wince at the scrutiny.

The booths to his left held only a single occupant. Conklin recognized him immediately. A wave of emotion caused Conklin to pause at the sight of the man who had been his WITSEC mentor. Bentley was now the most important person in his life. He was the only man who knew who he really was. He felt somehow Bentley would find a way to help him with his new dilemma.

Bentley hadn't changed at all. His gray-haired crew-cut head came up and a slight smile crossed his face. He stood and took Conklin's hand in a strong grip.

As expected, Bentley used Conklin's new name.

"Dan, how have you been?" He waved at the booth seat opposite him. Despite his current desperation, Conklin couldn't help but smile. Bentley always had that effect on him. He felt better just knowing he was about to unburden himself, to lay out an insoluble problem in front of this capable man.

"I've been good. And you?" Not used to talking to people, he surprised himself at how quiet his voice had become.

Bentley just nodded. "A little older, that's all. But it beats the alternative."

Perfunctory smiles seemed to be in order.

"Well Dan, what brings us here?" Bentley was always good at getting down to business.

"I need a favor. I mean, I need some help. I received a letter yesterday."

30

"From Denise."

The waitress brought Conklin a cup of coffee and refilled Bentley's cup. Conklin waited until she retreated, a habit he developed over the years. "You know about the letter." It was a statement, not a question.

Bentley clanked a spoon in the thick porcelain cup. "I knew. I wondered if you'd try to contact her. I almost brought it up before I turned you lose, but ..." He shrugged. "My experience in these things... Well you understood the risk. When it comes to feelings, nobody does the logical thing."

Conklin shrugged. "I tried to get a message to her." He saw Bentley nod. "I coded it carefully. She figured out my code because she found me and sent me a letter."

Bentley was silent for a moment. "Dan, we know all about your fake overdue library books. Really? 'Love Lives On.' Wasn't that it? Jesus, how stupid! Did you think we wouldn't find out?"

Dan Conklin dropped his eyes.

"And we knew she found out where you were and she wrote you that letter which you got yesterday. If she figured out where you were, why couldn't Vladoseev do it? Well, I guess he did find you, you idiot. That's why we had to sneak you out of the drug store and get you on that bus ride to this side of Timbuktu."

"How did he find out?"

Bentley paused a moment. Conklin saw him figuring, wondering how much to tell him.

"He watched her house. We didn't know that old Russian would go to all the trouble. After four years? He had someone dress up like a postman. He saw the letter with your address on it. We knew something was up. The regular postman came an hour later. US Postal workers put with a lot, but they sure don't like getting roughed up by federal agents."

Bentley stirred his coffee. He looked at his spoon. "You want to tell me about Denise?"

Conklin stared at his reflection in his own coffee cup, his eyes peering through the mask WITSEC's plastic surgeons had given him.

"Denise is not good. She's dying. Breast cancer. It didn't respond to treatment. It's spread." Conklin couldn't stop the tears. He wiped his eyes with a paper napkin. "I reach out to her and I find out she's dying. She said it's week to week now."

Bentley softened his tone. "What do you want to do?"

"I don't know. I want to be with her. Do you think you could come up

31

with something?" His napkin had become a wrinkled mess. He pulled another one from the chrome canister. "Being away from her these last four years has been hell. Maybe she could come here, I mean with me."

Bentley shook his head. "Impossible. I guess you know you can't go back. That was pretty close in Warhego. Was it a tall guy? Reddish hair?"

Conklin nodded.

"Nicolay Karolovsky. He's Vladoseev's top man. He's violent, Dan, a murderer. He'll kill you in a second if Vladoseev wants him to. You were lucky. We don't even have a good picture of him. I'm surprised he didn't go for your throat right there."

The ambient sounds of the diner framed their momentary silence. Conklin's tears dried on his cheek.

"You can't go back to Warhego, but..." Bentley sighed. "We might try something else. Something that might allow you two to be together. And this will help Denise too. You have to go somewhere else anyway. I know of a clinic. It's in Switzerland. They do cancer research there, but they only take terminal patients. They're working on new kinds of treatment. It's a wonderful place. They make patients as comfortable as possible. And their families..."

Bentley waited for his reaction. Conklin didn't move for an entire minute. His hands closed around his coffee cup.

"Denise is not a lab rat."

Bentley shook his head. "No, Dan. You got the wrong idea. This clinic works miracles. Their treatments reduce patient's discomfort and pain. Their aim is to help make their last days more comfortable. Less pain. You can spend some time with her."

Bentley paused, "My wife..."

Conklin heard a catch in his voice and saw his head drop.

"It was about a year after you went underground. My wife, Jenny... She had breast cancer. She was metastatic at initial diagnosis. You learn a lot of terms. Her doctors didn't even give her a year."

He raised his head and Conklin saw tears now in Bentley's eyes.

"Dan, I looked everywhere for a solution. I found this clinic and took her there. Her American doctors said she might not survive a trip to Switzerland, but she made it. At the clinic, they worked on her. They first made her comfortable. The kind of things they did for her... treatments, therapy... whatever it was brought her back. We knew it wasn't going to cure her. They told us that but... she actually got better. She even got up and walked... no cane, no wheelchair. We took walks together. It's in an old town and they have beautiful gardens. Jenny loved it. I loved it. After a year of watching her die slowly." Bentley covered his face with his hands and his shoulders rocked once, twice.

The few patrons in the diner may have sensed the gravity of their conversation. Except for stealing an occasional glance, they ignored the two men talking, drinking coffee and crying. The waitress refilled their cups and took away the two plastic covered menus as calmly as if she saw weeping men every day.

Bentley pulled out a handkerchief and dabbed at his eyes. Dan Conklin thought about what Bentley was suggesting. He hadn't seen Denise in nearly four years. He didn't know if she wore her hair long or short now. Or if it had fallen out from radiation or chemo, or if her pretty face had become lined with pain. A vision came to him: Denise lying in bed, body gaunt with weight loss and her eyes sad and red-rimmed with tears, surrounded by strangers or even worse, dying alone with no one there at all.

"Bentley, I want to be with her. I don't care what it takes. She's dying. I don't care what happens to me after that. I'm strangling myself living someone else's life. Thanks for saving my life, but it's just like being dead anyway. I don't know about this clinic, but at least let be together. A chance... to be with her. She wants me to be with her. She wrote me the letter."

Bentley looked at him across the booth. His hands folded around his coffee mug and tightened.

"Dan. Wylie." It was the first time someone had called him by his given name in years.

"You're alive, Dan. The fact that you don't like witness protection is not my fault. You had four years to make a better life for yourself. That's a rare opportunity. Remember you seriously broke the law and testified against Ray Suffield to save your neck. What you did hurt thousands of people. Some of them aren't doing too well either. You hurt innocent people. They got wiped out. You get federal protection. Maybe you're sorry for what you did, but it doesn't change the fact that you broke the law in a big way. Okay, you testified and helped put Suffield in jail, but that doesn't make you a saint, because you did it to save your own sorry ass."

Bentley's eyes were like ice and whatever humanity Conklin felt earlier had evaporated.

"Bentley, I know. A thousand times I wish I could take it back. What

I did, they were little decisions when I made them. It got away from me. Yeah, I loved the power, the money. I admit it, but I screwed up. I have to look at myself every day in the mirror, and see the guy who ripped off thousands of innocent people. I can't even see myself with what you guys did to my face. I'd throw myself off of a bridge, but you stashed me in a place where there's no bridge."

Conklin struggled to keep his voice low. He looked around at the other people in the diner. Apparently no one noticed the change in their conversation.

"Listen to me, Bentley. Denise is good. She never knew about what I did until it all blew up. And she forgave me. She stuck by me through all of it. It killed me knowing that she thought I'd died. You just don't do that to someone you love. If she was with me these last four years, things might have been different. I might have been able to redeem myself a little. She would have found a way to bring me out of this wretched hell I'm living in."

Bentley's eyes narrowed. "Then she's a lot better than you deserve."

Conklin's hand slapped the table. The coffee mugs danced in their saucers. "Damn it, Bentley, you don't know that. What gives you the right to be my judge? Denise thinks I'm worth it, that I'm worth saving. Maybe she sees something in me you don't know a goddamn thing about."

Bentley had to turn away from the heat in Conklin's eyes.

"Okay, Dan. Maybe she does."

The waitress left them alone.

Bentley spoke in an energized whisper.

"Dan. This could work for both of you. This clinic, they'll make her better for a while. Take her pain away. They did it for Jenny. You two will be together."

"It's in Switzerland?"

Bentley nodded.

"I guess we could try it. I guess I'd be safe there, but I'm an idiot because you already thought of that. You wouldn't even suggest it unless you've checked it out from every angle."

Bentley looked down at his coffee mug again.

"Dan, before we go anywhere, I need something from you."

A cold wind blew across the back of Dan Conklin's neck, perhaps from the diner's air-conditioning but more likely from those last words Bentley spoke. He knew what Bentley wanted, and he knew he had to give him something.

"Dan, it's time for you to come clean."

"What do you mean?" Conklin's voice shook.

Bentley's level stare and steady voice were worse than torture.

"Dan, you may be a great secret keeper but you're a terrible liar." Bentley let the silence hang like a storm-cloud.

"What... What do you want?"

"Dan your mere existence is expensive. WITSEC's strained resources have been keeping you safe and now you want more."

Bentley tapped his spoon on the Formica.

"The money, Dan. Is it really so hard to understand?"

The waitress refilled their cups on the chance that they might actually order something if she prodded them a little.

Bentley picked up his steaming mug and blew on it.

"I've let you go on now four years. It must be eating your insides up trying to keep this secret. There can never be any peace for you, and you know it. One and a half billion dollars. That's what we didn't recover. I know you have it. Now give it back. You can keep everything else we've given you. Like your life. We'll give you time with Denise. We'll help her. They can't save her, but they'll try. And you two can spend some meaningful time together. You can apologize to her. It could be the high point of what time she has left. You know you hurt her, more than the thousands of anonymous people you cheated. You hurt her, Dan. You showed the woman you loved what a real shit-ass you are, the man she fell in love with and wanted to spend the rest of her life with. There is absolutely no redemption for you without giving the money back."

Every one of his statements felt like a blow to Conklin's guts. His heart hammered a slow, heavy beat. He shook his head.

"I can't. I... Uh, I only have eight million."

Bentley's stare turned predatory.

"Dan," he whispered. "That's not nearly enough and you know it."

"Bentley, listen to me. It's gone. The one and a half billion is gone. It's scattered so far and wide I can't find it. I tried to tell you this four years ago. Ray told me to get rid of it. To hide it. He didn't want Vladoseev to get it, either. So he told me get rid of it.

"I had computer programs which allowed me to create spending accounts. It was easy to keep these accounts secret. I didn't want the IRS or the SEC to see every move we made... only what we wanted them to see. Suffield's group rarely looked at the where and how of things as long as they had enough money to spend. InCorps cash was my department.

35

"The computer could create accounts at institutions automatically without my involvement. The account information was encrypted so nobody could read it. If I wanted to retrieve these funds, I had to decode it."

Bentley held up his hand. "You're telling me that you don't know where that money is?

Conklin nodded. "I told you that four years ago, and nothing's changed. It's out there spread across hundreds of banks, mostly foreign banks, places where they have strict rules about privacy... hundreds of real accounts with hidden owners... all of them pointing back to Incorps.

"InCorps ran on cash. We had offshore accounts, some of them were strictly buffer accounts that put a layer between us and where we'd spend it. When the SEC investigators closed in on us, I loaded all the cash we had into offshore accounts and then transferred it into new accounts. Then the program gave orders to start passing the money around. The money went from account to account, with made up names, addresses, enterprises that looked like holding companies. And I don't know where it ended. Probably most of it is still there, but I don't know where to start looking."

Bentley thought for a moment. "How did you expect to get it back?"

"The computers didn't care how complicated the trail was. With enough time we could have discovered all the paths to the money. With enough time I could have gotten a list of all the account numbers and passwords. Remember, at that time I was coopering fully. I tried to help them get back as much as I could. We spent a month trying to unravel it all. And we got back, what, ninety-seven percent? Your guys seemed pretty happy with that at the time. The SEC guys told Treasury when to stop. Your guys stopped hounding me for more. And that's when you and WITSEC got involved."

Bentley said, "They stopped before all the money was recovered, a little less than three percent. One and a half billion dollars."

"I told the investigators that I didn't know where the rest was. And they believed me. Well, they believed me after they gave me eleven polygraph tests. Which I passed."

Conklin looked directly into Bentley's eyes.

Bentley shook his head. "Dan, are you telling me that a billion and a half dollars is lost?

"Yes, lost but still there. I don't know where the money went. I think I can get at eight million but I'll have to work at it. One of the many rules you gave me forbid me to use a computer to bank on-line and especially transfer money."

Conklin couldn't resist a small smile. "But I think I can do it again. It's like riding a bicycle."

"You mean you can fiddle around and scrape together eight million dollars?"

Conklin shrugged. "Probably."

"How 'come you didn't give us this eight million four years ago?"

"Your guys stopped when I told them that was done. Then you put me in a classroom and taught me to be a pharmacist. Bentley, you feds were happy with ninety-seven percent. The remainder is just a rounding error."

Bentley puffed out his cheeks. "I knew you held out on us. A billion and a half dollars... gone?"

"Bentley, I didn't hold out on you. I told you everything back then and took your polygraphs. What I'm telling you is that it might take forever to wring the international banking system for a billion and half dollars, but I think I know where about eight million is."

Bentley managed a grim smile. "If Vladoseev gets his hands on you, you won't buy him off with eight mil. He'll put you on a rack and every turn of the crank he'd expect another account number."

Conklin rolled his eyes. "There's nothing to remember, Bentley. Denise doesn't have enough time for me to get much... maybe about eight million. If I work all night."

They never ordered lunch, much to the waitress' annoyance. When Bentley and Conklin left the diner a government van pulled up. Some of the old cowboys stepped outside to watch them drive down the dusty road.

Chapter 7

Her alarm clock never rang. Pain and nausea, the dual realities of her existence, told her she had made it to another day.

Denise Oliver lay still for a few minutes taking inventory of where it hurt, shoulders, lower back and legs. The grinding throb from her right side had been so omnipresent that she no longer paid much attention to it. The sunlight at her window cheered some inner, undamaged place within allowing her to gather enough strength to struggle to a sitting position. She moved stiffened joints and let her feet plop on the floor.

Her scrawny legs underscored the point that there wasn't much left of her to haul out of bed.

She had smeared bar soap over her bathroom mirror so she wouldn't have to look at the death-mask her face had become. Last month, her coworkers' expressions had told her it was time to hide that face from the public, and after few days at home alone, she realized it was time to hide it from herself as well.

She shuffled toward the toilet but she really didn't have to go, but watching her urine steadily darken and decrease had become a macabre morning ritual for her.

A knock at her door distracted her. Her feverish mind marveled at how long it had been since her phone had rung or someone had knocked at her door. And why so early in the morning?

She put on a robe but didn't run a comb through what was left of her hair. She knew she looked ghastly and thought about ignoring the knock.

The knock came again like it wasn't going away.

Denise pulled aside a curtain to look. Outside her door a sharp looking woman dressed in navy blue business clothes stood rail straight, tapping her foot like she expected an immediate response. The woman wore dark glasses. Denise had an intuition that her visitor was a federal agent. Her heart fluttered a little at the thought. Who else could she expect besides the grim reaper?

She opened the door and watched her visitor's reaction to her appearance. The woman's mouth opened and her eyebrows rose behind the dark glasses.

"Yes?" Denise's voice had become gravely and deep like a woman twice her age.

"Uh, Ms. Oliver? Denise Oliver?"

"Yeah, that's me."

The woman quickly recovered. She took off her sunglasses, folded them and placed them in her jacket pocket. "I'm Agent Stacey Glasson from the Department of Justice. May I speak to you?"

Denise turned and headed into her living room, waving a hand for Agent Stacey Glasson to follow. She took a seat on a couch behind a glass coffee table and pointed to a chair for her visitor.

"Please have a seat, Miss, uh, Glasson." Denise tightened her robe around her and picked up a plastic baggie from the coffee table. She withdrew a hand rolled cigarette, lit it and drew. She had been about to ask her guest if she minded if she smoked, but concluded, it was her house, she was sick, and the Justice Department hadn't made an appointment.

Agent Glasson wrinkled her nose. "Is that marijuana?"

"Yes."

"It's illegal."

"Really? Where are their priorities? They should have outlawed cancer first." Denise blew a cloud of smoke between them and stubbed out the joint in an ashtray. She only wanted a few puffs, enough to quell the nausea that rippled through her abdomen.

Agent Stacey Glasson squared her shoulders.

"Ms. Oliver, I'm here to help you. But before I go any further, I need your assurance that you won't divulge what I'm about to say to anyone. We must keep this conversation strictly confidential. No, not just confidential. It must be kept top secret."

A flood of intuition filled Denise's head accompanied by emotions stronger than she had felt in years. The meager high from the joint faded and her heartbeat quickened.

"Ms. Glasson, can I call you Stacey?" A nod from Stacey. "I haven't spoken to anyone in a week. You're probably aware of my condition. If I understand the federal government, someone you work with, maybe even yourself has gone through my medical files and probably knows more about me than I do. So you know I don't have a whole lot of time. At the risk of being rude I need you to get on with the purpose of your visit."

Agent Stacey Glasson drew a deep breath. "I need your promise of confidentiality…"

"I promise. I won't live long enough to tell anyone."

Agent Glasson spoke with straightforward intensity, "Wiley Schram didn't die in a traffic accident three years ago."

Denise stared at her.

"I know this. I do now. He's in witness protection or something like that."

Glasson nodded. "We know he sent you a message and it gave you enough information to discover his location. You sent a letter to him, so he now knows of your condition. He contacted his witness protection team and wants the two of you to be together. He's asked us to facilitate it but you understand the risks, plus your condition is serious enough to complicate matters. We can make arrangements for you to see each other, but we have to keep him safe.

"My director who worked with Mr. Schram in our witness protection program has arranged for us to take you to a location, but you'd be better off not knowing where just yet."

Denise's heart fluttered again. She hadn't seen Wylie in four years.

"Wylie. How is he?"

"He's fine, but there are a few things we need to prepare you for."

Denise Oliver was already preparing for a wave of pain. Inwardly she cursed Agent Glasson for arriving before she could take her medication.

"Would you mind, terribly, uh…" Her head drooped and she closed her eyes. "…getting to the point? I told you, uh, uh, ah… I really don't have the patience…ugh… for your whole presentation." Her fists tightened and tears squeezed out of the corners of her eyes. A moan became a quiet growl as her insides cramped with anguish.

"Yes, of course." Agent Glasson proceeded as if the woman in front of her wasn't doubled over in pain. "We're taking you to a clinic…"

Without looking up Denise waved an arm in negation. Her voice sounded like it came from a well, deep and throaty. "No. No more treatments. Chemo, radiation, they aren't working for me. No clinics. Just let me see Wylie and die. Let me say, ah, hmmmm…" Another clutch of agony reduced her words to a progression of grunts, groans, deep breaths, sighs. "…goodbye to him," she whispered. "Just goodbye. And I'm going to die in my own bed and they can burn down the house for all the hell I care."

The tear-stained face she raised caused Agent Glasson's hand to fly to her mouth. She looked worse now than when she opened the door. Denise Oliver saw the federal agent's reaction and felt a surge of shame and regret. No sane person wanted to see anything this horrible in real life. She was a limping, blinking corpse, surrendered to death and late for her own funeral.

Agent Stacey Glasson took a deep breath, shrugged and plunged on.

"Ms. Oliver, we can't bring Mr. Schram here. This place is too exposed. You are being watched. By more than us. You are being watched by those who want to find Mr. Schram and harm him.

Denise nodded. She could not comprehend who'd want to watch her, but the realization came too late to matter.

"We have to take you and Mr. Schram to another location. Actually my director wants you to go to this place. For Mr. Schram and you to, uh, see each other."

Glasson went on. "We're doing this because of an arrangement that Mr. Schram and my director have worked out. At the clinic they'll make you as comfortable as they can. And you can be with Mr. Schram."

Agent Glasson waited a moment. Denise's pain diminished to an ache. She settled back in her couch.

"We'll leave as soon as you can get dressed." Agent Glasson looked around the room as if Denise's clothes were lying about.

"I don't get dressed anymore. I can't pull on my own clothes."

"Is there something I can do to help you?"

"Yes, there is." Denise's eyes bored into her. "You can hurry."

Chapter 8

Karolovsky was waiting in Chicago's O'Hare Airport when his cell phone rang. It was one of his guys hanging out in Denise Oliver's neighborhood. He listened for a minute, hung up and called Vladoseev.

"The Feds have picked up Denise."

"Are you certain it was Federals?"

"Black GMC SUV. Blonde female agent went to the door. Three guys in blue suits waited in the car. Thirty minutes they wheel her out on a gurney and into an ambulance. Our guy follows at a distance."

"They took her to the hospital?"

"No, they took her to Newark Freedom."

"The airport?"

"Yes, to a private hangar I think."

"The feds have Denise." Karolovsky could hear the frustration in his boss's voice. "First we lose Schram and now her."

"Boss, I got this covered. They're going to fly Denise somewhere but won't fly her commercial. She's on a stretcher, which means medical assistance. All medical assistance flights get priority with air traffic control. They talk on the radio, very chatty. We can get a list of all such flights out of Newark. She'll be on one of them, a guest of the federal government. Even if they use one of their own planes, they will certainly use the medical priority to get clearance. We listen and find out where her flight goes."

"We can do this?"

"Of course. Relax, boss. Leave it to me."

****

Daniel Conklin spent a sleepless night at the Marriott near Atlanta's Hartsfield Jackson Airport. While waiting for a limo, he stared at his reflection in the tinted glass window at the front of the hotel. He thought, she'll never recognize me. Denise would know his eyes, but not the anguish behind them. Then he chided himself. What she was going through must be a thousand times worse.

A limousine arrived and a beefy agent in a navy blue suit got out. Conklin knew instinctively this was his ride. The agent held the door for him. He climbed in the back of the limo and nestled into dark leather seats polished by the backsides of countless bureaucrats.

"Are we going back to the airport?"

The beefy agent who had held the door for him didn't reply but gave him an insect like stare from behind impenetrable Ray Bans. Conklin remembered from four years ago, federal agents, especially the lower ranks, liked to play Clint Eastwood.

Hartsfield Jackson Airport was only a couple of miles away, but they didn't head in that direction. Instead they looped through the maze of roads around the airport and headed west on Camp Creek Parkway. The limo turned north on I-285. Conklin was unfamiliar with the Atlanta area and in the madly zooming traffic soon lost track of where they were headed. When they exited the interstate he saw a sign that said "Naval Air Station" and concluded they were headed for a government facility. After a dozen traffic lights, they turned into what was obviously government property, surrounded by a chain-link fence.

The federal agent confused him further by stating, "Dobbins Air Force Base" in raspy voice, leaving Conklin to wonder if it was both an Air Force and a Navy installation. He shrugged. He had no choice in their destination, so why worry about it?

They did not go through any military checkpoint, but drove around for a few minutes between industrial buildings and unidentifiable structures. They parked in front of a huge building identified as "C-5 Maintenance, Lockheed Martin Aerospace," containing a hangar door massive enough to engulf one of the world's largest airplanes. They scuttled through the yawning portal like mice sneaking into a garage.

Conklin followed his escort through warehouse sized offices full of engineers working intently under suspended fluorescent lights. They descended in an elevator to an underground lobby that served as an entryway to a maze of tunnels. They boarded an electric golf cart and sped away through a tunnel that seemed to run for miles and crisscrossed and intersected more tunnels. Eventually they stopped at another elevator and ascended into a much smaller aircraft hangar containing a gleaming white Gulfstream G450 with an American flag on its tail.

A woman in a blue suit waited at the bottom of the rolling staircase. She held out her hand to Conklin.

"Agent Stacey Glasson. Justice."

Dan Conklin took her hand. A brief, unfeminine power grip made his fingers tingle.

"And peace," he said to her. He rushed up the stairs, past her quizzical look. After a second agent Glasson backed away from the jet, already making a call on her cell. The ground crew rolled away the staircase, and the Gulfstream's crew sealed the door.

He peered into a dimly lit interior. There were typical airline chairs near the front bulkhead. The back of the aircraft looked like a hospital room in a tube.

A sheet-draped figure lay on a gurney flanked by a man and a woman dressed in medical garb. Monitoring equipment blinked, IV's drained into the inert, recumbent, white-swathed form on the gurney. The two attendants retreated when they saw him. Conklin's knees wobbled as he stumbled toward her, to get his first look at Denise in four years.

Only her head protruded from the hospital linens, a scrawny, shrunken skull covered in mottled skin with patches of wispy gray hair. Thin dry lips pressed together as if frozen in pain. Eyelash-less eyes clamped shut, crusted with dried tears.

For a moment he felt like Bentley had played a cruel trick on him. This could not be Denise. Then he realized cancer had changed her appearance more than what WITSEC had done to him.

One eyelid fluttered, opened and looked at him. For a brief second there was no recognition as if the eye had seen too many strangers in the last few hours. Then she recognized him and with her eye she flashed some kind of message to him. And closed.

Daniel Conklin collapsed to his knees and buried his face in her sheets. A torrent of tears soaked into the stiff white cotton. He threw his arms across her inert form and felt the narrow mound of her body.

The sounds of the Gulfstream starting up blotted out his sobs. He felt the world move around him, a combined sensation of his emotions and the plane actually moving. Someone's gentle hands guided him away from her and into one of the chairs. His seatbelt clicked.

The Gulfstream accelerated down a runway and took to the air. All the window shades had been pulled down darkening the interior of the jet except for a few shafts of sunlight that rotated through the dust mote filled air like thin beacons.

The drone of the turbine engines lulled Conklin, relaxing the tension under which he had lived for so long. His eyes closed, and his head lolled to his shoulder. Unknown hands reclined his chair.

The Gulfstream outpaced eighty percent of its own noise, all but the muted blast of air against the fuselage. An indeterminate span of time passed.

Conklin awoke, his torpor faded and his tensions returned. He was on a jet bound for Zurich and Denise lay dying a few feet away. He thought of Bentley working behind the scenes, cranking the machinery of the Justice Department, providing protection, an airplane and medical staff to get them to Switzerland. Bentley had an agenda, and Conklin knew he would keep them both alive until he had what he wanted.

He lifted the window shade and saw a bleak red dawn rushing over a spotted cloudscape below. He lowered the shade and looked toward the rear of the plane. There Denise's gurney stood unattended except for the monitoring equipment hooked to her. Around him the Gulfstream's medical crew huddled in their seats wrapped in blankets.

Conklin unbuckled, stood and walked toward Denise. He raised the edge of a sheet covering her and sought her hand. Her hand felt surprisingly warm. Her thin bones seemed like tiny sticks wrapped in a pliant parchment. He felt her heartbeat, a pulsing, diffused throb.

"Deeny." He spoke in a voice so soft he barely heard it in his own mind. Her face was turned away from him so he addressed the wispy strands of hair dangling limply from the back of her scalp.

Over the North Sea Daniel Conklin tried to confess everything to Denise. He told her of his moral collapse, how he had evolved from brilliant businessman, to loophole finder, and finally desperate criminal. He had masterminded the huge corporate fraud that bilked billions from investors and trusted partners. He had been seduced by the excitement, the huge sums of money and how he had become a corporate demon, hell-bent on raking in even more money. Then his conscience had clicked in. He saw what InCorps had become and tried to turn them around. His goal had become just getting through the next quarter, with a promise, made to no one but himself, to guide the company back to honest ground. He talked about the tension, the panic that broke out among the company's executives when they were caught, of his decision to rat on CEO Ray Suffield, to go into witness protection, making the fateful choice of abandoning her, desolate after the staged accident where the whole world, including her, believed him dead. Then he told her of his four years of misery in the limbo of the federal witness protection program, how only thoughts of her sustained him, of his realization that his only redemption lay in their reunion.

His soliloquy left him gasping for air, heart pounding, as if the weight of what he had done lay on him still, crushing him with its enormity.

"Then your letter came, and you told me you were dying. Life was hell in witness protection, but God, what I did to you! You were in love with the worst crook in the country. I abandoned you... you thought I died. Then you were fighting cancer by yourself with nobody to help. I could barely live with what I had done. How could I live with what I had done to you? I don't deserve a wonderful woman like you."

His confession over, he fell silent,

Denise's inert form quivered once and a second later quivered again. Her head slowly turned, like she was making a terrific effort. Her ear rotated into view, followed by her cheek, and the full of her face, made awful by disease. Her face came to rest on the surface of the sheet, shrunken eyes closed, lips pressed together as if pain had become the engine of her existence.

Tears streamed down Conklin's face, and he made no effort to wipe them.

"Deeny, I thought long and hard about it. I know now we have to be together. No matter how much time we have, we have to be together."

Her hand squeezed his, a thin, weak compression of the fingers, not much more than a tremor. Her eyelids fought to open and when they did, her eyes gleamed like the thin dawn light seeping in from the Gulfstream's shaded windows. Her lips parted. Conklin bent to hear her.

A whispery hiss, "I know." A pause of a slow heartbeat. "I know." Her eyes closed and her hand moved no more. Conklin stared at her inert form. She knew.

Arriving in Zurich, Conklin and Denise were whisked through customs. Swiss cancer clinics were big business. Patients arrived at the Zurich airport routinely, destined for hundreds of facilities scattered around the region. The Swiss had elevated the customs process to maximum efficiency. Denise was semi-conscious so Conklin had to sign affidavits for all of her declarations. An ambulance took them directly from the airport to Klinik von St. Agatha in Schaffhausen, making the trip in less than an hour.

As soon as their ambulance stopped at the clinic's patient check-in area, several white-garbed clinicians rushed out and whisked Denise through glass double doors. Another aide showed Conklin a wood and leather library splendid enough for a monarch's country estate. There he filled out more paperwork. Once he completed the forms, they lay ignored on the antique wooden desk while he waited. Hours passed. A doctor came in wearing scrubs and a surgical mask that somewhat muffled his German accented English.

"Herr Conklin, I am Dr. Friedkin." He stripped off a latex glove and offered his hand. "We expected you much earlier than this. Like last year, perhaps?" His eyes crinkled above the mask as if Conklin needed to be told this was a joke. "She barely got to us in time. Another day or so and it might have been too late. The tumors in her lymph nodes, liver and along her right side are the worst. This accounts for her debilitated state. But I assure you, we've had some nearly as bad and have been able to help them. We will search for cancer in other parts of her body. Our treatments to remediate what we have found have begun already. This will make her feel better, almost immediately. We expect rapid improvement."

Dr. Friedkin launched into a highly detailed briefing that was way above Conklin's head, but his fluid torrent of words and confident manner somehow comforted him. When the torrent stopped, Dr. Friedkin excused himself and hustled out of the library.

Conklin sat in the leather chair and noticed afternoon shadows coming in through the high antique glass windows.

Evening fell in Schaffhausen, Switzerland.

He was alone again.

Chapter 9

"We lost her!" Vladoseev yelled into the phone. He lunged out of his chair like polar bear attacking a seal. Karolovsky was silent on the other end of their phone connection, glad he was not in the office.

"Kolya, speak to me."

"Boss, we tracked the Gulfstream from Newark to Dobbins, an Air Force base just a few miles outside of Atlanta, in the American Georgia. They were still using medical flight clearance. Easy to track. Then they pulled the plane into a hangar."

"Are they still there?"

"They did not stay long. Traffic coming into and out of Dobbins is light. They have the Lockheed-Martin plant there. They make C-130s and F22's. The Navy has F18's there, and they refuel military planes. Military planes, military security. Planes taking off all the time but few commercial or private jets."

"Can we track them off this military base, Kolya?" Vladoseev's voice had lost some of its anxiety.

"We are customers of an organization called Flight Stats and another one called OAG. They track all flights in the world."

"Even military flights?"

"No boss, but Denise Oliver is not on a military aircraft. She is on a Gulfstream G450, owned by a company called Med One. They do medical flights with planes set up like a hospital room. Very expensive and for rich people, but not a problem. The US government is paying for this. We grabbed their transponder number when they took off from Newark. Every checkpoint in their flight path gets logged in the OAG database. It's a simple matter to request an alert when that transponder number clicks off a navigational checkpoint."

"That's how you followed them to Atlanta?"

"Yes. It was all over Atlanta flight control, 'Gulfstream Med One to Dobbins' like they had nothing to hide. Nearby Atlanta Hartsfield is the busiest airport in the world and no little jet gets in the front of the line. But we're listening and we know where they're going. Then we got real lucky."

"What happened?"

"The US government has GPS tracking in all their vehicles: vans, SUV's, cars. The actual tracking of government vehicles is handled by a private firm and we are into their databases."

"How did we accomplish this? Don't these private firms have security?"

"Of course, but we contract with them to buy the tracking statistics. They sell some of their data, anything that doesn't have classified status. It's not like we are stalking government vehicles. Or so we say. We merely make a pest of ourselves with thousands of requests for data. Before long, the weary agency gives us access to their on-line database. It is then like the chastity belt is off and we are a fox in the henhouse."

"Henhouse?"

"Yes, where they keep the chickens." Karolovsky waited for his boss to make a joke about chastity belts and chickens, but apparently his Vladoseev's anxiety left no room for wit.

"So we know Denise is at Dobbins. It is unlikely the feds would drive Schram all the way from Nebraska to Atlanta. That means they probably fly him into Atlanta airport and stash him nearby until she arrives. With access to government GPS data, we look for federal vehicles heading from the Atlanta airport to Dobbins. The data is live and can be posted on computer screen maps. We spot a cluster of federal vehicles moving from the Airport Marriott and heading in that direction. Someone is joining Denise perhaps?"

"Wylie Schram!" Vladoseev practically sang the name.

"Who else? One federal car might be hard to spot but a convoy? That means one heavy-duty VIP. As soon as it arrives, OAG tells us her Med One Gulfstream rolls out and takes off."

"With Schram on board."

"Boss, it's a guess but I think a very good guess."

"So then what happens?"

"They take off, climb to altitude and poof... disappear."

"Disappear?" Vladoseev's voice falls.

"You know, Boss, we're not really watching the plane. It's what they call in English a metaphor."

"Don't give me English lessons, you *gamadril*."

"Easy, Boss. You'll blow a gasket. Another metaphor. English is full of them. We don't know where the plane goes because they turn off their transponder. OAG loses them. We lose them."

"This is the good news?"

"The good news is that the Feds go to all the trouble to put her on a Med One G450 at Newark. It is a very expensive airplane. They send her to Atlanta where she rendezvous with a cluster of federal vehicles. Putting two and two together."

"Karolovsky, one more metaphor…"

"We can be fairly certain she and Schram are now together."

"This is not the good news. Come on Kolya, give me the good news."

"Boss, I think the feds are believing we won't know how to track them and are using very little in the way of, uh, what is the word?"

"Subtleness. Subterfuge?"

"No, a simpler word."

"Deceit?"

"Cunning."

"That is a dirty word, Kolya. In English."

"No, Boss. It means being clever. They should have hired another medical flight company in Atlanta, flown her to Kansas. And then another flight from there. We would have gotten lost trying to track them."

"I am lost. Where are we?"

"You are in the Barclay Hotel in Manhattan." Vladoseev sighs audibly. "While I am in Atlanta in the Marriott Marquise Hotel ordering room service at your expense."

"Kolya, give me the good news."

"Well, Boss. They can't keep their transponder off for long or they'll screw up commercial traffic, so, when they turn it on, they click into OAG. We wait to get an alert on our laptop."

"Karolovsky, you are like an old man taking a piss. Why is this taking you so long? Did we get such an alert?"

"Yes we did. They show up on Flight Control in Washington, DC. Then Labrador. Then they are over the Atlantic and the North Sea. We'll have to wait to see which city they'll head for. I put my money on Zurich."

"Switzerland?"

"Yes, I know of no other."

"So then they can go off in a hundred different directions from there. Do we have assets in Zurich?"

"I don't think so. But consider that Denise has cancer. She's on a medical flight to Europe. They have a concentration of cancer clinics in Zurich. They have them other places for sure but I think that's where they are going. We just have to follow the OAG tracking. If it's Zurich, I'll leave tomorrow. Relax, Boss. Denise was in very bad shape when she left her house in New Jersey. When she lands, they can go few places but to a hospital where she'll receive medical treatment. They won't move around much after that. And the Feds think we could not track them! They land in

Zurich because her clinic is in Zurich. You can run but you cannot hide from Karolovsky, mighty tracker of sick people and embezzlers!"

"Another metaphor, Kolya?"

****

Evening fell in the Zurich suburb of Schaffhausen. Conklin had lost a day and he wasn't sure which day it was. A clinic orderly directed him into a black C-class Mercedes, and a driver took him to the heart of Schaffhausen's historic district. They stopped at a magnificent house where a large brass plaque announced in three languages that the house had once belonged to Johannes Von Müller, a famous Swiss historian.

A man who looked like a butler introduced himself as Gert. Gert took his coat and sat him at a dining table. Gert brought him a bowl of soup, some bread, and poured a brandy. He wolfed down the food and felt surprisingly better.

Gert pleasantly waved him up a wide wooden staircase. Apparently he had to carry his own luggage. At the top of the stairs, the hall was dark except for a single door spilling light onto the polished wooden floor. Conklin walked to the door and saw a wood paneled room with a massive four poster bed festooned with a white goose down comforter and giant lace-trimmed pillows.

Much to Conklin's surprise, a hot shower allowed him to fall asleep immediately.

He was back at the clinic at sunrise the next morning. Conklin entered through the glass doors and followed a sign, "Besucher und Familie" which lead to the library.

A strikingly beautiful woman waited for him there.

"Welcome to St. Agatha's, Mr. Conklin. I am Doctor Birgit Bauerle, the director here."

Fraulein Bauerle was tall and brunette. Smoky-dark eyes belied a stern, business-like expression behind stylish eyeglasses. Her near perfect figure was arrayed fashionably in a tailored black suit. Dr. Bauerle spoke perfect British-accented English, with a charming Teutonic trace.

She led him across the room to a kitchen, where the she invited him to, "…compose yourself here in the comfort of home."

She knew at once that her statement hadn't been gracefull, so she smiled and said, "Americans say this, '*Machen Sie es sich bequem.*'"

He knew little German, and in the last four years he had nearly forgotten how to speak at all. He stared at her for a moment. "Oh. 'Make yourself at home,' I guess. Uh, thanks."

"I will return later. Will there be anything else for now, Mr. Conklin?"

"Could you tell Bentley or Dr. Friedkin that I've arrived?"

She gave him a curious look. "I do not know Mr. Bentley. The Doctor is in the laboratory." She said 'doctor' as if the word meant 'Emperor' and 'laboratory' as if he were in the Himalayas.

"Well, I would like to see my, uh… wife."

"I'm afraid that is quite impossible. They have only begun her treatment."

Conklin felt his heart speed up. "When can I see her?"

Fraulein Bauerle gave him another curious expression. "Have they not explained our treatment to you?"

"No. I haven't been told very much. "

"The treatments begin as soon as patient arrives. The process requires around the clock monitoring. Until this phase is completed, contact is not allowed. It is a very sensitive procedure."

"Sensitive? How?" WITSEC had taken from him his ability to command. He dropped eye contact with her and stared at the floor.

Dr. Bauerle put a gentle hand on his shoulder. "Herr Conklin, I thought this had been explained. I've been traveling for the last month, and obviously no one has told you what to expect. Usually we provide a thorough explanation of what we do with our patients. But simply put, the first stage of the treatments requires complete isolation."

Bauerle's expression showed the strain of reducing a highly technical subject into layman's language and then translating into English. "Frau Conklin's condition is very grave. Her tumors are demanding more than her metabolism can produce. Doctor Friedkin's protocol involves shutting off the tumor's blood supply by reversing angiogenisis. Angiogensis is the body's process to produce blood vessels. His treatment works on the tumors but not normal tissue. Her body has been supplying blood to malignant tumors because they appear normal and are ignored by the immune system.

"Our treatment involves altering certain proteins of the enzymes, specifically an enzyme called VEG-F. We infuse a chemical that binds to the VEG-F and changes how it's read by cell receptors. The body's immune system recognizes any cell produced by the changed enzyme as foreign tissue and attacks them. No blood vessels are formed and anti-angiogenesis follows. With no blood supply the tumor starves and dies, allowing the immune system remove it as dead tissue.

"During the initial phase of the process, Mrs. Conklin's body must be maintained in a very specific chemical profile. She must remain completely motionless. We have hundreds of sensors in place to monitor this balance. Any unnecessary movement, even sensory stimulation, complicates this process, slows our progress, which none of us want.

"We have found this initial phase is not pleasant to watch, even for our clinicians who have seen many of these procedures. Frau Conklin is not conscious for most of this time. She rests and recuperates. Once her tumors die off, the body's natural balance returns and our treatment is less elaborate."

Conklin's forehead furrowed. "I know you're doing the best you can to explain this but most of it is going over my head. When can I see her?"

"A week from Thursday, if all goes well."

Conklin felt his knees buckle.

Fraulein Bauerle inclined her head. "Ah, we should have given you the orientation."

"Well, Bentley didn't tell me I couldn't see her for almost two weeks. I only saw her yesterday after ..." He stopped himself before he told her it had been four years since he had last seen Denise.

"Please, Mr. Conklin. Sit over here and watch this presentation. It will give you information on what we do here and what your wife is undergoing." She pressed a remote and a large LG television came to life. She handed him the remote.

A flourish of orchestral music filled the room and the television screen showed an aerial shot of the city of Schaffhausen. An announcer babbled in German. Fraulein Bauerle grabbed the remote from him, pressed a few buttons, handed it back and left the room.

"... built the clinic in the pristine forests of the former estate of Gottleib Schumann, the industrialist who ran the Goetze Industrial Conglomerate until his death in 2001." A helicopter shot zoomed over thick hardwood forests to reveal a post-Renaissance stone structure that Conklin recognized as the Klinik von St. Agatha.

"The clinic was founded by the G.I.C. for utilizing the oncology protocols developed by Dr. Hans Justice Friedkin, a Nobel Laureate in medicine for his work in cancer research. Dr. Friedkin's research focuses on terminal cancer patients, especially those with metastatic breast cancer.

"The work at St. Agatha improves the final days of these patient's lives, allowing them to spend meaningful time with their loved ones. It is hoped the work done here will eventually lead to a permanent cure."

Conklin watched the entire DVD and learned many things that neither Bentley nor Bauerle had mentioned. The treatments reduced the vitality of malignant tumors. Once the tumors began shrinking, the body's normal restorative functions produced rapid improvements in the patient's health and a renewed sense of wellbeing. The program went out of its way to remind him that the effect was temporary, that the malignancies always returned and the patient's decline resumed. But once the patient had been restored to sufficient good health, they could spend time with family and loved ones. The period of good health would continue for anywhere from two to four weeks. The scientists at the clinic had been able to increase the amount of restorative time by developing additional forms of treatment, but the patients' malignancies always returned, usually with renewed vigor.

Conklin learned, much to his alarm, that the world medical community considered Dr. Friedkin's techniques "experimental" and were not widely accepted. Major drug companies around the world had passed on the opportunity to form partnerships or provide funding in spite of the fact that he was genuinely helping patients. There were complaints from families of former patients. Despite the fact everyone was thoroughly informed and required to sign waivers, a few bitterly disappointed spouses and families filed lawsuits, which considerably reduced the resources the clinic had for continued research.

The video ended with several macabre vignettes showing patients, obviously in their restored phase; full of life and color, laughing, carefree; all of them appearing to be enthusiastic supporters of Dr. Friedkin's research. Sadly each vignette ended with a facial close-up: a freeze-frame smiling face with a caption of the woman's name, her age and the date she died.

After watching the orientation, Conklin sat on the lush leather couch, his mind attempting to absorb the flood of information. He was or soon would be with Denise again. She was still going to die, but they could have time together. She would be alive, awake, vital and laughing. The end of the program had advised him that in the patient's best interests they should both embrace this time with as much *joie de vivre* as they could muster. When the decline resumed, the patient would need the support of her loved ones all the way to the end.

For the next eleven days, Daniel Conklin followed a routine. Every morning, he arrived at the clinic. Usually he waited in the library, reading and watching television. The programs were mostly in French or German but he stared at the screen anyway, sometimes lost in his own thoughts. At midday he would make a small lunch in the kitchen and return to the Haus von Müller around sundown. After a few days, they handed him the keys to the Mercedes and he drove himself to and from the clinic. In many ways this existence reminded him of his days as a WITSEC fugitive; quiet, lonely, and waiting for something.

The big exception was that he had something new in his life that had been absent for years. After a prolonged assessment he identified what had been missing in his life.

Hope. And love.

During this period of waiting, he saw little of Fraulein Bauerle, and when he did, he'd ask about Denise. Her response was always the same; "She's coming along fine. You should be able to see her soon."

The afternoon before his second reunion with Denise, Fraulein Bauerle summoned him to her office. That's when Conklin realized she wasn't just an administrator. Her office walls were ringed with diplomas, degrees from Heidelberg, Oxford, and Harvard Medical School Department of Psychiatry. He saw certificates of studies, internships, fellowships, honorary degrees, awards, articles, and publications. The beautiful doctor looked about ten years too young to have achieved all this, Conklin thought. He sat before her desk and swiveled his head to take it all in. She smiled, and he saw dimples on her cheeks.

"Miss, I mean Doctor. This is very impressive."

"Thank you, Mr. Conklin. I can assure you it was all necessary to prepare me for my work here."

"You're a psychiatrist?"

"I do little clinical work, but my preparation is necessary to help our patients and their loved ones cope..." For a second, she hid behind her glasses. "...with what is coming."

Dr. Bauerle had stunningly beautiful eyes, but they were like deep wells full of hidden knowledge. Her face was much more than pleasant to look at, but she unsettled him at the same time. Conklin couldn't imagine what it took to help people face human tragedy.

He took a deep breath. "Her death, you mean."

She met his stare. "Yes. Well, Mr. Conklin, I thought we should have a little chat. You will see Mrs. Conklin tomorrow and..."

Conklin's eyes widened. "I will? I can see Denise?"

"Very likely, but I need to caution you. She still looks ghastly. But she is much improved from when she arrived. She has better color and more strength." Bauerle smiled slightly. "In the days to come you will be surprised. She will improve even more."

Conklin blinked, "She is… better?"

"Yes. As you know, our treatment is like fighting any illness. The body's energy is needed to attack the tumor's tissue. As her tumors shrink her body gains strength. She needs to build herself back up, but her progress is remarkable. I know she wants very much to see you."

Dr. Bauerle's smile returned. And her dimples. Her eyes flashed a trace of amusement.

Conklin shook his head. "You're beating her cancer when the other treatments failed."

Dr. Bauerle looked down at the report in front of her. "The treatment allows us to suppress certain semaphorins vital to VegF and angiogenesis. This is very delicate and requires us to masquerade, to disguise what we do from these cells. The malignancies are very defensive. After a while, they begin to produce semaphorin prototypes that see through our disguise, requiring us to alter the treatment to remain effective. In the last three years we've been able to adapt our approach against seven types of these semaphorin prototypes. But the eighth still beats us. When that happens, angiogenesis returns, creating new blood vessels, and the tumors grow again.

"Mr. Conklin, her tumors are shrinking because her immune system is now up to full capacity. Her body will continue to attack them until the anti-semaphorin treatments cease to be effective. Now we should see rapid restoration and in a week's time, Mrs. Conklin will look very good indeed."

"But it won't last," Conklin said.

Bauerle shook her head. "Ten days to a maximum of three weeks. That's where we are in the current stage of our development. Her body will reach equilibrium, and the cancer will appear to be defeated but it is only playing, like, uh the small animal that sleeps, what is it called? Opossum. It appears to be gone but is just playing Opossum. It awakens and mutates, producing a new prototype semaphorin and the tumors come back. We monitor this in our daily tests and apply new treatments for the next semaphorin. We defeat that and the cancer appears to sleep again. This cycle repeats until the eighth prototype arrives, for which we have no countermeasure. Mrs. Conklin will relapse unless by then we have developed a treatment for SP-8. SP-8 will rapidly build up undeterred and after that, she cannot possibly survive for long."

Conklin nodded like he understood, but he didn't understand most of what Bauerle had just told him.

"Before she…?"

"From that point before her cancer kills her." Dr. Bauerle said bluntly. "Unfortunately, and we don't quite understand why, but the body just gives up. SP-8 acts like a human growth hormone. Tumors return more virulent than before and the patient quickly dies. I must warn you that this stage is very disturbing to watch; a vital, seemingly healthy person wasting away in days."

Conklin felt a familiar numbness come over him. Years of isolation had subdued his normal emotions. But his return to Denise had taught him how to feel again. He hadn't seen Denise for four years. He saw her once on the airplane, and then she was whisked away from him. Two weeks would be a gift. Three weeks would be a miracle.

He looked up and Dr. Bauerle appeared to be blushing.

"Mr. Conklin, there is something else I need to speak to you about."

"What?" His voice sounded hoarse.

"Uh, breasts." Bauerle's mouth closed like a trap as if no further explanation was necessary."

Conklin blushed too. "Breasts." He could not stop himself from saying the word. His eyes dropped to Dr. Bauerle's marvelous chest. She took a deep breath, expanding that chest. As if to embarrass her even further, her nipples seemed to pop through her blouse and point at him. Her blush deepened, but her eyes took on a no-nonsense expression.

"Yes. Specifically, *your wife's* breasts." She highlighted the last three words.

"I, ah. Well, I uh.. uh." Conklin's eyes dropped and his forehead wrinkled.

"Mr. Conklin, Mrs. Conklin has no breasts. She's had a double mastectomy."

"I didn't know…" He stopped himself. Bauerle thought he was her husband, and what husband wouldn't know?

"You didn't know?" Bauerle's eyebrows arched behind her glasses.

"Uh, I mean, why is that relevant?" His eyes darted back and forth across the room, looking anywhere but at Bauerle's tits. Or her eyes.

Dr. Bauerle pressed her lips together. "Mr. Conklin, most people are unfamiliar with what happens here. Approaching death is a horrible ordeal, for couples in particular. Husbands watch their wife die slowly. Cancer takes many things away from these couples. Making love is one of those things. But then so is losing the patient's freedom, the ability to move without pain. And then one day the woman herself is gone.

"What is relevant is that here at St. Agatha's we see improvement in one hundred percent of the cases we treat... temporary improvement. For women who have been told they are going to die, it means their vitality returns and with that, a sense of wellbeing, even hope. Mr. Conklin, I am trying to say that their libido also returns. This phenomenon is quite often unexpected for both the patient and their spouses, but I can assure you the return of her health is psychologically connected to her libido."

Conklin's thinking progressed at a leaden pace. Dr. Bauerle was obviously trying to tell him something, and he just wasn't getting it. What wasn't he getting?

Dr. Bauerle took a deep breath. "Our women get better, Mr. Conklin. They get well for a while and want to resume making love with their husbands. Is that so difficult to understand?" She flushed deep crimson. Red circles glowed on her pale cheekbones.

"No, I guess not." He mumbled his words, wincing under her expectant expression while his brain searched for the missing piece of the puzzle.

"Well, Mr. Conklin?"

"Dr. Bauerle, obviously there's something you want me to understand, and I am just not getting it."

"Her breasts, Mr. Conklin. Most men want to make love to women with breasts, especially *you Americans*." Dr. Bauerle thrust her face forward as if this was both a distasteful cultural accusation and a repudiation of the American male.

"I've had this conversation with several of you." Presumably she meant American men. "I'll tell you that there will not be time for any reconstruction. Often our patients want to be perfect for their husbands but there just isn't time."

For a second it felt like a blow to the head where the numbness was immediate, and the pain would come later. Conklin blinked and felt his heart rate increase. He thought for a full minute while Dr. Bauerle's dark eyes bored into him as if his next words presaged a critical outcome.

Her voice took on the manner of a patronizing adult explaining the simplest concept to an unwilling child. "The healing time for reconstruction takes longer than she has..." Bauerle cast her eyes to the blotter on her desk. She took a deep breath.

"…to live, Mr. Conklin."

"Well, I suppose you're right. We haven't discussed it. I guess we haven't talked about, uh sex."

"She and I have, Mr. Conklin. She wanted me to broach this subject with you. How she will look to you. She won't be as perfect as she was before. She wants reassurance, like any woman."

However plodding his thought process had been, it ground to a complete halt.

"Me? With me? You've discussed it with her?"

"Yes, Mr. Conklin."

"I didn't think she would be well enough."

Dr. Bauerle smiled. It was a tight smile, but it was a relief to see the tension drain from her face. "She is very well indeed. You will be surprised when you see her tomorrow."

"Tomorrow." Conklin stared at Dr. Bauerle but saw only Denise as she had been five years ago, a vital, healthy woman. Lovely to look at. Wonderful to talk to and laugh with, innocent of any of the awful crimes he had committed and before she had been transformed by her disease. His memory drifted to the wonderful gift her body had been. They had been as natural together as any two people could be. But then his crimes and his secrets became a wedge between them. The thought of making love to Denise in her critical state had not crossed his mind, but that vacuum quickly filled with fear… and excitement.

He shook his head. "I want her as healthy as she can be. I want nothing to keep us apart."

Bauerle lowered her eyes and smiled.

"Very well, Mr. Conklin."

Chapter 10

"We got him, Boss!" Karolovsky's excitement came through the clear phone connection.

Vladoseev smiled. "Koyla, how did you do it?"

Karolovsky thought for a minute. How had he done it? He had landed in Zurich slightly hung-over from several of those tiny vodka bottles he poured down his throat. He then had reclined his business class seat and fallen asleep with his mouth open, causing one of the flight attendants to remark, "The Novocain's working but where's the dentist?"

"At the airport, I talked to the lady in a kiosk for visitor information. I told her I was looking for a cancer clinic for my aunt Matryona."

"You have an aunt Matryona?"

"Huh? Maybe I do. What of it? Anyway this lady was very helpful and concerned. Zurich has many such clinics. She gave me a catalog and asked what kind of cancer. I told her breast and maybe I blushed."

"You, Kolya? You blushed at 'breast?' Like a *Komsomol*?"

"Jesus, boss! I'm trying to tell you something. She showed me all the clinics for breast cancer. There are dozens of them. So I go and look at these clinics. Most of them have lots of patients coming and going. Very busy, but our guy is not there. I keep looking. I finally go to one in Schaffhausen."

"What is Schaffhausen?"

"Town nearby. They have two cancer clinics there. One of them no one is coming or going. Just staff, doctors and clinic workers. I wait nearby and watch the entrance. At dawn the next morning, guess who shows up driving a brand new Mercedes?"

"The wily Wylie?"

"It's him! I watch and wait. He leaves the clinic at night and goes to a big, old mansion. Next day he leaves the mansion at dawn and goes to the clinic. He's in a pattern, like he's waiting for something. Want me to nab him, boss?"

"Is there a pack of feds trailing after him?"

"If he's a billion dollar asset, there has to be, but I haven't seen them."

"I've been thinking, Nicolay. The feds are there already protecting him. This a very expensive project with them paying for a private jet and cancer clinic. Certainly he's going to have big bills to pay. Already they will be asking him for money."

"You think he may go to a bank?"

"He might. If he goes to a bank we have him and his money. How is this place, Schaffhausen?"

"Very nice, boss. Right on the Rhine. Ancient, picturesque. Lots of tourists."

"Well, keep an eye on Wylie and relax a little but not too much. If he goes to a bank, let me know."

"You're the boss, boss."

****

The night before their second reunion Daniel Conklin's insomnia helped him avoid a nightmare. He wrapped up in a fluffy cotton robe supplied by his host and sat in a leather chair in his sumptuous bedroom. A dim reading lamp turned to its lowest setting radiated a watery yellowish light. He stared through a dark window at a murky exterior. Ancient oaks outside rattled in the wind against a slate roof. The municipality of Schaffhausen was not big on streetlamps. It seemed he could peer into the night outside better than into his bleak future. He knew nothing about tomorrow or the next day. The gloomy window pane was as cryptic as a magic eight ball.

Dawn found him awkwardly sprawled in the chair, a nagging stiff neck his only reward for not messing up the bed. He limped through shaving and showering, grabbed a cup of coffee and drove to the clinic feeling frayed enough to require some treatment of his own.

Dr. Bauerle waited for him in the entrance lobby. She nodded a curt, "Good morning, Mr. Conklin. This way, please." She turned, pushed through a door which led them down a corridor flanked by empty hospital rooms.

They arrived at a room similar to all the other rooms except it was occupied. Bauerle stepped aside and the staff wordlessly vacated the room leaving him alone with Denise.

Arrays of monitoring equipment winked and chirped, showing colorful screens full of numbers and lines. The single bed was elevated allowing Denise to sit up.

And there she sat at an angle more recumbent than upright.

Despite Dr. Bauerle's warning Denise's appearance shocked him again. She was covered up to her neck in white sheets. Two incredibly skinny arms stuck out, battered with bruises from IV needles, plastered with sensors and wires. She retained the same ragged face he remembered from the airplane ride, only now she managed a diminutive smile. Over the horror of her appearance, Daniel Conklin felt his own face smile and he wondered how he had managed that.

He heard her voice, although raspy and faint, for the second time in four years.

"I can assure you I feel better than I look. I love you, Wylie."

He ran to the bed and buried his face in her chest. Her chest felt like a thin crate holding a live animal. Numbed by the feeling of touching her, he wondered if putting his weight on her was harmful. He sobbed into her sheets, feeling her hand land on the back of his head, stroking his hair. She patted him, and a long sojourn of tears without words passed between them.

Eventually the staff gently asked him to leave, telling him Mrs. Conklin was due another treatment. Someone pointed in the direction of the library. Lead footed he stumbled to the library where he had spent the last ten days waiting. He waited some more and at midday, he was summoned by a nurse who took him back to Denise's room.

Her color had improved from his earlier visit. She smiled broadly at this arrival, revealing dismal looking gray teeth, an unfortunate side effect of her medical ordeal. This time Conklin had composed himself, and he smiled back at her. They hugged and kissed for the first time in four years. The touch of her dry lips made him dizzy, and his heart beat like a jackhammer.

She whispered a few words to him.

"Wylie, I can barely talk. They're working miracles on me, but that tube they put down my throat is making me hoarse. It's only for a short time, but talking hurts. We'll have more time soon. I feel stronger every minute."

Conklin gulped several times and managed to croak out, "Oh, Deeny, Deeny, I love you."

It seemed funny to him that calling her by her pet name, now when she could hear and understand him seemed a thousand times more intimate than when he had said it on the plane. The realization that she was hearing her name from his own lips underscored the reality that they were together at last and that miracles of science and coincidence had allowed it to happen. The name came from an earlier, happier time, when the calendar held no threat and their future was unlimited.

She nodded. Her glistening eyes gave him an unspoken assent.

The clinic staff set a chair for him beside Denise's bed. They covered a bed tray in a starched tablecloth and set down shining flatware. They brought in with bowls of soup and a plate loaded with bread, cold meats and a cheese spread, but Conklin paid little attention to the food. Denise inhaled her food like a savage. She cleaned her tray before Conklin could take more than a few bites. He looked at her while he chewed and smiled. His smile felt rusty, like an artifact from his past, but, he reminded himself, now he had a good reason to smile so he grinned wide, stretching his plastic surgery scars. With her cheeks distended like a chipmunk facing a hard winter, tears flooded Denise's eyes and she stopped chewing and gazed into his face. She swallowed the load like an ostrich, touched her eyes and then her mouth and rasped, "Eyes and mouth still look the same."

He had forgotten that she had been seeing his altered face, the one WITSEC had chosen for him. It was the face of a fugitive, not the man with whom she had fallen in love. But they couldn't change his eyes, and to keep the world from seeing his smile, they had buried him alive in Lonesome Town. The realization erased his smile for a moment but soon it came back. Now even WITSEC couldn't change him anymore. He and Deeny would rebuild each other.

In a week, her color returned permanently and her hair grew back in short waves, still full of gray. An exercise regimen put some muscle on her bones and a healthy diet eliminated the dark circles under her eyes.

Watching her recovery Daniel Conklin witnessed a medical miracle. From a near skeletal corpse, her body rebounded with unbelievable vitality. In two days, Denise could push her own wheelchair, and on the third she stood and took a few steps.

The mysterious treatments continued. The clinic permitted Conklin to have meals with her. The rest of time they kept her behind the swinging doors. He spent this time waiting in the clinic's library. Perhaps to test his new found sense of freedom, Conklin used St. Agatha's library's computer and registered with breastcancer.org. He joined chat/support groups for families of cancer victims, rarely making comments of his own and mostly reading posts of others. At night he returned to the ancient house in the middle of Old Towne Schaffhausen. When he couldn't sleep, he continued his internet exploration of the dark world of breast cancer using the ancient desktop in Haus Von Muller.

And so a full week passed, during which Conklin saw Dr. Bauerle only once. On that single occasion, she informed him that Denise had defeated all her stage one tumors. Her body was in full recovery mode and each day would bring more miracles of restoration.

The clinic followed this announcement with a complete makeover for Denise – new haircut, makeup, wardrobe, nothing extravagant but the results were stunning. She dressed in her new clothes for their meals. The clinic added a thirty minute visit prior to their dinner, sort of a happy hour where neither of them drank much, but basked in the joys of being together. Although still gaunt, she exuded a new energy and her eyes shined with hope.

At the third of their happy hour sessions, as was customary, Denise and Conklin had the library to themselves. Since their arrival at the clinic, Conklin hadn't seen another patient.

They sat and held hands and looked at each other. Denise's cheekbones had lost some of their hollowness. She looked deeply into his eyes, trying to learn his new face. But on this day, their conversation was sparse, like both of them had something difficult to say.

"Deeny, we need to set some limits."

She nodded, "Okay."

"We need to discuss, uh. I don't know what it is… what to call it."

She nodded again. "Wylie, you're still my Wylie. Your face is different but it's still you. And you will always be Wylie, not Dan or Daniel or whatever they named you."

"Okay. Nobody knows us here anyway."

"The word is death. My death. It's coming. I'm going to die."

Conklin flinched but Denise continued.

"Dr. Friedkin told me what this treatment does and what it doesn't do. I'll get better. I mean, I feel so much better right now and it hasn't been but a couple of weeks. But SP-8, the eighth semaphorin prototype is out there lurking. They work very hard in the lab but they haven't cracked the code. The eighth prototype is the end…, will be the end for me."

His eyes dropped and he nodded.

"So we have the rest of August, maybe even some of September. What we don't have is forever. But few people get to take more than a week on their vacation so we should act like we're on holiday. People on holiday enjoy today and tomorrow and the next day. And, Wylie, we're in love." She looked at him. He nodded with tears streaming down his face. She placed a hand on his. Her hand was hot like a towel warmed in an oven.

"Wylie, we're in a lovely place. It's not like we have to worry about going back to dull and boring jobs. We can't travel because of the treatments but we can enjoy this place, local Switzerland. We can take it a day at a time. It's a beautiful place and it's ours."

He nodded. "Deeny, I love you. We won't talk about the future. We know what's coming. But I got to say something about the past. I've got to…"

Denise held up her thin hand, placing hot fingertips against his lips.

"Not now you don't. Four years ago you were swimming in a rip tide, Wylie. Maybe you weren't strong enough not to be swept up in it. You went along, did things and things were done to you. What happened then took you away from me, and for a while I hated what happened to you. But I knew inside my Wylie was a good person. Maybe not strong enough at the time, but you always were smart and no matter how bad it got, you'd eventually figure out a way to come back from it. Then I'd thought you died. There was something weird about it…, too many questions. But cancer came and I stopped thinking about anything else. After all the treatments there was no use in fighting it. Not without you. We were never to be together again.

"But you came back and just in time. We're back together for now. Maybe we won't have a long life together. But we have today and tomorrow. And whatever God has in store for us. I would trade everything I have in the world for just the next moment with you. There's got to be a reason. We must have something really important to do. We have to live and be happy with that moment. Today, tomorrow, whatever. We won't make plans for anything longer than two days from now. If we have one day in September, we grab a bottle of wine, some bread and cheese and sit out on that rock in the Rhine. Yes, I saw the promo video. You can almost walk to it. We'll go there and celebrate how beautiful life is."

Conklin's eyes continued to stream. His right hand darted to the table behind the couch where the clinic kept a box of tissues. But she reached out her arms to him so he blotted his eyes against her clean, green hospital gown which draped in roomy abundance across her bony shoulder. He held her gaunt body tight and it felt to him like a feather. Chest to chest he felt her heart pumping against his heart. The unused tissue dropped onto the surface of the leather couch behind her and they held each other until happy hour was over.

Chapter 11

It was normal for Conklin to turn in when he returned to the Von Muller Haus. Gert usually asked him if there was anything he needed. That evening Gert waited for him at the bottom of the polished staircase when Conklin came through the front door.

"Sir, will there be anything this evening?" His English was nearly as flawless as the impeccable mansion he kept.

"Not tonight, Gert." Conklin headed up stairs. Once in his room, he locked the door, which was not customary. Instead of getting ready for bed he dimmed the room lights, removed his shoes, settled into the leather chair and propped his feet up on a hassock. He folded his hands in his lap, laid his head back and closed his eyes.

After a moment he thought to himself, Body, it is time to relax. Mind it's time to relax. He repeated those two sentences while controlling his breathing.

It was time to talk to Dad.

Wylie Schram's father had been a CPA, a man who made numbers his life. The legacy he left his son was an awareness of the power of money. He had taught him the language, the skill and the craft of accounting. Wylie had gone beyond what his father taught him, mastering finance and economics, particularly investments and securities. His father had always been Wylie Schram's most trusted advisor. And then he died.

Wylie never believed in séances or that you could speak to the dead, but he believed in and had been a practitioner of mind control. He hadn't done it in nearly five years but tonight he was going to try.

Counting backwards from one hundred, he commanded his body to relax and allow his mind to go deeper. Gradually his heartbeat slowed. Tension left his body and his mind emptied of all thoughts.

When he felt he'd reached the alpha state, listened to the quiet in his mind. Silence wrapped him in a state of soothing comfort.

Using his imagination he slowly constructed a familiar scene: a wilderness lake with few roads and fewer people. The lake came from his childhood experience. His family owned a cabin on Sharbot Lake in Ontario, Canada. He imagined the lake's endless natural beauty, steep forested hills rising out of deep, clear water. Sunlight warmed him and birds sang in the trees. As he walked, the scene became more detailed and specific, matching what he remembered of the place. He kept his mind happy and empty, enjoying the serenity this comfortable setting brought.

When he was ready he approached the small log framed house sitting on a bluff above the lake.

A man sat on the porch. The man was reading a newspaper and did not look up. Wylie knew him. It was Fletcher, a Canadian who worked as a general handyman and caretaker for people who owned cabins in the area. Fletcher was known for his reticence so Conklin did not expect much of a greeting.

Fletcher grumbled, "It's about time. What's it been, four, five years?"

"About that. Good to see you, too."

"Hmmm… Your father's inside waitin' for you."

The porch boards creaked as he trod them. He remembered the sound and it filled him with a sense of nostalgia. He opened the door and stepped inside.

It was warm in the cabin and it felt good. His father sat beside a small fireplace glowing with yellow orange light. Wood smoke tickled his nostrils.

Dad was just like he remembered him, gray hair, glasses, face lined with wisdom. He smiled but kept his gaze on the fire.

"Don't get up, dad."

"I won't. It's been a while, son."

"I know, Dad. I should have been here a lot sooner." Wylie took the other chair and faced his father. Logs in the fireplace crackled between them.

"You've had a lot on your mind."

"My mind's been as empty as my life, Dad."

Dad nodded. "Things are different now, right? You and Denise are back together."

"Yes, but she has cancer."

"That's terrible."

"Yes it is, but what I came here for… I need to know what to do."

"You've got tough choices, Wylie. We've got secrets to keep, right? Nothing tops that."

"Yes, we have secrets. Dad, you helped me with them. You helped me hide the fact that I hid that money. You helped me beat eleven lie detector tests."

His dad looked at him. The expression in his dad's eyes showed no reproach.

"Wylie, you had a good reason for doing it. That money is other people's money. We're keeping it for them. Only for a little while. Until

67

we figure out the right way to give it back, right son? To keep it out of the wrong hands. We need to know who we can trust. We're still in agreement on that? That's why we did it… the only way we could do it, right?"

Wylie stared into the fire.

"Dad, I think I've figured out a way to give it back."

****

Bentley read the email, "Subject locked his door for the first time since arrival. Surveillance video shows subject appears to be taking a nap in the chair. Subject gets up thirty-five minutes later and goes to bed. While he's in the chair he does not move. Attached is the low-res video, which we sent because the subject doesn't move."

First Bentley requested the high-res version of the video but learned nothing from it. Schram truly did not move during his "nap." But locking the door to his room bothered him.

"Daniel, you got something cooking?"

****

The next morning Dan Conklin departed from his normal routine again. He couldn't see Denise until lunchtime, so instead of heading for St. Agatha's he drove randomly around Schaffhausen. He looked in the Mercedes rearview mirror and didn't see anyone following him, but he knew nothing about surveillance and assumed that whoever might follow him would be expert at remaining undetected. At least two factions might be following him, Bentley with the Department of Justice and Vladoseev, who probably wanted to torture him.

Both wanted the billion and a half. He could trust no one on this.

After driving more or less aimlessly around the picturesque city, he left the Mercedes near a wooded park on Hochstrasse and entered the Swiss Post Office on the same block. The Swiss Post Office clerk spoke English, so he had no trouble asking him where he could catch a taxi. He noticed they had a rear door and scooted through it onto Bocksrietweg. From there he casually strolled to the location the postal worker gave him. He gave the cabby an address for Migros Bank, AG.

At the bank he opened an account and deposited about 100 Euros and some change, about all the money he had in his pocket. He stuffed all the paperwork in his pockets and left. He has the bank call him a cab to return to where he parked the Mercedes. He arrived at St. Agatha's just in time for lunch with Denise.

Denise noted his upbeat attitude.

"You look happy, my love," she said tenderly.

Conklin let out a long breath. "Deeny, the staff here told me that in a day or two you can go out for a few hours."

"Right. We're going to dinner at... what is the name of the restaurant?"

"*Wirtschaft zum Frieden,* I think."

"Ouch, Wylie. Your German pronunciation is horrible." But Denise's eyes crinkled with humor. Wylie had to smile back at her and he told his first joke in four years.

"You're lucky I didn't spit on you!" They both chuckled.

"Wylie, it's so good to see you smile. I missed your twisted sense of humor."

"Seriously, Deeny. I've got some things I need to talk to you about but only after we drink a bottle of Worst-shaft-zoom-Freedom's best champagne."

After lunch, the staff took Denise for more treatments and Conklin sat in the St. Agatha's library at their desktop computer.

The meditation session with his father had enabled him to dredge up a few of the secrets Conklin had buried in his mind over four years ago. Using meditation he was able to "forget" many details that the federal RICO investigators wanted to know.

His federal inquisitors had never discovered how much computer savvy Wylie Schram had. Computers keep records of everything that's done on a keyboard. Schram had learned how to hide what he did on his computer from anyone who monitored the computer's logs.

He keyed in a very short program written in Intel machine language. The program contained thirty-six commands and could be entered into any command line, an original but seldom used feature of most personal computers. The program allowed the user to operate a PC keyboard and mouse, bypassing the system's key-logging registers.

After entering and assembling the key cloaking program, he ran a malware identification program and found several key-loggers on the clinic's computer. He erased his most recent strokes from the key-logger's logs.

He then logged on to the Breastcancer.org chat room and used another short program that allowed him to operate as an invisible user on that chat room's host's server. This made it possible to roam the internet without leaving a record in his computer's keystroke log where he had gone or what he had done.

He then pulled in text from several chat rooms to form a library of innocuous entries. Then Conklin "fed" the data into the logs. If anyone had this computer under surveillance, they would see normal, rather bland internet activity, certainly nothing that would arouse suspicion. Bentley's agents would grow bored after a few lines. In less than thirty minutes, Dan Conklin had made whatever he decided to do on that computer nearly invisible.

Conklin breathed a sigh of relief and tested his work by reviewing what the key logging programs were collecting from him.

Four years ago, Conklin had used his proficiency with mind control to bury an incredible amount of detail about where he had hidden the one and half billion dollars. In last night's meditation his father had revealed some of this information. He logged into his breastcancer.com ID and triggered the stealth program, which logged him into the site's server as an anonymous user. Then he opened up a browser and logged into an offshore bank account in a bank in Belize, as the registered the owner of the account. Four years ago this account had received a very hefty initial deposit. Having stashed a little over fifteen million US dollars, Conklin had assigned the funds to ultra conservative investments that had grown the amount about six percent per year. Conklin was gratified to see the assets in this one account were currently worth over eighteen million dollars!

He entered a funds transfer of less than two thousand Euros to the new bank account he had just opened in the Migros Bank, AG. He knew the Belize bank would send an email to confirm this transfer so he logged into his Gmail account corresponding to account's official owner, a fake investment company. He deleted four year's accumulation of correspondence and responded to the most recent with keywords and codes. He received confirmation within seconds. A small smile creased his face. He felt rich again, and now he had a mission.

It was time to go see Dr. Friedkin.

Chapter 12

"He went to a bank, boss. The Migros Bank, AG. He was in there about an hour."

"Hmm. Did he spot you?"

"No. I've been very careful. I even got a car that looks like one the Swiss would drive. It's like a minivan, European style. Wylie didn't see me but he did go into a post office earlier. He ducked out the back door, which means he is suspicious, like someone is tailing him. Then he gets into a cab. I ran back to my car and followed him to that bank. I can't do anything in the bank because it's like a fortress. They hold you in a glass booth while they look you over. The front door is always locked.

"An hour later another cab pulls up and takes him back to the Mercedes. His car is in a park full of nannies and kids. And cops. He jumps in the Mercedes and back to the clinic."

"Well, we don't know if he stashed any of the money in this Migros Bank but he just confirmed to me that he's still got it. How good is the security at the clinic?"

"I don't know but I'll bet it's got plenty of cameras."

"Koyla, you're still camera shy."

"You're damn right. I think they pictured me at that freaking drugstore."

"Don't worry about that. Still no federal tail on him?"

"Haven't seen any, boss, but they have to be here."

"Stay on him, Kolya. I think we grab them both when he comes out of the clinic with her. We'll have much more leverage with Schram if we have the woman too."

"What do we do if the girlfriend dies while she's still inside the clinic?"

"Then we grab him without her but just not now. The more he tries to slip around like he's a spy, the more likely he's relaxing, going to banks and poking around in his money. He's going to get careless."

****

At first, Dr. Bauerle stonewalled Conklin's request for an interview.

"Mr. Conklin, Dr. Friedkin does not make appointments. He is much too busy. We are running a race against time, and your wife could use a breakthrough in the lab."

Conklin held up a hand. "Dr. Bauerle, while I appreciate how busy you both are, my purpose is vitally important to the clinic and to his work."

Bauerle raised an eyebrow. "Exactly how so?"

"I will tell you both in the meeting. I will keep it very brief. It won't take more than thirty minutes. If you like we can hold the meeting over lunch."

Bauerle looked slightly ill. "I am well aware of your American penchant for conducting business during meals. The practice is not popular here."

Conklin shook his head. "Look, Dr. Bauerle, lunch doesn't matter, but I must speak to Dr. Friedkin as soon as possible."

Bauerle looked very stern. "I am afraid it is quite impossible. I am sorry, Mr. Conklin."

"Then I will take Denise out of St. Agatha's. There are other clinics nearby. Perhaps they will be more accommodating."

Bauerle went white. "Mr. Conklin! That is quite impossible. Mrs. Conklin cannot leave the clinic."

"I don't see why not. We're going to dinner tomorrow night at *Wirtschaft zum Frieden.*"

Bauerle winced at his pronunciation of the German name. "Mr. Conklin, we cannot allow you to take Mrs. Conklin out of the clinic during her treatment. She can go to dinner but must return here immediately to continue the treatment. You will put her life at risk."

"Dr. Bauerle, we are not prisoners here. We can leave whenever we want. I will demand a full refund, minus any expenses, of course. Even your Swiss police will not prevent us from going to our choice of clinic."

Bauerle was speechless for a few seconds. She slumped and dropped her eyes to her desk. "Very well. When did you want this meeting, Mr. Conklin."

"Now, Bauerle. Now would be fine."

Dr. Friedkin fumed when they entered his office. His desk was stacked with papers of the non-identifiable variety. The tip of his nose supported a pair of reading glasses.

"Mr. Conklin, what's this nonsense about taking Mrs. Conklin out of our clinic. You will kill her if you do that."

"Dr. Friedkin, I have no intention of taking Denise out of your clinic."

"But you told Dr. Bauerle…"

"Dr. Friedkin, I needed to see you. I don't have much contact with your staff and they rarely speak to me. Dr. Bauerle chooses to speak to me when it's in her interest, so it's not like I have a very clear status around here. Facing this lack of communication, I had to use firm measures to get this meeting. And believe me, doctor I wouldn't interrupt you if it wasn't important."

Dr. Friedkin appeared about to argue but instead looked down at his desk. "What is this about? A complaint?"

"Not at all. You do wonderful work here, in spite of keeping me in the dark most of the time." Both doctors appeared about to offer a response to that but Conklin moved on.

"You probably don't know much about me or what you do know may be incorrect. I ran a Fortune 1000 company for a number of years, one of the largest and most successful corporations in the world. I believe you've been told that I was a small town pharmacist.

The two doctors looked at each other.

"Did you ever wonder how a small town pharmacist could afford this clinic?"

They looked at each other again. Daniel Conklin continued.

"Your treatment here is very expensive. I estimate the cost is between six and eight million US dollars. For one patient, that is exorbitant by any standard. You could not afford to treat someone if they didn't come with deep pockets. You didn't ask for any money from me, and I haven't seen me a single invoice, so I believe that Denise's expenses are paid in advance. There's no way you could have very large cash reserves."

Both doctors appeared to have a response to that as well but Conklin held up his hand. "Trust me, I could write out your balance sheet within a few thousand Euros. You have no money. What you do have is a very impressive clinic. Lots of new equipment still in shrink-wrap and nowhere do I see any evidence of depreciated capital assets. You know, serviceable equipment but worn from constant use. And you have a very impressive staff. Everyone seems to know what they're doing. You must made a giant capital outlay to get this place operational, but now that you're up and running, you have no patients. I've seen the mail come in and it's nothing but journals. Maybe a few bills. The point is that your volume of mail is less than a country store, not that of a thriving clinic.

"Your deliveries are all equipment, supplies and provisions. Maybe you bank on line and have huge stipends arriving daily from many sources, but I don't really think that's the case.

"Before you let us come here, you received eight million dollars from a man named Bentley."

The two doctors froze. Dr. Friedkin blinked and looked toward Bauerle. Bauerle turned out to be a better poker player. Her face showed statuesque indifference.

Conklin thought, Got you, Friedkin.

Dr. Friedkin cleared his throat and checked his manicure. "Bentley. We know no one named..."

"Dr. Friedkin, someone made arrangements for us to travel here. On my end, it was a man named Bentley. I've been observing your operation for nearly a month now and I can assure you that I've seen much more than a small town pharmacist could ever understand. While I do not claim to be expert in medicine, I am a world beater in business. You need a king's ransom to treat a patient, and this clinic is living from ransom to ransom."

Both doctors bristled at his statement. Conklin allowed them time to respond. They didn't, so he continued.

"What you do here is miraculous. I also know your research continues. You're trying desperately to create a cure. You currently have only one patient, Denise, although you are sized to handle a much larger number."

"Mr. Conklin," Dr. Bauerle said. "Since you say you are not really a small time pharmacist, you may have even less medical knowledge than we first were led to believe. How can you estimate our capacity?"

"Walking around and observing your facility has told me a lot about St. Agatha's. I saw your parking lot. It's mostly empty except for my car and your staff's cars. You also have too large a staff for the number of patients. I can pretty much walk in and out of this place without seeing anyone. Your staff would be super busy if you were full of patients. When staff is super busy they are also super visible, scurrying around, coming and going. These people are expensive. If I were running things, I'd have everyone working over capacity. When a large staff remains invisible most of the day, it means they're hiding from supervisors. If your staff was properly deployed, they'd be frantically busy. But they are not. Your parking lot is empty. Maybe even a small town pharmacist could figure this out.

"I'm certain you are running on a shoestring. You haven't even asked me for more money. I haven't spoken to any accountants or administrators. I haven't given you a credit card, shown an insurance card. In fact you haven't asked me anything about myself. You just sort of took me in, put me in very comfortable accommodations, provided an excellent car, a

Mercedes for god's sake!

"Look, Doctors, you run a first class clinic, and what you've done for Denise is nothing short of a miracle. But I know I can help make you more efficient. Your revenue streams are too isolated. That eight million will last you about two, maybe three more weeks, which is more…" Conklin's voice broke. "than Denise has before she… After that if you don't get more patients, you will have to make cuts or close down."

Friedkin and Bauerle looked at each other. Conklin continued.

"Doctors, I believe in what you do here, but this operation is unsustainable. You must have very specialized staff and you have to keep paying them. You can't lay them off. They'll go get other jobs and they won't come back. There are many clinics and hospitals in Switzerland specializing in cancer treatment. Also Germany, France, Belgium and Italy are opening up new clinics all the time and they'll take all the clinicians they can get. Brazil, India, China, Japan and Indonesia are trying to recruit your staff right now and offering them more money than you can. Cancer treatment is a booming business and competition is growing. And yet if you can attract the patients you built this clinic to accommodate and charge reasonable fees, you are in position to capitalize on and be the leader in this industry.

"Let me cut to the chase. This clinic was built with higher expectations. Clearly you need more patients. You work miracles here. I've seen it with my own eyes. I've seen the testimonials on your video. So doctors, where are the patients?"

Dr. Friedkin had ceased to glare at him. Now he slumped lower in his chair. Dr. Bauerle's lips tightened, but her expression hardly changed.

Bauerle spoke. "Mr. Conklin, we don't cure cancer here."

"Yes, the video is very clear about that."

Bauerle continued. "The normal ways to treat cancer, radiation, chemotherapy, surgery… are effective. In some cases, patients appear to be cured. Some patients even return to normal lives."

"Right, but curing cancer is not as common as people believe. Even totally cancer free patients sometimes get cancer again later in their lives. I've studied the statistics."

"Mr. Conklin, our results are different. Although current medical protocols are able to defeat some cancers, many patients are not cured. Cancer can strike anyone and those who have had cancer are at higher risk. Tumors disappear but often return later and cancer patients can die of something else.

"Traditional oncologists offer the patient hope. That is the difference. They offer better statistics, ten percent, twenty, fifty percent or better. Everyone wants to live. When patients are diagnosed with cancer they are scared for their lives. Medicine errs on the side of hope. Patients all want to believe they will be the lucky one, the one who gets to go home to their families and live a normal life. But it is a lie and we all know it. The doctors know it, and the patients suspect it. We are all going to die, Mr. Conklin, and if nothing else gets us, we'll die of cancer."

Although Conklin didn't think Bauerle's joke was funny, he smiled and she smiled in response, flashing those amazing dimples. Then she returned to her stern expression.

"We do not offer hope at St. Agatha's. When we built the facility, we had such enthusiasm that a cure was just around the corner, at least for breast cancer. But when semaphorin-1 mutated into semaphorin-2, we had to face reality. The disease is far more complicated than we realized. SP-2 mutated through SP-7 and each time we eventually found a way to defeat it, but it's not a virus where we can build up an immune reaction. We're trying to kill our own living tissue. We may not even be close to a cure."

Dr. Bauerle rose from her chair and stood over Conklin and looked into his eyes. Her face, marvelously symmetrical and subtly proportioned seemed so beautiful to him. He could see tiny lines around her eyes that this close made her look older. And wiser and haggard from the struggle. He grew uncomfortable with the nearness of her. She radiated heat like a sunlamp. Her perfume tingled his nostrils like enchanted smoke.

"Mr. Conklin, we've never offered a patient hope. We only tell them the truth. We can make them feel better for a short time but they eventually are going to die because we cannot defeat the eighth prototype."

Tears welled in her dark eyes and she sat back on the front edge of Dr. Friedkin's desk. She lowered her face and covered it with her hands.

Conklin looked at the floor. He had intended to offer to make their clinic more efficient, possibly helping to fund them, but now he felt their frustration. Their dream of curing millions of cancer sufferers had ended in one defeat after another and all they could do was make their patient's lives a little better before the ultimate end.

Conklin straightened himself in his seat. He deliberately softened his voice.

"Doctors, I cannot help you in your research except to make your organization more efficient and to help you find new sources of funding. If you'll allow me a little access to your operation, I can suggest ways to cut your costs and give you more money and time in the lab."

They considered this for a moment. Dr. Bauerle stood and walked to the right of the desk, her hips passing within inches of Conklin's face.

Dr. Friedkin spoke. "Mr. Conklin, we've never had what you would consider typical administration. We never had the patient load to require it. Dr. Bauerle has done a very good job overseeing our business side."

"I'm sure she has, but that is not her specialty. I've seen all the diplomas on her office walls and her training is in medicine and psychiatry, not administration. Although she is smart enough to handle any task," Bauerle dimpled again. "... her talents are best used elsewhere."

"Quite so, Mr. Conklin. Let us consider what you are offering. We might be interested in studying a proposal."

Conklin shrugged. "Don't take too long, Doctor. If freeing you both up and having more operating capital leads to a solution sooner... I would be interested and so would Denise."

****

An hour later Bentley received a call from Dr. Friedkin.

"Yes, Hans. How is our boy?"

"This time you sent me a difficult one, Bentley."

"Really? Daniel? What's he up to?"

"Until yesterday, he was the model supporting husband. Today he's demanding meetings, asking questions and offering to 'help' us." Dr. Friedkin spoke the word 'help' with slight derision.

"What kind of demands?"

"First he threatened to take Denise out of the clinic if I didn't meet with him. So I met with him and he tells me that was just a ruse to secure the meeting. Then he tells me he is not a pharmacist but a business man who ran a big American company."

"Did he say which one?"

"No, but he claimed he could run this place better than us and made some rather shrewd observations. You know we're not very businesslike around here."

"Well, Dr. Friedkin, you staffed the place with medical people, not administrators. Sometimes I'm surprised Bauerle is able to keep the lights on."

"She does her best. Our government is very strict about compliance and licensing. We don't want a bunch of canton bureaucrats in here every month demanding to see the books. The first thing they'll want to see is where our money comes from."

"Neither of us wants too much scrutiny in that area, Hans."

"So what should I do with your boy Daniel? Is he who he said he is, a business tycoon?"

"Conklin makes Donald Trump look like Junior Achievement."

"What is that?"

"Dan Conklin could squeeze money out of a rock."

"Bentley, I find your metaphors baffling."

"If we turned him loose on funding St. Agatha's, your money problems would be over, but I'm not sure we can do that. I wonder what's motivating him."

"He thinks if we had more money, we could find a cure in time to save Frau Conklin."

Bentley was silent for half a minute.

"Jesus, Hans. I wish that were true."

****

After driving to nearby Dachsen, Conklin entered a quiet and nearly empty café. Lunch hour had passed and the sun heated Dorfstrasse in higher than normal heat. He ordered a double espresso and sat at a small wire legged table that wobbled precariously.

He waited twenty-five minutes and finally concluded that the man he had invited here would not show. A movement from the back of the café caught his eye. A man parted a bead curtain and strode into the room from the kitchen startling the waiter who had nearly fallen asleep behind the counter. The man also ordered *ein doppelter Espresso* and joined him at the quivering table.

He was medium height and build. His face had what was currently referred to as 'designer stubble.' The man's eyes darted all over the room and his shoulders twitched now and then.

Conklin had selected the man after an intense internet search.. Avoiding normal email, they communicated through LinkedIn messages and blog posts on www.breastcancer.org. The man's resume indicated he had served with Shin Bet, Israeli Internal Security.

"Herr Conklin, I presume?" His voice came from the corner of his mouth, raspy, muted and accented but not Swiss or French or anything Conklin could recognize.

"Yes and you are Zinsser?"

The man nodded.

Conklin didn't like to begin business relationships with a complaint. "Herr Zinsser, your arriving a half hour late does not make a good impression."

The man's expression did not change. "You noticed I came in through the back door?"

"Yes."

"I took some time to observe, to look around outside. You must know you are being followed."

"What? I mean, I guess I had suspicions. That's why I made these arrangements for here in Dachsen, but no, I haven't seen anyone following me."

"Tall, reddish hair. Eastern European. He's across the street watching you. This man doesn't think you will spot him so he's not exercising much caution."

Conklin thought about that for a minute. "I saw him a couple of weeks ago. Bentley called him Nicolay Karolovsky. He's supposed to be very dangerous. I had no idea how he could have tracked me from… where I came." He had almost said "Nebraska" but held back out of habit.

"Who is Bentley?" Zinsser asked.

"Bentley is a high level director in the American Justice Department. He runs WITSEC, the federal witness protection program."

"And you are in WITSEC?"

Conklin hesitated. "I was. I don't know what my situation is now."

Zinsser also hesitated. "Well that might explain the other tail."

"What?"

"Yes, Herr Conklin, you are being followed by someone else. The Russian doesn't know about them either. What have you done to rate such scrutiny?"

"Zinsser, if I hire you, that's one thing you can't do is poke around in my background."

Zinsser held up a hand, the back of which was covered with coarse black hair.

"Mr. Conklin, I am curious by nature. That's why we're having this meeting. Who does this Karolovsky work for?"

"A Russian named Vladoseev. Bogdan Ivanovich Vladoseev, now a New York City hoodlum."

"Ah, the new class of Russian gangster. America has become a haven for that bunch." Zinsser stared at him a long time. "Herr Conklin, what sort of help do you need?"

"Zinsser, I'm an amateur here. As you say, I've got these guys following me. If it is the feds, they're here to keep this Karolovsky from grabbing me, but the feds have their own agenda. In a month or so I may need to get away from them. I'm not sure how to do that. For now, I'd like to have some advice on surveillance. I want to know how they can track me. I know my room is bugged and probably the car. Perhaps even St. Agatha's."

"What is St. Agatha's?"

"St. Agatha's is a cancer treatment facility. Switzerland has hundreds of them."

"You are here for treatment?"

"No. My wife."

"Ah. And she has a month,"

Conklin nodded. "At this moment, I don't know what my plans are, but Karolovsky and Vladoseev have their own plans."

"To do what?"

"Kidnap me."

"For ransom?"

"Not exactly. I'm the one who would have to pay it. They think I have a lot of money."

"Have you?"

Conklin said nothing.

"Herr, Conklin, I'm not certain I can work for you."

"Why not?"

"I can help you with surveillance, but apparently you aren't free to tell your entire story. I don't know what I'm getting into. And maybe you can't trust me."

"Do I need to trust you, Herr Zinsser?"

"You are the goose that lays the gold eggs. The goose can trust no one"

Conklin thought for a moment. Their *doppelter Espressos* had cooled to frothy mud.

"Zinsser, I know I'm vulnerable, but I'm not helpless. I need information. What they can do is a complete mystery to me. I don't know their capability."

Zinsser was quiet for a long time. "You must have a lot of money, which is very motivating. And attracts the worst sorts. If this Vladoseev wants your money, and the American Federals are hovering over you, it must be an astronomical amount."

Conklin lowered his eyes. Zinsser flagged the waiter, who brought them new espressos.

"Herr Conklin, these men following you... they believe you have the money because it is too much to think otherwise."

"Like you said, Zinsser, they won't give up."

"And you still have this money?"

Conklin sipped his espresso and stared at Zinsser. "The feds couldn't get me to admit it and neither will you."

Zinsser shrugged. "What do you want me to do?"

"This should not be too difficult. First I want you to buy me ten iPhones. Then figure out a way to get them to me so that my watchers won't know. I assume they're tracking my cell phone and probably have something in the car. I know much more about computer communication than I do electronic surveillance. I've written down instructions for you how we can continue to send secure email and text messages to each other." Conklin pulled an envelope out of his jacket and placed it the table.

Zinsser ignored the envelope and looked out the front window of the café.

"There's twenty thousand Euros in there," Conklin said.

"I won't need that much."

"Loyalty is expensive..., but it's worth what you pay for it."

"Why don't I make a deal with the man across the street?"

"Are you a fool, Zinsser?"

"Not usually."

"That guy across the street thinks I have the money and so do the feds. It ought to be obvious to you... they don't have it."

Zinsser smiled and picked up the envelope.

"Herr Conklin, the goose can only stick his neck out so far."

Chapter 13

"Wylie, what are you up to?" Denise's question took him completely by surprise. He instinctively looked left and right.

"Whoops! I didn't mean to spook you, sweetheart. It's your eyes. You look so happy. I remember you had that same look when you were working on a big deal."

Denise read him like a book. Conklin chided himself to better guard his emotions.

He smiled. "Honey, I'll tell you about it soon. It's a little surprise. And I am happy. You look spectacular and we're going out for the first time in a long time."

Denise was resplendent in a new smoke-blue silk dress, matching heels and borrowed jewelry. She took delicate steps and Conklin protectively steered her toward the limo. She still looked very thin, but her skin glowed with new vitality and she could not stop smiling.

Their driver held the door, and Conklin gently helped Denise into the back seat. He climbed in beside her. When they were underway, Denise held his face and kissed him with surprising strength. Her lips felt wonderful. Conklin's head spun like gyro.

When they broke she stared at him, her eyes moist.

"You do look happy, Wylie."

"And why shouldn't I be?"

"You should. We both should. My god, a few weeks ago, I was so depressed, so lonely for you. Now I feel like I'm in a 'Heaven Can Wait' movie."

He chuckled. "I know, sweetheart." She rested her head on his chest. They watched Old Towne Schaffhausen slip by past the limo's windows.

Wirtschaft zum Friden was all white plaster and wooden beams inside. The enthusiastic headwaiter led them to an elegant table in the center of the room. Conklin stood by the table and held his hand up as the headwaiter pulled out the chair for Denise.

"Excuse me, sir," Conklin said.

"Yes?"

"We'd like that table over by the bay window."

The headwaiter was well trained. He showed no change of expression. "I am afraid that table is booked. Is there anything wrong with this table, sir?"

"No, but my wife has been in the clinic for a month and she'd like a look at your beautiful gardens."

"Ah, we welcome any patient from St. Agatha's. We will offer a vase of fresh flowers instead. Will that suffice?"

"No sir. With all respect, we would like that table over by the bay window. It is the same size as this one and whoever reserved it can have this table when they arrive. And they can enjoy that vase of fresh flowers as well."

"This is a very unusual request. We've have you booked at this table, sir and here you shall be served."

Denise who looked concerned. "Wylie, this table…"

Conklin held up his hand. "Sir, I am afraid that you must accommodate us at that table near the window. Otherwise we will walk to Wirtschaft zum Beckenburg, just a few blocks from here. I'm told they have a view of the Rhine."

Conklin had prepared himself to deal with the haughty pique the Swiss showed when a visitor questioned some detail of their extensively well-organized country.

"Impossible, sir. I must confer with my staff. This is quite upsetting." He hustled off.

"Wylie, why all this fuss over the table?" Denise whispered.

He gave her a quick grin. Another white-shirted waiter hurried over. "This way sir and madam."

At the table by the window, the waiter again held Denise's chair. Wylie discretely palmed a twenty Euro note into his hand. Shortly a giant bottle of Pellegrino appeared and the waiter poured sparkling water into crystal goblets.

"Deeny, look at this garden."

"It's nice Wylie, but…"

"Honey, keep looking at the garden. I have to tell you a few things."

Instead Denise looked at him.

"Deeny, keep looking out the window. I believe we're under surveillance which means that table over there is probably bugged."

"What?"

"Keep looking out the window. I've been in witness protection for all these years and hardly paid attention, but now we have to protect our privacy. We're going to have some time together and I don't want every episode of our life analyzed by federal agents."

"Is that why we're talking to the window pane?"

"They have video cameras and experts who can read lips."

Denise was silent for a moment. "Wylie, what's going on?"

"Our federal government at work."

"What, here in Schaffhausen?"

"Yes, even here, even with two people who aren't dangerous and threaten no one. We're under surveillance. For the last four years I've behaved with perfect compliance with every witness protection demand they made. At the same time just about every personal decision was taken away from me. I didn't get to choose where I lived, what I did for a living or even what I looked like. Sure, I did it to protect myself but it was like a prison anyway. Now, here with you I feel like myself again. I feel in charge of things and it feels good. I'm not going to passively submit to every whim of our omnificent federal government. I just have to beat them at their little games, and I'd like our conversations to be private. That's all."

The waiter appeared with another bottle of bubbles and two champagne flutes. This time it was Phillpponat Royale. The cork popped loudly.

Denise leaned over the table slightly. "I love that sound!" she said.

Conklin leaned toward her. He savored the look in her eyes and said, "I love you, baby."

The waiter poured them each a glass of champagne and left them a pair of menus. Denise and Conklin studied them.

Denise mused, "I can't decide between the 'Tater vrooom Wasser-baffle or the Zee gen-case Pan 'O Cotta mitt Tomato-en Cool-eeze."

Conklin's nostrils spurted champagne bubbles. He grabbed his napkin. "And you said my German was terrible!"

He lowered his menu. "Before we call the waiter over, let's use a trick football coaches use. This way we won't get a crick in our necks talking to the window." He raised the menu until it covered his mouth.

"Deeny, my witness protection handler thinks I've hidden a lot of money. From InCorps. That's why we're getting all this surveillance."

Denise raised her menu in a similar fashion. "It's not true is it, Wylie?"

"Sure, it's true. It was my job. For most of my career I hid money. Most of the time it was legitimate. InCorps had nearly sixty billion in convertible assets when the Feds came down on us. Some of it was cash. I cooperated, helped them recover most of those assets. They recovered about ninety-seven percent and actually concluded their whole operation was a huge success. All except Bentley, my witness protection handler. Bentley's high up in the Justice Department, a director level, maybe even assistant to the deputy secretary, whatever. He took a personal interest in me and is obsessed with trying to recover what's left. He helped us get here, in St. Agatha's. Years ago his wife had breast cancer. They found this place."

"And she died here." Denise said.

"Yes. Bentley helped us be together again, and I owe him a lot for that."

Denise's actuarial mind went to work. "Wylie, what they didn't recover, that's over a billion dollars. How did you hide that much?"

"Well, actually it's not difficult. You move it around from bank to bank. Most of the world's wealth is virtual anyway, and there's millions of fund transfers every day. The feds recovered all but one and a half billion, but Bentley thinks I'm holding out on him."

"And he's manipulating you again, right? He got this for us and he wants you to give him the rest of the money."

"That's his game alright."

"Wylie. Are you holding out on him?" Denise's stare was intense. A couple of weeks ago her eyes had been clouded with pain and disease. Tonight they were vibrant and as clear as a child's.

Conklin nodded behind his menu.

After a moment, Denise's eyes twinkled. "Wylie, how exciting!" she whispered.

"You're not angry with me?"

Denise lowered her menu. "Where's the camera?"

"Uh, you mean the surveillance camera. I don't know."

She looked over at the table where the head waiter had tried to seat them originally. The restaurant had filled up since their arrival. Other patrons now sat at the original table. They looked Swiss.

"Wylie, it would probably shock the hell out of that Swiss couple over there, but I feel like going over and yelling into the hidden microphone and telling this Bentley character to go piss up a rope."

For the second time, Conklin sneezed. "Deeny, not while I'm sipping champagne. This is too good to be snorting it out my nose."

She shrugged and laughed. "I have my Jersey Girl moments. Wylie..."

He turned his head toward the window. She followed his example.

"Wylie, I'm not going to let this guy intrude on the small amount of time we have. What's he going to do, kill us?"

"No, he's protecting us."

"Protecting us? From what?"

"Vladoseev."

Denise squinted. "The Russian gangster?"

Conklin nodded. "There's a guy tailing us who works for him. Vladoseev wants the money as much as Bentley."

All the humor evaporated from her eyes. "So we're in real danger."

"Yes. Somehow Vladoseev tracked us here. He's biding his time, trying to figure out how to nab me without bringing down the feds on him."

"Wylie, you sure know how to make things exciting." She was smiling again.

"That's not the reaction I expected."

She smiled. The waiter came over and emptied the champagne bottle. They managed to place their dinner order. The food was superb and Denise ate with the same gusto she had shown at lunch.

"I don't think they can read our lips when our mouths are full," he said.

She smiled with distended cheeks. "Wahghag garful yabib."

Conklin smiled. "Exactly what I was thinking."

Night had descended on Old Towne Schaffhausen by the waiter had taken all their dishes. Conklin summoned the waiter and discovered to his amazement the bill had been paid by St. Agatha's. The manager came over and thanked them profusely and apologized for the misunderstanding about the table. Conklin had a question for him.

"Sir, can you ask our driver meet us at the rear entrance and can we exit there?"

The manager looked perplexed and even a little irritated by the concept but when Conklin's hand placed a hundred Euro note in his hand his face became all smiles again.

"Of course, my dear fellow. No problem at all." He hustled off and returned after a few minutes.

"Please follow me."

He led them through wood paneled rooms to the kitchen, frenetic with cooks and waiters and noisy enough for a factory. They walked through a back room filled with cigarette smoke, a sort of lounge for the help. The limo driver was waiting for them when they exited through the back door. As soon as their seatbelts clicked the limo rocketed through the alleyway.

Conklin did not know the driver's name. "Can you take us out to the rock?"

"Park am Rheinfall?"

"Yes. Thanks."

"Sir, I'm supposed to have you back at the clinic by nine o'clock."

"We're not going back to the clinic."

"But, sir…"

"No arguments. Driver, what's your name."

"Thomas." He pronounced his name like Toe-moss.

"Thomas. From now until we're finished for the evening, you earn double."

"Rheinfall it is, then."

Denise looked concerned. "Wylie, I have a treatment scheduled."

"When is that?"

"Eight o'clock in the morning."

"We'll be there in plenty of time."

They stood alone looking at the spectacular waterfalls below Schloss Laufen, arms around each other. A full moon rose over the river. The thundering water made too much noise for conversation, or surveillance, so they just held each other. Denise felt like a feather to him, much lighter and thinner than he remembered. Like something lost and regained, she seemed hardly there at all, but the warmth from her was as he remembered and it radiated into his body. He pulled her tighter, a matrix of life both fragile and tenuous. She looked up at him, her tears streamed from the corner of her eyes, leaving silvery streaks down her cheeks. A torrent of water surged around the rock in the middle of the Rhine. They held each other like the intensity of their embrace could slow the relentless ticking of the clock. For a moment they ignored muted warnings buzzing in the back of their minds and the torrent of events that surged around them.

Back at Haus Von Mulller, Denise went around his room studying every shelf and piece of furniture. Eventually she found the closet and opened the door. She took out a filmy black shift of Chinese silk and grinned at him.

"Ah, evidence of premeditation."

"Guilty, my love."

She disappeared into the bathroom. Conklin undressed and donned his own robe. But when Denise opened the bathroom door, her face formed a mask of sorrow. She emerged wearing the black silk robe which hung from her shoulders like an ill-fitting curtain. Tears streamed down her face.

"Oh, Wylie. How can we make love? I look worse than a corpse."

He went to her and wrapped her in his arms.

He forced himself to feel more confidence than he really had. "Honey, you're much better than before. And we're together."

His left hand sought the light switch. Their robes fell to the floor. Moonlight coming in the window showed him what he feared to see, what he had refused to even think about. He saw what Denise had seen in the bathroom mirror, for her a living reality. All that evening she had cloaked her body's secrets beneath fabric and makeup. But now her naked body shined in the moonlight. Her skeletal frame was wrapped in thin muscles and translucent skin. Conklin desperately focused his memory on how she had been before. His guilt flared. When he had abandoned her he had left behind a beautiful woman. His departure stole what could have been their best years together. Cancer had taken her youth and now wanted her life as well. Their beautiful love had turned into a freak show of denial and compromises.

But moonlight and memory allowed him to see more, to see within her. In her eyes he saw the woman who loved him and who needed his love beyond any desire of the flesh. Conklin clamped his arms around her skinny body and felt the rush of her breath. Not so tight, he thought.

The feel of her lips restored the same warmth that first kiss had brought. And it saved them.

They made their way to the bed and with strength she backed him onto the sheets. They rolled and her body was amazingly alive under him. Suddenly he too was amazingly alive, all parts of him. His hands roamed her body because it was her. He felt her empty and scarred chest, her belly, legs, the small of her back, all the time kissing her face, her neck, and again those amazing lips.

The morning found Deeny and Wylie tangled up in the bed sheets just as they were tangled up in each other.

The dawn's light streamed in through the wavy glass of the Haus Von Muller's window, promising them a day with too much to think about, too much left unsaid.

And one less day to live.

Chapter 14

"Boss, I just couldn't get them. I followed them to the restaurant and meant to nab them when they came out. The limo driver parked across the street. I thought maybe I'd stuff him in his own trunk, but they never came out. I waited a long time. The driver left and I went inside. They were gone."

"Must have gone out the back. Do we need a team there, Kolya?

Karolovsky thought for a moment. "Boss, now I'm seeing federal agents everywhere."

"I knew it! It's just too much damn money. Koyla, the federals went to a lot of trouble to get him there. They used private jets getting the woman to this clinic. They got a lot invested in Wylie Schram. They have to have a lot of agents watching his ass."

"Boss, Schram is walking around like a free bird. Driving that damn Mercedes everywhere like he owns Switzerland. Not even looking over his shoulder."

Vladoseev was silent. "Koyla, my friend. You are in the field. You will tell me what you need. This guy is smart. He duped the whole world, never forget that. He's got billions of my money, while I have to live in a hotel, like a gypsy."

That prompted a laugh from Karolovsky. "You, boss, a *tsygan*? You live in gold room at the Barclay Hotel in Manhattan. Your limo's so big it has its own zip code. People think you are double dating black teenagers going to the prom."

"Koyla, you must be politically correct. You'll never make it in broadcast TV."

"Yes, Boss. The feds are very good and if we bring over more people, the feds will too. It's not like Schram is going anywhere. Not while his Denise is in this clinic. I've been thinking and asking a lot of questions. This clinic, St. Agatha's, people talk about it like it's different."

"Different?"

"Yes, they don't save anyone there. They have a treatment that makes the patient feel better for a while and then they die. You remember how she looked in New Jersey? Denise looked very good when she stepped out of the limo last night and she's not been there a month. But in New Jersey, she looked like one of the 'Walking Dead.' You saw the pictures."

"She looked good?"

"Still very thin but she had color in her cheeks and spring in her step.

Like springtime in Grodno."

"Ah, Kolya. Do you miss the flowers?"

"Seriously, Boss. Denise looked like she was healthy woman. These two were out on a date. Dinner at this fancy restaurant and afterward... Well they gave me the slip so I waited at the Von Muller house. They showed up late, got out of the limo arm in arm. I could have shouted, "Get a room," but they already had a room. Went into the house and didn't come out 'til morning. And then back to the clinic."

"What about the clinic?"

"Everyone dies. They only take terminal patients, make them feel good for a while and then they die. Everybody dies. That's what they say about St. Agatha's."

"So Denise is going to die. We knew that. How long?"

"Less than a month."

Both men were silent for a moment.

"Kolya, in Grodno, the flowers in springtime, they were truly beautiful?"

"Yes, Boss. All the fields covered with them and the bees made so much noise you could hear it everywhere."

"And still there's a price on your head so you can never go back there."

"There's no going back, Boss, for either of us."

"Kolya, there is no hurry. They are not going anywhere. Wylie Schram is chained to St. Agatha's for as long as Denise is alive. The feds are there, even if they're not sitting in black SUV's sipping Dunkin Donuts coffee. So it means more hiding in the bushes for you. You must be ready when the opportunity presents itself."

"Boss, the bills come to you and you pay them. I'll tough it out."

****

Denise made her eight o'clock treatment at St. Agatha's clinic but just barely.

Conklin sat at the computer in the library reading St. Agatha's patient histories, a privilege he had just recently acquired. He was studying the chronology of Glenda Klappenfelter, who had died last year.

Dr. Bauerle burst in, body language radiating indignation.

"Good morning, Dr. Bauerle." Conklin said as pleasantly as he could.

"Mr. Conklin, please come with me."

Conklin returned to reading Frau Klappenfelter's medical history. "In a minute, Dr. Bauerle."

"Mr. Conklin, I must insist. You have a phone call."

He tore his eyes away from the screen and studied Dr. Bauerle. She loomed over him with a hand on one hip, body cocked at an angle, shoulders back, lacking only a tapping foot to complete the picture. She looked both fierce and magnificent.

"Bauerle, there is no one who would call me here. It's probably a salesman selling life insurance."

"It is," she said curtly, "your mister Bentley." She twirled and strode out of the room. Conklin could not help but watch her butt flexing rhythmically under the tight, dark blue skirt. He rose to follow her.

Once inside her office he closed the door. She walked behind her desk, and he stood in front of it as if he were a schoolboy called to the principal's office. Her eyes were unreadable behind her glasses.

"Bauerle, you're angry I kept Denise out overnight."

Bauerle's eyes widened and her head reared back slightly. She looked down at her desk. She quickly raised it again and her dimples made an ultra-brief appearance. "Mr. Conklin, you are not the first to keep your wife out against the rules. And you certainly won't be the last. Actually, we sort of expect it now. It is dangerous and irresponsible of course, but otherwise understandable."

"Okay....." Conklin looked at the phone on her desk. No blinking lights. "You said I had a phone call?"

"When he calls us, you will take it in here."

"When he calls us? You mean you summoned me here and there's no phone call?"

"There will be, Mr. Conklin."

"When?"

"I told you... when he calls us."

"So you do know Bentley?"

"He is apparently an associate of Dr. Friedkin's."

"And you know Bentley yourself?"

"I may have met him once or twice." She stared at her desk again.

"So why did you both tell me that you didn't know him? What's his connection to St. Agatha's?"

Dr. Bauerle said nothing. They held each other in a stare-down.

"Do you know what Bentley does? For the American Justice Department?"

Dr. Bauerle said nothing and at that moment the phone rang. She gave

Conklin another unfathomable look and left the room, closing the door and leaving him alone with a ringing phone. He walked around the desk and picked up the receiver.

For the second time in two days, someone asked him the question he least wanted to be asked.

"Daniel, what are you up to?" The voice was Bentley's.

"Bentley. I might ask you the same question."

There was a soundless pause. "Daniel, what makes you think you can ask me questions?"

"Why shouldn't I? I have lots of questions, and they keep me up at night."

"But not last night."

Conklin's hand tightened on the phone "Bentley, you're an asshole. How many cameras did you plant in my room? How many of your agents did you allow to watch?"

"Daniel, calm down. You're the one who took Denise there. I guess you figured out you're under surveillance. You're a WITSEC client. No matter where you roam, you always will be. But for your information, I shut the cameras off at the Haus Von Muller. I wouldn't let anyone watch you."

"But you had the restaurant bugged... cameras and mikes. Probably the limo and our driver, he's your guy too, right."

"No, the driver's not our guy but did you forget, there are other people in the world who want to find you?"

"Apparently they already did."

"You saw Karolovsky?"

"I know he's out there. How did they track me here?"

Bentley didn't answer for several seconds. Conklin stared at Dr. Bauerle's framed diplomas on the walls of her office.

"Daniel, I don't know how they tracked you."

"How many feds do you have here in Schaffhausen shadowing me, Bentley?"

"They're not shadowing you. They're between you and Karolovsky."

Conklin thought about that. "Bentley, please tell me why you haven't grabbed him and stuffed him in a sack?"

"We can't just grab him, Daniel. We're not on home soil. If we get caught with Karolovsky, you're out. You know what that means?"

Bentley waited for Conklin to say something.

"Daniel, it means the end of you and Denise. Every service in the world in in Schaffhausen. Every television camera in the world, every microphone…"

"Jesus, Bentley. What kind of game are you playing? This is my life and Denise's."

Bentley sighed. "This is your game, Daniel. I didn't start playing with gangsters. That was you four years ago. You knew the risks when you went to Switzerland. I'm with the Justice Department, not the State Department. If I had enough on Karolovsky, he'd be in prison in the US. But I don't and he's free to walk around that town just as you are. But you are a protected witness and you have to stop sneaking around like a spy. If you make it difficult for us to protect you, we may not be there when he grabs you. Do you know what you can expect if he does?"

Conklin didn't answer.

"He'll torture you. That's what Karolovsky did for the FSB. He was one of their chief interrogators. That man has a monster's heart. His boss wants the billion dollars and Karolovsky will do anything for Vladoseev."

Bauerle's digital desk clock ticked over a new number.

"Daniel, are you still there?"

"Yes, Bentley. You probably know I'm here because you probably have a camera in the desk clock here. You probably have a camera in Bauerle's bra."

Bentley chuckled. "Now I'm watching that video! Look, Daniel. I want to know what you're doing. You're showing way too much independence. After four years of being a perfect little witness. You threatened to take Denise out of the clinic and then offered to work for them. A few days ago you disappeared for a couple of hours. You locked your bedroom door at Von Muller. What's going on?"

"Bentley, I have a question for you first. I know your wife was here but what's your connection to St. Agatha's?"

"Daniel, I'll answer that, but I don't want you to get the idea you can interrogate me. What I do for my government is classified. I have a lot of secrets to keep. I'm sure you understand."

"Cut the crap, Bentley. Your connection with St. Agatha's has nothing to do with the Federal Government."

Bentley sighed. "Witnesses! After we save your life and hide you in the middle of nowhere, why do we think we've tamed you? Daniel, sometimes I forget how smart you were, I mean are.

"Jenny and I both went through what you're going through. God! After watching her slowly dissolving away with breast cancer, those first weeks were amazing. She came alive again, just like Denise. We had time together, weeks of joy, like last night was for you. Only it gets better. We did things we couldn't have done, things we used to do. We made the mistake of being happy. You know, for a while we forgot she was going to die. I was seeing her alive. Have you ever watched anyone die?"

"No, Bentley. I wasn't there for that part."

"Right, you weren't. Well, it's horrible. We loved each other and for thirty years we were in love until breast cancer started killing her. But Dr. Friedkin brought her back. It was a miracle, a goddamn miracle. I wanted to help him. I would do anything to help him. Hell, I knew the good part wouldn't last. But, goddamn it, I couldn't accept the fact that she was going to reach a point where Friedkin could no longer save her.

"I went to Dr. Friedkin and asked what he needed. I learned the thing he most needed was patients! Unbelievable! The most marvelous treatment in the world and they lacked patients. There was no waiting list and no money. The treatments were very expensive. They couldn't take on indigent cases. They had to have rich patients, with millions of dollars. Back when Jenny was there, it cost five million to treat her. As you know, it's more now."

Conklin was tempted to ask him where he got the money. "Eight million, Bentley. That's what you squeezed out of me."

"Yeah, eight million. I started finding patients for them. Rich people, patients who could pay. At first I had the foolish notion that if I could find them a lot of money, Dr. Friedkin could save Jenny but he put the kibosh on that. She died after her cells began producing the sixth prototype. I guess you know about the different semaphorin types."

"Yeah, only now they're up to eight prototypes."

"I know. I follow what they're doing. After Jenny died, they learned how to beat the sixth, then the seventh. I would have given anything, just for another day with her."

"But the time you had…it wasn't enough, was it Bentley?"

Static on the phone line stretched for a few seconds. "No. It never could be. Not when you love someone. Not enough time at all."

"Bentley, is that why you want the billion and a half you think I have?"

Bentley's voice regained its authoritative tone. "You have it, Daniel. And you're messing around with it. Which means you're messing with me. I know what you did. Four years ago you hid it from us and from Vladoseev. You are the only person who knows where that money is and you're the only one who can bring it out from the mysterious mattress you

94

hid it under."

"Just for the sake of argument, what makes you think you're going to get it now? All this time you still don't know where it is but not from lack of trying."

"Daniel, why don't I grab you myself and stuff you in a sack? Would that be enough incentive for you to cooperate a little?"

"Not your style, Bentley. You're a master manipulator. You need to squeeze it out of me."

"Daniel, if you wanted to play ball you would have done it already."

"Bentley, what if we're on the same team? What if I want what you want? If this could give Denise one more week, don't you think I'd do it?"

Bentley thought about this for a minute.

"Daniel, you don't trust me enough to do that. And that gives us one big problem."

"What's that, Bentley?"

"I'm running out of time. You have vast resources at your fingertips. A billion and a half could buy a pretty good disappearance. The only leverage I have over you is Denise. What can I do with you when she's gone?"

Conklin thought about this for a minute.

"I can promise you, Bentley, you won't have that problem."

Part Two

Chapter 15

From the news archives of Associated Press:

November 12

Former InCorps CFO Wylie Schram was sentenced to fifteen years in prison and ordered to pay sixty-five million dollars as part of a plea deal with prosecutors for his testimony against former InCorps CEO Raymond Suffield. As CFO of InCorps, Schram violated SEC statues, made numerous false statements and issued falsified records to auditors, intended to mislead investors and artificially inflate the company's stock price. Without the plea deal, Schram faced up to 120 years in prison for his actions.

December 5

Last evening Philadelphia police investigating a traffic accident on Interstate 76 discovered the body of former InCorps CFO Wylie Schram, who apparently died instantly when he lost control of his car and slammed into a bridge abutment. Schram was supposed to turn himself into Federal Authorities on the following Monday to begin serving his prison sentence for securities fraud. According to the medical examiner, the accident was alcohol related.

January 26

Despite the death of federal prosecutor's primary witness, former InCorps CEO, Raymond Suffield was sentenced to a total of a hundred and forty years in prison and was ordered to pay fines and restitution of slightly over a hundred million dollars for defrauding InCorps investors. Chief witness for the prosecution, Wylie Schram died in a car accident last month, but his previous testimony had been enough for the jury in this case of massive investor fraud that brought about the collapse of highly successful InCorps Corporation, whose stock price lost eighty percent of its value and brought the DOW down 300 points in a single trading day.

****

From Dr. Hans J. Friedkin, PhD, A.M., RSI, VQR – Journal of Research

Additional tests have determined the detailed structure of an essential piece of the telomerase enzyme, which provides a significant contribution to the development of tumor cells. The actual physical shape of this protein may indicate how this enzyme promotes reversion to type following nucleic-synapse manipulation (NSM), the process that had initially shown so much promise.

It appears that the telomerase catalytic protein subunit seems to "anchor" the DNA strand near the end of the chromosome, where it lays hidden, waiting until the beneficial effects of NSM treatment have run their course. The tumor cells have their own immune system code which produce a prototype semaphorin sufficiently altered such that the NSM no longer is effective. Subsequent to the discovery of the prototype we altered the NSM to deal with it. Chart 6 shows the specific difference between the initial semaphorin and the prototype. They appear to be nearly identical but different enough to render the NSM ineffective.

But also it was discovered that after some time, the second NSM treatment was neutralized by the arrival of a second prototype for which a new altered NSM had to be developed. Thus far in our research, we've seen the tumor produce eight different forms of the semaphorin in sequence. We've been able to produce alterations to the NSM treatments to deal with seven of them. Additionally we've been able to time the arrival of each prototype such that we can at least offer what appears to be a continuously effective application of our treatment. The widest variance appears between the sixth, seventh and eighth, which is why we cannot predict how long the patient's restorative period will last. After the third week of treatment, we begin looking for the eight semaphorin prototype.

Since there is no apparent benefit to further treatment, we halt NSM when the eighth appears. That is when our patients begin their decline, which at first is so subtle that days can go by before they feel any detrimental effects. But quickly, the effects of their restoration wear off. Patient condition quickly deteriorates to pre-NSM levels, and their cancer progresses, now more vigorously, due to a peculiar effect of the eighth prototype which acts on their tumors like a HGH, human growth hormone.

Another peculiar effect of the eight prototype is its ability to eliminate any possibility of spontaneous remission.

Throughout the broad history of treating cancer patients there are many reports, even among premature metastatic cases, where the patient actually undergoes a spontaneous remission. Some of these cases occur after traditional therapies have failed. Unfortunately, although medical science readily admits the occurrence of spontaneous remission, we have yet to properly study the phenomenon. We do not know or understand a single reason or cause for it, yet there must be some similarities among spontaneous remission cases.

But at our clinic, we have never had a single case where NSM has been applied, and subsequently the patient goes into long term remission. Thus it appears we've found a way to treat tumors and make the patient better temporarily, but in so doing, we've quite unintentionally discovered a way to prevent the possibility of spontaneous remission. It seems that the application of NSM makes fatality a certainty, although we have not studied enough cases to be certain. Additionally we have not determined any process or mechanism by which NSM alters the tumors' development such that spontaneous remission becomes unattainable.

The most difficult part this research is the tragedy we've endured with our patients. The patent's mental state naturally improves as soon as the NSM effects are felt. The typical gloomy outlook of a terminal cancer patient is replaced with one of hope, which none of our clinicians have the callousness to dash. The positive effects seem to last from three to four weeks, during which their tumors shrink, their bodies recuperate and they exhibit all symptoms of recovery. After this period of improvement, the decline is even more rapid. The cancerous cells restore their vitality and the patient's condition cascades into an accelerated march toward termination.

****

From the journal of Brendan Macbean:
I didn't see it coming.

Old age overtook me the night before my forty-ninth birthday. I was a full leap year shy of a half century and suddenly my mirror showed me how much I had aged. My sparse hair now had more gray, and somehow had I ignored all those wrinkles.

The reason for this sneak attack was obvious. Love had done a number on me.

My lovely Parisian, Betty, had come into my life and given me twenty-three months of real joy; an interim where my life was care-free and abundant. But love with a French woman proved slippery, and somehow I managed to let this most precious thing slip through the grasp of my soon-to-be gnarled, old fingers.

There are no fools like fools in love, and maybe we both just let it slide. Euphoria made us ignorant, and we never saw the end coming. Nothing could have been more obvious had we not been blinded by the light of our own joy. She lived in Paris, and I lived in Atlanta. Neither of us would commit to moving and that lack of commitment may have presaged the end. The breakup might have been obvious to Doctors Phil or Laura or anyone else not in love.

In the early days we could ignore the four thousand, three hundred and eighty mile gap that separated us. The exaltation we felt when we were together hid the obvious trap fate sets for lovers. Eventually our euphoria diminished and the time between visits grew longer, the transatlantic phone calls shorter. The end crept up unheralded and our conversations turned perfunctory, waxing eloquent with what was left unsaid.

Alone and on the eve of my near half-century, having just endured twenty months of self-denial after my last conversation with Bettye, nothing could have saved me from a night of unconstructive self-reflection, the conclusion of which was that my old man's hands had been unable to hold on to the love of my life. But why hadn't an old man's senility spared me the realization that it had probably been my last chance?

I grew tired of my own whining.

The solution was to pretend to feel good, even if I didn't. Thorough re-invention of self was in order. One of my less orderly friends suggested a tattoo, but I opted for a more traditional approach. In succession I launched a fad diet, took Tae Kwan Do lessons, worked out until my joints ached. I managed to lose ten pounds, but I never acquired a six-pack stomach or bulging biceps. And as far as Tae Kwan Do, my instructor, Master Kim Suh said I had something he called "bulgul-ui jeongsin" or *indomitable spirit*. It was obvious I lacked the coordination demanded by the sport. While self-defense may have been my goal, what I got mostly was self-injury.

Still Tae Kwan Do was a lot of fun. Most afternoons the martial arts gym crawled with ten to twelve year olds, for whom I became a favorite sparring partner. Their conquest over a grown man brought them great pleasure, I'm sure. Or maybe gave them "bulgul-ui jeongsin."

A week and a day after my birthday, I suffered a brutal defeat at the hands of what was probably a red-shirted fifth grader, or one deliberately held back for academic reasons. While dabbing Neosporin on my mat-burned knee my phone rang. It turned out to be Bud, my old boss at the television station, and I could not have been more surprised.

It hit me suddenly that several years had passed since I had last been an on-screen television reporter. The TV Swanson saga had obsessed me to such an extent that when layoffs came to the station, Bud Chaney, the newsroom boss, handed me a pink slip. I felt I had put together a pretty good story about Swanson, but Bud wouldn't put it on "The News at Six" saying that there were just too many loose ends. After the layoff, it had taken me a while to gather up all those loose ends. My efforts resulted in a Newsweek commission, a bestselling book and a follow-on string of freelance jobs. It had all turned out okay for me but I still fumed over losing my job in television. I enjoyed being an occasionally on-screen reporter. Admittedly I was not a big-market talent, not the square-jawed type that anchors the news. One reviewer referred to me as an "Aw shucks Opie with fruit-jar glasses and male pattern baldness." A particularly witty anchorman coworker referred to me as "Our newsroom's version of Charles Martin Smith." I had to look that one up. Mr. Smith is a fine actor who played the character Terry Fields in "American Graffiti."

I'm not sure I saw any resemblance.

But for nearly twenty years, I had chased local legends, folksy tales and occasional outright weirdness, producing spots that the Atlanta TV viewers enjoyed. Bud Chaney had labeled my work "Kittens, babies and freaks" and made every effort to squeeze all the art out of it. Consequently he wasn't one of my favorite people. So why would he call me after all this time?

"Bren, what're you up to these days?"

"Not much, Bud. You?"

"Same old, same old." Bud cleared his throat and hearing that sound over the phone brought back a host of obnoxious recollections. He seemed to have one of those throats that always needed clearing, and the mental image of him orally manipulating phlegm-wads made me wince.

"Look, Brendan. What are you doing for lunch tomorrow?"

I usually ate something like yogurt and granola but admitting that might make *him* wince.

"Well Bud, Savannah Guthrie is flying down to interview me for the Today Show," I smirked. "But for you, I'll ask her to reschedule."

Bud had no sense of humor. Jokes, regardless of how weak, always derailed his train of thought. Another reason we didn't get along.

"Macbean, you always were a smartass. How about 11:30 at Pero's?"

"Sure. I'll see you there."

You can find Pero's in a strip mall on Northside Parkway, a section of Atlanta between Buckhead and Vinings. I arrived a little early and notwithstanding the intervening years, didn't have any trouble spotting Bud when he came in. He landed heavily in the seat across from me.

"Bren, you're still balding and bespectacled."

And you look to have packed on about thirty pounds, I should have said but my stress-free lifestyle gave me enough social grace to pass on such opportunities.

"Rogaine and Lasik surgery. Bud, being unemployed, I can't afford them. Good to see you, too."

My non sequitur stopped him. All he could do for several seconds was stare at me.

"Don't give me that. I get a weekly 'Brendan Macbean' progress report from your old buddies down at the station. Apparently you-all stay in touch. Especially the women."

Bud cleared his throat and rolled his tongue back and forth. The waiter came over and took our orders.

"Bren, you're still pretty active. Writing, magazines and such?"

"Yeah, I have some things going."

"Are you too busy to take on something for the "'News?'"

A heavy tingle crept up my back. It was my turn to stare back at him. "Television?"

Bud milked it. "It's what we do."

"I mean, what is it? Tell me about it."

Bud smiled and checked his manicure. Perhaps I sounded a little too eager, but I'd trade my departed mother's antique furniture, now in storage, to get back on television.

Billy Pero himself brought our food. For me a slice with pepperoni. For Bud a special pizza with everything. Mr. Pero stood around and shot the breeze with us. This nearly gave Bud an anxiety attack trying to hold his appetite in check. After Billy turned toward the kitchen, Bud went after his pizza like a half-starved pit bull.

He spoke through mouthfuls of cheese and dough, "We got this segment, "Deep News" where we do in-depth investigations on high profile people in the news."

I was very familiar with Deep News, hosted by an up and coming young TV star, Shelby Chadwick, a drop-dead gorgeous woman with a magnetic voice, penetrating eyes and an on-screen presence clearly too big for the Atlanta market. The camera loved Shelby, and so did most males between thirteen and eighty. She was a heart throb for me too and I often caught her spots. I barely held my crush in check because I was a little jealous of her. She had what I badly wanted back. She was a television journalist with a job, admittedly much more mainstream than myself. She probably had someone to do much of her research so she could focus on looking spectacular. But Shelby was a real pro, and I think everyone expected her to be swept up to New York soon.

But my heart flopped with disappointment. Bud wasn't going to offer me an on-screen opportunity, just a chance to write for one of the station's biggest stars. He wanted me for my research skills. He knew I was a bulldog when it came to digging. Hell, I had lost my job over it, but I'd just be one of several supporters hovering in the background near the real on-screen talent.

But I almost said yes on the spot just for the chance to meet Shelby. She was way out of my league, not that I'd ever get an opportunity. She might take pity and throw the little balding, bespectacled Charles Martin Smith lookalike researcher an occasional smile.

Then I thought about working under Bud again. My former boss liked to argue and disagreed with every idea I had. After the years of freedom from Bud, working under him again sounded like pure torment.

Bud's feeding frenzy slowed. He had consumed all but the crumbs. He stared at his empty platter like he was going to pick it up and lick it, but he shrugged and started filling me in.

"Bren, do you remember, the big InCorps scandal, about four or five years ago?

"The 'Hole in the Wall Street Gang?'"

"Yeah. That's what everybody called it. Do you remember the names of the guys who went to jail?

The Hole in the Wall Street Gang had been a national news sensation and held the nation in a TV headlock for months. Two C-level execs had conspired to defraud millions of stockholders and filled their own pockets while they did it. Millions of investors bought into the rapidly rising company. When finally exposed, the company's stock fell and brought Wall Street down with it. But at the moment, I could not recall the names of either of the two execs. I shook my head.

"It's the old three year rule." Bud nodded like he had coined the term.

When a TV story gets stale, the ratings fall faster than the proverbial rock. No matter how big a story is few people can stay interested longer than three years. The normal lifespan of a big story is a few weeks. After the guilty get punished, the story dies. If the media doesn't continuously bring up new angles, we all get too bored to remember the details. The perpetrators lose their celebrity and we forget about them.

"Schram and Suffield." Bud prompted. "Schram was the money man and Suffield was the CEO."

My memory began supplying a few details. "Suffield went to jail, right? And Schram...."

"... Accepted a reduced sentence in return for testifying against his boss. Only he died in a car accident. Suffield goes to federal prison for the rest of his life."

I sat and waited until Bud decided he'd give me the rest. He sat there pinching up his last few crumbs looking very much like a cat playing with a chipmunk.

"Shelby came up with the idea of reviving this 'Hole in the Wall Street' thing, but management kind of frowned on it. I mean, the story is more than four years old. It was a big deal at the time but just like 9/11 or the war, our viewers lose interest. Today nobody gives a flip. Only Shelby got her way. She goes to my boss, tells him we had an obligation to keep this story alive, to make sure we all stay diligent. All the pain and anguish, the public outcry. We need to hoist these guys to the rafters and get congress to pass a bunch of laws."

"Shelby went over your head?"

"Yep." Going over Bud's head was a sure way to doom your career. It was strong testimony about Shelby's prestige that she got away with it. Beauty, personality and brains, all of which Bud lacks, gave her a lot of power at the station. Anyway, he looked like he had decided to shrug off Shelby's end-around. Television can only handle so many prima donnas and Bud, although powerful, was off-screen, which means he could no more fire Shelby than he could take that last slice of pizza home in a foam box.

My middle-aged memory began coming up with some of the details of the story.

"Wasn't there some connection with organized crime?"

Bud nodded. "Yeah, one of the Russian gangsters, Bogdan Ivanovich Vladoseev. Rumors said he bankrolled InCorps stock run-up with some heavy buys. The Feds never came up with hard evidence, but there was some stories floating around."

"You think anybody's interested now?"

"No. But like I said, Shelby is. She dug around and came up with something."

Another unpleasant memory of dealing with Bud; he was a surprisingly poor communicator for someone who held a management job in television.

"Bud, you got *me* hanging in the rafters. As if watching you eat pizza isn't torture enough. What's this about?"

"Ray Suffield is in federal prison, so Shelby tried to go see him. She used their website… The Bureau of Prisons has an 'inmate locator' app. Anyway it showed Suffield was at some federal facility in Louisiana. Shelby tried to make an appointment to interview him and she hit a wall."

"What'd they say?"

"They said he wasn't listed in their rolls and she should go back and use the locator again. She did and the next time it said, 'In Transit.'"

"Transit, like he's going somewhere?"

"Right. It seems that he was being transferred. But he stays in transit for a couple of weeks. He should have arrived at 'that somewhere' by then. Shelby presses the BOP officials. They tell her that he's still at Oakdale but his visitor's privileges have been suspended because he misbehaved. After that they give her excuses and more bullshit than a cattle ranch. She went up the chain of command but finally got stonewalled. Add to the fact that Shelby's busy, in high demand. She gets pressured to take more assignments. She put her intern on it, but you know how interns are."

"So you want me to find out where the Feds have stashed Suffield?"

Bud took a breath before replying. "Bren, that's part of it."

"What's the other part? You know the bad part."

Bud looked hurt. "Why do you think there's a bad part?"

"Whatever you want to call it; bad, disgusting, disgraceful, distasteful. Too hard for an intern and too tedious for Ms. Chadwick, who is otherwise busy with more important assignments."

The expression that crossed Bud's face told me that I had plucked a righteous string. Bud looked like what he had to tell me, he'd rather skip lunch than tell me. Which is saying he really didn't want to say it out loud. I did the calculation in my head. Shelby's the star. She's the big concept person and needs a gopher to do her bird-dogging. The TV station had other reporters but I heard that they were expanding their news coverage and everybody has too much on their plate. And maybe the InCorps story was a complete dead-end anyway. Plus if it's too hard for a college intern, why waste employees' time on it? Especially an expensive employee, who made more money for the station in front of the camera than sitting in a cubicle poking a touchscreen.

Bud could not hold it in any longer.

"Macbean, Shelby asked for you. Specifically for you."

Chapter 16

From the journal of Brendan Macbean:
I've lived in Atlanta all my life and could not imagine living anywhere else. The people of Atlanta are like my extended family, but like many families, we're often dysfunctional.

Atlanta is a successful city, expanding in all directions, sometimes at such pace we can't get out of our own way. We're characterized by an exuberant lifestyle, divisive politics and a complicated culture partly derived from a chaotic history some of us would rather forget.

Atlanta is full of people who weren't born here, folks who moved here to capitalize on the growth or the climate. Very few of our welcomed newcomers move here solely for the renowned Southern Hospitality. Atlanta is a fun town, you can do business here and you Yankees can leave your snow shovels behind.

Speaking of Yankees, I have yet to meet a one who didn't move here without bringing along an opinion on how to make it better. "Youse guys know what youse guys need down here?" I keep telling them, "Thanks, friend, but the more *y'all* try to make it like where *y'all* came from the more it's going to be like where *y'all* came from."

There is one aspect of Atlanta I wish I could change, one characteristic of my beloved hometown no one likes, can ignore, or fix.

There's a great divide running straight through the heart of the city, and almost everything cultural, political, economic, or social falls on one side or another. You see, everyone knows that until 1863 the South had slaves, and that legacy will haunt us forever. Historians will point out the inconsistencies in this indictment. Prior to the early 1800's slavery existed in almost every state, but today we often ignore the facts. Today Americans choose to think it only happened in the southern states. This allows the rest of the country to focus all the guilt on the folks who happen to live those few states, ignoring the massive and continuous population redistribution, typical of American culture.

During the chaotic civil rights era, clashes between whites and blacks occurred almost nationwide, and still do. But with every passing decade the indictment of racism seems to concentrate more and more to the South and since Atlanta is the heart of the South, we get the brunt of it.

We, the people of Atlanta, newcomers and natives alike, welcomed the aforementioned growth while ignoring our slower evolving social development. We allowed this cultural divide to develop by accepting stereotypes, often created elsewhere, by people who don't know us and have little understanding of who we really are.

Atlanta's people fall on one side of the wall or the other based entirely on their race. Every social misfortune brings with it its own ready excuse. If you're white, it's because the other is black, and vice versa. You just don't, won't, can't, understand. And once we're cataloged into our racial stereotype, we despair of ever understanding.

Nobody wants it this way but we're forced to participate. As much as we'd like to accept each other and treat everyone evenly, we're never allowed to without receiving the insidious label of racism or insensitivity. And that ends any dialog. You must be hopelessly, politically incorrect or behind the times, as if this division was a new development. We're issued an off-the-shelf pre-judged attitude and our own conclusions summarily dismissed on how we feel about our neighbors.

Individually we may love our fellow man as an equal. Publically the media portrays us as a lynch mob ready to stereotype blacks or whites for just about any transgression, and the facts and the truth and what is in our hearts be damned.

Most of us are weary of this; of the need to tiptoe around our differences rather than just embrace and enjoy each other. Maybe my friends from the north have something to teach us after all, because up north it seems like they don't really care if your ancestors were Irish, Polish, German, Asian, Indian, African, any or all of the above. Northerners can innocently ignore all their own imperfect social development and ascribed the blame and guilt to the South, thus empowering themselves, with typical Yankee hubris, to form lofty opinions on what Atlanta needs to change.

However from time to time individuals arise who breach the divide. Through sheer force of personality and celebrity they are viewed apart from that which smites the rest of us. These individuals truly are loved by folks on both sides.

Shelby Chadwick is a knockout beautiful woman who spans our invisible wall. The molds that forged Vanessa Williams, Halle Berry, and Tyra Banks outdid themselves in the creation of Shelby. Naturally, the TV station wants an on-screen personality to appeal to all people in their market. If affirmative action ever produced results everyone could agree on, the hiring of Shelby Chadwick blasted the practice off the scale.

Beautiful women come in all guises, but unless you lived under a rock where the rest of us wish you'd remain, Shelby makes you forget about race.

The day arrived for me to meet Shelby. That morning I managed to shave my face baby-butt close without major wounds. I splashed on enough cologne to make my eyes water. Alas I could do little to improve my slovenly appearance fallowed by isolation from the bright lights of television. My mirror told me I looked like a schlump, but I forgave myself because nobody ever confused me with Elvis.

The television station had not changed much since my departure. Driving up to the familiar building overwhelmed me with a tidal wave of nostalgia. When I entered the front door into the rather plain visitor's lobby, I received another wave, this time coming from an old friend. Misty Holden had been the station's receptionist when I worked here last and she still was. Her mother had given her a stripper's name way back when the Johnny Mathis' song hit the charts. I used to kid her that her mother should have completed the sacrilege by giving her the middle name of 'Just.' She'd been at the station longer than anyone and was one of my favorite co-workers. Misty gave me a big hug and a bulls-eye kiss that would have made her husband blush.

"Mac Bean, you old stranger! Where have you been keeping yourself?"

I hugged her back and said, "Here and there, around."

"Making yourself famous, too, haven't you?" We walked back to her desk in tandem, arms around each other. She sat me down in an adjacent chair and resumed her seat behind the desk.

"I don't know about famous. I just…"

"…been all over national magazines, writing sensational articles. Haven't you been on Oprah?"

"Not yet, but I do have some unreturned calls."

We chatted it up for a few minutes, catching up on the years since our last meeting, wondering how we'd ever let our busy lives keep us from each other's company. For a while I forgot my anxiety over meeting Shelby. Finally Misty brought us both back to business.

"You're here to meet 'Our Girl.'" I had no idea how old Shelby was but to Misty, every female who stood in front of the camera was a girl.

"Right." I was afraid to say more about it. Was I coming back to television to work with their brightest star? I couldn't afford any assumptions.

Misty handed me a sheaf of papers. "Brendan, I took the liberty of filling out your application. It's a station requirement that new employees fill one out. I remembered you hate paperwork, so I did it for you. Oh, I took the liberty to fill in your recent experience myself because I know how modest you are. Anyway, here it is and if you want to make changes, have at it."

Misty continued after taking a deep breath, "Here's your form for a badge. You got to get a new picture taken. We can't use the old one. The calendar hasn't done you any favors."

"Thanks a lot!" I said but my mind was reeling. New employee?

"Here's your parking pass. Hang it on your mirror. Here are a couple of forms I couldn't fill out, like the company insurance form, 401k and stock purchase. Just go through them and bring it all back to me."

Bewildered to the point of speechlessness, I took the forms from her and didn't even glance at them. Without anyone asking me if I would like to have a job at the station, or take the job they were offering me, or accept such or such a salary or so much as a "by your leave," it seemed like I was back in television.

And before I could stammer out any of my famous witticisms, Misty yanked me up by the arm and led me into the newsroom, where another wave of nostalgia made my knees buckle. More than just a familiar place, the newsroom charged me with an unexpected spike of electricity. Everyone who worked at the station worked here in a vast matrix of cubicles, even the news anchors. Here were the men and women who rode the news desks, the writers, the producers and directors, camera operators and off-camera staffers. Here also worked the roving reporters, the sports reporters, and the weathermen, all the pros needed to broadcast an entertaining product. As usual everyone was rushing around or had their heads down over a display. The newsroom had a palpable energy and just being there gave me a boost.

I was immediately surrounded by crowd of coworkers both old and new. Some of them I didn't know but who knew me. I felt I was receiving way too much attention but... what the heck? Take it when you can get it. Misty allowed the glad-handing to continue for a full five minutes and then dragged me over to the big conference table in the corner of the vast room. Someone had hastily written "Macbean" with a Sharpie on a tent card and set it on the table.

"Thanks for reserving a conference room." I said.

Misty raised an eyebrow and gave me a smirk. She hustled me into a chair and left me there wondering what came next.

Chapter 17

From the journal of Brendan Macbean:
What came next arrived immediately. Shelby Chadwick strode up behind me, placed her hand on my shoulder and spun my chair around. She stood smiling down at me looking hotter than a Krispy Kreme doughnut. I struggled to my feet with more creak than the Tin Man before the oil treatment. She was dressed in a light gray suit accented with matching blue earrings and pendant. I couldn't remember the name of the gemstones, but they teamed up with her luminous eyes in a mystifying way. She held out her hand and said, "Tanzanite."

A strong tingle, her hand in mine. I stammered, "What?"

"The gemstone is Tanzanite. My image consultant says the color makes my eyes look bigger on camera." She said this with a young girl's exuberance enhanced by a brilliant smile. "I just think it's pretty. Mr. Macbean, it is such a pleasure to finally meet you." String music seemed to accompany her voice.

The conversation had gotten off on an unfamiliar thread, but the kind of charm she poured over me came from the Old South, of which I had received at least a cursory education. So I smiled back and tried to lay it on just as thick.

"Ms. Chadwick, the pleasure is all mine."

The image consultant got it right. Shelby had lustrous, non-typical blue eyes backlit by a contagious energy. Tight cheekbones rode above her girlish smile executed with her wide, expressive mouth. Ok, if I stare too long at that face, I'll make both of us uncomfortable, but I felt myself falling hard with infatuation.

"Please call me Shelby." Her lips parted with unabashed pride in her orthodontist's skill. My face began to cramp up with the effort to out-grin her so I backed off a little.

"And you can call me Brendan but my friends call me Bren."

"Okay, but I can't call you Bren."

"Oh, why not?"

"You know you're famous where I studied journalism. Professor Glenmore called you the last of the true Southern TV journalist."

I didn't know any Professor Glenmore or how he could know me.

"Professor Glenmore?"

"At Duke. We studied your story, 'Tiger in Georgia.' He called it the definitive "Southern social documentary."

Her statement left me open-mouthed and staring. I didn't remember the piece, didn't know if I'd done it five years ago or twenty. And then I remembered that the tiger was Tiger, Georgia, a town way up in the Georgia Mountains. But I couldn't recall why the place was special enough to make a documentary about it. Whatever it was, it certainly wasn't why we were here. So I just nodded like a dumbass.

"So, Shelby…" Saying her name to her face seemed awkward. "Why can't you call me Bren?"

"Because you're my hero and you're Macbean. You'll always be Macbean."

I tried to hide behind my glasses.

Shelby knew how to get down to business. "Bud said he spoke to you about my project."

"Yes he did without giving me a whole lot of detail. Something about you getting the run around with the federal prison system."

She gave me a penetrating look with her Tanzanite eyes. Her magic smile disappeared. My heart fluttered. Would I ever get used to just looking at her?

"One prisoner in particular… Raymond Suffield."

"Of the Hole in the Wall Street Gang," I offered.

"That's what they called it."

Infatuation aside, I quickly focused my attention. I'm a reporter… an investigative reporter. This was what I got out of bed for every day, and why I had come back to the station that had fired me. The awareness that I was talking to a stunningly beautiful woman receded to somewhere in the back of my mind, not forgotten or ignored, just held in check. For a while.

"Miss Chad…. Shelby…" My voice came out a little breathlessly, but I pushed on hoping she didn't notice. "Let's talk about why you wanted to interview Suffield."

She nodded and her voluminous hair didn't move. In television, you get used to the phenomenon.

"Back when that InCorps thing happened, it was the biggest story on the news. But people forget and they don't think about it anymore, about how millions of folks lost their money. I think it needs a revival, like a Dateline or Sixty Minutes treatment. I want to resurrect Hole in the Wall Street Gang to make people aware. I want to look at the economic and political impact InCorps had on this country. I think there are big heads that should have rolled and didn't.

"The InCorps scandal was the stroke that broke our financial system. A lot of our leaders who should have been preventing this, didn't. And they still have their jobs. It woke up a lot of politicians, when InCorps crashed. Suddenly everybody wanted to look closely at the companies where folks were putting their money; investments, savings, pensions, IRA's and 401k's." She said this with a sort of cadence, like it was part of a polished presentation to execs who approved projects. Or rejected them.

"The scrutiny made everyone nervous. Lots of big money men and politicians had been exploiting the lack of regulation for years and did so with the regulators looking the other way. When the scandal broke, more scandals followed. Big corporations did everything they could to calm their stockholders. Congressmen called for investigations. Accusations flew everywhere. The American economy slumped. We lost our confidence. We lost our savings and our jobs.

"InCorps was the first big company caught defrauding their shareholders. Their CEO and CFO, Suffield and Schram found themselves under indictment and would have both gone to jail if Schram hadn't died in a car wreck."

"Schram dies and his boss goes to prison." I added.

"A lot of people wanted a lynching."

"The mob always wants a lynching. Federal prison is supposed to be tough. I wouldn't like it."

"Nor would I." The thought of such an exquisite creature behind bars made me cringe.

"But Shelby, the story's a little old. InCorps went under five years ago. The Treasury agents confiscated all their assets, and the SEC auctioned it off. Individuals got burned, of course. Smaller investors lost every penny they had in InCorps. We heard a lot of screaming but it all died down and we all forgot about it. Old news is hard to sell to the viewers."

"You're trying to tell me nobody's interested. That's what I've been running into around here. Our viewers are bored with the stock market. Years and years of a wimpy economy, a do-nothing Congress and political mudslinging. But the reason Schram and Suffield were able to pull off this caper in the first place is because, back then we were pretty much the same as we are now... complacent. We're not as fat as we used to be, but we're still pretty dumb and sort of happy. What Suffield and Schram did was a very dark crime and we're asleep at the switch again. We're primed for somebody else to do it to us again."

She strode back and forth, and when she stopped she put her hands on her shapely hips.

I took a deep breath "Okay, Shelby, this story needs a comeback. So, you tried to get Suffield in front of a camera again? At federal prison, I guess."

"Yeah, I tried. I called the Federal prison in Oakdale, Louisiana, and they told me he wasn't there. What, not there? Are you kidding me? So I told them, their own website says that's where he is. Gave them his inmate number. They told me they were going to check. I felt I was in the twilight zone. This guy is the most famous inmate they got and they act like they didn't know him? Oakdale's not that big. Then I got cut off, so I re-dialed and made the same request. Got put on hold... and so on. Repeat as necessary until the pesky reporter gets frustrated and goes away."

"You didn't give up there, did you?"

"You bet your sweet ass, I didn't." I guess her language startled me. She noticed and the girl actually blushed. Amazing!

"Macbean, I feel like we're old friends, comfortable enough to use my water cooler language. We're going to work together. We have to communicate, shorten the formalities, make something happen and have some fun."

That sounded good to me. Besides I liked the way Shelby said 'Macbean' like my first name was 'Mac.'

"I finally got through to the BOP administration. And they said that he was there at Oakdale after all and they were sorry for my trouble, but, his visitor's privileges were suspended. Indefinitely. That made me more than a little annoyed so I went up the line again. I even pushed hard enough to have our boss's boss get involved, all the way to our corporation's board member who is the public relation liaison to Congress. We invoked the freedom of information act and everything. The feds said they'd get back with us. They never did."

"So Suffield's at Oakdale, but no interview. Right?"

"Oh, he's at Oakdale all right. Nobody can see him. Then our boss put me on the steroid story and I don't have any time for what Bud calls, 'pet projects'"

"That's Bud, alright." Shelby's the brightest star we have and she has to focus on very big, news stories. Our television station, under orders from the network, put Shelby on the steroid story and she had been running weekly interviews with baseball players along with their managers, their lawyers and agents. I guess that kept her busy.

"Now I've have no time to fool around with the Bureau of Prisons, and everybody else around here is busier as hell. Interns don't have the guts for hard news."

I knew what she meant. Good journalists are all royal pains in the ass. Not everyone has the temperament.

"But the InCorps story is too important to just let it drop. I try to interview a high profile criminal, and I get the runaround. Why?"

I tried to think of something logical. "Maybe they're hiding him for his safety. Probably some folks out there who'd like to break his arms."

Shelby nodded. "Sure, they should protect him but why the dumbass act? First he's there then he's not. If they're trying to hide him, they're bungling the job. Usually they're more upfront with the press. They're making me suspicious."

"Shelby, what usually what looks like a government conspiracy often turns out to be just plain old government inefficiency. It's obvious they don't want you to see him, but it's like they don't want to give you something to argue against. Okay, I'm here now, and I may be even a bigger pain in the ass than the rest of you. You want me to try to set up the interview?"

Her smile reappeared, this time in earnest. "Not exactly, Macbean. I want you to do the interview."

A powerful swoon swept over me. I think I held my mouth open long enough for her to count my molars. Was this my chance to get back in front of the camera?

"Uh, I guess I could do that." Cough, cough. "I'll need a place to set up my laptop, a cubicle with network connections, access to the Internet… you, know, all that stuff."

She gave me a curious look, vaguely similar to the one Misty had given me earlier.

"Mr. Macbean… Bud calls you the world's foremost smartass, but I just think your brain works different than the rest of us. So every time you say something dense I'm going to call you 'Mr. Macbean.' Instead of just 'Macbean.'

"This," she patted the big conference table and held up the hastily created tent card. "… is your office."

Chapter 18

From the journal of Brendan Macbean:

I got busy immediately after Shelby left my "office." I saw no point running down the same paths she already covered. I went straight to another source. I called a friend of mine in the FBI.

My briefcase is loaded with years of ignored paperwork and business card accumulation. After a painful search I found her card and dialed the number.

"Agent Pamela Stratton, please,"

I met Pam at a writer's conference in New York a few years ago. Writers are constantly looking for ways to beef up their realism. Pam held highly attended seminars teaching what could be told about the inner workings of the FBI. Her career had provided her with many stories about criminal investigations. Agent Stratton was a cute girl in a man's world. Besides teaching she was also my classmate in other seminars. We became friends sharing a beer and a burger after the classes.

"Agent Stratton." Her voice was feminine but abrupt.

"Pam. It's Brendan Macbean from Atlanta. How's the weather in D.C.?"

"Raining and bureaucratic. Brendan, how the hell are you?"

"Great. Sunny and hot, here, but that's Atlanta."

"Is this a friendly call or do you need something?"

"Friendly… and I need something."

"Yeah, you're always friendly when you are pouring alcohol down a girl's throat." I hadn't seen Pam in a few years but her grating Yankee voice contrasted the image of a short, curvaceous bottle-blonde with a big smile and intense eyes that could charm a snake. The Glock on her hip somehow strangely enhanced her femininity.

"Your linebacker of a husband would toast me like a Pop Tart if I ever made a move."

"What makes you think I need protection?"

"Pam, you'll always need it. Men think you're flirting with 'em when you say 'Halt, dirtbag!'"

"Okay, Boy Scout. What can I do you for?"

I briefly told her what I was after. There was a ten second pause while she considered her response.

"Brendan, that's Bureau of Prisons, not FBI."

"Yeah, I know. But BOP is giving us the runaround. We brought out our heavy hitters and went up the line as far as we can go."

I heard the clatter of a keyboard. "Suffield's still in Oakdale. I'm not looking at the public access database, either.

"They won't let us see him and I don't know why."

"Protection. Keeping Suffield low profile. We, the Feds are worried about potential threats. Did you check with his lawyer?"

"His lawyer is out of the picture. No more money coming from Suffield. His lawyers cut back to an annual visit."

"Tough world isn't it." She did not sound sympathetic.

I thought for a moment. "Suffield is right where he belongs. We want to talk to him about how he scammed the public and why."

"I wonder if he could be linked to an ongoing investigation."

"Yeah? So?"

"If he were linked to an investigation, the FBI could get access to him."

"Aren't you guys investigating the Russian gangster, Vladoseev? He's the bankroll guy," I said.

"That's Treasury. They do their own investigations but come to us only after they screw up."

"Extortion, smuggling, drugs, money laundering?"

I heard more keyboard clicking. "I can't promise you anything, Brendan, but let me make a few calls. I'll find out who's holding Suffield's leash."

"Thanks, Pam."

An hour later she called back. "Macbean, thanks for the steaming pile of horseshit I just stepped in. I figured if the FBI wanted to interview Suffield, all we had to do was ask, interdepartmental cooperation and all that. I ask two questions and nearly lose my job."

"Jeez, Pam, what happened?"

"They're not letting anyone see him. He's only allowed 'cleared' personnel, The official reason is security. Somebody is trying to get to him. Or they have other reasons for keeping him isolated."

"Somebody like Russian gangsters?"

"Brendan, I'm not commenting, and you're never going to see him. My face still hurts from the door they slammed in it."

"Pam, I don't want you to get in trouble."

"Too late for that, Boy Scout. Listen, I went up the ladder until I finally hit a nerve with someone big. The top floor guys at the Hoover Building started questioning me. What investigation was I pursuing? Who are my supervisors? They wanted names of agents and file document numbers. I backed off. I could get fired if anyone found out I was poking around where it didn't concern me... and especially for talking to reporters. Then I got frog-walked to the office of the Director of Security and Operations."

I felt a tingle of fear creep into my gut. Pam had gone out on a limb for me and someone was sawing it off.

"What is Security and Operations?"

"I had never heard of it but this guy supposedly reports to the Deputy Attorney General. Higher than that it's more than your nose that bleeds. Anyway, this guy is a big hitter, and he starts dressing me down. He knows my supervisor, my record and dangles my career in front of me. I can't say we have FBI investigations without giving active file numbers, so I stood in front of his desk with my thumb up my ass. He so spooky he doesn't even have his name on his door. I'm standing there getting grilled by a DOJ director and I didn't even know his freaking name? What could I do? Suddenly getting fired sounded pretty good compared to a chicken-wire pen in Guantanamo. So I laid it all down for him. I had to give you up, Macbean."

"Jesus, Pam."

"Brendan, I love you but I won't go to Cuba for you. I told him you wanted to interview Suffield. That you're doing a story on the Hole in the Wall Street Gang."

"What'd he say?"

"He said, have this Macbean call me. Here's his number." Pam gave me a phone number and she had one more tidbit of information to give me.

"Ask for Bentley."

Chapter 19

From the journal of Brendan Macbean:
I didn't get to call Bentley.

My home phone rang at 3:30 in the morning, jolting me out of a deep sleep. I instantly thought of Bettye.

In the days of our long gone romance, she used to call me when she woke up. For her it was sunrise in Paris, five hours earlier for me. I never objected to those phone calls. I loved being woken up by her sexy female voice, soft and musical and French. Her calls instantly chased sleep away and gave me just what I needed. We would murmur sweet nonsense to each other for a few minutes, and then she would hustle off to her day and often as not I'd roll over for a few hours more sleep with nothing but good dreams until dawn.

Near the end of our relationship those calls grew further apart and their content less enriching, but even after six hundred nights without a wakeup call from Bettye I still answered the phone with a soft whisper, sounding hopeful and needy.

"Hello."

The caller oozed West Coast ennui. "Macbean, did anyone ever tell you, you have a bedroom voice?"

"A what?"

"Who were you expecting a call from, Agent Stratton? Should her husband know about the two of you?"

"Who is this?"

"Bentley."

My brain struggled like a drowning person to come awake.

"Macbean. Are you there?" I shook my head and looked for a cup of coffee that wasn't there.

"Bentley or Mr. Bentley. I was going to call you."

"I don't have time to wait. I'm on a plane by the time you get around to making the call. Look, Macbean, I understand you want to interview Ray Suffield. Right now that's a bad idea."

Ah, pushback. It always brings me to full alert. "And why is that, uh, Bent... Mr. Bentley?"

"Just Bentley."

"Why is that?"

"Why is it a bad idea or why is it just Bentley?"

"Bentley, you're enjoying this more than I am. You're in a hurry to get on a plane, but you thought you'd call and play with my head first."

I heard him chuckle, muted as if he covered the phone.

"Ok, Macbean. Ray Suffield is under special protection. We think he's being targeted for violence, which sometimes happens to prisoners, even in federal prison." His tone was slightly patronizing, more than if he was just trying to get my goat.

"Yeah, so was Michael Vick. And he was interviewed in prison. Just not by the A.S.P.C.A. You guys even let NBC into Guantanamo. Look, if you can't protect prisoners in federal prison under your total control, with the glare of TV lights and guards present, 'I don't know what the hell kind of unit you're running here.'" I did my best to imitate Jack Nicholson in "A Few Good Men."

He gave me another chuckle. "Mr. Macbean, I don't run the prisons, but I do have some say about high profile federal prisoners. Suffield is under a threat watch and we're not going to allow any interviews."

"So why did you call me, Mr. Bentley?"

"Bentley. I called you because you're the kind of guy who'll keep pushing until you break something. You called agent Stratton and she started asking questions in places she shouldn't have. She won't get in trouble. This time. But eventually someone will. I just want you to stop harassing our hard working federal employees. We don't want to have to fire someone because of your lack of judgment."

"How do you know about me?"

"I read your stuff and some of it is not bad. Makes me wonder why you're not more famous. My guess is that you probably suffer from bouts of depression which keeps you out of the field for long periods, typical of obsessive-compulsive types. But when you do come out and get into gear, you seem to be a 'Tom Petty' type."

"Tom Petty? Oh, 'I Won't Back Down.'"

His amateur psychoanalysis grated but I was on a mission. I wasn't going to let this federal asshole intimidate me. "Bentley, you have to be a pretty good politician to get to your level. I specialize in harassing federal employees. But bureaucrats like you are out of my league."

He chuckled again. "Too bad. You start pestering me and things could go very dark for you."

His threat sounded a little like a joke and it made me think he could be played with a little. It's amazing how one minute you're groggy with sleep and the next your brain is running at full speed.

"Bentley, you work for the prison system?"

"No, Department of Justice. The Attorney General's my boss."

"Hmm... That's a little grandiose. Your boss is more likely the deputy Attorney General."

"Okay, Macbean, from the same movie you quoted earlier, 'Is there a point somewhere in our future?'"

His Jack Nicholson was better than mine, so I stayed on the theme.

"We're on the same side here. You want what I want. You're a government employee. You work for the Department of Justice. Which means certainly you're a patriot."

"Sometimes I wonder," he said dryly. "Again, the point?"

"The point is you have a job to do but you are much more than just the job. You find a way to do what's right, get the job done, shun the typical government routine and cut corners out of expediency."

"In your own words, Macbean, that's a little grandiose."

"You called me, Bentley. At three damn thirty in the morning. Where are you, Timbuktu?"

"No, right here in the good old USA."

"Bentley you called me because you want me to convince you. You need me to convince you."

"Thank you, Nathan Jessup."

"'I would appreciate it if he would address me as colonel or sir. I believe I've earned it.'"

I heard another low chuckle on the phone. I had him laughing and it made me smile, a rare time when someone got my sense of humor!

"Bentley, do you believe Ray Suffield received a fair sentencing?"

"He's a criminal. His conviction says so. He defrauded millions. There's bad guys seeking to end his life for taking what they think is their money. He's serving a buck forty years and probably won't ever see freedom. Yeah, he's getting what he deserves."

"He did his crime five years ago. What does the average American think of Ray Suffield today?"

"The average American doesn't give a rat's ass and probably doesn't remember who Ray Suffield is."

"That, Bentley, is my point."

More silence on the phone so I unrolled my thesis. "Bentley, the average American doesn't want to remember the Hole in the Wall Street Gang, Suffield, Wylie Schram and that Russian gangster."

"Vladoseev," he offered.

"Whatever. We were all shocked when their big scheme came

crashing down. America was shaken to its core. Financial markets collapsed and we lost faith in the system. What followed the InCorps disaster was fear, devaluation of our pocket money, the very thing from which Americans derives their sense of wellbeing. We don't like being broke. We especially don't like people taking our money. We want guys like you to punish the crooks and keep punishing them so we can forget about the assholes who scared us, and blissfully go back to buying stuff, drinking beer and watching ESPN."

"'You want me on that wall. You need me on that wall.'"

"Exactly," I said. "But like any good medicine, it doesn't taste good. Letting Ray Suffield slide is not really good for us. We need a reminder not to let our guard down so that it never happens again, blah, blah, blah. That's why I want to stick a camera in his face and make him answer tough questions. Nobody ever did that. He's never faced the cameras. And then we do this again four years from now. Are you getting my point now, Bentley?"

I waited for Bentley to reply. I waited a long time listening to the hiss of the landline.

"Macbean, is it you who wants this or Shelby Chadwick?"

My turn to pause while I thought about that.

"Bentley, I'm getting old. I just turned forty-nine."

"For a TV personality of your ilk that's way past your prime. Maybe you're vulnerable to a little feminine persuasion."

"Who isn't, Bentley? I admit Shelby could get a boost out of this story but she's doing that steroid series for the network. Millions of guys would rather have her asking the questions, and sure, I admit it, this is her idea, but she thought I have the chops to do it right."

"You are not going away easily are you, Macbean?"

"No, I am not, Bentley. I don't want anyone to get fired but we're all just doing our jobs. And don't get pissed and hang up on me because I can be a pain in the ass like nobody's business."

"I'll bet you can, Macbean. Okay, I'll wake up some more people. You can have Suffield for a few hours but it'll be up to you to make him talk."

"You're going to let me do the interview?"

"Against my better judgment."

"When do you think you can arrange it?"

"Delta has a direct flight to Lafayette that leaves at eight-thirty AM." And my landline went dead.

Chapter 20

From the journal of Brendan Macbean:

Forget any good dreams until dawn after that. I had to catch a plane at eight-thirty. I had too much to do and was too excited to sleep. I went online and bought two plane tickets to Lafayette. Then I called Bud and woke him up. He was even more unsociable at four in the morning than his usual miserable self.

"Macbean, I'm going to kill you."

"You'll have to wait. I'm going to federal prison to interview Ray Suffield."

"You what?"

"Ray Suffield. I've got the interview."

"What'd you have to do, kill somebody?"

"You having bad dreams, Bud? All that killing."

"You're an asshole. What do you need?"

"Just Tony." Tony used to be and still was our best roving cameraman. Two years ago he was a young and eager rookie. Experience since then made him better. I knew he'd be willing to bolt out the door at a moment's notice, especially for this kind of story."

"I'll call him." Bud said.

"No, Bud. I'll call him. I know you actually like waking people up before dawn."

"Macbean, you're a worse asshole than me."

"Bud, you don't mean that, but look who I work with."

I called Tony. He was, as I expected, thrilled to be on this story. We agreed to meet at the airport and he'd bring all his stuff. Tony would take care of any technical issues. He would bring everything we needed, allowing me oto focus on the interview. I waited until six to call Shelby but she didn't answer so I left a message. Since this started out as her story, I wanted to make sure knew I was going. I was sure she would call me when she got the message.

I live a mere twenty minutes from Atlanta Hartsfield Jackson Airport, contrary to most Atlantans. The extra time gave me the chance to study the history of the InCorps scandal and the two principles, Ray Suffield and Wylie Schram.

Long before InCorps existed, Ray Suffield ran a small petro-prospecting firm in Dallas he had inherited from his dad, who along with his grandfather had been successful during the development of the Texas petroleum industry. Later one of the giant oil corporations bought the family business. Suffield had then turned from oil prospecting to speculation.

The process of rendering crude oil into gasoline and other petroleum products requires quite a progression of events from exploration, drilling, transportation, refinement and final product delivery. Sitting on a lot of cash from the sale of his company, Suffield looked for the most profitable place to invest. Big oil companies buy their raw crude months in advance and the price of crude varies according to perceived future demand. When Russia, China and India and Brazil began their recent hyper-development, they began buying a larger portion of the world's available crude. Ray Suffield began leasing tankers to transport the crude from oil producing countries to the ones where the demand was growing and where those same countries were building refineries. He branched into oil storage and eventually bankrolled the worldwide spectrum of oil production, providing loans and leases to petroleum exploration, equipment leasing, and well drilling. He brought in the brilliant financial wizard, Wylie Schram, to handle the money end of the business and soon had every major petroleum corporation in the world using InCorps services. InCorps went public at sixty dollars a share and for ten years their stock more than doubled the S&P 500 average returns. Millions of investors bought in. InCorps became part of everyone's portfolios turning Ray Suffield into America's newest billionaire.

InCorps' spectacular success brought a host of imitators, resulting in increased competition which put pressure on their growth and profits. Suffield and Schram surprised everyone by continuing their domination. They were on the covers of Newsweek, Money, Fortune, Forbes, and in the Wall Street Journal as the new wizards of Wall Street. For a cover shot, Time Magazine even dressed Suffield up as Butch Cassidy and Wylie Schram as the Sundance Kid.

But beneath the balance sheets, corruption was afoot. Competition crimped their profits which lost them leverage. Their hold on the market began to weaken. To keep the bad news under wraps they fooled analysts with inflated balance sheets. Investors were told about oil tankers that didn't exist, fictitious oilfield outputs and refinery production. They began missing a few payments. The SEC brought in auditors and in very short order InCorps was spiraling down like a diving pelican. In a month the stock lost eighty percent of its value and in another month no one in their right mind would buy it. This brought about intense focus on all segments of the energy industry and eventually other industries. Worldwide markets reeled like the iceberg-struck Titanic. Suffield and Schram who Time magazine had once called Butch and Sundance had been renamed The Hole in the Wall Street Gang.

In the end Wylie Schram spilled his guts to the feds and later, more literally in a car crash. Armed with Schram's testimony, prosecutors offered Suffield no deals. He pled guilty and went to federal prison for the rest of his life. Federal agents investigated Vladoseev, but he was never indicted. I decided to keep the Russian out of the interview because of the shortage of evidence and because it might distract viewers from what I really wanted from Suffield.

But there was plenty left to talk to him about. Americans had been legitimately outraged at the crimes committed by the InCorps' top two executives. What followed was a full scale panic. InCorps and later Enron caused a general collapse of the stock market. The real estate bubble burst, which caused endless bank scandals and painful audits of American corporations and financial institutions. In spite of our fascination with bad news and tragedy, we don't like to be put in the middle of a real crisis, especially where our wallets are concerned.

After these economic catastrophes, financial news in general maintained a dour profile for years. At that point, it is human nature to start looking for sunny horizons. As long as we've thrown the crooks in jail, we'll gladly put celebrity scandals and sports upfront and the Hole in the Wall Street Gang behind us .

Except for people like Shelby, that is. The problem with burying stories of the recent financial collapse is that not very many criminals really got punished. Only a few of the guilty got exposed to the light of public scrutiny. You can't steal eighty billion dollars and collapse the economy without help. Congress and all those regulatory agencies are supposed to keep watch over operations like InCorps and Enron, Fannie Mae and Freddie Mac. They let us down. Whether we want to or not, we needed to know more about this. We need to get the names of the others who were involved. We need to know how a couple of clever dudes hoodwinked billions out of millions so, in the words of The Who, "We Won't Get Fooled Again."

Shelby was right, and now I was delighted she gave me this mission. I was as eager as any caped crusader to bring the whole ugly mess to the light of television journalism, name names, point fingers and be the pain in the ass I was always meant to be. If we could attract enough attention with this interview the investigation would spread and some big names will have to answer tough questions on the nightly news.

Hours later, Tony and I landed at Lafayette Regional Airport. In addition to our carry-on bags, Tony brought the tools of his trade loaded into two big cases, which we checked as baggage. Delta charged us a huge fee for what they called oversized bags. Seeing Bud's face when I handed in my expense report would be priceless.

We settled down for the hour plus drive to Oakdale, Louisiana. The drive goes north on I40 and then west on state 106, through the town of Oakdale and back into the pine forested countryside where Oakdale Federal Correctional Institute is located.

Oakdale is a class of detention facility where the inmates are housed in more comfortable quarters than your typical penitentiary. At Oakdale they have rooms instead of cells. Some of the inmates even have a room to themselves and I suspected that Ray Suffield was one of those.

I had had extensive exposure to prison life researching the Ted Swanson story but his was a state maximum security facility with bars and dingy walls, more familiar to us when we think of a prison. Oakdale FCI was a minimum security prison made for inmates who weren't likely to ravage each other, riot or take hostages, which resulted in more freedom for them. These federal prisoners were still incarcerated and had very strict rules of conduct. Inmates at FCI's were expected to behave themselves and act with decorum. If they didn't they got knocked down to a more brutal environment. I assumed the inmates knew this and toed the line.

Oakdale FCI sat out on a flat field surrounded by tall pine forests, a wide grassy buffer area and a high double chain linked fence. There was a guard who checked our names, looked in the trunk and told us that there would be a more thorough inspection inside. We followed the signs and parked in an empty visitor's parking lot. The reception area was a sandstone building with a low flaring metal roof. If you ignored the razor wire topped chain linked fence, it resembled the headquarters of a moderate sized company. Once inside it was all Federal Bureau of Corrections décor, industrial tile floor, institutional green/gray walls, and fluorescent light fixtures every eight feet.

Standing in front of a reception desk was a tall, pleasant looking gentleman in a dark blue suit. He leaned over like his shoes were glued to the floor and extended his hand.

"Mike Ferguson. I'm warden here at Oakdale."

"Brendan Macbean, and this is Tony Gianelli, my cameraman." Tony set down his equipment cases and warm handshakes crossed between the three of us.

"Mr. Macbean, the director of Bureau of Prisons called me this morning to tell me of your visit. I can take you to the room we've set up for you but Mr. Suffield won't be available until after lunch."

"Oh, well, thank you Mr. Ferguson."

"Call me Mike. Everyone here does."

"Okay, Mike. I guess we'd like to set everything up. In the interview…, uh, where we're going to do the interview."

"Mr. Macbean…"

"Call me Brendan."

"Brendan. Wouldn't you like to have some lunch, first?"

We had arrived near lunchtime, but I was too keyed up and couldn't even think of eating. I glanced at Tony and he gave me a rueful look. Of course, Tony was young and skinny. He probably thinks of eating all the time. The problem was I could let him go eat while I set up the equipment, but that wasn't our roles. If I set up cameras and microphones we'd all strangle ourselves in the resulting tangle of wire.

"Mike, I don't know how much time I have. We've flown in from Atlanta this morning because Bent…"

He cut me off. "Brendan, you have as much time as you need. Mr. Suffield isn't going anywhere." He smiled like even he didn't know how old that joke was. "We were asked to give you every courtesy and as much access as you needed. You have the run of Oakdale for as long as you want. Within reason, of course." Mike Ferguson slackened his tie and took off his suit jacket, slinging it over the back of the empty reception desk chair.

He rubbed his hands together. "So, let's go have some lunch. Tony, leave your cases here. I'll have someone take them to the interview room."

Wow, I thought. Bentley not only gave me an opportunity, he really got us the VIP treatment.

Mike Ferguson led us through a pair of double doors and down an office-lined hall that reminded me of a modern university faculty building. As we walked, the smell of cooking grew stronger, and if I had any preconceptions about prison food they were dispelled by the marvelous aromas wafting up the corridor. Tony picked up the pace.

We entered a cafeteria which look more like a college campus than a prison. Sparkling clean tile, bright fluorescent lights, round tables, a gleaming stainless steel and plastic sneeze guard serving line. Everyone, about fifty men by my estimate, looked up as we entered and I noticed that they all wore the same clothes in lieu of a uniform: khaki pants, white logoed polo shirts, sensible footwear. The inmates looked like business men at a corporate retreat. I saw no shaved heads, tattoos, or facial piercings. No one gave us more than a curious glance and after a few seconds they all returned to their table conversations.

The thought went through my head you really had to have a good lawyer to get this billet. It was a prison, but there was less suffering and regret going on in this place than at a typical Atlanta Falcons game.

In the middle of the room I saw what looked like a small traffic light suspended from the ceiling. The green light glowed cheerfully.

Mike Ferguson saw my interest. "Brendan, in federal detention we have lots of rules. One of the traditional rules is a ban on conversation during meals. We found this rule almost impossible to enforce, so we allow some slack here. I put up this light and permit the inmates to talk to each other... quietly. As long as the noise level remains low, the green light stays on. Our cafeteria monitor," he nodded to a guard sitting in a corner reading a magazine. "...can turn on the yellow if the buzz goes up. If it goes to red, we cut off the talk, everyone gets an infraction on their record and a fine."

"A fine?

"Sure. They all have jobs and get paid. The money is tiny by outside standards. And they don't actually get paid real money. The inmates aren't allowed to have much real money. We pay them to work here but what they actually receive is a credit at the commissary. With that credit they can buy the kind of stuff they're allowed to have: toothpaste, candy, cigarettes, although smoking is only allowed outside."

I must have had an astonished expression on my face. Mike Ferguson smiled.

"Oakdale is minimum security but there are lot of little rules that govern what happens here, actually thirty-eight pages of little rules. The inmates' lives revolve around the handbook, but little of what people think of prison life resembles what we have here at Oakdale."

"It looks very orderly," I said. "And kind of comfortable."

"We like it that way, thank you very much. It's just easier on everybody."

We went through the serving line picking up the usual plastic tray and institutional crockery plates, stainless utensils wrapped in paper napkins, a knife, fork and spoon. The warden continued his cheerful audio tour.

"When we serve steak, we give them steak knives. Nobody smuggles knives back to their cells. Nobody gets stabbed in the shower at Oakdale. They can shower in their rooms, and the only multi-person shower is in the gym."

Mike Ferguson recommended the fried flounder so that's what I got, along with wild rice and a salad. A Diet Coke completed my choices. I noted Tony added the Black Forest Cake to his tray. I shrugged. Tony was obviously not worried about his waistline.

We sat at the warden's table. I looked around the room and did not see anyone who looked like Ray Suffield. I actually didn't want to engage him here because I preferred to meet him on my terms, in front of a camera with lights and microphones and a bunch of difficult questions on the tip of my tongue. I did notice a guy staring at me. I didn't know who it was and dropped my eyes instinctively. I looked up and he was still staring at me with an unreadable. It wasn't hostility, just curiosity, like he knew me. I used to be mildly recognizable years ago when I was on-screen, but that was only in Atlanta. The years had changed my appearance and apparently my comfort level at being recognized. The man stood and walked over to the guard who Mike Ferguson had pointed out as the lunch monitor. The guard looked up from his magazine, at the inmate and then over to our table. The guard shrugged with practiced nonchalance and went back to his magazine. Then the inmate walked over to our table. He stood there for a second and cleared his throat. The man looked to be in his early fifty's and as harmless as a gardener.

"Mike, permission to speak to your guest."

"Pete. Do you know our guest?"

"Yessir. Well, I met him a bunch of years ago. He came to Mansfield, up in Ohio when I was doing ten for bad checks."

"Sure, Pete. Mr. Macbean, this is Pete Hagamire. He's been with us a couple of years and might be going home soon."

Pete Hagamire stuck out his hand. "Mr. Macbean, you may not remember me but you came up there a lot to visit Ted Swanson. I worked in the office. I sometimes escorted you to the interview room."

I shook his hand. I didn't remember him, didn't remember who had escorted me. I did not remember very much about Mansfield except nervous interviews with that vicious murder.

"Pete, it's nice to meet you. This is a better place than Mansfield."

Pete seemed to think that was funny and let out a chuckle. "Right you are, Mr. Macbean. This is a different thing entirely. I was up there doing ten years and when I got out I hadn't learned my lesson, obviously." He looked around at the cafeteria. "I did some mail fraud and that's federal." He glanced at Mike Ferguson. "But it was a stupid thing to do and hopefully I'm a lot smarter now about things like that. Warden Ferguson encourages us to 'fess' up and get on with our life.

"I wanted to thank you for that book you wrote about TV Swanson. It had a big influence on me. Old Ted was a lot badder than I ever was but your book helped me realize that any kind of crime is a terrible thing and hurts a lot of people."

A host of dreadful memories surfaced. Ted Swanson's story had been an appalling tragedy. During his sorry life he had destroyed many other's lives. I never realized that writing about it might have the effect it had on someone like Pete Hagamire."

"Pete, I had no idea. You are certainly very welcome, and I thank you for telling me that."

"Your book is one of the most popular ones in the library, Mr. Macbean. I'll bet there's jailbirds all over the country who have read it at least five times."

Mike Ferguson frowned. "Pete, we don't use that kind of language here."

I wondered what language had annoyed the warden.

Pete looked chastened. "Right you are, sir. I meant 'inmates' not the word I used."

Mike Ferguson smiled again. "Okay Pete. No harm done."

There seemed to be nothing else to say. I stared back at Pete Hagamire while a feeling of numbness crept up my spine. Pursuing the TV Swanson story had turned my life upside down and brought in a bucket of money. I felt proud of the book, but writing while it I got too close to a profound human tragedy. I don't think I'll ever get over it, but now I felt amazed that the story had inspired the man standing at our table.

Mike Ferguson said. "Pete, anything else?"

Pete looked flustered. "No, warden, sir. I just wanted to tell Mr. Macbean, thank you."

His head nodded. My head nodded, and he shuffled back to his table. I watched him mutter something to his tablemates and they all turned to look at me for a few seconds.

"Pete's probably going to be paroled this winter. His mistake with the mail was minor and while he's been here he's kept himself straight. If he hadn't had that prior conviction he might have just gotten probation."

"He said you encouraged them to 'fess' up?"

"Yes, I do. I've been a warden for a long time. Working here is my reward for having worked at places like Mansfield. Prison warden is a frustrating job. You see the worst the human species can produce. For many of them you can't do anything. You can just tell about some prisoners. A lot of the inmates in places like Mansfield are just what they seem, ruthless, hard-core animals without a shred of decency, completely incapable empathy for their victims. You can work with them for years and offer them all the education and rehabilitation in the world, but in the end you will see absolutely no change. Except they learn to be better conmen. Nothing changes inside them. They're still hardcore animals who would cut your throat for no reason at all.

"Brendan, these guys here at Oakdale are completely different. Yes, they all messed up... made big mistakes. They hoodwinked, defrauded, stole, cheated, just plain screwed their fellow man, but they're not violent. They can come here, serve their sentence and get out with a good chance of not coming back. Most of them were successful in business or at a profession. Most of them will be successful again after they go home. Very few will wind up in trouble again, but to be certain of that I make a lot of demands on them. One of things I encourage is for them to acknowledge their crime and understand how their actions affected their victims. Are you familiar with AA, Alcoholics Anonymous?"

I shook my head. "I've heard about it, that's all."

"Many people think AA is old fashioned. Even medical science has come up with new ways to cure alcoholism and other forms of addiction. But modern day treatment often overlooks the concept of personal commitment. AA may be old fashioned but for those who follow the plan, it can work. A long time ago, AA invented a program of rehabilitation, the twelve steps to keep alcoholics on track to recovery. They reasoned that you can't change what has become habitual without turning yourself over to a higher power. You simply have to behave differently. You have to become a different person. Same with criminals. Anti-social behavior is really a form of adaptation. Rehabilitation requires fundamental change in the person.

"Criminals simply can't rehabilitate unless they sincerely admit there's a problem and understand why what they did is unacceptable. Penitentiaries like Mansfield are full of crooks who don't consider themselves bad people, or if they're bad, they're proud of it. So why do we expect they'll rehabilitate? The awareness required to admit guilt can only result after you thoroughly educate the criminal, get him to step outside himself and see what he did as bad. Then they can acknowledge their crime. It ought to be plain to everyone that a criminal can't rehab if he won't admit guilt."

I nodded agreement. "What's different about your program?"

"You'll admit this is a better place than Mansfield?"

"Much better."

"It's a privilege to be here. You have to have a good lawyer who'll persuade your judge to send you here. The judge has to agree you have potential to go clean. After you get here, you have to continually validate that potential. You have follow my rules and based on my evaluation of you, I may let you stay here. If you don't, you could get sent to a real mean place, like a max security prison where we dump society's human garbage."

"That's a pretty strong statement."

"Yeah and I'm talking to a reporter. Go ahead. Quote me." Mike Ferguson's face lost most of its friendliness. "Here, we can work miracles with these guys, but we don't accept self-delusion... none of this 'I was framed' crap. You have to willingly admit your guilt. Then you work on understanding how you hurt your victims. They are *your* victims..." he stressed the word, "which means you're willing to take ownership of your crime and of the reparations you must perform. If you can't grasp this concept you haven't demonstrated the depth of character needed for reintegration into society."

"Sounds good, Mike, but how does your approach sit with the ACLU."

He smiled. "They climb all over me and have filed a bunch of complaints, even a few lawsuits. The ACLU accuses our program of everything from racism to corruption. They think we operate this place to provide a cushy landing for the politically connected. But they can't say anything negative about my results, which are the best. The ACLU should go focus their attention on what's not working at places like Mansfield or other Ultras."

"Ultras?"

"Ultra-security prisons. Look, Mansfield and other prisons like it have a difficult mission and unless an inmate really sees the light, the chances of coming out of there and going straight... well the statistics are terrible."

"And your results?"

The smile came back to his face. "At Oakdale, our guys never come back."

"What about a guy like Suffield."

Mike Ferguson frowned. "Suffield is a peculiar case. I didn't want him even though he does admit his crimes, which is almost a bare minimum getting into Oakdale. Suffield's a smart cookie and seems to know what the score is here. He walks the walk and talks the talk, but I have doubts. His lawyers got him a marvelous concession, but he hasn't proved to me he belongs here. Also he's under the watchful eye of some high ranking Justice Department officials."

"Why's that?"

"They think he's still under a threat. Not from inside. We have a small number of inmates, less than two thousand, and very few guards. Our men are on a short leash. One or two mistakes and you're out of here. So, everyone behaves themselves. But a few of our inmates made some bad enemies, like Suffield. There's his connection to organized crime."

"The Russian guy, Vladoseev?"

"Yeah, whatever his name is. We carefully control all outside contact with our inmates. A couple of months ago, a lawyer applied for a visitation. In the beginning, Ray had lots of lawyers and lot of lawsuits. But when he saw this guy's name he said absolutely not. Apparently it wasn't his lawyer. We reported it up to Justice and they sent an investigator."

"A guy named Bentley?"

"No, not Bentley. Bentley is big stuff in the DOJ. The guy they sent was just an investigator. Nothing ever came of it or if it did, they didn't send me any memos."

The conversation slowed. I realized I was scraping my plate. Mike Ferguson watched me and asked, "You liked the flounder?"

My empty plate gleamed with cleanliness. I grinned. "Better than the Fish Market in Atlanta."

"I doubt that, but we try to keep things civilized. Are you ready to meet Ray?"

I nodded.

Chapter 21

From the journal of Brendan Macbean:
Mike Ferguson led us to the prison library. The guard at the gate had warned us we'd be more thoroughly searched inside. Someone had carefully unpacked all of Tony's equipment and laid each piece on a wide table. The foam linings of the equipment cases had been removed and placed on the floor next to the cases themselves. With a great deal of agitation Tony fussed over his cameras, cables, mikes and mixers and finally acknowledged the prison search had done no damage to his equipment.

"Where is Ray?" I asked.

Mike Ferguson said, "We'll call him up when you're ready."

We decided to set up in the main part of the library with shelves of books as a background. Tony set up three cameras in a triangle so they could simultaneously capture my face, Ray's face and more distant shots that put both of us in the scene. During the interview Tony would 'rove' with a fourth camera. Later Tony could edit snippets into the final version. After roaming around the room looking for the right spots, Tony placed microphones at strategic locations. He set out lapel mikes for Ray and myself.

"When it's time to bring Ray Suffield in here, I'd like Tony to video him walking from his cell to this room."

Mike Ferguson looked thoughtful for a second.

"We don't allow cameras in that area. And we don't call them cells. They're just rooms. There are lots of security reasons we don't allow people there. You probably want to hear those reasons, but they usually invite argument, so let me simplify things by saying no."

Mike Ferguson saw the drama play out on my face and offered, "You can film him walking down the hall just outside of the residential area. How's that?"

"That will have to do," I said.

Tony carried the camera into an interior foyer marked with a sign that said, "Residential Wing D." In a few minutes, we saw convicted felon Ray Suffield, the former CEO of InCorps, the leading member of the Hole in the Wall Street Gang, enter the building through double glass doors. As he approached us, Tony backed up and I grabbed him, behind his back by the belt, gently guiding him down the hall, toward the library.

Ray Suffield strolled with all the confidence and nonchalance of a

133

Wall Street executive. He strode past the cafeteria, glancing in as he passed. Tony's camera automatically turned on a bright light when the ambient light dimmed. Ray squinted and gave a bemused look directly into the camera.

The warden introduced us and we shook hands.

Ray Suffield was dressed the same as the other inmates I had seen, white shirt over khaki pants. He looked like a very fit middle aged man. He had close-cropped graying hair and reminded me of the actor, Brian Carney, who played the GEICO executive who talked to the gecko in the old commercials. He seemed to have a lot of energy and kept a tight smile on his face.

After the nice-to-meet-you banalities Suffield got in the first shot. "Mike told me you wanted an interview. I said that's fine as long as I have final edit approval." He held my hand in a firm grip. The statement completely stopped me in my tracks and my expression must have showed it. His smile widened, showing gleaming white car salesman teeth.

"Just kidding, Mr. Macbean."

I felt the hot flash of having just been had. I tried to show a good face. "Sure, Mr. Suffield, but if I were you, I'd save my best stuff for the camera."

His face turned mock serious. "Best stuff? Don't worry. I got lots of good stuff." The wide smile reappeared.

High profile celebrities often demanded final edit approval before granting an interview, but we hadn't planned to give Ray Suffield any say in how we presented him which is why his remark threw me for a loop.

"Can I call you Ray?" He nodded. "Ray, before you say anything else, I'm going to make a statement and it will be the last thing said that's record statement. In fact, nothing in this interview or any conversation leading up to it is off the record. I'm a journalist and I intend to produce an informative piece for television news, the contents of which will be anything currently in the public record, plus anything we talk about on camera plus any information that may come to light right up to the moment we broadcast it. You are free to answer my questions anyway you want, but anything and everything, including what we say here may be used in our final presentation."

He took the seat facing me looking reasonably relaxed. "Wow, Brendan. That's quite a speech."

I nodded to Tony and he nodded back. All our cameras red lights came on. We were rolling. I felt a tingle of excitement. I was finally getting to interview the one person who had remained elusive to television journalists for four years. And I was getting in after the networks had tried and failed, which ought to be a genuine embarrassment to them considering the clout national television has in America.

I sat opposite Ray and fixed my face in my most authoritative television journalist expression, made somewhat difficult because of my glasses. In television, appearance was the god we all knelt before. I had not been blessed with anchorman good looks. I couldn't wear contact lenses so if I were to see anything, I had to wear the heavy lenses I had worn for the last forty years. Trying to look like Brit Hume contorted my facial muscles, but still I felt exhilarated.

"Mr. Suffield, you have been serving a prison sentence for four years. Other than the information that came out in your trial, we haven't heard much about you. You haven't granted any interviews. Why is that?"

Ray Suffield looked thoughtful. "That's complicated, I guess. You have to get permission for everything here. My legal people worked with the courts so I don't get much direct contact with anyone outside this facility. If someone wants to see me, it often doesn't come to me directly. It's not like I'm hard to find." He smiled at his own quip. "But I haven't reached out to any news media and if they've reached out to me, either the authorities or my attorneys have squelched it and I haven't heard about it."

"So it's not like you refused interviews?"

"No. Not at all." He shrugged. "But what's the point? Someone wants to see me they have to go through channels and I'm not sure what those channels are. My guess is that the reluctance comes from the justice department. They're the ones making the rules. There's been nothing to refuse."

"You received plenty of publicity before and during the trial."

"Exactly and that wasn't too pleasant."

"Ray, this seems like a pretty nice place for a prison."

He shrugged. "If you have to go to prison, I guess it's a lot better than some other places."

"What are the cells like here?"

Ray's smile was slight, a tiny upturn of the corners of his mouth. "Well, we don't call them cells and anyway I don't have much experience with jails. They're like the dorm rooms I remember from college."

"Do you share a room?"

He shook his head. "Some of the guys have roommates. I don't."

"Still, Ray, it must have been difficult going from a penthouse in

Manhattan to federal prison."

"It's a shock, but in those days I had a lot of shocks. My arrest, then the trial and sentencing. Before I had to report to federal prison, I had a few months to get some of my affairs in order. I had to face the final days when I knew going to jail was inevitable."

"When did the reality of going to prison settle in?"

"When I turned myself in to the federal authorities."

"In New York?"

"Yes. I went to the federal court building and the US Marshals were waiting for me when I arrived. They took me in along with some other prisoners."

"What was that like?"

"We were processed like immigrants. We went through examinations, turned in all our possessions. We were stripped, showered and given an orange jumpsuit with the words "Federal Prisoner" on the back. Almost like going into the army again. Except for the uniform."

"No more VIP treatment?"

He shook his head. "Not any more. Not for me. We were put into a cell where we waited for a few hours before they loaded us on a bus. The bus had wire screen on the windows and two armed guards. The bus drove south and made stops in North Carolina, Atlanta, Alabama. Maybe some other places. When they finally pulled into Oakdale, it was just me and the two guards. They took my traveling coveralls and gave me these wonderful khakis," he added with slight sarcasm.

"Did you settle into prison life?"

"Warden Ferguson runs a tight operation. The guys here are pretty well behaved. I don't know much about other places but here you can either make friends or people let you alone. I was isolated the first two weeks and gradually they let me mingle with the other inmates. One thing the warden doesn't allow is for the other guys to give you a hard time over anything."

"Anything?" I asked.

"Well, like if people know what you did that landed you here."

"Like defrauding millions of people, some of whom may have been friends and family of the other inmates?"

I worded the question as a challenge, but Ray didn't rise to the bait. "Yes. Exactly that. No retribution. No messing with each other. If you have a dispute, we have weekly councils. If it's more serious you have to take it to the warden."

"No one gave you any trouble over what happened with InCorps?"

"Mr. Macbean, everyone in here has committed a federal crime. Whatever they think about me or InCorps, the guys keep it to themselves. That's the rule around here. If someone wants to be unfriendly, we let them, but if you start a ruckus, you get demerits. The warden only puts up with so much of that and if you don't straighten up you get transferred."

"What happened with InCorps was four years ago. Do you think people outsides these walls have forgotten?"

"No. But I'm not Michael Vick, either. Football fans wondered if he'd go back to the NFL. Well he did and it turned out okay for him, at least for a while. I don't think I attract the same level of interest."

"So forgive and forget?"

"I just don't know. I can't forget what happened and I doubt anyone who lost money with InCorps will either."

"Mr. Suffield, you were indicted on over a hundred securities and exchange violations, fraud charges and other felonies like extortion and racketeering. You pled guilty to eighteen felony counts."

Ray sat there with a neutral expression on his face. He might have been listening to his doctor telling him his health was normal. Finally he shrugged. "Eighteen out of a hundred. The rest were dropped."

That was not what I wanted. He seemed to be avoiding getting emotionally involved.

"A few years ago, you were one of the most hated and reviled men in the country. Americans were screaming for vengeance. In the final days before your arrest what did it feel like to be Ray Suffield?"

His expression changed. He slowly lost his confident smirk. Pain crossed his face like a shadow. His eyes dropped and he stared at a place between his knees. He looked at me with saddened eyes.

The camera caught it.

Ray's voice rasped. "It felt horrible. My whole enterprise had been built upon a good reputation, my reputation, my father's. My family had a good name. InCorps was a company that traded real value. We made money for people. We pushed a profit motive, and we delivered. Nobody invested in InCorps who didn't think they would get back a solid return. InCorps was a good name. Ray Suffield was a good name. I think that losing my good reputation hurt worse than... anything else."

Good, he was feeling bad about it. I bored in.

"Your investors, the people who trusted that name, would like to know how it all went sour. How did you go from a legitimate business to being a convicted criminal?"

Ray Suffield winced at the word 'criminal' and looked like he might raise an objection.

"Criminality has degrees, Mr. Macbean... especially in business. We're governed by rules. We have procedures to deal with rules, even avoid them. Business laws, taxes, regulations, fees, guidelines, each one of them has an authority, a policeman, a watchdog, to make sure we're in compliance. InCorps tried to follow every rule we had to follow and find loopholes if it would save us money. Every business does this. Regulations take profits."

"But rules prevent fraud, dishonesty and cheating." I added.

"Yeah, they're supposed to." He looked straight at me. "And sometimes they don't. InCorps' practices were not fraudulent or criminal. Some of them were more like loopholes, like we all do at tax time. Our business was based on leverages and privilege. We bought the production of an oilfield in Turkey for example. We sold the oil to a refinery. We leased space on an oil tanker to bring the crude to that refinery. Every segment of that process involved laws, local and international laws. Every time you move a product there's an official collecting a fee along the way. The bigger you get the larger your staff has to be to keep track of it all. Does that make sense?"

I nodded.

"So we tried to make sure everything was legal. It's the cost of doing business, a significant cost."

"Okay?" I wondered where he's going with this lecture in international commerce.

"It's much easier when profits are high because you have cash flow and considerable margins. When we began, we achieved very high profits. We grew fast. More business came our way. Every segment of what we were doing helped other businessmen, other companies. Other companies wanted to do business with InCorps because we got the job done. We were the IBM of international petro-commerce, and we had everybody scratching their heads trying to figure out what we were doing that was so special."

"And at the time, what you did was above board?"

"Certainly. We were making money. We paid our dues. And our tributes."

"Did your competition figure it out?"

"Not for a while. But our lead only lasted a couple of years. You can't keep what you're doing a secret, and all we really did was cover most of the operation of oil mining and delivery… like a one stop shop. Eventually other companies figured it out and duplicated it. Competition undercut our prices. Our margins got pinched. We grew ten straight years and gradually we found ourselves in the middle of fierce competition. Our profits went down and covering all those costs… well, it got harder to make payments."

"So what did you do?"

"Cash keeps the business moving. We'd borrow and pay off the debt. We had to find more sources to borrow from, which was where Wylie Schram came in. Wylie was amazing at raising money. He figured out tactics that restored our cash flow even with all the competition. Our profits came back. I asked him how he did it and he showed me all this confusing accounting stuff. I'm no accountant. I had no idea but he told me it was all above board. He was very persuasive. With Wylie running the finances we squeezed out an eleventh and twelfth year of growth and profits. What he did seemed like a miracle and the investment money kept rolling in.

"And what Mr. Schram did was on the up and up?" I asked.

Ray Suffield nodded. "It had to be. That was my policy. But we had to borrow more money. We're talking millions here that had to be paid back in a short cycle. InCorps was a dynamic, thriving business. And growing. Millions of dollars were invested every day. We were raking in the money and we were spending like any big, vital company, but as we borrowed more our cost of borrowing rose and our lenders shaved our credit rating. That is a common dynamic in any enterprise, even for IBM."

If this were live TV, our viewers would have vanished at this point. Viewers were not going to sit still for an economics lesson. I said, "Okay, Ray, business got competitive. Your corner of the market got crowded. What caused InCorps to go shady?"

He gave me a look of polite exasperation. "What I'm trying to explain… there are degrees. At the one end you have legitimate businesses, with triple A ratings and large amounts of money coming in. At the other end of the scale you have totally illegal activities, conmen try to sell you the Brooklyn Bridge or swampland in Jersey, the guys that steal money from little old ladies. I'm not trying to be flippant here. Most businesses operate somewhere in between. Even Fortune 500 companies punch up their financial statements when it's time to announce quarterly earnings. That's why we have auditors. That's why Wall Street analysts rate companies, their stock, their bonds, even their debt on the basis of the data. Wylie Scchram was doing things with our money that seemed too good to be true but from my seat, the CEO's seat, one day we were pinched for cash. The next Wylie had it fixed and we had a thriving business again. I said, thank God! And the money kept rolling in."

"So you were unaware of what Mr. Schram was doing?"

Ray Suffield shook his head. "No, I'm not saying that at all. I was the boss. It was my responsibility. I'm not sure I understood that what he was doing was shady. But when we got audited, we didn't have the reserves we said we did. We didn't have the cash we said we did. We didn't have the signed contracts we said we did. The more you looked at it the shadier it got. Wylie had total authority to do what he wanted, but he did so under my authority and our board. But I can tell you this. We liked what he did, and in the haste of the moment, he saved our butts. Our ongoing success made me trust him. We had investors to serve and creditors to pay. There came a time when trusted creditors shied away from lending us money, so we had to find new creditors. Wylie found them. We borrowed and we paid back. I didn't ask where it came from. Maybe if I had paid closer attention...." He trailed off.

There is a time in an interview where silence is a powerful tool. It seemed to me that we had arrived at that moment. I wanted very much to hear the end of that sentence. I let him think about it maybe too long.

But instead of saying anything, Ray Suffield seemed to reset himself. He closed his mouth, sat up straight in his chair and gave me a very direct look. I knew what that look meant. He had clammed up.

I wasn't going to let him clam up.

"Mr. Suffield, if you had paid closer attention..." I paused, "What?"

He waited a long time. I wrote on my note pad, "Edit this pause."

Finally Ray Suffield dropped his eyes. He blinked first.

"I didn't pay attention to his money sources. Some came in from venture groups I hadn't heard of. Some of the money looked like it came from overseas."

"Did you look into it then?"

"No."

"The terms?"

"Not really." Ray Suffield's eyes drifted away.

"Why not?"

"Because I didn't want to know where it came from. I didn't want to suspect that Wylie was getting the money from rough customers."

"Rough in what way, like gangsters?"

"No, not that, but people and groups who would play rough, in a business sense, if you owed them a favor. Or who might take advantage of a situation in which you were vulnerable."

"What kind of advantage?"

"Ownership. Equity in the company. Takeover. That kind of advantage."

"And more?"

"Possibly."

"Did you feel threatened?"

"Our business was threatened."

"Did these people, these sources of money communicate with you directly?"

"Yes." Ray Suffield's eyes dropped and returned.

"Did they make threats, Ray?"

"No, but I knew what they were thinking, what could happen to InCorps. When we were on top we called our own shots, dictated our own terms. We needed cash immediately and these new creditor slash investors, they'd tell us what was what. Their demands got bigger and we'd have to give it to them. It's not like a physical threat. More like they had leverage to take something away from you. Like bigger returns. We made less money. Our company was vulnerable."

"If you suspected that, why didn't you give Schram's activities a closer look? Or put a stop to it."

His voice raised a notch, like an uncle answering a pesky question.

"Because we were still raking in the cash. I was good at bringing in business. I let Wylie do what he did, which was raise money. I knew we were losing control. InCorps paper was becoming junk. We were getting riskier and riskier and we tried to hide the fact we weren't triple-A anymore. But I thought that we could wean ourselves to a back to a safer place. Maybe if some of our creditors were a little rough, when we got stable we could ease them out and get InCorps fully legit again."

"So what happened to that idea?"

Ray clasped his hands and looked at the ceiling. He let out a long breath. "I should have written memos, made a paper trail, but I never told anyone about what was making me nervous. We all felt the pinch, the anxiety. We just never talked about it. Wylie and I never made specific plans to pull back. There was too much going on all the time, but we were becoming more vulnerable. When you get in certain situations, people notice your weakness. They're kind of like vultures. When a corporation like InCorps starts getting salty, they jump on the opportunity."

"What kind of opportunity were you?"

"Buyout. Hostile takeover. Leveraged stock deal. Raising capital to take us over. We got squeezed even more."

Ray Suffield was talking his jargon again, not mine. "What do you mean, Ray?"

"InCorps could be had. All some smart guy needed was to go around after us and buy our paper, our debt. When you own the debt, you make the rules. That's what they were doing."

"Who did this, Ray?"

"Actually it was more like a group. This group of corporate raiders put the squeeze on us, made demands, wanted higher rates. Wylie had pledged too much of InCorps for the credit. We were in a world of hurt unless we wanted to trade away the company. I had no idea who these guys were. At the time."

"Ray, tell us who they were."

I saw a brief momentary flash of panic cross Ray Suffield's expression. He got his emotions under control and gave me a condescending shake of his head.

"Ray, I'm sure the justice department wants to know who these people are," I said.

"The justice department already knows. It's an ongoing investigation. I'm under a gag order."

"That's bullshit, Ray."

His head snapped back. "You can say that on camera?"

I shrugged. "I can say anything I want, Ray. And no one is restricting your right to free speech. You have total control, remember? Only I get to edit out what I don't like, and I don't like this pile of crap."

Ray Suffield squirmed in his seat and looked behind him as if someone stood there. Tony moved the roving camera to Ray's left and zoomed in. Ray followed the motion and like a startled deer and stared directly into the lens.

Perfect.

"I liked your story about how business pressures made you get risky but when I asked to name some names, I get the silent treatment. You're happy to blame it all on Wylie Schram, but that's not how journalism works. I have to check everything. Who was lending you the money? Whose signatures are on the contracts? What pressure did they apply? What decisions did you make, you, Ray Suffield, that turned InCorps, the biggest moneymaker of the new century into the world's biggest scam and put the blight on American business?"

Ray's eyebrows came together. "Mr. Macbean, I think this interview might end a little early."

"We're not done until I say we're done, Ray. Suffield." I added. "Mike Ferguson is very sincere about his program. Maybe, I show him what we have so far. I'm in no hurry to wrap this up. We can go at this all day and the next day. And the day after. Mike Ferguson won't mind and the food is pretty good here. We can stay at this until I get a little more candor. Out of you, Ray."

At the mention of the warden's name, Ray Suffield pulled his feet under his chair like he was going to stand up. Then he went slack. He lowered his eyes and stared at his feet. "Look, Macbean. I'm still in a vulnerable situation. I'm aware of the warden's program..." He paused and thought about what he was going to say. "I'm trying to follow the program." He leaned forward and whispered.

"Federal investigators. Treasury. Back before I came here, they wanted me to give up the same answers. But it's not the same as airing them on television. So it's me and Wylie Schram. Everyone knows what happened. You want other names, you can go to Treasury. See if they want to give them to you..."

"Ray, Americans are a forgiving bunch of people. I think a lot of them don't think you received a stiff enough sentence. Some of them may like to know you just didn't take their money and destroy their life out of greed. If InCorps were being held hostage by some strong-armed threats, maybe they might cut you some slack."

"What kind of slack is going to do me any good?"

"Your piece of mind. It might let you look at yourself in the mirror again."

I could see my words were having some effect. He stared into the camera lens like looking into a mirror, his face slackened like he was growing old before our eyes.

Perfect.

"I know the collapse of InCorps hurt a lot of people..."

"Grandma's and grandpa's life savings," I said. "They got nothing left thanks to you. What they saved their whole life for went up in smoke." My face closed with his until we were literally only a foot apart. "What did you and Wylie Schram do to grandma and grandpa's life savings?"

Ray Suffield took a deep breath and let it out and it sounded like the fierce his of a big truck's brakes.

"Someone bought up our debt, InCorps' paper. I can't tell you who it was. But once they had it, they could start calling our notes. Shut down our whole operation. We negotiated. We pleaded. We promised them we'd give up major stakes in the company. They could seize our assets. They had us."

"You couldn't pay them off?" I asked.

"With what? We didn't even have our operating capital. It was all committed. These guys wanted their money. Right here. Right now. They didn't care if they shut us down. If we wanted to stay in business we had to give them the keys to the treasury. It would have led to liquidation of the company. At the time we were sitting on nearly eighty billion in assets. Cash, contracts, notes. Property. They could have locked our doors."

"Didn't that happen anyway? Millions of people lost their investments. Who got rich when InCorps fell?"

Ray shook his head. "Nobody got rich. I wanted to save the company but we couldn't hold it anymore. We tried to delay our creditors. Buy time until we came up with another strategy."

"What happened?"

Ray Suffield took a deep breath. For a moment he looked incapable of speaking the words encompassing the tragedy that had been InCorps' downfall, which proceeded the gigantic calamity of the American economy, the disgrace of our own federal government, exposing their system-wide lack of oversight, the frightful plunge of the Dow, the worldwide realization how fragile and vulnerable we all are.

Ray took a deep breath. "The feds stepped in. We got audited, investigated. Analysts dropped a dime on us. Our stock price fell like a bomb. The SEC condemned us and cut us up like a roast turkey. They auctioned off our assets like we were trinkets at a garage sale. They left us with no cash to pay our creditors. Nobody got any money because there wasn't any fucking money."

Ray was angry now. His eyes blazed with unwanted tears. He wiped them with the back of his hands.

"We weren't the only ones. Other corporations, some bigger than us were just as hollow. InCorps had a dozen tankers full of oil rolling on the high seas with nowhere to go. Oil wells stopped pumping, gas stations went dry and entire industries caught the plague. Auditors got busy and a widespread credit malaise swept the country. Our biggest banks and financial institutions had feet of clay. They stopped lending money they didn't have. Bond ratings dropped. Credit got frozen worldwide, and businesses choked due to lack of cash. People started storing money under their mattresses again and little old ladies got thrown out on streets."

"And everyone blames Ray Suffield."

"Why not? I'm still here. Wylie Schram was the lucky one."

"He died violently in a car crash."

"Yeah. I had to face the world's anger while Wylie died. All those news cameras followed me around. I couldn't take a crap without someone screaming at me.

"Look Mr. Macbean, I ran InCorps. I didn't run the rest of the country. I didn't run Bear Sterns, General Motors, Bank of America, Chrysler, Enron. The weakness of the world market became evident when the mortar crumbled and the bricks started falling. Huge amounts of cash had been flowing around the world and cash feeds business. When cash shuts down, businesses shut down. What I'm trying to say is that, yes I'm responsible for InCorps. But I wasn't the only one who had problems and swept dirt under the rug. There are other guys, big names, just like me who had a hand in it."

"People in power, you mean. But most people want to make you the villain. You and Wylie Schram, Bernie Madoff, Ken Lay, Jeff Skilling."

"And we did it. Okay?" He looked directly into the camera, only this time it wasn't deer in the headlights. His eyes blazed red and fierce. Tony zoomed the handheld in for a close-up. My spine tingled again. God! This was going to be good!

"I admit it. You hear me? I'm guilty. My responsibility. Wylie too, but it was me." More tears streamed down his face. He was not faking it now. I felt a lump in my throat too, but I had to control myself. This was journalism not therapy.

Ray Suffield turned his head to wipe his eyes on a sleeve. When he looked back at the camera, they were red but dry. I had to get him moving again.

"Ray Suffield, the people who were hurt in your scheme…"

"Look, Mr. Macbean. It wasn't a scheme. I didn't set out to hurt anyone. Neither did Wylie."

"Okay, but when InCorps went down, people got hurt and you actively tried to hide it, right?"

"Yes, you could say that. Okay, we were trying to hide it, but it was to prevent a selloff. There would have been panic over our stock and what we tried to cover up seemed like a temporary situation."

"But it's illegal, right?"

"Yes, it's illegal, but, I'd like to state for the record, it is also standard practice for nearly every business in the world."

"So we should haul the rest of the CEO's to jail, too?"

Ray lowered his face again and shook his head. He sat there for a full minuet and I knew, if I had anything to do with the final edit, I'd let never edit out his silence.

"Ray, are we supposed to feel sympathy."

I intended the question to be a challenge. Ray looked up and stared at me for a moment and then he lowered his eyes again, looking defeated. He raised his head and stared at Tony's handheld.

Ray's eyes shined like a lighthouse, but his voice was a whisper.

"No. I'm not asking for sympathy. I would like to apologize to everyone who put their trust in InCorps and lost all their money. For what I did, there is no excuse. No forgiveness."

In all my years of television journalism, I had never captured a moment like this.

Tony and I were bone weary hours later, when we finally got to the Days Inn in Opelousas. Tomorrow we would return to Atlanta with the interview of the century.

Chapter 22

From the journal of Brendan Macbean:
We caught a midmorning flight back to Atlanta and headed directly to the station. Bud was waiting for us at the front door.

"So you come sneaking back from your little boondoggle. Up all night doing Bally's in the Big Easy while pretending you're interviewing somebody in federal prison?" His voice dripped with oily innuendo.

I must have given him a glassy stare, easy for me since I wore glasses. "Geez, Bud. Where's the love? We got some good stuff here."

Bud looked at Tony. "That right, Tony?"

Tony gave him a thumbs up, "Macbean's back, Bud. He nailed it."

"We'll see. Let's go to a conference room and see what you got."

"Hey, Bud. I need to return some phone calls. Tony will set up and I'll be along in about fifteen minutes." Last night at the Days Inn I had discovered two messages from Shelby but was too tired to return them.

"From Shelby?"

"Yeah, not that we're trying to keep you out of our conversations or anything."

"She's here. She's probably already in the room."

"I thought she was in New York."

"She got back last night. Hey look, Macbean. We're all glad you decided to come in 'cause you got some big-time explaining to do."

"For what?"

"Going off on that interview with Suffield without giving me time to clear it with the GM. We got a chain of command around here. You're not free-lancing anymore. And you used our resources." He nodded toward Tony. I opened my mouth but Bud resumed his tirade. "The network is genuinely pissed *you* got the interview with Suffield. They told Shelby to get down here and take over. They called me and told me to pull you off the story and put her in. They were throwing their weight around like a two-horned rhino."

"Bud, you remember, I called you first. You were pissed I woke you up. Remember?"

Bud's look told me all I needed to know about how much support I was going to get.

"Look, Macbean. I should have told you to wait."

"Well, you didn't. Anyhow waiting wasn't the plan. The guy I talked to who set it up? He's in the Department of Justice. He said go and I went.

I only had a few hours to get ready."

"Well, it was a bad move for you, but I sucked up to them until I thought I'd puke. They were real hot. How dare we send in some old worn out has-been whose career bottomed out and couldn't write? Gonna fire us all they said. We shoulda called them and they'd send Chris Hanson or somebody. Somebody with a name."

"Gee, Bud. I hope you're not in serious trouble."

"Asshole. You always get everybody into trouble."

"Don't bother to thank me. And let's take a vote. Everybody in this room thinks you're the asshole, not me."

I looked at Tony but he had enough sense to keep his opinions to himself. Bud wasn't used to people talking to him like that, but I really didn't care. I had gotten in to see a man nobody could get an interview with and I had aced the interview.

"Calm down, Macbean. If you nailed it like Tony said we may be able to save your job, but it has to be super good."

"Thanks for going to bat for me, Bud." I made no effort to hide my sarcasm.

We all hustled to the conference room.

Shelby Chadwick was there waiting for us dressed in a tight fitting dark red business suit, accessorized like the network news reporter she aspired to be. To me she looked good enough for the cover of TV Guide. She gave me a ferocious smile, walked over and crushed her boobs against my chest in a Kodiak-style bear hug that lasted an eternity. I found my breathing apparatus strangling in the forest of her hair while mentally disabusing my spontaneous arousal.

"Macbean, you did it!" She pulled back and planted a full-on-my-mouth kiss that both resuscitated and defibrillated me. Later I thought I remembered someone shouting, "Clear!" during this episode. Bud and Tony stood awkwardly, their faces half struck between shock and envy. A flurry of emotions overwhelmed my body's physical reaction. I had not had that kind of contact with a woman since Bettye and I broke up, and as different as this woman was, it brought back sad memories.

Bud completely lacked empathy for the moment. "You two want us to wait outside?"

We both faced him while still embraced. Did I detect a blush in Shelby's cheeks?

I let go of Shelby, sat and scrunched my hips under the table just in case my traitorous libido needed more time to subside. I tried to take charge. "Okay, Tony. Show us what we got." But my voice sounded a little husky.

Tony waited until everyone settled into chairs. He fed his camera feeds into the monitors and the audio into the room speakers. We watched the entire interview with Tony fast forwarding through the dull parts. This was a standard technique familiar to television pros and TiVo sports fans. At the part where Ray Suffield broke down, Tony fed the different cameras' perspectives back and forth, again and again from a different camera.

Without much comment, we watched the raw highlights of the interview several times. Each time my excitement rose higher. Damn, this was good television!

At the end we sat in silence. Even Tony and I were stunned with what we had captured of InCorps CEO Ray Suffield.

Bud took a deep breath and said, "God, I may finally get an Emmy."

Although I had conducted the entire interview, until this moment I hadn't appreciated the full extent of the emotional impact we caught. Ray Suffield projected the image of an intelligent, respectable corporate executive. He came off highly sympathetic, just a man caught in circumstances but underneath it all there was an unmistakable artifice that made you feel wary.

What we had was ultra-high quality television but it was also very rough and needed serious editing. But the interview was sensational. With the right promotion viewers would swarm to the Ray Suffield interview like ants to a Claxton fruitcake.

Chapter 23

From the journal of Brendan Macbean:

Bud excused himself after ordering us to put together a rough-cut version and to have it on his desk in the morning.

Shelby, Tony and I started brainstorming. Editing extracted the true magic of television. We would manipulate what we had to fit how we wanted the piece to air. We could heighten the drama, emphasize some moments and diminish others. Without changing the content we could mold what we recorded in ways both subtle and dramatic.

We divided the recording into segments and sequences. We created a timeline, jostling parts, evaluating which bits made the most logical progression. We could edit the sound, the lighting, tempo and sequence.

For the final broadcast much of what we recorded would be cut out because there wouldn't be time to air it all. Local news segments ran three to five minutes. Even with a series, where you showed pieces of a longer television article on successive days, you could only show a few minutes a night or risk losing your viewers. A big network show like 60 Minutes aired three of four articles in a single program. Dateline could keep a single story going for more than an hour but they constantly had to tease their audience before and after the. You had to be careful with the viewer's attention and if they sensed you were manipulating them, they might go watch something else.

We decided to make a sampler of the highlights. This would be a short, focused version of a news piece designed to sell our managers on the value of what we had recorded. We'd let our executives decide what to do with this incredible exclusive. We had Ray Suffield in front of a camera answering hard questions. It was platinum television and we were going to get promotions, awards and voted into the broadcasters' hall of fame.

Or so we all thought at the time.

While we put together our video presentation, the afternoon flowed into evening. Tony's stomach reminded us of the time by growling with leonine ferocity. The three of us looked at the clock on the wall. It was closing in on eight o'clock.

Shelby tittered in a drawling version of a Southern Belle, "My, my how the time does fly when working with two handsome men, like ya'll boys."

My own stomach started harmonizing with Tony's. "We're almost done here. Why don't we call in a pizza and finish up?"

Tony looked relieved. One of my symptoms of middle age was indifference to a regular meal schedule. I had pushed the young cameraman beyond his glycemic limit.

Shelby said, "Mr. Macbean, you can't be serious. You expect this future Emmy winner to order pizza? You are beyond crazy." She gave me a stern look.

"I, uh. Well..."

Shelby saved me. She put a manicured hand on Tony's shoulder. "Tony, you order a pizza and finish up. Macbean and I are going to celebrate. We'll meet back here in the morning. That okay, honey?" She moved her face right into Tony's grille and tilted her head like she was going to French-kiss him. Instead she gave him a 'Nobody says "no" to Shelby' smile.

Guess what Tony said.

"That's a deal, Ms. Chadwick."

"Tony, call me Shelby or I'll fire your ass!" she said in a passable impression of Bud. She brought out still another smile, her 'Everybody laughs at my jokes' smile and we all laughed.

I was developing an impression that Shelby's smiles hit like a wrecking ball and mere mortals forgot how to say 'no.'

She also built up momentum fast. It seemed like less than a minute had passed and we headed out the door. At a television station there's always around-the-clock activity. Plenty of people saw Shelby towing me out to her car, which turned out to be a fairly new BMW 750i. She handed me the keys and skipped around to the passenger side. I got in the driver's seat and experienced the frictionless leather, noted the polished burl walnut trim and breathed in new car scent which merged intoxicatingly with the essence of Shelby. I didn't need to adjust the seat since she was on the tall end of the feminine spectrum and medium height was a stretch for me.

I turned to her and faked my 'I'm completely comfortable with this' smile.

"Where to?"

Obviously my smiles lacked the same power as Shelby's. She gave me an unfathomable look and turned her head toward the windshield.

"Macbean, this is your celebration. Make the most of it."

Her tone summoned a sense of urgency. My instincts told me I was on the edge of blowing it, without knowing what 'it' was. I guess I summoned all the gumption I had and made a decision. I backed up her hundred thousand dollar car and headed toward Bacchanalia. What the heck? Bud was going to pay for this.

It didn't take us long to get there. What took a long time was driving around the seedy parking lot, shared by two other restaurants looking for a spot where car door dings couldn't happen to Shelby's midnight blue Beamer. Bacchanalia was arguably Atlanta's finest restaurant but not very impressive from the outside. It was located in a strip mall wedged in between the Atlanta Waterworks and the outskirts of Midtown. Bacchanalia shared a parking lot with two other eateries favored by the torn-jean and sandals set who filled the parking lot with cars of their ilk. Where we were going was snootier than anything within a hundred miles. My Charter Club sport coat and ten year old tie might barely cut it at Bacchanalia. However I was escorting one of Atlanta's brightest celebrities, a famous TV star, a woman who looked good enough to walk down a runway at a New York fashion show.

Normally you have to have reservations for Bacchanalia weeks in advance, but I discovered the rules are different for public icons. As soon as the hostess saw Shelby, we were given a high profile parade in full view of the entire patronage. A few diners stuck their arms out and asked for autographs which I endured with bemused good grace. Actually I enjoyed watching Shelby work the crowd, and in a few minutes, the spontaneous media event ended and we were seated in a quiet corner. Except for the occasional, grinning rubbernecker, Shelby and I were left pretty much alone.

Fantasies I had in plenty, but never had I allowed myself to dream that I could take this beautiful woman out to dinner. But here she was sitting across from me, smiling her powerful smile. I allowed myself a few luxurious seconds to gaze into her picturesque face, trying hard not to shake my head in wonderment. Slowly it dawned on me that she liked it. Shelby was not only used to being looked at, she wanted it. She could choose from a catalog of good looking men and expect them melt before her, but tonight I was the one she wanted to celebrate with.

"You hit a bases loaded homer, Macbean."

I opened my mouth to decry such a statement, but the waiter showed up at that moment with a two hundred dollar bottle of champagne in a table-high silver bucket glistening with ice sweat. Waiters must have clairvoyance on their resumes to land a job with Bacchanalia. With a flourish he de-foiled, unwired and popped the cork with a thunderous "Pop!" The room erupted in a chorus of murmurs. I blushed self-consciously. The waiter handed me the cork like it was the pope's ring and I was supposed to kiss it. I took the cork and nodded and he proceeded to make pouring champagne look complicated. His penultimate act was to hand Shelby a delicate flute dancing with gold bubbles. She sipped daintily and smiled with exquisite satisfaction.

"Excellent, Bryce." She pronounced the word like an aristocrat. Aristocrats expected excellence and made no big deal about receiving it.

I guessed our waiter's name was Bryce. Bryce's ultimate act was to hand me a similar crystal-encased golden fountain and I sipped as daintily as I could manage. Ahaaa..., tasted good to me. I fought the urge to rub the tip of my nose.

"We must be celebrating, tonight." Bryce said in a nasally voice.

"We must be." I tried to give my response the same treatment Shelby gave the word 'excellent.'

"Hmmmm." Bryce held that descending note a little longer than a Mayfly's life. He vanished in a swirl, trailing white apron strings.

When I looked back to my dinner partner, she was holding her flute across the table to me. "To Brendan Macbean: unsung television journalist, the people's hero returns to the glory he deserves."

I slugged back a generous swallow of the best product to ever come out of France. Bettye had taught me to like this stuff. I smiled back at Shelby.

I had a speech prepared. "Shelby, thanks for giving me this opportunity."

"Oh, don't give me that humble crap, Macbean. It was a long shot. It was a dead possum and you brought it to life. I rode that thing as far as I could... got nothing out of it. Then they had me so busy I can't think straight."

"High profile projects, Shelby."

"Yeah, for sure, but I just couldn't get anywhere with Ray Sheffield."

"Shelby, you brought me in. I used to live for this stuff. You know that. You gave me another shot. I got lucky."

She almost looked angry. There was a fire burning behind her eyes. "Look, Macbean, nobody gets that kind of luck. Those guys at Dateline and 20/20 have been trying for years to talk to Suffield. You're on the case for a couple of days and you get the interview we could only wish for. You were always my hero. Now you are my real, big, strong superhero."

I blushed again. I emptied my glass of bubbly and so did Shelby. Bryce was there in a thrice, refilling our glasses.

I stopped looking at the most beautiful woman in television and stared instead at the energetic effervescence in my champagne flute. "I'm very proud of the interview I did with Suffield. Very, very proud of it. It's great television. But it is bigger than I am. We shouldn't kid ourselves. I'm not a big enough star to ride this to national television. You are. Shelby, I want you to take this."

Somehow my pride, the truth and the champagne collided to give me goose-bumps. What I had just said rang the heavy bell of fate in the back of my mind. It felt like a transcendent act of generosity and I expected to be elevated to sainthood, but it felt like I had mindlessly opened the cage of a wild beast and there was no way to get it caged again.

Shelby eyes widened, like a thunderclap had temporarily deafened her. Just as quickly she composed herself. She shook her head.

"What do you mean? Me? This is your triumph. You did this Macbean. This can get you back permanently. They'll give you Bud's job if you want it."

I laughed and shrugged off the moment. "That's one job I don't want. You'd have to be Bud to do Bud's job. And I not sure I want permanent. I know what it's like to work for the station. Doing freelance, I had freedom and flexibility."

And it was a lie. We both knew it. The truth was I didn't mind being low banana. I didn't want her kind of celebrity. I was proud of being the best journalist on the planet... for now. For just this moment, when last week my idea of fun was wrestling fifth graders on the Tae Kwon Do mat.

I could see the wheels turning behind her Tanzanite eyes.

"What do you think they'd do, dub me in asking your questions?"

"No. that might be a little grotesque. You bring me in as second fiddle. You do all the narration. We could get some video of you at the prison. Maybe the two of us in planning meetings. More of you than me, but you take the lead. It's your story. I just went in did the interview under your supervision when our window of access was this small." I held up two fingers close together. "If we do it right, nobody will even know I was there."

Shelby gave me a skeptical look that lasted only a few seconds. I saw the Tanzanite turn smoky and I knew behind the smoke was fire.

Chapter 24

From the journal of Brendan Macbean:
For the rest of the evening we spoke no more about the Suffield interview. We had an excellent dinner as you always get from Bacchanalia, plus service that is miles above any other restaurant in Atlanta. I let Shelby do most of the talking and got filled in on her biography. Shelby had been born in Birmingham, Alabama, the daughter of a pro baseball player and a surgeon. Her family moved to Atlanta when her mother took a teaching position at Emory Hospital. Her life had been a string of beauty pageants, sports and cheerleading, private schools and finally Duke University, where she studied journalism.

Throughout my career I had been in and out the public eye as an occasional on-camera personality, but it always surprised me when anyone remembered my work. Shelby had developed admiration for my TV spots. I had to admit, this mild hero worship felt really good.

It was mutual. She had risen fast in the rough world of television news. She had the brains, ambition and looks to be a star. It was wonderful to spend an evening with this beautiful and charming woman. For us time flew by and it seemed the dinner was over in moments.

I wish I could remember more but memory of our dinner date was erased by what happened next.

After paying the enormous check, we strolled through Star Provisions, the gourmet gift store that serves as an entrance to Bacchanalia. Shelby walked on my right and surprised me by taking hold of my hand. She pulled and guided my arm around her. This sent confusing shockwaves through my brain, but it felt breathtaking. We hobbled to her car in tandem. I pressed the key button and gallantly opened the passenger door for her.

As I pulled the car toward Huff Road, I noticed an orange dash light had come on indicating we were out of gas. It was late and heading back toward the TV station where I would have picked up my car might have risked getting us stranded. Running out of gas was an old trick guys of my generation used in high school to make out with girls. I guessed today's generation just made out, but darn it, it was her car!

"We're out of gas. There's a Race Trac on Marietta Avenue."

Shelby said nothing so I turned left on Huff. A few minutes later we pulled up at the all night gas station near the intersection of Marietta Boulevard and Bolton Road. The offices of the Atlanta Waterworks were across the road but the rest of the neighborhood had fallen into seamy urban blight. I had used this gas station place many times. The pumps were the automatic kind where you didn't have to go into the actual store, which was somewhat forbidding with bars on the windows and an omnipresent assembly of unsavory characters hanging out around the front door.

The Beamer's gas tank door was on the right side of the car instead of on the driver's side like where a sensible Japanese car would have it. I parked and pushed the button to open the refueling door, got out and went through the credit card swiping routine to activate the pump. Although Shelby didn't tell me to use premium, I did, figuring that Bud was going to pay for it. I took the opportunity to stare at her through the passenger side window. She was occupied reading messages off her cell phone. The gas nozzle clicked off.

When I turned around to replace the nozzle in the pump I saw what horrified anyone who watched the local TV news.

At first all I saw was the black gorge of an automatic pistol, just inches from my face.

"Tell-da-bitch-getta-da-car." The voice sounded youthful, low, unnaturally paced.

I saw that the automatic was held horizontally, an awkward angle popularized by actors playing hoodlums on crime TV shows. I saw the hand holding the pistol, wavering slightly, dark knuckles shining in the fluorescent lights, a thin wrist protruding from the sleeve of a grey sweatshirt, a hood hiding the man's face in shadows.

"Tell-da-bitch! Getta da car!" Louder and the barrel of the gun reached toward my forehead.

For some reason, I said, "Don't you know who that is?"

The hoodie inclined slightly toward the BMW's windshield.

Tae Kwan Do.

My left hand flew up inside his gun arm gun and slapped his wrist toward the Atlanta Waterworks. The pistol fell without discharging on the beautiful hood of the BMW 750i, sliding toward the front of the car. I swung the fuel nozzle, still in my right hand and smacked it against the side of his hoodie, rushed forward, smashing my shoulder into the man and he fell backwards like a toppled fruit stand. I stood over him and squeezed the handle of the fuel nozzle, dousing him with four seconds of gasoline, premium unleaded, that Bud was going to pay for.

He lay on his back not moving. I looked through the window at Shelby. She gaped with wide eyes and her mouth formed an "Oh!" She held her smart phone close to the windshield and I guessed she had videotaped the action.

And the next thing I saw was the parking lot filling with Atlanta Police cars, flashing lights and scurrying people. I'm fuzzy about the sequence of things from that point on. It seemed the police had responded in record time. A pair of cops held the hooded man on the ground like alligator wrestlers, bending his gas-soaked arms behind him. Once the handcuffs were on, they rolled him face down in the pool of premium unleaded.

A van showed up from our television station and Shelby did an on-the-spot telecast while I sat in the back of an ambulance and was checked over by some paramedics. It turned out I was fine, since he hadn't shot me and I had managed to not crap in my pants when I saw the gun.

The police stashed the mugger in the back of a cruiser. They retrieved the gun from the asphalt in front of the BMW. They took my statement, Shelby's statement, the operator of the Race Trac's statement. In a few hours we would be today's heroes on the morning news but for now we were bone-tired and wanting to go home.

Except that's not what happened.

We didn't all go home.

By two in the morning, TV news and the police had had all they wanted from us. Shelby and I climbed back into her car and we headed toward the station.

"Macbean," she said in a tired voice. "Can you take me home?"

I could and did.

We drove in near silence while she directed me in monosyllables. Her house was in an upscale neighborhood across from where Paces Ferry ended at Atlanta Road. We drove around her neighborhood until she reached across, pressed a button and I saw a garage door open and a light, the brightest spot in the shadowy early morning gloom.

Her garage was nearly empty and I had only a moment to think about it when she exited the car, opened a door and disappeared inside the house. I followed her, my mind a blur of avoided assumptions. The interior of her house was as gloomy as the street until she turned on a light. I found myself standing in a glittering foyer that would have made the cover of a decorator's magazine proud.

"Macbean, I'm going to take a shower and when I get out, remind me to call the engraver."

She disappeared again, down a hallway, leaving me alone to parse her imponderable statement.

I thought, Hmmm, you engraved a trophy or a plaque and… uh, okay.

I followed the sounds of running water and soon inhaled the scent of an exotic soap. My clothes fell in a vertical pile on white marble tile and a moment later I plunged into the fog… of shower steam and imponderable possibilities.

Shelby stood in her shower, her head encircled by a plastic bubble that looked like it belonged in a modern remake of Barbarella. She was gloriously naked. Shelby spent long hours at the gym and her lean body exhibited exquisite muscle tone. I slid in beside her and felt the hot water stream against my body. We hugged and lathered each other running our hands over breasts, backs and buttocks. Shelby's breasts were full and firm and they spiked my chest while my erection swung clumsily against her thighs. She worked her hands over my back and slowly knelt running her lips down my chest and abdomen, and eventually swallowing the entirety of me.

We both groaned.

Out of the shower we dried each other with thirsty towels. Her mouth was on a level with mine and we kissed sloppy kisses arms wrapped tightly around each other, marching sideways like crabs that won't let go toward her enormous bed, where we collapsed crosswise on a folded silk counterpane. The cover had been laid back and I briefly wondered if she had a maid.

Briefly.

We rolled against each other passionately, alternating between giving and receiving. My mouth slid down her remarkable torso against breasts, nipples, ribs, the cords of her stomach while my hand snaked between her legs and found her labia. I don't know what I did, driven by arousal and instinct, encouraged by her movement and moans. A moment later, her hands pulled my head upward to her and again I was swallowed whole.

Imponderable.

I lasted longer than I thought I would. We drove against each other slowly, spreading each millisecond into chasms of pleasure, our voices animalistic in the blind need to express our ecstasy. We felt a tide of irresistible pull, and when the flash and concussion arrived we seemed to sail over the edge and never hit bottom.

When my lungs were no longer heaving I heaved myself off her, plowing my face into her crisp white sheets.

Shelby lay with her forearm covering her face, body skewed, spread and spent. "Oh god, Macbean. No wonder all the girls at the station love you."

Chapter 25

From the journal of Brendan Macbean:
I awoke a few hours later feeling glued to Shelby's crisp white cotton sheets. Prying loose felt like pulling Velcro. I made my way to the bathroom, where I found my glasses and returned to the tousled, empty bed. On the nightstand I found a three by five ivory card. Her calligraphic script was neat and even as if she had indeed gone to the engraver.
"My hero!
There's coffee in the kitchen.
Love Shelby."
There was no comma after the word, 'Love' rendering her meaning indistinct. Did it mean love 'from' Shelby or was it a command to 'love' Shelby? At the moment both messages worked.
Like a hound I found the kitchen by sniffing for coffee. There stood a nearly full thermal carafe resting confidently on a highly figured granite countertop. Shelby had proffered a stainless steel travel mug with the logo of "Interstate Batteries" embossed on the side. That seemed to fit into my plans: I intended to both drink coffee and travel.
The elation and excitement of last night filled my brain, but now I faced heading to the TV station where Shelby and I worked with a very close knit crew. Even as I sipped her excellent coffee, I could feel a contagion of rumor and innuendo building.
I looked in the garage and saw Shelby's midnight blue BMW parked there and wondered how she had managed to get up, dress, make coffee and leave without waking me. But it had been the weight of her BMW keychain in my pocket that helped drop my pants to the floor last night. So I donned those pants and equally rumpled shirt, refilled my Interstate Batteries coffee mug, managed to get the garage door opened and headed toward the station.
The guard at the gate to the TV station parking lot definitely smirked at me so I flashed him a smile full of un-brushed teeth. But it occurred to me that the front-desk sentinel Misty Holden would greet me with even more irony if I walked in dressed in yesterday's clothes that looked like I had slept in them… even though I hadn't.
I lost my nerve.
I parked Shelby's Beemer next to my Toyota and threw her keys under the floor mat. I would text her a message later after I was far away from

the station.

In my own car I headed to my place and arrived just as a dreary fatigue settled over me. I made another pot of coffee while noting how bland my kitchen was compared to Shelby's. A hot shower revived me a little and as I strode naked into my own bedroom I saw the phone winking at me indicating I had a message.

I pressed the speaker button and dialed the code. The message was two days old. Well, I hadn't been home and who calls me anyway?

I heard a little static, some recorded phone fumbling and the voice.

Her voice.

Her voice was accented and hoarse, but I instantly recognized who had left me a message. "My Brendan..." A pause and a cough. Goosebumps formed on my arms. "My Brendan, I know it has been a long time. I will be in Atlanta on Wednesday. Can you meet me at the place we went? Ten o'clock? Please, it is important. Merci."

Bettye. She always called me, "My Brendan" and the way she pronounced my name made me shiver every time. Love with a French woman in a language made for love. I looked at myself in the mirror. My faced flushed with shame and guilt. I had just showered off the residue of love making with another woman.

Meet her. Wednesday. Today was Wednesday and, according to the clock next to my bed it was twenty minutes to ten.

I dressed in a hurry and was out the door in five minutes. 'The place we went' was the Silver Skillet on Fourteenth Street where for years, Bettye and I breakfasted after making love all night long. She loved the simple atmosphere of the place and even the food which surprised me considering her typical French disdain for American cooking. Fortunately 'The Place' was only fifteen minutes from my place. But any trip in Atlanta is subject to the whims of traffic and I arrived at the Atlanta landmark ten minutes late.

I hadn't given a thought to whether I would comply or refuse Bettye's request. We hadn't spoken a word in two years. I hadn't given a thought to the propriety of what she had asked me. I had reacted with instant assent, but now my mind filled with questions. Why had she come to Atlanta? Why did she want to see me after not even a French post card for two years? Why had she not given me more notice? But most importantly why was I so eager to see her? Her simple summons had completely erased the elation I felt after last night with Shelby.

I parked on the west side of the building and carefully gingerly side-stepping the perennially torn-up sidewalk in front of the restaurant. I paused at the door, my heart pounding like a hammer, took a deep breath and opened the door.

A cheerful bell announced my entrance. Somebody in the kitchen shouted, "Sit wherever you like."

The place was almost empty. A couple of Georgia Tech students held hands across a Formica topped table. An old lady occupied the corner table in the rear. Barely able to hold her head up the old woman seemed to be falling asleep over an untouched glass of iced tea. A second later her head came up and she stared at me. My knees buckled. Although her head was covered in a raspberry colored beret, I could see her once lustrous auburn hair had disappeared, to be replaced by a skullcap of gray and stringy strands. The skin of her face sagged from her sharp cheekbones and her eyes had the distinctive doomed look I had seen on faces of condemned prisoners on death row. As I staggered toward her those haunted eyes filled with tears. Tears streamed out of my own eyes. She struggled to get up.

"No. don't get up, Bettye. I'll hug you where you sit."

I tried.

My arm circled her shrunken body. I buried my face in her beret.

What had happened to her?

I finally slid into the booth and we held hands across the Formica like the two Tech students.

She took a deep breath. "My Brendan…" It was still that husky, smoky French accented voice that years ago had made my blood hot, but now it sounded of strain and ruin. "You look so fit and healthy." She made no effort to smile.

That left me with nothing to say, but that didn't stop me from trying.

"Bettye, I, uh… Bettye…" She pulled her thin hand away from mine and held it up. I saw her wince as if the movement hurt.

"I know how I look. My Brendan, I have much to say to you. So much you deserve to hear."

I nodded.

"My doctors call it stage four breast cancer. I have been fighting this for two years. Yes, even before we ended. My doctor recommended an immediate double mastectomy. After that I had chemotherapy, radiation, hormone treatments. I've tried it all. Endured it all. With every new treatment, the side effects are worse than the disease. Except they let you live a little longer. Headaches, cramps, blurred vision, nausea. This is what I've lived with for the last two years.

"My god, Bettye. Why didn't you call me? I could have helped you."

"No, My Brendan. I did not want you to know. I just couldn't face you after the surgery. You always were such a tit man." She gave me a tight smile. Dull gray teeth flashed between her lips.

"Bettye, I would have done anything for you. You must know that."

"I know. I barely had the courage myself. I couldn't put you through it. I was so disagreeable. And how horrible I looked! I felt it was better to break your heart than watch you worry about me. The operations, treatments. Many times I was ready to die. But I could not bring myself to die."

"Where are you now? What do your doctors say?"

"It is not good. I have tumors in my lymph nodes and along my spine. My doctors have told me I am month to month but..., the way I feel, I really don't want to live another day."

"Bettye, I can't believe it. You must have someone here look at you. We have the best doctors in..."

"No, Brendan. We must face the facts. Your doctors do not have any magic pill that will save me."

"Then tell me why you are here. You were going to die in Paris and I'd never know what happened."

"No, my Brendan. I wrote you a letter. As part of my estate, you would have received a letter explaining everything."

"A letter. What can you say in a letter?" I felt a little cruel saying it like that. But I hurt for a long time after we broke up. Now she shows up wedging herself into my life again and I could do nothing but drop everything and rush to her.

"Brendan, we loved each other and our life was full of possibilities. It was a shock to me when the doctor told me I had cancer. It meant the end of everything..., of you and me. The cancer got between us."

"Because you let it. I could have helped you."

She nodded. Tears streamed down her cheek. "I let my cancer come between us. I wanted to save you the pain. Maybe it was wrong. I don't know."

Bettye lowered her eyes. She shook but whether it was from a sob or pain I couldn't tell.

"Why did you come here? To see me? To tell me this? Jesus, Bettye, I'm really confused."

She nodded. "I know. I know you loved me. It must be terrible to see me like this but there is a reason I came. Recently, something has happened to give me a little hope."

"Hope?"

"Yes. Quite unexpected, a man came to see me, an American."

"A doctor?"

"No, no… an American." She said that like an American was the stark antithesis to a doctor.

"I think he is some kind of official. He came to see about a clinic in Switzerland. It is near Zurich."

"What kind of clinic? What can they do that doctors in France can't do?"

"Brendan, doctors all over the world are trying to cure cancer. But the treatments are so difficult and often the patients die anyway. At Klinik von St. Agatha they have found a way to kill the tumors without killing the patient. They are able to temporarily shrink a patient's tumors. They restore the damage the cancer has done so that they can live for a time as a healthy person."

"What? That doesn't make sense. They shrink the tumors and you get better?"

"Yes, you do recover, but Bentley was very specific. The tumors go away for a while but they return. It is only temporary. The disease reasserts itself and the patient dies."

"Bentley?" For the last minute my brain was like a runaway train, unable to analyze all the information. When she said this name the train swerved as if on a high speed curve and everything flew off the tracks.

"Yes, the man who told me about St. Agatha's… his name was Bentley."

"It couldn't be. I spoke to a man named Bentley Monday morning. He works for the Department of Justice."

"He is some kind of government official here, but he helps St. Agatha's find patients."

"Why do they need to find patients if their cure is so wonderful?"

"They do not have a cure. He was very specific about that. They only make you better for a short while. And it is very expensive."

"How expensive?"

"Over six million Euros."

"My god, Betty. Who has six million Euros?"

"I do. And I would spend it all to live like a human again. Even if just for a week."

"But then you die. Again." There were a thousand better things to say but my emotions were like a tornado. Part of me wanted to embrace her like the old days and part of me wanted to run away from her.

Because she hurt me.

"Then why do it?"

Bettye's eyes blazed with sudden fury.

"I want to live!" she said and pounded her fist on the table.

The waitress came over to take our order. I asked for just water. The waitress went away.

Betty lowered her voice. "Brendan, I have never wanted to live more than I have since I saw this man. In a month or two, perhaps less I will die. I want to die, not to live like this another day." Her hand circled her head, an odd gesture, airy and halo-like. "But to be healthy again, even if just for a short time. And to spend the time with someone I love. Oh, god. I would give everything for that."

"With someone you love...." Tears flooded my eyes. "With me."

I got another napkin out of the chrome canister on the table top.

"Yes, with you. Only you, my Brendan. You beautiful, stupid man." She smiled a painful smile, as thin as her bony neck and cheekbones.

I couldn't meet her eyes. They were slightly bloodshot and full of tears but they were the gray eyes I remembered. Cancer had turned her flesh into jerky but the Bettye I loved and who loved me was still in there reaching out for life, for me. Too many thoughts clamored for attention. Too many questions, but the one that slipped out of my mouth surprised me.

"Bettye, when?"

Those eyes speared me with their intensity.

"Our flight leaves at four this afternoon."

Chapter 26

From the journal of Brendan Macbean:
She had called it "our flight."

Bettye didn't come home with me. From the Silver Skillet she took a cab directly to Atlanta Hartsfield Jackson Airport. She told me Delta operated a comfortable facility for patients traveling with medical conditions.

I went home and packed, and spent the next few hours totally avoiding imperatives any sane man would have attended to before he flew off to Switzerland with a woman who had dumped him two years ago.

I didn't call the TV station.

I didn't call Shelby.

I didn't call Tony to go over editing notes on the interview with Ray Suffield.

I didn't call Bud who had just given me my highly coveted job back.

I did reflect on the folly of what I was doing.

Two years ago Bettye had dumped me and that still hurt. Now I understood what her reasons were and although I hated her decision not to let me help while she fought cancer, I guess it was better than being dumped for another man.

I guess.

Our flight took off at a few minutes before five PM, Atlanta time. With Bettye beside me, I stretched out in first class comfort. I don't know how far in advance she made this reservation but I checked with the airlines and my ticket cost over eleven thousand dollars if purchased today.

We didn't talk much. Our earlier conversation had exhausted what little energy she had and probably took an emotional toll as well. I had thousands of questions, about her, about us and about this mysterious clinic, but most of my questions begat more questions. I guess anyone who abandons his life work to attend to the love of his life has a lot of faith in the outcome.

I guess.

We flew mostly over land, following along the east coast. Within a few hours I saw the sun set through the window on my left. We still had Nova Scotia, Greenland, Iceland, Scotland and Europe to cross.

During the first hour of darkness I beat myself up over my decision to foolishly toss away my golden opportunity. Two days ago, I had nailed the biggest interview in recent television history. What Tony and I had captured on video could have won awards and certainly would have rekindled my career.

Television is tightly controlled by big corporations and highly political. When a low-level like me finds a diamond, the big bosses want to cut and polish it. Giant careers come with giant egos. TV stars don't mind stepping all over careers like mine. Rarely do they allow a local reporter to outshine them. Which meant that if I was to receive any credit for the Ray Suffield interview I had to stay and fight for it. By boarding this plane with Bettye, I was speeding away from my career at six hundred miles per hour, and thrown away the best piece of television journalism I had ever done.

But by the time it turned too dark to tell if we were over land or sea, I put the entire episode behind me. Or so I thought. Shelby and the network executives would fight like hyenas over the giant beast I had slain, and it was unlikely they'd save any leftovers. They would laugh at me if I tried to stand up for my rights.

In less than a week I had mourned my lost youth, contemplated sedentary middle age and had both laments overturned by an abrupt career opportunity. Now I could not see what my life would be like a week from now, and longer than that promised only tragedy. Somehow my lack of a future aligned me with the fate of the poor sleeping woman beside me. Neither Bettye nor I could predict much beyond this flight. This woman, the love of my life, who I thought I had lost, had returned, and our lives for worse or worser were linked. I guess that thought silenced my raging doubts and worry.

I guess.

I slept beside Bettye while the interior of the Boeing 777 grew dark and the roar of the turbines blotted out the dreams that should have come. Occasionally I woke, checked the video monitor of our flight path. The airplane icon inched a little further along the curved line toward Zurich and the giant question mark that awaited us.

Somewhere between Scotland and Denmark the airplane came awake. Lights came up with the sun, again on my left. The flight attendants scurried around to serve us breakfast which in first class began with a glass of juice. Bettye thirstily drank hers but after feeling the texture of the tiny tablecloth the attendants spread across our tray tables, she sniffed at the rest of the airline's offering.

We deplaned at the Zurich airport, the last passengers to get off due to Bettye's medical VIP treatment. The Swiss take pride in their efficiency.

Airport attendants wheel-chaired her through customs by the numbers. My previous experience with European travel occurred mostly at Charles De Gaulle Airport where you're subjected to lines and multiple inspections of your passport. As we exited the security area we spotted a limo driver holding a sign for Mlle. B. Le Boutilliere. He bowed, announced in French he was from St. Agatha's, noted the look on my face and repeated the statement in English, but I had caught the meaning. The driver immediately took over the wheelchair duties leaving me with nothing to do but meekly follow along.

The driver took us directly to St. Agatha's but I don't remember the trip much. My body was still trying to figure out where it was. Zurich is an ultra-modern city with a fast moving freeway system. Our driver rattled on about how taking A4 and A1 added twenty kilometers to our route but avoiding two border crossings into and out of Germany.

"Fine," I said. "As long as you know where we're going."

He gave me a curious look in the rearview mirror and a shrug which from the back lost much of its emphasis. It took us nearly an hour to get to St. Agatha's which was located on a splendid country estate complete with iron gate and long winding uphill driveway. We pulled under an elegant porte-cochere. The driver opened doors for both of us appearing to be on both sides of the car simultaneously. White coated orderlies manhandled Bettye into a wheelchair.

We were greeted by a tall, stunningly beautiful brunette. Did I say stunningly beautiful? No wonder they charged eight million dollars to come here. They're hiring Victoria Secret models as hostesses. The drop dead gorgeous woman introduced herself as Dr. Bauerle. This babe was a doctor? Gorgeous, only if you liked six foot tall German brunettes with smoking-hot brown eyes, more curves than a Swiss country road and a dimpled smile almost as wide as Shelby's. God help me where did that thought come from?

"Bonjour, Monsieur Le Boutilliere." Her delicately boned hand grasped mine.

"Good morning, Doctor. My name is Brendan Macbean. I'm here with Mademoiselle Le Boutilliere." I tried to give her a confident smile but obviously neither of us knew what to make of the situation.

"Oh, you are not Madame's husband?"

"No, Doctor Bauerle. Did I pronounce your name correctly?"

"Close enough." Her cheeks dimpled briefly. "You're not French?"

"No, American."

"Good. We have another at our clinic."

"Another American? Great! We'll talk American."

She smiled again. "Mister Macbean. You will have to fill out a form."

"Just one? The Swiss are well-organized!"

I turned around to see if Bettye was enjoying this conversation as much as I was and discovered she was not there. My head twirled looking for her.

Bauerle spoke, "We've taken her back to our treatment facility. We cannot waste any time, of course."

I suddenly felt guilty. While I mindlessly flirted with Bauerle, Bettye was fighting for her life.

Dr. Bauerle's authoritative voice brought me back to earth. "Follow me, Mister Macbean."

I followed her through double glass doors into a European-modern style lobby and into another room, a contrasting old fashioned wood and leather library. There was another man in there hunched over a computer. Bauerle pointed to a large wooden desk and laid a few forms on it.

"Mister Macbean, please fill these out. We didn't know you were coming."

I nodded. The forms really did just ask for the basics, repetitively... name and address, the standard phone numbers, place of work... Did I still have one? They also wanted emergency contacts but I couldn't think of anyone. It took twenty minutes and when I finished I looked around. Bauerle had vanished but the man sitting at the computer was staring at me. I stared back, not out of rudeness but because he looked vaguely familiar. For several seconds his name hovered on the edge of my awareness only to flit away.

"Excuse me, have we met?"

"No, Mister Macbean although I know you from your writing."

That startled me. The Atlanta television viewers may know me from the local news but I've been out of the spotlight for several years. Recognizing me is rare. Recognizing me for my writing is rarer still. And in Switzerland? At that moment, I couldn't remember the name of the town we were in.

"From my writing?"

"The book about TV Swanson. Your picture on the jacket cover. Weren't you on Good Morning America?"

"Not that I remember. Anyway, that was ages ago."

"Great book."

"Thanks." I rose from the desk and walked over. He met me halfway, and we shook hands standing on a giant red and brown Asian rug.

"I'm Daniel Conklin." The way he said it sounded off a note. Daniel Conklin wasn't the name hovering in my memory. His face had a bland, masklike characteristic.

"Nice to meet you. Dr. Bauerle mentioned there was another American here. I'm curious. They don't have other patients?"

"No, just my Denise and your wife, I guess."

I let the word go. The explanations could go on forever and I had a vague notion Conklin and I might share a similar status.

"It seems strange. I'd think St. Agatha's would have a waiting list."

He gave me a look, odd and unreadable.

"Mr. Macbean, have you had the orientation?"

"Call me Brendan. I know it seems strange but twenty-four hours ago I had never heard of the place."

I knew as soon as I said it I had made a gross error. My statement raised questions even I couldn't answer. He stared at me with palpable curiosity. I saw his face work through a handful of inquiries. I leapfrogged them all with one of my own.

"Daniel, do you know much about what they do here?

"More than I did a couple of weeks ago. I'm a pharmacist and you'd think I'd be able to figure out some of their secrets but I just have the basics. I live in a small town where you can't get cancer treatments. Most of the drugs we dispense are for prescriptions our folks get after they go to a big city doctor. I've read some of St. Agatha's information but I don't really speak the language. They have a million terms most of us never hear of. I've been reading a lot on the internet chat-rooms like breastcancer.org. I've learned a whole new vocabulary. Dr. Friedkin's treatments attack tumors on the cellular level."

"Dr. Friedkin?"

"He's the head of St. Agatha's. He used to be real big in worldwide cancer research. Over the years, he's developed his methods which have been highly effective in killing malignant tumors."

"Why isn't he more mainstream? You said he used to be big in cancer research."

Conklin paused for a second.

"Brendan, the problem here is this place is for terminal patients. People look for places where they're offered some hope. Millions of cancer victims all over the world, many of them get well and live. Not with

169

Dr. Friedman's patients. They all die. Admittedly he hasn't treated that many, just a little over a hundred in ten years. They're all dead except for Denise."

He shrugged his shoulders and dropped his eyes. "And her day is coming. We both know that."

"Why do they let him operate at all? Don't the Swiss have an FDA here?"

Conklin shook his head. "Nothing like that. They have a lot of cancer treatment facilities in Switzerland and the Swiss have very strict regulations, but St. Agatha's is different. The Swiss authorities let Dr. Friedkin operate his clinic as a research facility. Believe me he does his patients a lot of good. He takes only terminal cases and he makes them better for a while."

"Then they die."

"Yes, they all do and St. Agatha's isn't shy about telling you that."

He led me to a comfortable leather couch and pressed a DVD remote control.

"Here, this might help."

A large flat-screen TV came to life and Conklin returned to the computer. I sat on a leather couch and watched an hour long program about St. Agatha's. The program ended with a ghoulish collection of freeze frame pictures of smiling women who had died.

St. Atatha's wasn't shy about it at all.

I felt slightly less ignorant than before, only now I had a thousand questions.

Conklin returned and took a chair opposite me.

"Their orientation leaves you with a lot of questions, doesn't it?"

I nodded. "I thought that montage of dead people at the end was a little disturbing."

"Yes, but I think that's their way of not sugar coating it. Everyone who comes here dies. Dr. Friedkin works on terminal patients and his methods are extraordinary. Your wife will get better. It's amazing, but in the end she...."

"How is your wife?"

He nodded without smiling. "Amazing. When she came in, she was this close to death." He held up two fingers close together. "Dr. Friedkin brought her back. But I knew nothing when I came here. I didn't know what would happen. What to expect."

"How long had you been fighting it... her cancer?"

Again, he showed me his inscrutable look. "Years. A long time. Denise was a few days or a week from dying. A little over two weeks with Dr. Friedkin, she was able to get up. Now she can eat without throwing up. We went out to dinner last week. We go all over the place. But she has to come back here every day for more treatments."

The first question that came to me I blurted out without thinking about it.

"Why didn't you bring her here sooner?"

Conklin shrugged and I read the gesture as if I had asked the unknowable.

"Two weeks? I have to wait two weeks?"

"Just about. I don't know what condition Mrs. Macbean is in."

"Bettye. Not, Mrs. Macbean."

That look again. "Okay. My Denise was very far along. Her cancer had metastasized. A long time. I didn't know. I mean we didn't know. We got her here just in time."

"How do they do it? The video said something about VEG-F."

"It's an enzyme that produces blood vessels. Friedkin uses nucleic-synapse manipulation to alter the tumor cells. The cells produce proteins called semaphorin which specifically call for the creation of new blood vessels. The alteration prevents the tumors from producing blood vessels. The tumor's die."

"What keeps his treatment from blocking blood vessels in healthy tissue?"

Conklin shook his head. "I don't know. I think, from what I've read, there is a gene modifier that's slightly different in malignant tumors. He targets all the cells that carry that modifier. I don't know how he does it."

"The tumors die and the patient gets better?"

"Right. But after a short while the tumor starts producing a prototype semaphorin. Tumors make more blood vessels and regenerate. He's developed a process to target SP-2, as they call it. After more time a third prototype shows up."

"Sounds like a vicious cycle."

"It is. There are eight prototypes and he can't beat number eight."

"They get better and then they die."

Conklin pointed to the TV. "They want to make sure you understand. All his patients die."

"That's why the parking lot is empty."

"That's why it costs eight million dollars."

"Jesus." I said.

We both sat there for a moment.

"I can't see, uh, Bettye for two weeks?"

"About that. It depends." he said. There was no cagey look in his eye now. He may be hiding something about his relationship with Denise. Heck, me too. But he told me the straight skinny about the clinic, cancer and Bettye's chances of survival.

I exhaled like I had been holding my breath.

"Two weeks."

Chapter 27

From the journal of Brendan Macbean:
Fatigue and jetlag descended on me like a summer storm. Conklin suggested I go to where patients' guests were housed, the Haus Von Muller in Old Towne Schaffhausen. Fighting brain fog I found my way to the lobby and outside. The limo driver had waited patiently for my return. While he waited he had apparently smoked a dozen cigarettes. I stared at the pile of butts surrounding his feet. The driver shrugged. I headed toward the rear door which he hastened to open for me.

"To Von Muller Haus!" I uttered with as much panache as I could muster. The driver gave me another look, but he seemed to understand and we headed thither, I guess.

I saw nothing on the way except the inside of my eyelids. The wide comfortable leather seat in the rear of the limo proffered the Swiss antidote to jetlag. I slept most of the way and apparently some time after we arrived. The driver woke me with gentle assertion.

Afternoon shadows had darkened the cobblestone courtyard that formed the turnabout in front of Haus Von Muller.

"Sir, shall I bring in your luggage?"

I nodded and stretched. Getting out of the car became a major chore with my legs tingling but I managed.

Von Muller Haus looked like a Swiss stucco and wood mansion, old and magnificent. At that moment I lacked the capacity to appreciate the details.

Inside I was met by an elderly servant type dressed in what I guessed was Haus livery. He bowed deeply and spoke in a stentorian voice.

"Bienvenue à Von Muller Haus, Monsieur Le Boutilliere. Mon nom est Gert. Pendant que vous êtes ici s'il y a quelque chose que je peux vous donner, n'hésitez pas à demander."

At my hesitation, he switched to English.

"Welcome to Von Muller Haus, Monsieur Le Boutilliere. My name is Gert. While you are here if there is anything I can provide, do not hesitate to ask."

His French was French and his English, British. His slight bow was nothing but Teutonic.

"Thank you, Gert. I'm with Mademoiselle Le Boutilliere, a patient at the clinic, but my name is Brendan Macbean.

Gert showed considerable consternation over the name problem.

173

Apparently to upset the applecart in Switzerland all you needed was to expose a flaw in their preparation. We finally got it straight and he bowed again.

"Welcome to Von Muller Haus, Mister Macbean," he repeated. "Your room is upstairs, end of the hall on the right." He pointed upstairs. Obviously his duties did not extend to carrying my luggage or showing me the room so I schlepped my own bag and laptop case up the dark wooden stairs, down the dark wooden hallway, over a dark wooden floor which creaked at every step. The last door on the right was dark and wooden and I entered without knocking.

With the sun falling on the other side of the house my room was gloomy. Curtains were pulled across the two windows and a dim nightlight beamed from the cracked bathroom door. A four poster bed with the coverlet pulled back beckoned me and I longed to be absorbed in its downy depths. To my right a desk and chair lurked in a shadowy corner.

And in the chair sat a man staring at me.

My suitcase and laptop case fell to the floor. My heart froze as I turned slowly toward him. I had no idea who he was but found myself oddly familiar with his manner of dress. In television where image is everything, we dress in power clothes, dark tailored suits, complementing shirt and tie that display authority and confidence. This man dressed as a power broker and obviously American. He was athletically fit, his head covered in gray close-cropped hair, an easy smile on his face and his eyes reflecting an intelligent curiosity.

The only intelligent thought that came to my buzzed-out brain was, I should know this man. If the situation had allowed me a few more seconds, I might have figured it out, but when he spoke I knew at once who he was.

"Macbean, what am I going to do with you?"

I stood glued to the floor feeling weak and shaky. "Bentley. Who else but Bentley."

"Smart guy."

"I haven't been called smart in weeks. Smartass, yes."

Bentley chuckled. "God sure works in mysterious ways, doesn't He?"

"Is that the game you're playing?"

"Sure, Macbean. But I'm not good enough to play God. People like you mess things up. Here you are, unexpected and unwanted. When I spoke to Mademoiselle Le Boutilliere, I didn't know you and you didn't know me. Now I know you and what you are and I don't think I can have you here."

"You can't have me...? Why is that up to you?"

"The mission, Macbean. It's too important. There's a delicate balance here."

"Mission?" I shook my head. "You know the problem, Bentley? You Washington guys need to get out more. Talk with real people. I'm a real person and I don't talk like that. I don't know what you're talking about and I'm too tired to decipher your federal bullshit."

Bentley rose from his chair. He was half a head taller than me and although he was ten feet away, at once I felt a menace.

"This is no game, Macbean. There's a mission. You 'real' people don't have a clue what really goes on. Your lives center around eat, sleep, watch TV and get laid. You don't know anything about what it takes to run the world. If it weren't for people like me arbitrating your lives you'd be scratching your ass and killing each other with clubs."

I thought for a moment. "Look Bentley, I don't want to be on your damn wall. Not now.'"

Bentley smiled. "Doesn't matter what you want. I've got responsibilities. You already know too much and now you're the only person who can totally fuck things up. I never intended you to get involved here. You call it a game but lives are at stake. Your life, not that I give a rat's ass about that, but I like you. You have chutzpah and you're smart. And from what I'm able to tell, you are what we need in the media... a genuinely honest journalist. So I'm going to give you a little advice. Before you totally ruin what's going on here, I need you to go back to Atlanta and put your life back together. What's going on here is delicate, subtle. A house of cards. A line of dominoes. Wouldn't take much to knock it all down, but there's too much at stake to let that happen. Your showing up here totally messes up what I thought I had carefully put together."

"Bentley, what are you talking about?"

He pointed a finger at me. "I gave you Ray Suffield when nobody could get an interview with him. You wanted to get back into television didn't you? I gave you a pot of gold and you pissed in it. Even as we speak, your buddies back in America are ripping your brilliant work to shreds. What they're going to do to your interview will turn it into a typical piece of shitty TV journalism, totally meaningless and totally acceptable with all the real substance and relevance removed. And everybody in America will swallow it whole because they're used to bullshit, watching senseless crap and thinking it's great. And what do you get out of this? You won't get squat because you created a masterpiece and left it to the rag pickers to cut up. And your buddies will manage to completely erase you in the process."

It was hard to stand there and take it because everything he said was true. Neither Shelby nor Tony would stand by me or fight to include my name in the airing of the interview. Shelby was bent on a career. Passing the interview off as her work would be a springboard to what she wanted most in the world. And the network would sensationalize it to the max and plaster her pretty face all over the screen. Everybody wins but me.

"Macbean, are you listening?"

I nodded.

"You were a big hero the night before last, right? Didn't you subdue a carjacker at a convenience store? Didn't the local TV news show up and interview you. Didn't your precious Shelby film the whole thing on her cell phone?"

I nodded like a bobble-head.

"Would it surprise you to know the network killed the spot? Your heroics never made it to the local news."

"What? Bud wouldn't pull that spot even if was about me."

"Bud doesn't like you."

"He's just jealous."

"The big boss told him to pull it and he did. Why do you think they did that?"

I thought for a moment. "Because they can't have me getting even a shred of publicity in advance of airing the Suffield interview. They're going to put Shelby in take me out. She's already been on the network news with the steroid story. It'll be good for her, but I have to disappear. Totally."

Bentley waited a few seconds, maybe to let me think about what I had just said. When he spoke, his voice was gentler.

"And you did, didn't you? Macbean, you totally disappeared. You have a few days to go home and fight for your spot. Get your ass on the flight back to Atlanta. Get in their faces. Save your career. There's nothing for you here but a chance to wreck something really important. In America you can be a hero."

He smiled a wicked smile.

"I want *you* on *that* wall."

Chapter 28

From the Journal of Brendan Macbean:
I don't remember Bentley leaving. I don't remember crashing into that big fluffy bed, but it must have happened.

I awoke hours later in total darkness feeling a peculiar state of mind, somewhere between numb and erudite, with the residue of unfathomable dreams and disconnected memories. A silent blackout surrounded me and even the nightlight from the bathroom seemed to have gone out. I fumbled for my cell phone and lit it up.

Three AM, local time. Great. I was out of sync with the rest of Schaffhausen if not the rest of the world. I wanted coffee but waking up Gert seemed a bad idea. I and took a leak and settled for some bathroom water from lead crystal drinking glass.

Now what?

I fired up my laptop. The Von Muller's wireless internet connection information was spelled out in seven languages on a placard on the desk. The Swiss think of everything.

I immediately went to my TV station's website and confirmed what Bentley had told me. The Ray Suffield interview was plastered over the home page as if they were hyping the second coming. The network had pulled out all the stops. They cancelled popular sitcoms and gave it their choicest piece of primetime. Shelby's pics, bio and credentials were linked, including a totally fabricated story about how she finagled her way into federal prison and sweet-talked warden Mike Ferguson into granting the interview. I half expected a roving video of her confronting a guard.

I searched the entire website for "Macbean" and came up with zilch. Big surprise there. I searched the website for the attempted carjacking incident, which should have headlined their local crime-watch page. More zilch. There was no mention of what happened at the Race Trac gas station.

I unclenched my jaw and spent the next ten minutes getting over the shakes.

Bentley's words resonated in my head. What else could I do?

Yesterday I had willingly made the decision to abandon the best piece of television journalism I had ever done. I had chosen to go with Bettye, the love of my life when I could have told her emphatically 'no.' Notwithstanding Bentley's near-direct order to return to Atlanta, I was barely in a position to do anything else but what I had come here to do. I was going to stay and spend the next few weeks with Bettye and had better own up to the fact that I had flushed the rest of my life down the toilette.

The east coast of the United States was now past ten AM so I thought I'd call Shelby. Her ring bounced immediately into voicemail. I shrugged. She's a big celeb, so I left her a message.

"Shelby. This is Brendan. I just checked the network website. Good job, girl. You deserve it. As crazy as my life has been the last few days, it's even crazier now. I'll explain if I ever see you again. Bust their chops, babe. Go to the top where you belong with my blessing. Love you."

When I closed the phone there were tears streaming down my cheeks. I felt like I had just killed my own dog, but there wasn't time to cry about it. It was time to kick some ass.

Bud did answer his phone.

"Jesus, Macbean. You really stuck your dick in it this time."

Did he mean something by that? My mind filled with a host of replies, none very appropriate.

"Bud, why did you pull the carjacking spot?"

"Where are you?"

"Schaffhausen."

"Where the fuck is that?"

"Switzerland."

"You mean like in Germany?"

"Yeah, Bud. Like in Germany, you dumb-assed ignorant asshole."

"No use trying to sweet talk me. You call to save your job or something?" He was never good at sarcasm.

"Speaking of jobs, what kind of job did you do on the Suffield interview? Is that the job you're talking about?"

"Look, after you pull a two day disappearing act, what do you expect?"

"It's only been forty-five hours, not that it matters. I did expect somebody to stick up for me, maybe keep my name in there. But not you. That's never been your strong suit."

"Nobody around here's got enough 'strong suit' to save your ass, you idiot. You were given back your job and you pissed it away." His nasally voice rose in timbre. "And besides, Shelby said it was your idea."

I had the shakes again but I deserved a little anger.

"We talked about a lot of things. She thought it would better if we shared it. I never thought you'd totally scrape me off the Suffield interview without asking me. And be in such a hurry to air it. And why did you pull the carjacking spot? What's going on, Bud? Did the network bosses make you their prison bitch again?"

"Look, Beanbrain. I don't even have to talk to you but you've been around long enough to know they can do whatever they want. Even if I liked you, I couldn't stop them from throwing you under the bus. And I never liked your sorry, balding, glass-eyed ass. If it was up to me you would have never seen the inside of this station again."

"And you never would have gotten the Suffield interview."

He was silent for a second.

"Hasta la vista, Macbean. Don't call here no more and have fun in Germany."

"Wait a minute, Bud. Do you know Matt Drudge?"

"What about Drudge?"

"He's a friend of mine. We share stuff all the time."

"So what?"

"So here's the story: I do the impossible, get an interview with Ray Suffield. Then I nail the interview. But the network isn't happy with the choice of interviewer so they decide to fake the interview, putting Shelby in and cutting me out. That's a pretty crummy, phony thing to do. But it's exactly what we expect those monster power brokers to do. A story like this could destroy what little credibility and integrity this network has. What if I give Drudge the story? He's got some enmity with this particular network. He's always eager to prove them a bunch of hacks."

"He's got some what?"

"Enmity, Bud. I know it's a big word. Means hostility."

"You smart-assed jerk. Even Drudge won't do anything if he can't prove it."

"I give Drudge Mike Ferguson, the warden at Oakdale Federal Prison. Mike's a real straight shooter and I believe we connected when I was there. He knows who came and did the interview. He knows it wasn't Shelby. Drudge gets the expose he's been looking for. Heads roll and one of them is yours."

The seconds ticked faster than Bud's thought process.

"You won't do that. It would ruin Shelby's career."

"Shelby's on your side now, so I'm calling Drudge after I hang up on you."

I hung up on Bud.

Chapter 29

From the Journal of Brendan Macbean:
I didn't call Drudge. I just wanted to rattle Bud's cage.

I reviewed my conversation with Bentley and tried to figure out what was going on. He had surprised me in my room, catching me at my weakest. Just like when he had called me at three-thirty in the morning. Bentley chose to attack when his victims can't fight back.

I was here because of Bettye. Bentleuy had recruited Bettye as a patient for St. Agatha's. But he was a Department of Justice official who had some responsibility for federal prisoners. Warden Mike Ferguson knew Bentley as some kind of higher-up in the Justice Department. That's how he got me the interview with Suffield. What connection did he have with St. Agatha's? Was his selection of Bettye as a patient coincidental or did he uncover her because he investigated me? I concluded that he could not have selected Bettye because of me. I had only first spoken to him two days ago and he had approached Bettye long before he knew anything about me.

St. Agatha's patients had to be selected from a short list. They had to be terminally ill and have lots of money. I knew nothing about St. Agatha's recruiting program. I made a mental note to ask Conklin about it. He'd been around longer and may have more answers.

But something nagged at me. Bentley showing up here at Schaffhausen had nothing to do with me or Bettye. He said I'd mess something up if I stayed here. My instincts would not quiet down.

Dawn was not far away so I opened my door on the chance I would catch the scent of brewing coffee wafting up the staircase. I didn't have to wait long.

I made my way to the bottom of the steps and found a dining room large enough for a formal dinner. It was quiet and nearly empty. Daniel Conklin sat at the end of the long dark wooden table sipping coffee and reading a newspaper. He looked up and stared at me. It seemed that since I had arrived in Switzerland, I was getting stared at a lot. An enormous gilt-framed mirror stood next to a large, dark wooden buffet. A glance at in the mirror told me why I attracted scrutiny in this particular instance.

My normal but not overtly meticulous appearance had been severely compromised by an array of fashion and tonsorial disasters. My mother had taught me to at least run a comb through my hair before going out in public. Mother would be rolling over in her grave, but last night I had fallen into bed without so much as removing my clothes or brushing my teeth. According to the mirror, some trickster invaded my room while I slept, unfastening random buttons on my hopelessly wrinkled and un-tucked shirt, unzipped my trousers and had done my hair in a Bride of Frankenstein style.

I stood before the mirror and took in the spectacle. Even jet lag could not dull my appreciation for how ridiculous I looked. I turned toward Daniel Conklin and said, "Trick or treat!"

We shared a chuckle.

I straightened myself up as well as I could without my shaving kit. The coffee was served in an enormous silver vessel with an alcohol flame gently waving under it. I drew a cup and sat across a corner of the table from Daniel Conklin.

"Rough night?" he asked.

"The roughest, according to my appearance. I smelled the coffee. I guess I didn't expect to run into anybody this early."

I took a sip and it was the best coffee I've ever tasted. Conklin noted my appreciation and nodded.

"They serve a good brew here."

At that moment, Gert entered. He was impeccably dressed in his butler's livery. He took one look at my appearance and said, "Good morning, Mr. Macbean. May I offer you the Haus valet service?" He managed to ask this question with perfect British intonation except for the word, 'Haus.'

I blinked at him. "You have a valet, here?"

From his sudden change of expression, I guessed my response put Gert into an instant quandary.

Conklin tried to help. "Brendan, the Haus Von Muller provides a service, like dry cleaning in the States."

"Oh, okay. I'll leave these on the bed." I padded my wrinkled clothes.

Now Conklin looked disquieted. "No, that's not how it works. You have to hang your clothes on a hanger and place them in an armoire near the back door. They will be cleaned and pressed and you can pick them up the same evening.

"Oh, okay. Thanks, Gert. I will use this service, of course."

Gert looked only moderately comforted. I had the feeling I was digging myself into a hole but could not figure out why. I was a guest here, wasn't I?

Gert wasn't going to cut me any slack. "Very good, sir. And I hope soon." He raised his eyebrows and sniffed as if I smelled bad in addition to looking disheveled.

"Look, Gert. I apologize for my appearance. I smelled coffee and came down for a cup. I didn't expect to run into anyone."

Gert frowned. "Sir, you only had to ask."

"Ask? For what?"

"Coffee, of course. Or valet service." Gert looked anything but accommodating.

"Well, great, Gert. It seems like I haven't read the rule book for Hoss Van Halen, but I'll go get one from the etiquette section of the local rare book store. Once I acquaint myself to your convoluted set of rules, I'll try to behave with more decorum."

Gert straightened up and stared down his nose at me. "There are many hotels nearby who will accommodate you as you are, *Herr.*"

For a moment I thought he had called me a name then I realized we were in a foreign country and in one of Switzerland's German Cantons. Where I sat I could have head-butted him in his crotch but that would have dislodged my recently patted-down jangly hair. I guess neither of us was having a good morning.

I stood and faced him. Fortunately the butler wasn't much taller than me. I tried to keep my voice calm but felt increasing agitation. "Gert, maybe I should go to one of those hotels. Perhaps my room won't be broken into by strangers in the middle of the night. Maybe those rowdier hotels has better security."

Gert's eyes looked about to pop out. "Preposterous! Such a thing has never happened. Not here. We have no intruders in Von Muller Haus!"

"Well, right after you greeted me last night I went to my room. There was a man in there. I had no warning. Why didn't you tell me I had a visitor?"

Gert looked doubtful. "I know of no visitors. No one came here. We have only you and Mr. Conklin."

I considered this and felt myself cooling down. Bentley would come and go as he pleased. Anywhere he wanted to go. That was his game, to sneak in and out like a spy. Surprise gave him the advantage. He would never try to explain himself to someone like Gert.

"Gert, I do not know your full name. I profoundly apologize for anything inappropriate. I meant no disrespect for you or your beautiful house. I am especially sorry if anything I've said or done disrupts the order of your establishment. From this moment, I hope our relationship can improve and we can be at least on friendly terms."

Gert bowed slightly, a movement confined to his head. "Sir, my name is Gerbert Goetze, but I am called Gert. If you have had an intruder, we shall investigate."

"There is no need. It turned out he was someone I knew. His visit was brief but unexpected. If you had known he was here, I'm sure you would have told me. There will be no further incidents, I am certain."

"If you are certain, Mr. Macbean." His expression implied if I had an intruder it was my fault.

"Thank you, Gert. I'll refill my coffee and return to my room after a word with Mr. Conklin.

Gert nodded to me and then to Conklin and strode out of the room with exaggerated dignity.

Conklin smiled when I turned to him. "Brendan, Gert is not a servant here. He owns Haus Von Muller. It's been in his family for nearly a hundred years. He's a chum of Dr. Friedkin's. St. Agatha's is built on an estate co-owned between the Goetze and Schumann families, but the whole relationship is complicated."

"Well, that explains his people skills. Whatever happened to the customer is always right?"

Conklin smiled and then looked concerned. "You had an intruder?"

"Yeah. It was kind of spooky. Some guy I've never met, only talked to on the phone. Once. He helped me get an interview a few days ago. Then he shows up in my room last night. Maybe the last person I expected to be here."

"What?" Conklin look thoroughly confused. Well, anyone would be. I thought for a second. Would it even be possible to explain what had happened to me in the last few days? I decided to take a gamble.

"Daniel, less than a week ago, I didn't have a job. I used to be a television journalist but I got laid off several years ago. You read my book about TV Swanson. Since then I did some freelance work but it was pretty much hit or miss.

"Then, out of the blue I was offered my job back, specifically to try to get an interview with one of the worst criminals in the last few years, a guy who nobody in the news business could get near."

Conklin sat up and his head twitched, almost like a double take.

"Worst criminal. Who are we talking about?"

"Ray Suffield, CEO of InCorps." At the mention of the name, Daniel Conklin did a triple take, if that's even possible. As he reached for his coffee cup, I saw his hands shake. What was this? Was he one of the millions who invested in the company and got cheated out of his money? But I didn't think it was money that caused his hands to shake. He had the eight million for St. Agatha's, didn't he?

"What...what happened?" His voice shook a little. Puzzle pieces floated around in my head but formed no picture.

"I tried to get permission to interview Suffield. He's at a federal prison in Louisiana. I got stonewalled like the rest of them. I called a friend of mine in the FBI and asked a favor. She started going up the line. The next thing I get a phone call from a big shot in the Department of Justice. A guy named Bentley."

Daniel Conklin froze like a wax statue of himself. If I had stuck him with a cattle prod he could not have looked more pole-axed.

"And to my surprise, Bentley smoothed the way." I told Conklin the rest of the story omitting the filling station mugging, my one night stand with Shelby and the network stealing the interview. I also left out the two year hiatus in my relationship with Bettye.

"And then Bettye tells me that a man came to see her. She said he was an American official. He offered her the chance to come to St. Agatha's."

I ended my narrative but Daniel Conklin said nothing. His eyes took on a faraway look.

Sunlight streamed in through the dining room windows. A bright shaft of light struck the side of his face. I could see a tiny white line across and slightly above his cheekbone heading in the direction of the corner of his eye. It was a scar from very skillful plastic surgery. Over the years I had interviewed many Hollywood types, actors and actresses and had seen similar lines where they had had surgery to keep their appearance youthful. So what? Conklin had had plastic surgery. So had thousands of others.

"Then last night, this Bentley guy shows up in my room. Scared the living crap out of me. I never met him in person so at first I don't know who he is. Then I figured it out. A weird coincidence that a guy named Bentley helps me get the interview and it's this same Bentley who talks Bettye into coming here. So he tells me to go home. He tells me I'll mess something up. Something too delicate and too important. 'Go home,' he said."

Conklin remained silent. He had composed himself and now he looked like a man who could keep secrets. Much better than me. And better than Bentley, apparently. Bentley should have thrown a bag over my head and shipped me back in the cargo bin of an Air Force C-130. But Bentley may have over done it. Enjoyed the moment just a little too much. Just like with Gert, Bentley's pompous attitude got my dander up.

"This guy Bentley. He's shown up three places in my life where he isn't expected. First he's a DOJ officer. Then he's shilling for St. Agatha's. Last night he's a spy."

Conklin meets my eyes but says nothing.

"Daniel?"

"Yes?" His voice even, controlled.

"You asked me a question. Let me ask you one."

"Yes?" he repeated.

"What? As in what's going on?"

Conklin didn't respond. He sat there sipping his coffee. Between sips he gave me a calm smile. He took another sip and drained his cup.

"Brendan, can I show you something?"

"Sure. What?"

"First go up to your room. Take a shower. Change clothes. Come back here. We'll take a drive."

My first instinct was to say no. I felt the need to drive this interview until I had my answers. My better nature prevailed. I didn't even have the questions yet, so I decided to put Conklin in control. A second glance at the mirror made his advice seem all the more reasonable.

I ran back up the stairs, did a quick cleanup, shave, shower, new clothes, and at the end of it, I not only looked better, I felt at home, even in Swiss time.

Conklin had a snazzy black Mercedes Benz C-class waiting outside.

"Wow. Nice wheels," I said.

"Not mine. The clinic lets us use it."

"How better to spend eight million dollars?"

I climbed into the passenger seat. Conklin started the engine and pulled out an iPhone. He dialed a number. A few seconds passed and he said into it, "Entschuldigung. Falsche Nummer."

He put the phone back into his pocket and took out another iPhone. He set this iPhone screen side up on the Mercedes console and without explaining this behavior, drove out of the Von Muller Haus courtyard.

I now had a chance to see some of the city of Schaffhausen. Narrow streets and sixteenth century architecture characterized Old Towne, but the ancient city quickly gave way to modern buildings with bustling street traffic and occasional glimpses of the Rhine River.

My whirling thoughts could not focus much on sightseeing. Conklin seemed to anticipate I was about to ask him a bunch of questions and he put a finger to his lips in a "hush" sort of way. His finger circled the air between us like I was supposed to notice something in the interior of the car. He tapped his watch like we needed to wait. So I held my peace.

He parked the car in a short, awkward parking lot with white painted car slots at odd angles, quite a contrast to how parking lots were laid out in America. Looking around, I noticed the centuries old buildings had been laid out at odd angles as well. The neighborhood looked more suited to pedestrians than cars.

Conklin shut off the engine and hastily exited the car. As I followed him I noticed his head swiveling like a man looking for something.

He ducked into a coffee shop. The place was crowded with people coming and going every second. A queue held about thirty men and women shouting orders in a chorus of languages, grabbing espressos, sipping and departing. The café held about four small tables mostly ignored by the bustling clientele. We took a table by the front window and were shielded from the sun by large gilded lettering on the glass. If I could read backward from the inside, it would have said, "König Bohnenkaffee." We sat conspicuous with nothing in our hands while the crowd swirled around us.

Conklin leaned in over the table, motioning me to do the same. I gave him my good ear.

He shouted, "The car's bugged. That's why I didn't want to talk. Same with Haus Von Muller."

I gave him a look and cupped my hand around my mouth. "Bugged, like in spies and surveillance?"

He nodded. He ducked his head toward the window and peered between the gilded letters. Apparently he didn't find what he was looking for because he resumed staring at me.

"Who bugged the car and the house?"

Conklin mouthed the word, "Bentley."

It was good that there was such a commotion in the café because I needed to think about what he just told me. If we were in a quieter place our conversation might have provided the commotion.

So Bentley bugged the house and the car. And Bentley had something going on here. Bentley was concerned I would mess it up. Conklin was aware of the surveillance and knew something about Bentley. Conklin must know about Bentley's business. Conclusion: Bentley was the bugger and Conklin the buggee.

Conklin stared through the glass again. This time he found what he was looking for. He motioned to me to look out the window.

He shouted through the crowd noise. "Across the street. Behind a bench under a red and white striped awning. Man at a table. Tall, red hair, blue polo shirt, jeans."

I saw the man. He was reading a newspaper. He glanced up frequently but I could not tell in which direction because he wore sunglasses.

I mouthed the word, "Who?"

Conklin leaned in and said, "Nicolay Karolovsky."

"Russian?"

Conklin shrugged. "He's not working for the Russians. He works for a Russian named Vladoseev, a New York, uh. I don't know what he is. Underworld, mobster, gangster."

I had to ponder that for a minute. Conklin was being followed by the mob, and the feds were snooping on him. Conklin was the center of a lot of attention. If my presence here was messing up Bentley's operation, Conklin was the operation.

Conklin waved for me to look again at Karolovsky.

"He sees something he doesn't like. Look."

Karolovsky wasn't looking in our direction. He directed his gaze up the street.

"Two guys looking in a store window, the music store."

A block up the street, somewhat obscured by a phalanx of pedestrians. The two men were engaged in an animated discussion and pointing at something in the store window. The two men looked like musicians, bulky, wrinkled clothes, long hair and John Lennon glasses on one of them. Even to my untrained eye, they looked a little too much like musicians.

I looked back at Karolovsky and he was still staring at them over the edge of his newspaper. I looked back at Conklin, who was looking at me.

"Feds," he mouthed.

Conklin stood up and gave me a "Come on" gesture. I followed him out the back door of the König Bohnenkaffee. We emerged in an alley and sprinted for the Mercedes. He quickly sped out of the parking lot and we headed back to Old Towne. Instead of returning to Haus Von Muller, we went to a park on the Rhine River where the Canton had built a viewing area to allow tourists to get a good look at Rhinefalls, a spectacular waterfall, a huge cataract split by a giant rock sticking out of the surging water. The noise here was louder than the coffee shop but steady enough for us to converse. We took seats on a bench.

Conklin spoke first. "The feds can't spy on us here. Oh, sure they can look at us but they can hear a word." He pointed at the falls.

"Brendan, I know you're confused about what's going on. I also know you're a reporter and probably have more than a mild curiosity for things like this. You're about to pummel me with questions but I'll warn you. I can't answer all of them."

"Okay," I said. I did have a zillion questions but at that moment, I hardly knew where to start. But after a full minute of thinking about it, start I did.

"Karolovsky is trailing you."

"Yes."

"Why?"

"I won't tell you why. It's the part I can't talk about."

"The feds are trailing Karolovsky?"

"No, but I'm certain they're here under Bentley's command. I think they're here to keep Karolovsky from grabbing me."

I thought about that for a while. "The feds want to keep Karolovsky away from you?"

He nodded.

"What will Karolovsky do to you?"

A shrug.

"He works for a Russian gangster?"

"Vladoseev."

"You have something Vladoseev wants."

"Can't talk about that."

"Look, Daniel, I'm going to figure it all out anyway. I won't stop until I do."

Conklin nodded. "I guessed as much. So did Bentley."

"Because Bentley's protecting you?"

Conklin said nothing.

"What does Bentley do for the Department of Justice?"

Conklin stared at Rhinefalls for a long time. "Bentley is very high level and reports to the Deputy Attorney General. He's in charge of DOJ operations."

"What does that mean, operations?'

Conklin shrugged, which meant he wasn't going to answer.

"What does Bentley do for St. Agatha's?"

Conklin smiled. "Bentley raises money for them. I know it sounds weird but he goes out and finds patients for them, terminal breast cancer victims who have a lot of money. You know what St. Agatha's offers. It's not exactly a mainstream service. They don't advertise but they need patients and money. Bentley recruits patients for St. Agatha's."

"Is that an official mission of the US Department of Justice?"

"No. Completely off the reservation."

"And he uses DOJ resources?"

"Absolutely. American taxpayers pay for everything Bentley does but he won't funnel DOJ money directly into St. Agatha's. Bentley is too ethical for that."

"Ethical? What he's doing over here is legal?"

Conklin shrugged. "Bentley will fly all over the world to talk to a potential client for St. Agatha's but he won't pilfer government money to fund their research. I know it sounds crazy, but Bentley's a boy scout and walks a line."

"But not when it comes to breaking into my room or threatening me."

"Bentley is a piece of work, all right. He wields the power of the US government without much oversight. He can move mountains for you or he can drop them on you."

"I've experienced that. He granted me the interview with Suffield and nobody had been able to get close to the guy for four years."

Conklin looked away at the river. As far as sightseeing goes, it was about as enticing a view as any I've seen.

"Why does he help St. Agatha's?"

"His wife was a patient here a few years ago."

And all St. Agatha's patients are dead. Except for Conklin's Denise and my Bettye.

"So, Bentley got you to bring Denise here?"

Conklin nodded.

"You and Denise paid St. Agatha's price?"

He nodded again.

"Eight million dollars on a pharmacist's salary? Are you kidding me? Did you know Bentley before Denise got breast cancer?

Conklin stared at the falls. That told me as much as if he had said "Yes."

"And Bentley is protecting you from Vladoseev's henchman?"

"I'm not sure. I only suspect that's why they're here."

"What's your connection with Bentley? Bentley recruited you for St. Agatha's and protects you from Vladoseev."

Conklin said nothing so I speculated out loud.

"You and Bentley have a history, maybe related to his job. And he gets you and Denise to come here and somehow you come up with the money since Bentley's scruples won't allow him to open up the US Treasury. That's a lot of money for a drugstore man. Bentley has bugged Haus von Muller and your car. He has agents standing between you and a gangster. I think whatever Vladoseev wants from you, it's the same thing Bentley wants from you.

"And, Daniel, my new best friend, what else could it be besides money? A lot of money."

Chapter 30

From the journal of Brendan Macbean:
We drove to the Von Muller Haus to retrieve my laptop before heading for St. Agatha's. Conklin disappeared almost as soon as we arrived at the clinic. He told me his usual routine was to meet up with Denise after her morning treatments.

On my own I wandered the halls of St. Agatha's. I found there were not many places I could wander. Nearly every door off the main hall was marked Nur Zugelassen, which I interpreted, "you can't go in there." I did run across Dr. Bauerle's office and stuck my head in. She was not there. Her office was just a plain, windowless room made fancy by the large number of diplomas. I would have loved to explore her walls of fame but felt like an intruder. So I left her a note to look me up and headed for the visitor's lounge.

In the visitor's lounge I found a kitchen through a door marked, Wohnzimmer. Ah, a kitchen! I hadn't eaten in a long time so I explored the Wohnzimmer, which later I found out translated, 'lounge.' Hmm, I thought the lounge was where the leather couch was. But the Swiss call that a "Besucher im Wartezimmer."

The kitchen seemed well stocked for heavy snacking. I made myself a giant sandwich, grabbed a Diet Coke and parked my elbows on the table. I hadn't realized how hungry I was. The sandwich before my eyes wafted rich scents of dark rye bread, mayonnaise, grainy brown mustard, Black Forest ham and, what else? Swiss cheese. I stuffed my mouth with a cheek-stretching wad of food. Fate chose that moment for Dr. Bauerle to walk in, and she caught me in the act of mastication.

My mouth froze.

She smiled. "Please continue, Mr. Macbean. Before you choke."

I chewed through that massive first bite feeling mayo and mustard stream across my cheeks. I looked around for a napkin. No luck. Bauerle walked over to the counter, returned and handed me a paper towel. Demurely she sat down across the table from me.

My mouth finally empty I didn't feel I could say a word until I took a gulp of Coke. Gulp being the operative word. The soda foamed in my mouth, reached for my nostrils and a belch formed in my stomach. Bauerle saved me ultimate embarrassment by carrying the conversation.

"Mr. Macbean, I suppose you'd like an update on Mlle. Le Boutilliere."

I nodded.

"Well, we have just begun the treatments, but she came in better condition than some of our patients. She is responding extremely well."

"Dr. Bauerle, please call me Brendan. This is good news. When can I see her?"

"Two weeks perhaps, Brendan" The way she pronounced my name was not at all French, like Bettye's version. Bauerle's voice was deep and German. It sounded like, 'Breen-down.'

"Two weeks?"

"This is a delicate phase. It may be as much as a month before we allow our patient to see their loved ones but Bettye is showing great promise. We will see."

"A month…" Urgently I had an ache to see Bettye as she used to be, in the old days when we were lovers. I wanted to hold her warm and soft body, feel her yielding in my arms, the heat from her face radiating into mine when we kissed.

My need for her felt immediate and I had to wait two weeks?

What kind of relationship did we have? Could we still call it love after a two year hiatus where I had completely given up on her? Now, considering she was near death, physically changed and fighting for her life, she still had enough gas in her tank to show up unannounced and plead for me to be with her. I felt a sense of responsibility, of course, to stand by Bettye in sickness and in health, but I wasn't sure from where such an obligation had sprung. We had never exchanged vows, made commitments or even promises. I even sensed that her cultural notion of love might be foreign to mine, perhaps even to the point of dispensing with vows or commitment. By necessity our long distance love had been completely based on assumptions. I keenly felt her need for my support, but was this what I wanted? I wanted healthy, normal love, with commitment and vows and continuity. But, God help me, making those demands now would kill her and I was powerless to ask for anything.

Surprisingly, I discovered that it was possible to muse while masticating, and to think about love while under the keen observation of a beautiful woman. My sandwich had disappeared and my plate seemed empty even of crumbs.

"Two weeks," I said.

Bauerle may have noted the emotional commotion distorting my face. Her expression changed from detachment to compassion.

"Brendan, our patients start to feel much better as our treatments take hold. Cancer has made them feel terrible. Lots of pain and discomfort every moment of their lives. Body functions like urination, bowel movements, even normal breathing are affected by the disease and even more by traditional therapies like radiation and chemo. And because we are not bombarding them with radiation or chemicals, they do feel good again. Do you know what the first thing they want to do is?"

"See their loved ones?" I offered.

She shook her head. Brunette locks waved and rustled against the crisp white collar of her blouse. "No Brendan. They want to sleep. They want to rest and recuperate. We let them rest and then we start them on physical therapy. To rebuild their strength. Then they want to see their loved ones. More than anything Bettye wants to get to the stage when she will want to see you and welcome you to her arms. It will be when she has enough strength to give you a big hug."

Bauerle gave me a beaming smile. It was a sales job, I know, but Dr. Bauerle had depthless eyes and a wide mouth. She looked beautiful beyond belief. She noted the tears in my eyes and somehow conjured a tissue. I could only nod my head. What else could I do? At that moment, what I wanted most in the world was beyond my power to bring it closer. Worse, considering the conflict that had just passed through my brain, I probably could not identify what that one thing was.

"Thank you, Dr. Bauerle. I completely trust your judgment."

Bauerle stood and gave me a matronly pat on my shoulder. She turned and left leaving behind a tantalizing hint of fragrance. God, what was wrong with me?

I returned to the leather couch library/lounge/visitor's waiting room. The room was empty so I turned on the television. I've always been good at figuring out remote controls. The large LG HDTV was set to receive DVD input but I soon had it switched to cable box input. After that my audio-visual skills failed and I was unable to decipher the bewildering cable menu. I wanted to find the channel that would allow me to view my network's broadcast of the Ray Suffield interview. As my frustration reached crisis level, Daniel Conklin walked in.

"Brendan, you look a little frustrated."

"I am. I can't find a channel that will allow me to watch an American TV broadcast."

"Hmmm. There might not be one. What's up?"

"My interview with Ray Suffield. It will be broadcast the day after tomorrow at three AM local time. I want to watch it. I don't recall there's a TV where we're staying. Do you think St. Agatha's will let me watch it here?"

Conklin thought for a moment. "Brendan, I have a key to the place. I'll clear it with Bauerle. But first we have to figure out a way to get the broadcast. Let me check the internet."

He went over to the desktop system where he sat when I first met him. In a moment he had Google up. His fingers clattered over the keyboard. His head nodded.

"It looks like the broadcast is available from a streaming channel. We have to create an account."

"Do you need my credit card?" I offered.

Conklin smiled. "No need. St. Agatha's will foot the bill this time." He smiled at me. "I have some privileges around here. And like what you said earlier, what better way to spend eight million?"

"Wow! Daniel. You're a genius. Will I have to watch it on the computer screen?"

Conklin smiled again. "Not at all. HDMI connection from the computer to the set. Hand me the remote, please and I'll see if it works."

Never argue with a master. Conklin clicked the remote. The image on the computer monitor was displayed on the set.

"Oh, okay. Great. Thanks, Daniel." I had a flash of inspiration. "Why don't you join me?"

He smiled again. This time I saw a gleam in his eye.

"I wouldn't miss it for the world."

Chapter 31

From the journal of Brendan Macbean:
I had been there less than twenty-four hours and already had a date. Conklin invited me to have dinner with him and Denise. We would meet her in the lobby of St. Agatha's at six PM. Conklin drove us back to Haus Von Muller where I re-shaved, showered and dressed in clothes even Gert would have approved of. Years ago, Bettye had gently chided me on my attire. From the many trips to Paris, she had guided me to an appreciation for fashion and propriety. Unfortunately, such appreciation did not make me a clothes horse. When left to my own devices, I reverted to casual dress, but since we were to have dinner with the recovering Denise, I wanted to dress in the best I had brought with me.

I stood in the entrance foyer of Haus Von Muller looking splendid, at least in my own mind, waiting for Conklin to descend the stairs. Gert emerged from a door down the hall. He saw me and stared for a full thirty seconds. Without changing expression, Gert nodded and exited through another door. Well, now I felt even better.

Conklin came down the stairs and immediately I knew I had overdressed. He wore a nice shirt and casual slacks, appropriate for lunch at the club, maybe. But he had been here longer than I and maybe knew something about propriety in Schaffhausen.

"Macbean, you look splendid," he said cheerfully.

"Looks like I over dressed."

He smirked, "Tonight there will be no weddings. Or funerals."

"Wicked and totally inappropriate. Daniel, I'm beginning to like you."

"Shall we go?"

He started the Mercedes. Once again he pulled out a cell phone made a call and apologized in German for a 'wrong number.' Then he pulled out the other iPhone and consulted the screen.

"Does your horoscope give us a favorable aspect?" I asked.

Conklin looked thoughtful for a moment. He reached toward the radio and turned on station playing what sounded like Polka music. The car filled with lively accordions and thumping tubas. He cranked up the volume. Before he spoke, he leaned his head toward me and gestured for me to do the same.

Conklin smiled through the loud music. "Do you know about GPS tracking devices?"

I needed to shout. "Yes. We use them at my TV station. We have vans.

We can see where they are."

He nodded. "Just like that. The feds have one on our car. They know when I'm going someplace. They watch a screen so they can follow me. I have an iPhone app that allows me to select certain GPS tracking devices in the area."

"Okay. How does that help?"

"These guys are my protection. I want to make sure they're in place. Look." He showed me the screen on his phone. "That black dot is the Mercedes. Fed car number one is moving. See that blinking green light?"

His phone screen showed a familiar GPS display. A blinking green light moved.

"They work in a team. One of them will follow us to St. Agatha's. We don't leave until they're in place. See, they're stopping a couple of blocks away."

The blinking light had progressed through the maze of Schaffhausen's streets on the GPS screen and stopped.

"Do they know you're tracking them?"

"They might figure it out, but so what? No big secret here. We're helping them aren't we?"

"I guess. I've never been under surveillance."

"Don't get used to it."

The Polka music blared on.

"Okay, what's the deal with the other phone? Wrong number, or should I say 'Flasche Nummer?'"

Conklin gave me a wicked smile. "For backup they track my old cell phone. This one..." He held up the iPhone. "They don't know I have another. If I stopped using the old phone, they might get curious. Don't want that."

He silenced the radio. My ears deflated a little.

The sun cast lengthening shadows as Conklin eased the Mercedes out of the turn-about and into light commuter traffic. We drove to St. Agatha's. By now I was getting used to the route and more familiar with Schaffhausen. We left the car in the porte-cochere and entered the clinic.

From down the hall I heard the sound of giggling women coming from Dr. Bauerle's office. Daniel and I poked our heads in. Seated in front of Dr. Bauerle's desk was what looked like a pale, thin twelve year old dressed in a Roaring Twenties costume. Dr. Bauerle and the girl were rocking in their seats, laughing over some unknown joke. Bauerle looked gorgeous when she laughed. Okay, I'll admit it, I had a crush.

Daniel went forward, bent and hugged the twelve year old who turned out to be Denise. She turned to look at me and I hoped I didn't look as shocked as I felt. Denise looked like somebody's grandmother in a child's body, decades older than Conklin, and her Roaring Twenties outfit was really an evening shift that hung on undernourished, child-like shoulders. The slack skin of her face glowed with color and wrinkled with mirth over the joke she shared with Bauerle. Bauerle looked up at me and her smile widened.

"Ah, Brendan Macbean, the famous TV reporter." Denise stood and held out a skeletal hand covered in parchment like skin. I shook her hand as if were made of crystal. She responded with a strong grip.

"Ma'am, my fifteen minutes of fame occurred years ago," I said trying to hide my reaction to her appearance. I don't know what I expected but certainly didn't expect a spry septuagenarian.

"Relax Brendan, I feel a thousand times better than I look." Her wide smile briefly erased those extra decades.

"And you must be Denise Conklin." I said.

Her smile turned wry. "I guess that will do for now." Her remark reminded me we all hid a few secrets.

Conklin chimed in. "What were you girls laughing about when we came in?"

Bauerle said, "That will have to remain between us girls for now, Mr. Conklin."

Denise headed for the door. "Come on, guys. I'm starved. As you can see, Brendan, I need to put on a few pounds." She laughed heartily.

Conklin followed her. I turned back to Bauerle. "Are you joining us, Dr. Bauerle?"

She smiled. "Not tonight, Brendan. Perhaps another time."

I nodded and chased after the Conklins.

We drove to a restaurant called Sommerlust, which despite its erotic sounding name meant Summer Fun. We all like fun, don't we? Summer Fun was a grand country house on the Rhine surrounded by colorful gardens. No, they weren't playing Beach Boys music inside. The ambience was more Mozart-like and just what you'd expect for the European countryside.

A maître de met us at the foyer and seated us in an outdoor veranda with a stunning view of the Rhine. I glanced at Denise and saw childlike delight on her face. The exuberance she displayed for life forced me to reevaluate of my first impression of this lovely woman.

"Oh my god, you guys! This is so beautiful." Denise clapped her hands together. She and Conklin exchanged the look true lovers exchange. They were sharing a moment and I suddenly felt like an intruder. Their time had limits and I was using it up.

A waiter appeared dressed in white tie to take our drink orders. Suddenly I didn't feel so overdressed.

Conklin ordered for the group. "Jason, there are three of us, that should be at least two bottles of Piper Heidsieck, if you have them cold."

"Of course. We knew you and Madame were coming, Monsieur Conklin." Jason the waiter winked at us and hastened away.

I noted, "He's French or he sounded French. I thought everyone here was German."

"Yes, he's Swiss of course. Probably hails from one of the French Cantons. Everybody in Switzerland speaks two of the three languages. French and English or German and English. German or French is their main language depending where they were brought up. It's an amazing country."

"Yes, considering we Americans can hardly speak our own language."

Denise smiled. "But you, Brendan are very articulate. I read your book."

"My gosh! You read it? Really?"

"Really. It's in St. Agatha's library."

I guess my mouth hung open for a moment. "I had no idea. I never got a lot of fan mail from women. That's a pretty despicable story. Lots of violence and bad language."

"And realism. It's a story that needed to be told. That experience must have put you through hell," she said.

I nodded.

The waiter showed up with the first of two apparently, bottles of Piper Heidsieck red label champagne. Tall crystal flutes were passed three ways and soon the golden bubbly was tickling our noses. Conklin raised his like he was about to offer a toast. For some reason, my heart began fluttering. What could he possibly toast in their present situation?

"To life and our new friend, Brendan." His words made me feel abject humility. I sipped and felt the blonde elixir change gears on my palate.

"Gees, you guys are amazing," I said quietly.

Denise lowered her head. "Life makes you amazing."

"I know. I'm coming to grips with that."

They both looked at me.

I stammered on, unsure what I was going to say.

"I'm still getting used to the idea of being here. At some stage of life, people go through this, but Bettye and I are not that age."

"None of us are," Conklin said.

"Right. But here we are and if there's a chapter in the manual that tells you how to deal with it, I haven't read it."

Denise snorted champagne. "God that's funny!" She held her napkin to her nose.

Conklin said, "Brendan, there is no 'normal' way to feel about it."

"Of course you're right. But I'm just getting used to the idea Bettye's going to die. And now I'm getting all this information about how she's going to get better. My brain is numb about it."

Conklin's eyes narrowed. "But you've known about it for a while haven't you?"

"No, just a couple of days."

They both stared at me. My answer wasn't what they expected. So I told them more of my story, how Bettye and I weren't married and that we'd broken up two years ago. I hadn't had any contact with her until she showed up sick and invited me to come to St. Agatha's with her. During the telling I noticed a curious change come over them both. Daniel and Denise kept exchanging glances at each other almost like my story had some connection to theirs, more than the obvious similarities. My assumptions about them and their assumptions about me meshed in a confusing way. It was another puzzle piece, but where did it fit?

Denise put her hand on my arm. "Brendan, I can imagine what you're going through, but you showed a tremendous amount of faith in Bettye. You dropped everything just to come here and support her. That sounds like love to me."

The second glass of champagne began limbering our reserve.

"But it's so hard, my God, what you're going through... and you're comforting me!"

She smiled and I saw what Daniel saw in her. She was beautiful, I just hadn't noticed it at first. Her incredible strength was stronger than the grotesque mask cancer made her wear.

"I think I see some of it. I have to be strong for her. Bauerle says Bettye's coming along. She's getting better. I'm going to see her soon."

Jason, the waiter pulled the cork on Piper Heidsieck bottle number two. The other diners looked up at the loud pop

Denise clapped her hands. "I love that sound!" And we all laughed.

Dinner progressed on a happier note. We worked our way around the German concept of fine dining. I ordered the Kaninchenbraten gefüllt mit Dill Kräuternockerl in Weinsauce because I loved the way Jason pronounced it.

The rabbit cadaver arrived headless, thank God, laid out on its elbows and knees, over a thin, besotted sauce. The three of us scrutinized my entrée for a silent thirty seconds.

"Beatrix Potter's final chapter." I offered.

Our hearty laughter lasted a full minute longer than the scrutiny.

"Oh God, Brendan! You're so funny!" Denise wiped her eyes with her napkin. The best way to encourage me was to get me drunk on champagne and laugh at my jokes. I loved them both.

We started nibbling at our entrees. My Kaninchenbraten was incredible once I got past the notion that Easter would be canceled because of me. We ate with smiles on our faces until I came up with the perfect mood killer.

"So, Daniel, Denise, what's your story?"

I instantly regretted my question. I knew how secretive Conklin was, and surely I should have known Denise would be in cahoots with him. Conklin turned away in his seat like I had slapped him. Denise dropped her eyes but kept a devilish smile on her lips.

Conklin shook his head. "Brendan. We're in a different situation. We can't tell you much more than you already know."

"Look, Daniel, I'm sorry. We had our little chat earlier. I guess I should have realized you couldn't talk about it. I'm a reporter. Asking questions is automatic."

Conklin nodded. "And I…" he paused and dropped his voice. "…keep secrets." He smiled and our dinner atmosphere limped back to an uneasy kind of normal.

Our conversation toward the end of dinner kept within the boundaries we imposed, avoiding our dark areas. I felt my connection with them growing. A congenial atmosphere returned, and despite my previous gaffe, everything was going extremely well. Until I came up with another perfect mood killer.

"Daniel, Denise, this is a wonderful place, and I'm enjoying the heck out of your company. When Bettye is well enough, I want the four of us to come here."

They both look as if I had stepped on their grave. A chill wind rustled our tablecloth. It seemed to come from a tall window where outside the darkened Rhine rushed across a bleak landscape. What did I say this time? The silence was thick and foreboding. It felt like we must sit here like wax statues until I figured it out and fixed it. And in a few seconds, even my muddleheaded brain worked through the haze.

We were all here playing a part in this masque. I was the jester. Daniel the noble hero. Denise the doomed heroine. She pretended to be full of life, but she wasn't full of life. The sand in her hourglass fell, each grain a moment made precious by its rarity. Daniel's life would darken without Denise in it and that reality clung to him like the chill from the river.

They could not make plans like the one I had suggested. For them, this moment had to be enough.

Soon it would be my turn to wear his mask.

We drove to Von Muller Haus in somber silence. Daniel and Denise crept up the stairs arms around each other. Their fate hung over them like a lead cloak, halting their steps, shrouding their dreams.

I waited in the foyer, giving them the space they needed.

I stared at a tall ancient clock standing on the floor next to me. It banged away the seconds like a hammer stroke. It surprised me to note that in Switzerland, the land of fine clocks and watches, the Von Muller Haus held a genuine antique from Colonial America. The clock had a highly figured face faded by the very time that it had cadenced through the centuries. "Tempus Fugit" scrolled above its Roman numeral twelve. On the bottom of the clock, in barely visible ink, italics of ancient script had been penned to proclaim an enigmatic message.

The message read, *"Immortal dost thou know, Time will soon give thee to Eternity? Where, Oh! Where then! And what shalt thou be forever? Nath. Dominy, E. Hampton, Long Island 1787"*

The epitaph gave me a chill.

What do we know about our next minute? Or day? What the week will bring or a month or a year? With an abundance of time do we forget how precious it is and how the sands falling through our own hourglass will transform us?

In twenty-seven hours I would watch my career's finest achievement broadcast to the world under somebody else's name. I felt a morbid fascination, like watching a surgeon removing my heart while I was still alive and awake. I was the organ donor and someone else the recipient. A revelation entered my head that maybe my life's work wasn't journalism. Perhaps this was my work, being here, putting the pieces of a puzzle together, scraping under lies to reveal hidden truths and taking the mask from the hero.

Twenty-seven hours before my career was removed, but I would still live.

What would Daniel and Denise give for another twenty-seven hours?

Chapter 32

From the journal of Brendan Macbean:
Twenty-seven hours later, closing in on three o'clock in the morning, Daniel Conklin and I sat on opposite ends of the leather couch watching the streaming broadcast on the big LG in the library of St. Agatha's. Without calling attention to it I had lowered the lights in the room. In a darkened room we're drawn to the light, the television. I wanted to watch Daniel Conklin watching the broadcast.

A countdown clock superimposed over the network's famous logo ticked off the seconds on the screen. Instead of having to watch a bunch of lead-in commercials, we had the opportunity to watch the network pros getting ready to go live. We saw the two prominent news reporters sitting, chatting at their desks, microphones off, amid the bustle that usually takes place in a television studio just before to going live. Shelby Chadwick and Chris Hansen leaned toward each other. It flashed through my mind that all the hundreds of management about the production had already been made. Who should anchor? Which set to use? How to introduce Shelby? I didn't give Conklin a running commentary on the insider's perspective of television broadcasting. In fact my whole agenda had shifted away from my fascination with how they were going to carve up my magnum opus. Now I wondered how Daniel Conklin would react to watching Ray Suffield answer hard questions about the collapse of InCorps.

The camera zoomed in for a close-up of Shelby's face. It was standard practice for the director to evaluate how she looked, how close they could zoom, which angles were best and so on. Shelby saw the camera's red light and looked straight into the lens. She looked confident and unabashed.

I had a brain flash: Shelby knew I was watching. From whatever dark hole I had crawled into, Shelby would know I'd have to watch it. She wanted me to know she got my last voice message. And now the look on her face said to me, "Macbean, your career is over, baby. You gave the best work of your career to me. I love you and thank you for it, but the mantle is passed. I'll do my best to make you proud.

And I added my own thought. And thanks, dude for making an exit, graceful or otherwise.

Fifty ways to leave your lover?

Conklin exclaimed, "My god, what a beautiful woman! You worked with her?"

"I did, briefly. That's Shelby Chadwick. Currently she's a reporter for the Atlanta station but she's expected to go to the network soon. Maybe she already has. She's done several pieces already for the network news."

"You're lucky to be in the same room with a woman like that."

I smiled. "You're right. She's stunning in person but I have to add, she's a serious pro."

Conklin just nodded and stared at the screen. The digital clock counted down the last seconds and the broadcast went live.

"Now live! An exclusive special report. The Ray Suffield Interview with Chris Hansen and Special Correspondent, Shelby Chadwick."

The camera faced Chris Hansen who looked grave and sincere. The lighting was perfect and the camera slowly zoomed in. The network's image consultants worked overtime to get the atmosphere right. I felt eager about what was coming.

"Good evening, America. Four years ago our country faced the largest most widespread economic crisis since the Great Depression. The collapse of the giant American economy was due to a pandemic of greed and corruption, rampant within the largest and most trusted corporations in the country. The first of a series of scandals to hit Wall Street was the collapse of one of America's most dynamic and fastest growing companies, InCorps. The downfall of InCorps exposed the soft underbelly of American business and financial institutions, exposed widespread accounting fraud, corruption and executive greed on an unprecedented scale.

"Two major villains of the financial meltdown, the men who built the gigantic petro-conglomerate InCorps were Ray Suffield and Wylie Schram. Wylie Schram died in an alcohol related traffic accident and Ray Suffield pled guilty to numerous charges and went to federal prison for the rest of his life. For four years Americans have wanted to hear from this criminal to better understand how a few men could bring down the largest economic force in the world, the American stock market and plunge the most prosperous country in the world into year after year of recession and massive unemployment. For four years, Ray Suffield has remained silent, hiding in a federal prison in Louisiana, protected by the US Department of Justice from answering the serious questions we've waited so long to ask him.

"Tonight, thanks to the monumental efforts of one courageous young woman from our network affiliate in Atlanta, Georgia, Ray Suffield has to face the cameras and tell America why he did what he did. Shelby Chadwick…."

The camera panned to Shelby who sat straight and unafraid facing Hansen, looking like the bold crusader she was, the journalistic warrior who would not take no for an answer.

Hansen continued. "Shelby Chadwick is known to many of us, working tirelessly on a series of special reports on the drug crisis in professional sports. Still she found the energy to chip away layers of protection the federal prison systems had erected to hide the true nature of Ray Suffield's crimes from the American Public."

He went on to give a brief biography of Shelby.

"Shelby, tell us how you were able to get permission to interview the most hated man in America when more famous newsmen have been stonewalled for so long."

Shelby turned to face the camera. "Thank you, Chris. I've been working on this for years." Her voice carried all the beauty of an American Southern accent with enough educated sophistication to make us believe every word.

"Phone call after phone call, writing letters, email, a massive, collective effort to bring this man in front of the camera. I have to thank my team back in Atlanta for the many hours of work it took to pull this off. Last week we were finally granted limited access to take our cameras into Oakdale Federal prison in Louisiana to interview Suffield who, with the help of high ranking Department of Justice officials, dropped out of sight and went into hiding before he could face the American people and tell us why he brought down our economy."

Shelby herself was facing the American people looking knockout beautiful, radiating heartfelt sincerity and gigantic determination. She walked us through how she took her crew to Oakdale. They showed drive-by footage of the federal prison complex, Louisiana sun shining off of chain link fences topped by razor wire. Then they showed Shelby herself, dressed in a dark blue suit wearing her Tanzanite baubles, spike heels clicking on the polished floors of the prison wing which held the library. Obviously they received permission to go there again and shoot this additional footage. The screen showed Shelby taking a seat in the library setting notes on the table. She looked fit enough to take on the world.

The scene shifted to Ray Suffield walking down the corridor, past the cafeteria, glancing in momentarily and casually continuing on down the corridor. Goosebumps rose on my arms and neck. This was my footage. I remember grabbing my cameraman Tony's belt and backing him through the library door so he could keep shooting Suffield. Our footage had been very skillfully edited and I half expected to see the camera pan around to show Mike Ferguson introducing Shelby and Ray. Of course they didn't show that because it never happened.

The view shifted to a stern looking Shelby, apparently giving Ray a carefully worded preamble similar to how I had opened the interview. Her statement was not exactly what I has said but re-crafted by network staff writers to improve on the original. Ray's response seemed natural and totally responsive to her statement. There was no way a casual viewer would suspect that Shelby wasn't really there and that it wasn't really her questions driving the interview. Even the lighting and atmosphere of her do-over shoot matched our original.

The camera switched back and forth, Shelby delivered her questions in an ever increasing cadence. Ray's responses seemed measured at first. The editor patched in more snippets of him squirming. Tony and I had filmed plenty of squirming. Tension between her and Ray seemed to heighten as the interview proceeded. My footage had been edited by a master. Shelby had been well coached and she executed her role with laser precision.

I fully realized this no longer was my work. What we watched sitting on the leather couch of the library in St. Agatha's Clinic was the work of the network television pros who had taken my raw material and polished it into award winning journalism. You could almost hear Emmy and Pulitzer nominating delegates furiously scratching notes, and they didn't need to know how to spell Macbean.

Warning bells went off in my head. This ultra-slick presentation of which I had made a limited contribution had seduced me like everyone else who watched, but I remembered my real agenda had changed. I glanced over at Daniel Conklin. He had been irresistibly sucked into the broadcast. I knew what Tony and I had captured, but he knew something more from a different perspective. I saw his eyes glisten as emotions within him forced through his reserve.

In the darkroom of my imagination the pieces of the puzzle began to form a picture. I watched Daniel Conklin shake his head, a movement made slight by his incredible reserve and compelling need to hide. He had hidden these four years, accepted exile, a punishment even darker than that of Ray Suffield. Conklin knew Ray Suffield intimately. I could see it in his eyes. And he knew Ray Suffield had lied... to me, and ultimately to Shelby, in response to her highly crafted surrogate questions.

And he lied to the naked eye of the camera.

The interview concluded with Ray's emotional breakdown, and this time I viewed it as the sham it was. Telepathically I heard Ray Suffield's laughter as he had just pulled off another great scam on America, behind locked steel doors, shielded by the barbed wire and tempered glass windows of Oakdale Federal Prison.

At the end the network announcer tried to liven up our mood, promoting the coming television schedule. We fortunate Americans could look forward to more TV nonsense, reality shows, sports and sitcoms. Conklin's hand shook as he picked up the remote and shut off the set.

In darkness and silence he stared at the black screen for seconds and finally turned to me, his face wet with tears.

His voice shook. "That... is not how it was at all."

I took a deep, shaky breath.

"Then, Wylie, tell me how it really was."

Chapter 33

From the journal of Brendan Macbean:

Wylie Schram, aka Daniel Conklin gave me the "Please don't call me Wylie" look, a plea to maintain plausible deniability. If I didn't call him Wylie, he could still pretend to be Daniel. But who knew the truth? I knew it and certainly Denise knew it and certainly Bentley and the list would have to include Vladoseev and Karolovsky. The rest of the world thought Wylie Schram was dead and the crock holding this load of bull hadn't leaked a drop in four years. No one else had seen the collected evidence the way I had. So no one else was even looking for Wylie Schram.

"Brendan, it's better the world never finds out. Wylie died in a crash four years ago. End of story."

"Stories this big never end. It's better even than TV Swanson's. Or Ray Suffield's so called interview."

"Nobody knew about Swanson until you told them. Everybody knows about InCorps and the Hole in Wall Street Gang. It would kill me as surely as if you pulled the trigger. I don't think you'll do that and I'm pleading with you not to."

"It's okay. You're Daniel to me. Nobody wants to hear this one anyway. Shelby was wrong... We're better off not knowing."

He looked a little relieved. "It's just that I've hidden it so long. Now it feels like my pants have fallen down. I feel exposed."

"Trust me... I won't tell anyone."

"Yeah, but now you're going to ask me a bunch of questions. Things I've been hiding for years."

"Well, I think it's what you want. At least about Suffield lying in the interview."

Daniel Conklin nodded. It surprised me how easily I reverted to thinking of him as Conklin and not Schram.

The room remained dimly lit with the television off. We got comfortable on the leather couch. A good reporter would be taking notes, but, with a gulp, I realized I wasn't a reporter anymore. It was just two guys talking.

"We never lacked investors. Ray and I worked like a good ham and egg team. He knew the petro business and I raised cash. Many people don't know this but there are thousands of investors out there looking for places to park their money, for short and long terms. A lot of investors end their weeks with tons of cash and want to park it over the weekend, or a week, a month or a quarter. And they want the highest returns they can get. InCorps, gave them a place. If you had two mil, and needed it next Wednesday, give it to me and I'll give you back an extra two or three points."

I did some quick, crude math. "You mean like fifty thousand dollars?"

Conklin nodded. "The longer the better, but there was always risk, and timing was important. Investors would call up and ask what the return on some amount would be for three or four days and I'd give them my best guess based on what we had going. I also knew when, say a tanker was coming in and we expected a big payoff. I knew what to tell these investors, the money men, when they asked. Computers handled everything. Everybody who sent us their cash knew what the risks and returns might be. Sometimes we didn't make the number they expected but not very often. We were hot and good at what we did.

"Ray knew oil but he didn't understand cash or investors. Or timing. We weren't squeezed by competition. It was Ray. He started bringing in guys who wanted to invest really big chunks of money…"

"What's really big?" I asked. It occurred to me that big for me would be a thousand dollars but that might be nothing to these guys.

"Thirty million. Fifty. The kind of money you went after when you needed to make a strategic move." He said this with a calm voice like he was used to handling lottery sized money most of us would never see in ten lifetimes.

Conklin gave me an intense look. "Ray would bring in these guys' money at the wrong time."

"There's a wrong time for fifty million?" I asked.

"Sure. It's the wrong time when we couldn't pay back what they expected. Ray would come in and tell me, so in so has fifty million. I'd tell him it would come handy at the end of the month. He'd say, no, the guy wanted it back next week and he still expected a big return anyway. You see, these guys expected us to take it in and turn it around, give them three or four or five points anyway. We couldn't always do that and InCorps was expected to take up the slack. You don't run a business that way. I'd ask them to wait a month or four months and they said, no. You did it for us last month, you got to do it for us now. There was no trying to talk them out of it."

"Who throws chunks of money around like that?"

"Not people who you had a 1099 on. Ray wanted to hide these investments from the IRS and the SEC. That's where we clashed. It's

John Wilsterman

illegal. But I found out Ray was getting pressured by people who break your arms instead of twist them."

"Like Vladoseev?"

Conklin nodded.

"I told Ray we can't take money and keep it quiet from the Feds. We'll go to jail. As it turned out we couldn't keep it quiet. Rumors started making the rounds and some of our strategic investors pulled out. Vladoseev demanded what Ray promised him. Ray paced the office like a hunted man. He kept asking me how much cash we had on hand. It seems like he constantly needed to make payoffs to Vladoseev.

"Rumors don't circulate long before the SEC starts sniffing around. And then the IRS. Then RICO. And that's when the shit hit the fan. Suddenly I couldn't raise enough cash to lease another tanker or buy crude or any of the other deals that were the mainstay of our business."

I thought for a minute. "Your board of directors…"

Conklin snorted. "Our board of directors never looked at anything. They rubber stamped everything we brought them."

"So you and Ray pretty much did what you wanted. It was all on you two. And your stock was selling like hotcakes and soon it was too hot for anyone. What did you do?"

"One day I told Ray we were both going to jail. He had been handing over our operating cash to this gangster. That Russian son of a bitch could have bought stock like everyone else but that was too tame for him. He just wanted cash. In less than a year our liabilities dwarfed our assets. InCorps couldn't even be carved up and sold. Our decline didn't last long enough to liquidate."

"So you hid some money?"

"Ray came to me with the idea we could start over. With RICO closing in he'd let InCorps crash and burn. We'd go to jail or plea bargain to lesser sentences or probation. We needed what he called 'seed money' which we could use to start operations again. Ray knew how he could do this if he had some money. Our business premise was still sound but the seed money had to come from our cash accounts which would be seized as soon as the SEC found them. We were under subpoena to turn in all our bank records. I had about twenty-four hours to move this money overseas. I figured out how to do what Ray asked. I had computers that could handle massive banking transactions, like account creation and money transfers. If the SEC didn't know about these new accounts they would never know where to look. All these transactions were buried in a mass of traditional looking transactions we conducted every day. The banks and account numbers were hidden from the feds under a haystack of detail."

"If you hadn't done anything, the investigators would have found your cash accounts?"

"Yes, that's what auditors do. When they found the accounts there would be a lot less money in them. And I was going to tell them I didn't know when or how the accounts got depleted."

"You were going to lie."

Conklin nodded. "Brendan, we had seventy billion in tangibles, like contracts, capital goods, buildings, real estate, notes and bonds. When the feds raided us, I turned it all over to them and they recovered ninety-seven percent of it. All but a billion and a half."

"That was the money you blasted overseas."

He nodded.

"You lied to them about that money."

He nodded. "More like I told them the truth, just not everything. The cash was placed in accounts and the account information came back encrypted. I had apps that could straighten it all out but the feds thought they could de-encrypt it themselves."

"They must be the worst interrogators in the world."

"Well, they were quite thorough. Days and days of interrogation. Eleven lie detector tests…polygraphs. I told them all I knew… that there were no more accounts which I knew about."

"And they believed you."

"Eleven lie detector tests. All positive."

"You fooled the polygraph tests. How?"

"I hid it in my brain."

"Huh? I mean… uh… Huh?"

"Brendan, are you familiar with meditation?"

"Not really."

"There's a form of meditation developed by Jose Silva sixty years ago. Silva called it Mind Control. It's like meditation. You use the unconscious part of your brain to strengthen and support your mental capacity. I did not want my conscious brain to be aware of these accounts. Your brain hides information from you all the time. You just don't 'know' it. Using Mind Control I could retrieve the data but consciously I wouldn't know the specifics. The feds suspected I had the info but in all their interrogation I told them I didn't. They never asked me if I could retrieve the specifics. When they asked me if I knew of any more accounts, I said no. They asked me if it was on my computers and I said it was all there. Both statements were true."

"How do you retrieve it?"

"Same way you hide it. You relax your mind to a state between Beta and Theta, slow down brain activity somewhere between conscious and unconscious. That state is known to neurologists as the 'Alpha state.'"

"Okay...."

"Brendan, you're already familiar with the Alpha state. It's how you feel when you're waking up. You level of brain activity is entirely suspended between asleep and awake. When you initiate Alpha from consciousness you retain the ability to use your free will to govern all activities of your mind. You can determine what you think about in a way that directly contrasts your inability to control that function when you're unconscious. What your unconscious mind thinks about sometimes manifests itself as dreams or at least so it appears to your conscious mind."

"Okay, what I did was 'think' about a series of pictures of comfortable and familiar images... I imagined a place that felt safe to me and filled with things I was comfortable with. Like a cabin my family went to in Ontario, Canada on Sharbot Lake. My father and I loved it up there. Where we spent many happy times. I always felt safe and secure, so it seemed to be an ideal place to hide the information about hidden bank accounts. In a fantasy way, I mean. I turned all the account numbers, passwords and amounts over to my father for safe keeping."

"Huh?" An overused word, but I was finding it very useful.

Conklin smiled. "I know it sounds like mumbo jumbo."

"Well, how about implausible?"

"Whacko, goofy and airheaded," he volunteered. "Beads and headbands with 'California Dreaming' in the background."

"All that and more," I added.

"Look, Brendan. When you were a teenager did you ever have a fantasy about a girl?"

"Uh, well, I guess so."

"Did you tell her about it?"

"No."

"Tell anyone else?"

"Mostly no, I guess."

"We're good at keeping secrets, but polygraphs work on the principal that you get nervous when you lie. If that girl you fantasized about ever looked you straight in the eye and asked you that question when you were hooked up to a polygraph, the needles would fly off the chart. But in a casual setting you might have calmed yourself down and denied it with as much aplomb as you could muster.

"My father passed away when I was just starting my career but he was someone I could always trust. For the purposes of meditation I built this fantasy about him and the cabin out of my memories of a place where I could feel safe and unassailable. I needed a person I could trust who had the absolute moral rectitude to keep my secret. My dad. And I had to know very little about the secret itself other than he had the information.

"To hide money from the Feds, what I asked him to do went against his ethics. So I had to concoct a rationale to get my memory of him to cooperate."

"Huh?" There was that word again.

"I wanted to hide the information. I wanted to say I didn't know about the accounts. I knew how I was going to retrieve the information but I didn't want to 'know' the information. So I meditated to bring myself into the Alpha state. Then I imagined I was at the cabin at the lake with my dad and I explained everything to him. He, or my memory of him refused and encouraged me to turn all the money over to the feds. You know, he wanted me to do the right thing."

"Your dad refused?"

"Yes."

"And this is your dad who had died, like you had a recent conversation with him."

"I know it sounds confusing. It wasn't my dad, it was my memory of dad. In many ways my memory of him was more perfect that the man himself had been, but even so I had to concoct an elaborate justification before 'he' would agree to hide the information. Hiding money from Treasury officials was not something my dad would agree to so I told him there was a higher purpose but at the moment I didn't know what it was. He could keep the information from me until I had given him a plan that would pass his moral standards."

"Jesus, Daniel. This is all just a fantasy."

"Exactly. But real enough to beat eleven polygraphs."

"How did you get the information into your head without your conscious memory receiving it?"

"That was tricky. I had the data stored on my computer. I programmed it to use computer speech to 'say' the data out loud at a specific time. When it spoke the account numbers, bank names, ID's and passwords, I imagined

I was temporarily deaf. I could not hear what the computer was saying but 'Dad' did and wrote the numbers down. On a virtual piece of paper, I guess."

"All in your imagination."

"Yep."

"And he's not real."

"Nope. Just a Fig Newton of my imagination."

"And you dreamed the whole scenario up."

Conklin looked perturbed. "Brendan, dreams are different. Dreams are subconscious thoughts which leak into your conscious awareness. You wake up with a vague memory, which you recognize as a dream. This is the opposite. I control what's happening when I'm in the alpha state. I imagine in vivid detail a scene where I control the outcome. It's more akin to your fantasy about the girl. You make up what happens and it adds to your experience, makes you happy."

"Sort of. Not like the real thing."

"Not with this either but creating mental scenes can be useful."

"Useful," I wondered aloud.

"Eleven polygraphs."

"But you said your fantasy dad would not give up the information until you came up with a plan that would pass his moral standards."

"Right. I did. Finally. He gave me the data."

"You have the billion and a half." My heart began to beat like a heavy sledge.

Conklin looked pensive.

"Brendan. I'm a money man. Do you think I'd put this money where it would sit idle?"

"It's worth more now?"

He nodded.

"How much?"

"Two billion. Three hundred eighty-five million. Four hundred thousand."

He took a deep breath.

"And growing."

Part Three

Chapter 34

Each day brought Nicolay Karolovsky closer to total, screaming frustration. Initially he had enjoyed the charming Old Towne Schaffhausen, but in the last week he had grown bored with the unchanging routine and the lack of progress on their objective. His annoyance with the situation had ridden up on him like tight underwear. He was tired of the Swiss, the food, and his accommodations. And especially he was tired of chasing that *ublyudok*, Wylie Schram.

"Oh, and boss, now he's got with him a new little buddy," he told Vladoseev on his twice daily call. "They go to coffee together and the feds show up. They go to dinner in a fancy restaurant and the feds show up. Schram is under federal protection and it's like they got no care in the world. I expect to see them prancing around in milking jackets and lederhosen singing 'Edelweiss' from the Sound of Music."

"Calm down, Kolya. Anyway, you are not in Austria."

"So, what's the difference?"

"It is not the same. In the movie the Von Trapps were in Austria."

"Boss, what are you babbling about?"

"Koyla. Calm down. Who is this new little buddy?"

"He's obviously an American. Short, balding, wears glasses. The clinic took in a new patient and he came with her."

"And she's another American as well?"

"How the hell would I know? That damn clinic didn't hand me a newsletter. I can't just walk in there and ask questions. There's a fence around the place and the feds are parked at the gate."

"Wylie and Denise are still there?"

"Of course. He comes and goes like he owns the place, driving that big black Mercedes. Last night, the two guys snuck into the clinic after midnight for god's sake. Alarm went off on my phone telling me they were on the move and I had to jump out of bed like a fireman."

"Ah, good. I'm glad that program our friend gave us is working. Was it a crisis or something? Is Denise dying?"

Karolovsky sighed. "Boss, I'm trying to tell you I have no fucking clue! Except I have to spend the night in the car and so did the goddamned federal agents. In the morning the new buddies go out to coffee again and back to the clinic. The place is like a fortress. We can't get near them."

"What do you think they were doing? Are they having a threesome with the hot *bryunet* doctor?"

Karolovsky let the question hang for a few seconds. "Jesus, Boss. She wasn't even there. I can see the parking lot and it was empty except for the night staffers' cars and their Mercedes. I guess if there was a medical emergency there would be more staff. Wylie and the new guy went in there for something. It is definitely not their usual pattern, but hell, I just don't know."

Vladoseev thought for a moment. "It seems that Wylie has the run of the place, otherwise he would need someone to let him in."

"Here's the thing, Boss. Denise is going to die. If we don't grab Wylie now, the federal agents will scoop him up as soon as Denise *peynet vedro*."

"How does she look? Did you see them when they went out?"

"Through binoculars she looks fine but I'm not a doctor. She's thin and got no boobs but walks like she has energy."

"A far cry from a month ago."

"Yes, Boss."

"So maybe she's not going to kick the bucket soon."

"The point is we don't know. As long as she's here, Schram is here and when she's dead he's going to disappear."

"Can you do anything between the clinic and the house?"

"His commute is worse than a state funeral. He gets in the car and the feds fall into line. They drive in a convoy. At least two teams. Maybe more. As soon as he pulls out, they're in front of him and behind. And I think they know I'm here."

"Of course they do. Don't worry. They won't do anything to you, or so my new friend assures me. International incident and all that."

"Don't be so sure, Boss. I wouldn't count on any deal you made. Those guys don't play by the rules. They could bag me in an alley or something. Typical federal *fignya*. Unless they got guys I haven't seen, it's just the two, three teams, maybe a couple of geeks in a hotel room with electronics. They stick close to their cars. We know when they're moving but we can't track them. The feds probably got bugs in his bedroom and all the local restaurants."

"Are you able to listen in?"

"Nope. It's not like the radios when they were watching Denise's house. But then they didn't know we were watching. Look, Boss, I don't know what we're supposed to do here. With the help we're getting from you-know-who, why don't we just grab the guy? Denise is going to die and after that Wylie will bolt. What are we waiting around here for?"

There was a long pause as Vladoseev thought about this.

"Kolya, I think our new partner wants us to figure out a way to get the job done. Why else we get all this information? But it has to look right. Not make a big scene or get police involved. That brings reporters and TV cameras. It has to be the right move. Have patience and do not get so frustrated. You're going to make a mistake and get into trouble. You're not going to be much good to me after that."

"I'm not much good here as it is. What you need is a miracle worker not a, uh well, whatever you call me."

"Partner, agent, henchman."

"That last one sounds evil."

"And evil is what we will be when we get our hands on Wylie Schram."

"I am in total agreement Boss but I'm tired sitting in this car all day. I'm tired of the Best Western Hotel and most of all I'm tired of Wurstsalat."

"What in hell is that?"

"Greens, boiled eggs served with sour sausage. *Bog uzhasno i kislyy.* Yehch!"

"Well you won't have to eat the worse salad for long. I think the day has come we collect our little accountant. While we are talking, I think of a plan."

"Excellent, boss. Let us hear of your plan."

The next day, Karolovsky drove to Zurich to meet a man named Arnie. Their rendezvous occurred at the Starbucks at Kalanderplatz. Arnie looked to be about forty, was much shorter than Karolovsky, and he had the perfect face for a sneak thief, completely unmemorable. Karolovsky had no problem spotting him in the crowded coffee shop and marveled at his boss's vast network of dubious characters. Arnie sat in the back corner, near the restroom and was receiving absolutely no attention from the other patrons. He dressed in what looked like his painter clothes, sturdy, dirty and practical.

Arnie already had a table so Karolovsky stood in line to get his usual, a grande bold pick of the day, no room for cream or sugar. His cup of coffee as usual was hot enough to melt the floor tile if he spilled it. He strolled over and towered over the shorter man seated in the dark corner.

"Arnie?"

Arnie nodded. "And you?"

Karolovsky smiled. "I'm me. When I call you, I'll say it's me so you will know who it is."

"I don't like it you have my phone number and I don't have your name or your phone number."

"You don't have to like it." Karolovsky sat his coffee on the table and next to it he placed his phone so that Arnie could see the screen. Arnie stared at the screen which displayed a photo of a red brick building. Arnie squirmed in his chair and looked up at the merciless eyes of the tall man standing over him.

Karolovsky took a chair across the table.

"Nice house. I also know where your children go to school. Arnie made a move like he was going to get up but Karolovsky laid a heavy hand on his arm.

"Relax. You're going to get paid a lot of money."

"What do you want?"

"Where's your phone?"

Arnie laid his phone on the table. Karolovsky picked it up.

"Piece of shit. When are you going to get a decent phone? Okay, here you go." He keyed Arnie's phone for a couple of minutes and set it down on the table. Karolovsky picked up his coffee and winced. Still too hot.

"There. That's what I need."

Arnie looked at the screen. "What's this?"

"Welcome to the twenty-first century. It's a list of what I need."

"This is mostly hospital supplies," Arnie said.

"Ought to be easy to get since there are so many hospitals around here."

"Some of these are Schedule One and Two narcotics."

"So? Are you a narc? Arnie, if I could get this stuff myself, I wouldn't need you."

Arnie shrugged. "It will take me at least a week. How do I contact you when I have all this?"

Karolovsky showed him the picture of his house again.

"Two days. I'll meet you back here at five PM. No excuses. And be prepared to stay out all night."

Arnie shook his head.

"My duties are limited to getting what you need. I don't stay out all night. Your boss should be able to get you somebody else. I don't do, uh… field work."

Arnie turned away from the fire building in Karolovsky's eyes.

"Arnie, do I look like I'm going to get someone else?"

Arnie didn't answer.

"Two days. Five o'clock."

Karolovsky picked up his still scalding coffee and left.

Chapter 35

Daniel Conklin entered Dr. Bauerle's office. It was midmorning, and upon arriving at St. Agatha's he had gone to see Denise. She had not spent the night with him at Haus Von Muller. Her doctors had stepped up her treatments to three times a day and told him they required her to remain at the clinic.

Dr. Bauerle rose behind her desk looking composed. She gave him a restrained smile. Conklin immediately sat down in the chair in front of her desk. He was not smiling.

"Yes, Mr. Conklin?"

Conklin slumped a little. "I just came from Denise's room."

"Yes, Mr. Conklin?"

"She had a bad night."

"I know." Bauerle's voice was calm.

"She said she felt terrible. Back pain, cramps… headaches." Conklin clenched his hands in his lap. "What's going on, Dr. Bauerle?"

Bauerle glanced down at the paper on her desk, and then raised her eyes to meet Conklin's. She took a deep breath.

"These symptoms are consistent with the return of her tumors, of course."

Conklin stared at her mouth, that wide, beautiful mouth that belonged on a magazine cover.

"So soon?" he said in a barely audible whisper.

"I'm afraid so, Mr. Conklin."

"I thought we would have another week, maybe more."

Bauerle walked past him and closed the door to her office. As she returned she trailed a hand, touched his shoulder and continued to her chair behind the desk. A faint waft of perfume followed her.

"Daniel…" The use of his first name added a touch of intimacy. "You've read the case histories, our patients' reports. We usually don't grant access to these records, but you have helped us. So you know what to expect, more so than many of our clients."

"But so soon?" Again it was all he could say.

"Yes, Mr. Conklin. Unfortunately." Bauerle dropped her eyes again.

Conklin straightened up. "Dr. Bauerle, you mentioned the case histories. On average your patients' restoration lasts nearly three weeks before serious symptoms return. You've had exceptions, of course, but Denise has had a little over a week… nine days. Please explain."

Bauerle took another deep breath. "The restoration period seems to be proportional to their initial condition upon arrival. The closer they are to death, the longer their recovery time takes and the shorter the period of restored health. Denise came to us in very poor condition. We helped her recover but as we've mentioned many times, the tumors persistently attempt to renew themselves by producing mutated semaphorins. Quite rapidly, her tumors ran through SP1 to SP7 while we applied the treatments to overcome those strains. She is now expressing SP8 and we have no effective treatment for it. As a result, her tumors are growing. SP8 is an ugly mutation and acts like a human growth hormone. Her tumors are growing with extreme vigor. We have not developed a reliable response for SP8. We're trying a few experimental treatments but without success."

As if knowing she spoke too many words Bauerle halted leaving her mouth open. Conklin silently let the seconds stretch. His eyes focused on a spot somewhere between them. He finally met her eyes.

"What's the prognosis?"

"We can't be precise. The headaches and back pain are preliminary symptoms. She felt these before... before she came here. I'm sure then her doctors advised her on proper treatment. But..." Bauerle's voice dropped. "But our patients are different. Their situation is different."

"How so, Dr. Bauerle?"

"We all know this day is coming, Daniel. Our patients have been through conventional treatment and endured all the side effects associated with it, pain, nausea from chemo, burns from radiation. They've dealt with the periods of uncertainty, of waiting for doctor's reports, the sleepless nights, their loved ones tip-toeing around them. It is agonizing for everyone. They come to St. Agatha's to put all that behind them. Our patients choose not to resume any conventional treatment."

Daniel Conklin stared at a diploma on the wall behind Bauerle. More seconds ticked by. His hands twitched and he made an effort to hold them still.

"So we make her comfortable and watch her die."

As he said it, he heard echoes from more than a hundred ghosts. The ones who came before him, the husbands who sat in this chair and heard Bauerle issue the death sentence. Bauerle was no rookie when it came to handing out bad news. She had become adept at it and faced him with open eyes. She appeared sympathetic but offered no hope or denials.

Conklin stood and slowly turned toward the door.

"Daniel…" Dr. Bauerle said.

He paused only for a second but then opened the door and headed in the direction of Denise's room. He quick-walked down the corridor, passing clinic staff, but stopped just a few feet from her door. He started shaking. He wrapped his arms tightly around himself to stop the shaking. She would be waiting for him. He could visualize her head coming up as he walked through her door. She'd offer him a tentative, strained smile, waiting to hear words… words Dr. Bauerle could not offer.

He turned around and ran back, down the corridor, through the staff-only doors, through the lobby, past the library where he saw Brendan Macbean standing in the doorway cheerfully waving. He charged past him.

Outside healthy sunshine hit him in the face just as his depraved act of cowardice hit his conscience like a sledge hammer. Tears streamed across his face as he walked toward the Mercedes. Out of habit he pulled out his iPhone but set it on the console instead of checking his federal escort.

He drove around for almost an hour without knowing where he was going. Eventually he managed to quiet his mind. Eventually he found the courage.

He headed back to St. Agatha's.

Back to Denise.

He picked up his iPhone. The screen told him his federal escort occupied their familiar positions behind and ahead of him. He nodded and mentally thanked them for their predictability and levelheadedness.

He pulled into the entrance to St. Agatha's and turned off the Mercedes. He glanced at his phone again and noticed his federal escort cars settle into their customary locations outside the gate. The screen held his eye for a second longer as a red number traced along the road, representing an unknown vehicle approaching. The vehicle turned into the driveway.

Conklin looked in the rearview mirror and for a moment thought of quickly ducking into the lobby, but the mirror showed only a yellow DHL delivery van snaking its way up the drive. He got out of the car just as the van pulled to a stop in front of the clinic.

A man in a tan uniform came around the front of the van and held out a clipboard to him.

"Sie für eine Lieferung unterschreiben?" the man asked.

Conklin pointed to door where deliveries were made. He felt a sharp prick on his neck a few inches below the ear. The overhead sun swirled, bathing his face with warmth as he swooned into the arms of a very tall man with reddish hair.

Chapter 36

The faint stirrings of consciousness came upon him slowly. Numbness kept him from opening his eyes so he lay prone and felt the complete relaxation of having been heavily drugged. He lay in a room that was as quiet as a tomb, but large enough so that the air produced a slight reverberation. The room was partially dark. The air he breathed had little movement but it wasn't stuffy. The surface he lay on had a slight resiliency. There were no restraints on his wrists or ankles, he was dressed, and the drug was wearing off.

He assumed he had been snatched by Karolovsky. And there was another man, the man with the clipboard. Was that Vladoseev? Somehow Conklin doubted it. What he remembered was that the man looked nervous, completely uncomfortable with his role as a kidnapper. His act with the clipboard was forced. Conklin had no idea what he had said but he assumed it was a request for a signature. He remembered nothing else.

He dredged up from memory a book he had once read, a Jack Reacher novel by Lee Child. The hero had been shot by a dart from a compressed air gun that injected him with a narcotic causing immediate unconsciousness. Reacher had been out for eight hours. He could assume he had been out for a similar period. Therefore it was night. Vladoseev and Karolovsky would be anxious to start interrogating him. They would not want him unconscious any longer than necessary.

He opened his eyes slowly and waited until they adjusted to the gloomy light. He seemed to be in a box-like featureless room. He rolled over on his back and saw a low ceiling. Slowly he sat up. Turning his head he saw a single door about eight feet away which was closed. On the floor next to the door was a red Igloo cooler. The cooler reminded him he was very thirsty.

Before he moved he took ten deep, measured breaths, which brought on a wave of dizziness. He waited until it subsided. He still lacked the capacity to stand so he crawled over to the cooler on his hands and knees. Inside the cooler was a liter of mineral water and a red Powerade.

He tore the top off the mineral water and swallowed it in successive gulps. The water refreshed him. He tentatively stood and tried the door. It was not locked. The door opened to a small bathroom containing a toilet and sink. No window. No mirror. No cabinet. Two rolls of toilet paper and one roll of paper towels. A small cake of soap wrapped in Best Western logoed paper.

Conklin looked around the larger room and estimated the size to be about fourteen by twenty feet and about eight feet high. He could not see very well in the dim light but the walls seemed to be covered with quilted pads, the kind movers use to wrap furniture. The surface beneath the pads was hard but not too substantial. The whole room seemed unsubstantial and temporary.

While he pondered this his bowels cramped, suddenly, severely, doubling him over. Suddenly his abdomen felt like it was about to explode, and he staggered to the toilet. Just in time he managed to mount the commode while his intestines voided themselves. When he thought he could give no more, his bowels cramped, jittered, cramped and brought forth even more.

Exhausted, he managed to clean himself up. The light switch near the door turned on a fan but no light. Thank god the toilet and sink worked.

Conklin staggered out of the bathroom. What light there was came from tiny cracks in the oddly composed walls and ceiling. Whoever built his prison had done so in haste with an obscure purpose. The bowel emptying ordeal had left him ravenously thirsty again so he opened the Powerade and sipped it while he looked around. The red liquid was still fairly cool so his kidnappers must have recently put it in the room. Before he knew it, he had emptied the bottle of Powerade and held it vertically to drain the last drop.

His stomach gave a gastrointestinal version of a shrug and he emitted a giant belch.

Except for the curses he hurled upon himself, his mind brought forth a single word. The word was PEG or polyethylene glycol. He remembered other words from the storeroom of the pharmacy where he worked: Golytely, Colyte, Nulytely, Trilyte. Last year the small town doctor he saw had recommended a colonoscopy. The day before the procedure, his boss had cheerfully donated an Imperial gallon of the stuff and he had to drink the entire amount before nine PM. He had finished drinking the four liters of the stuff, but it took him until four in the morning before he finished with the commode.

He felt the warnings of another intestinal tsunami and he raced back to the bathroom.

Thirty minutes later he staggered out of the bathroom, left the fan running and stood sore-assed in the middle of his dark prison. Rectal eruptions visited him twice more, and when he thought he might shit his lungs out, he made his last trip.

Once again in the middle of the floor he lay down, drained of energy and fluids. He actually dozed.

The sound of power tools woke him. He listened to a drill making eight runs as if screwing in eight screws. Or removing eight screws. A piece of the wall moved, a gap appeared at the end of the room and Karolovsky strolled in carrying two folding chairs and a shop lamp trailing an orange extension cord. He set the lamp on the floor and opened the two chairs.

Conklin had been so preoccupied with voiding his guts he hadn't prepared for this moment very well. It occurred to him he might have made a break for it but didn't know what awaited him outside the room. He felt completely unprepared for what would happen next.

Karolovsky sat in one of the chairs and gestured to the other one. The shop lamp on the floor cast an upward-pointing light making the Russian's face seem ghoulish.

"Sit, Wylie. Let's talk." He gave Conklin a friendly smile.

Conklin took the chair. His exhaustion caused him to slump a little. Karolovsky handed him another bottle of water. Conklin stared at it suspiciously.

"No. Is okay. No PEG. See it's unopened."

"Why did you do that?" Conklin's throat felt scratchy.

"What? The shitting? Just a precaution. If you're smart, it will have been completely unnecessary. If you're stupid… well, you'll figure it out."

"Where am I?"

"We're still in Schaffhausen. You can wrap this up and can go back to Denise in a couple of hours."

Conklin took the bottle of water and sipped it slowly. "What kind of place is this?"

"Oh, you like it? I'm quite proud of it, you know. I followed you from Atlanta so I've been here about as long as you have. Plenty of time to get things ready. Did you spot me? I tried to be careful. But we I knew this day would come so the first thing I did was find a place like this. It's a big warehouse. Nobody was using. I rented it dirt cheap and started building my little room. The neighborhood is real quiet. A lot of empty buildings. Places just like this. Nobody comes here, but you never know. Somebody might wander by. See a light. Hear a noise.

"So I went to the nearest, what do they call it here? FX Ruch AG. Bought some two by fours, plywood and screws. Also bought some mover's blankets. And there you have it. A little room! Framed and covered with plywood with the blankets tacked on to keep someone from seeing light and hearing noise. I built it next to the bathroom you've become so familiar with.

"No. It's not escape proof. It's not as sophisticated as some facilities I have worked in, but I don't think we'll need it for long. I know a smart guy like you would figure out how to get out, so let me tell you a few things. I've got nothing else to do and as soon as we work something out, you go back to Denise at the clinic and I get out of your hair. Otherwise, I'm just outside this little room. And I'm not going to let you go until we have something worked out."

"What do you want?"

"Not smart, Wylie. Don't pretend you don't know what we want."

Conklin nodded. "How much?"

Karolovsky smiled. "That's more like it. I knew you're a smart guy. Well, we want it all. It's as simple as that." He sat back in his chair and folded his arms.

Conklin shook his head. "What shall I call you?"

Karolovsky thought for a moment. "Do you know 'From Russia with Love?'"

"The James Bond film?"

"And book. The villain's nickname was 'Red.' The character is really an Irishman, which I am not but it's okay to call me 'Red.'"

"Okay, Red. You say all of it but you don't really know what 'all' means, right?"

"Oh, but I do. You see, all means all. My boss…"

"Vladoseev."

"Look, Wylie. My best wish is that you go to your little woman in a few hours. You need to go back to her quickly, right?" Karolovsky gave him a wink. "Names can be dangerous. He's my boss and I call him Boss. Got it?"

Conklin nodded. "I guess we are all something we're not."

"Exactly, so when I said all of it, I guess we both have to accept that there's really a number. You know what it is. It is when the boss says that's enough. He will know. That's what we want and if you think you can negotiate, we're done talking. Okay?"

"Sure, Red. But I need to explain something. Vlad… your boss thinks I have something of his. The federal agents think so too and that's why they put me and Denise up in this fancy clinic and posted guards while she goes through her treatment.

"But I'll tell you what I told them. I don't have it any more. Before I got arrested, I scattered it across a hundred banks in a hundred countries. I didn't keep the account numbers. They were on my computer and the feds trampled all over the records. They stuck me in hiding for…"

Karolovsky's fist smashed into his cheek hard enough to knock him backwards. His folding chair folded under him and he landed on his over-used anus.

Conklin felt the back of his head hit the floor but he was amazed how painless the punch had been. He blinked and stared up at Karolovsky's face leaning over him and smiling.

"Wylie, I went to school in Russia and learned how to punch *fignya khudozhnika* like you without doing too much damage. So you can still talk without the bullshit. Hopefully you will appreciate the seriousness of our discussion."

Karolovsky yanked Conklin's collar up and used his other hand to reset the folding chair.

"We try this again." He kept a firm grasp of Conklin's collar and looked in his face. "Wylie. There is only one thing you can say before we move to plan B. You must say, 'Yes, of course, Mr. Red. I will gladly give your boss everything.' Then I bring in a computer and you start giving. If you have anything else to say you better wait until you are done before you share it with us. Okay?"

He let go of Conklin's collar and took his seat in the other folding chair.

Conklin shrugged. "I can't." He lowered his head.

Karolovsky sighed. "Wrong answer, Wylie."

He produced another syringe and jabbed it into Conklin's arm. In seconds blackness erased the glare of the shop lamp.

Chapter 37

From the journal of Brendan Macbean:

The days that followed watching the Ray Suffield interview settled into an uneventful routine. Bettye was held captive inside the part of the clinic where I wasn't allowed so I most of my time in the clinic's library. St. Agatha's allowed Daniel Conklin to be in Denise's room and he frequently spent the entire day somewhere else.

The library was quiet with just myself, so it was easy to lapse into woolgathering. After the sandwich incident I feared Dr. Baurele would bustle in and find me napping. When Conklin was here he dominated the computer, but with him gone, I could use it.

I sat at the computer and the monitor came alive. I stared at the screen. Apparently someone had recently reviewed St. Agatha's previous patients' history because the records of one Glenda Klappenfelter were displayed. I immediately felt guilty for accidently poking into someone's life. This was supposed to be doctor-patient confidential. Conklin appeared to have access to the clinics secrets. He must have been signed in when he left.

I swallowed my misgivings about voyeurism and scanned the summary of Glenda Klappenfelter's fight for life. She had checked into St. Agatha's about fifteen months ago, at a time when her doctors had declared her terminal and no further treatment recommended. She had had malignancies in her lungs and liver. Dr. Friedkin's treatments had cleared those tumors, and she spent a blissful three weeks as a restored, healthy woman. She and her husband, Sebbi went out to dinner, went on picnics by the Rhine. They even took a day long boat excursion to Kreuzlingen. A photo showed Glenda and Sebbi laughing and hugging each other.

Three carefree weeks of health before her tumors came back. There was a lot of term-laden description of how her cancer mutated the enzyme that generates blood vessels which I knew about but didn't understand. What I did understand is Dr. Friedkin's treatment only went so far. The cancer always came back.

And so Glenda Klappenfelter spent ten days of increasing pain and debilitation before she died, her malignancies growing at an astonishing rate with nothing to hold them in check.

The horrid truth about what I was doing here pelted me like a lead hailstorm. This is where Bettye was right now. Dr. Friedkin was shrinking her tumors so we could go on a picnic. And then she'd spend her declining days in St. Agatha's death chamber. Except her body wanted to live and so did she and so did I. At the end of Mrs. Klappenfelter's life they were injecting her with massive amounts of morphine to fight the pain. She had gone to sleep with a cannula over her nose and mouth so they could pump enough oxygen into her to keep her alive for one more breath, even as her lungs worked overtime like a sprinter's lungs trying to finish a race. And it was not enough. Her days shrunk to hours then minutes, and in her last seconds, according to Sebbi's comments, she managed to squeeze his hand. When that pressure went away, Glenda Klappenfelter, a woman loved by her family, was gone.

The screen I was reading went hazy contrasting my own thoughts which became crystal clear like reading the message on a magic 8-ball. Is that what my next few weeks would be like?

The icosahedral die floated up through inky liquid with its enigmatic message, "It is decidedly so."

In front of me, the computer screen went blank and a message displayed: Sitzungszeitlimit."

I moved the mouse and hit keys but it kept asking me for a password. I didn't have one so I headed to Dr. Bauerle's office. I had a million questions to ask and I hoped by the time I arrived, the chaos in my head had cleared.

As I left the library, I saw Daniel Conklin burst through the clinic's doors. He gave me a look of complete fury. I immediately knew I had been caught reading confidential files and he was rushing to chasten me.

I gave him a kid in the cookie jar grin but he whizzed by me, his face still dark as a thunderstorm and headed out the front door. At the glass door entrance, I saw the black Mercedes heading down the driveway scattering leaves across the asphalt.

Geez, I thought, sorry, Dan. Obviously he hadn't charged out of here because I was poking around in the medical records. He drove off in a huff of unknown origin but it didn't take a genius to figure it out. What bothered Conklin was the same thing that bothered me.

I turned around and headed to Bauerle's office. When I arrived, she was bent over her desk, head in hands, elbows on the blotter. She raised her face to me. I had never seen her without her glasses. Her stunning beauty was marred by smeared makeup and tears streaming down her face.

From deep within me I suddenly felt enormous sympathy for Dr. Birgit Bauerle. An endless parade of tragic figures funeral-marched through St. Agatha's. She and Dr. Friedkin tried to help these heroic women and supportive husbands, boyfriends and significant others, but the end was always the same. From time to time, one of their patients must touch her more deeply than the others. The need to stay aloof was paramount but so was human compassion. She tries to steel herself against liking them, loving them, knowing the tragedy that's coming, the return of their wife's pain, her suffering and ultimate death. Another grieving husband marches numbly off into his own quiet desperation, followed by the arrival of another couple, sick but full of hope that the doctors of St. Agatha,s can make them like they were before cancer, alive, happy and full of joy. But all Bauerle can offer is the chance to say goodbye and to feel a few last moments of happiness.

How can Bauerle not feel for them? Without knowing what I was doing I went behind her desk and bent over her, putting my arm around her shoulder, patting her hair. She partly turned toward me and wrapped her long arms around my waist, buried her face in my shirt and wept for how many thousands of women.

I don't know how long we remained like that. I felt awkward and helpless against her waves of grief. Dr. Bauerle never shed tears for her patients. Not in public, anyway, but bravely she had tried to save every one. And after all those courageous battles, all losses, life was setting her up for the most brutal defeat of all.

I could feel her heat against me, her wet and hot face. Against the onslaught of love she had no defense, and Bauerle, the woman, had fallen in love with Daniel Conklin. She couldn't completely know Daniel and Denise's story, but something about them had touched her. And about him. Dr. Bauerle loved him. There could be no doubt. I could feel it in her heart which was now beating hard against mine. She was fighting with her last ounce of strength to save the woman who, if she lived, would take away the man she loves.

Her sorrow did have its limits and she pulled her face away from my tear-stained shirt, looking up at me with sad, red eyes.

"Mr. Macbean," she gasped. "Sorry you have to see me like this." She smiled thinly, not deep enough to show the dimples, but at that moment she was the most beautiful woman I had ever hugged.

"It's okay, Bauerle. I don't know how you do it." As usual, in a crisis my wit had abandoned me.

She nodded and wiped her eyes on a tissue. I had a flash thought that they must use a lot of tissues around here. She found her glasses, put them on and became Dr. Bauerle again.

She took a deep breath. "You came in here for a reason. How can I help you?"

"Dr. Bauerle, I think whatever it was I came in here for can wait."

I left her office and stood for a moment in the corridor. To my left was the library and front entrance to the clinic. To my right were the doors marked, "Nur Zugelassen."

On impulse I turned right, pushed the double doors open and entered the inner sanctum of St. Agatha's.

I don't know what I expected. I had been in hospitals before and I've been in churches. St. Agatha's Clinic had originally been a church. The hallway before me looked like the typical administrative part of a church, vinyl floor, smooth institutional walls, doors to rooms on both sides and fluorescent lights in the ceiling. Staff bustled by completely ignoring me. I walked slowly down the hall hoping to not ruffle anyone's feathers.

The rooms I passed were set up like hospital rooms but empty and dark with lonely looking beds perfectly made with tight white sheets wrapped around them. I finally found a room with a patient quietly reposing atop the slightly inclined bed. I paused in the doorway, my heart pounding. Multiple IV's snaked into the patient's arm. Her hand rested on the bed but nervous fingers tapped lightly against the sheet. The patient's head turned toward me and she smiled a thin, pain stretched smile.

Not Bettye but Denise.

"Brendan. Come in. Where's Wylie, I mean Daniel?" Her voice rasped like she had a sore throat. Nervously I walked to the bed and stretched out my hand to touch hers.

"Wait!" she warned with an urgent hiss.

Too late. As soon as I touched the cool skin of her hand an electric spark shot between us like a flashbulb had gone off in the darkened room. I jerked my hand back.

Denise smiled. "I know. It's worse than a carpet shock. When Daniel first came to see me during a treatment, he made the mistake of trying to kiss me. Lips are really sensitive."

It felt closer to being electrocuted than a carpet shock. I shook my hand to clear the tingle that lingered there and fully expected to see first degree burns on my finger tip.

"It has something to do with what they're pumping in my arms." She glanced at the multiple IV's in her forearms. "Where's uh, Daniel?" she repeated.

"Denise, I don't know. A while ago he left in the Mercedes."

She gave me a look. "You know who he is, don't you. I can't stop calling him Wylie."

I nodded. "He's Daniel. Wylie died four years ago. That's the way it has to be."

The expression on her face became very grave. "But you're a reporter. This is the biggest story of your life."

"I was a reporter." And for some unknown reason my eyes spurted tears. Denise watched me as I moved to the table by her bed and pulled a tissue. Note to self: Remind Bauerle to order more… this ain't over yet.

She raised her hand about an inch, dragging cables and tubes. She let it settle again on the white sheet.

"It must be hard to give up," she said. "Something you love so much."

I nodded but said nothing.

"Denise, how are you?"

She looked down at the white sheet pulled across her flat chest. "Not good."

I tried to take a deep breath but my lungs wouldn't cooperate.

She raised her eyes. "I had pains last night. Headaches. Wylie's gone to check with Bauerle. When you came in I thought it was him coming back with…"

And I had seen him leave with a thunderous look on his face. He had run outside and sped off in the Mercedes like a hellhound was on his trail. And Bauerle had been in tears when I went in.

Unfortunately, Denise read my face like a billboard. I saw her lips pull into a straight line and she squared her chin. She glanced away… looked back at me.

She said in a whisper, "I guess we all have to go sometime."

Tears spilled out her eyes like they were pumped by her heart.

I said nothing. I knew nothing.

"You probably have your own conclusions." Her lips trembled.

"Denise, I don't know anything. I didn't ask Bauerle. She wouldn't tell me anything if I had."

She nodded and looked at the far wall.

I don't remember ever feeling more useless than I did at that moment. I now know why the doors are marked "Nur Zugelassen," "Only Approved." I had barged in here where I wasn't approved.

"I'll go and see if Daniel has returned."

Denise didn't move. She stared away from me, thinking her own thoughts. I left the room and headed back through the double doors.

I ran by Bauerle's office, which was empty, to the clinic's front doors. I looked out and saw the black Mercedes parked again in its usual spot, across from the entrance. Good, I thought. Conklin's back. He needed to go straight to Denise. I saw motion to my right. A delivery truck was leaving through St. Agatha's front gate.

I opened the front door and walked across the drive-through entrance. The Mercedes was empty. I looked around. No one in sight. I put my hand on the car's hood. Hot. Conklin had just pulled up, but where was he? He had not come through the front doors.

I looked inside the car. The keys were still in the ignition and Conklin's iPhone was on the seat. I picked it up and looked at the screen. The screen was black but came to life as soon as I touched it. It showed the same GPS screen Conklin had shown me a few days ago. The green numbers on the screen were the GPS numbers for US Federal agents parked in their usual spots outside the gate. There was a red number inching away from St. Agatha's location, presumably the delivery truck I had seen leaving through the clinic's gate.

But where was Daniel?

I walked back to the library with my heart pounding and sat down at the desk. Conklin's GPS app now showed the red number snaking along Gabenstrasse, a nearby street. I touched the red number and it highlighted on the screen. I quickly wrote it down. A dropdown menu offered an "info" button. The red number belonged to the local DHL delivery fleet. I seemed to remember it was yellow and red. Okay, nothing suspicious there. I had seen DHL trucks come to the clinic. Here in Schaffhausen they were as common as UPS or FedEx trucks back in the US.

I slipped Conklin's phone into my pants pocket and headed back to Dr. Bauerle's office.

Chapter 38

The sound of a woman's screams summoned Daniel Conklin out of a well of unconsciousness. Her screams grew louder.

He opened his eyes slowly trying to dispel the effects of whatever Karolovsky had used to drug him. He lay on a bed with his torso elevated. Straps restrained his arms and legs. A firm pillow supported his head and a harness across his forehead prevented all but minimal movement. He felt like he was glued to the mattress. There was a large HD TV in front of him and the picture showed a woman strapped to a hospital bed, similar to how he was restrained, except her head wasn't elevated.

She was completely naked. Even her pubic hair had been shaved. The videographer had gone to ultimate effort with camera position, lighting and acute focus, to produce a finely textured, high definition presentation. The camera moved across her body showing every close-up detail of how they had prepared her. Wires ran across her pink skin with contacts taped at her feet, legs, crotch, abdomen, chest and around her head. Alligator clips pinched her nipples. Wires ran into the corners of her mouth and into her nostrils. Her body was slim with good muscle tone and she might have been attractive except an expression of abject terror contorted her face into a mask of animal fear.

Conklin could move his eyes, and he looked down at his own body. He too was naked. Wires ran across his body to taped contacts, like an EKG. Just like the woman on the television. Alligator clips pinched his nipples and he slowly became aware of the painful compression. Wires also ran into the corner of his mouth and into his nostrils. He felt wires around his penis and scrotum.

A monstrous noise startled him: the sudden hum of a large transformer creating a massive jolt of electricity. The woman bucked and quivered on the bed, arms and legs whipping uncontrollably within the range allowed by her restraints. She screamed and writhed, panted and screamed again. His own body jerked and it took a moment for him to realize he had not actually been subjected to the electricity that surged through the woman's body.

But he was being forced to watch.

Another jolt came and more screams from the woman. He closed his eyes and the sound intensified. Someone turned the volume up to a painful level. It felt like the speakers were right next to his ears. The noise physically pounded his eardrums, so overwhelming the actual sound distorted to an insane thunderous nightmare. He opened his eyes and the volume was lowered. Apparently Karolovsky wanted him to keep his eyes open.

The electricity surged again and the woman screamed. Sweat streamed across her skin and spittle spewed from her wired mouth. How long this went on, he couldn't tell. Hours at least. No one could endure such levels of pain and live or even remain conscious. Her intense shrieking eventually wore out her vocal cords and all she could utter was a hoarse guttural roar.

Obviously they rested her between bouts of torture, but the rest periods had been edited out. The scene cuts were obvious and each new scene began with the woman pleading for the torture to stop, begging in a language he didn't know, tears streaming down her face, her voice distorted by her worn out larynx and the wires in her mouth. He nearly lost his mind watching the wretched woman's unendurable agony. No one asked her any questions. No information was being sought. Her torture was apparently solely for his review.

His turn was coming.

It felt like an entire day passed with nothing but the gigantic, grotesque, explosive buzz of the transformer, the screams of the woman, her body jerking, the tearful pleading, over and over again. By now he knew each scene by heart. He knew when the episode of torture ended only to be rewound for him to watch again, her voice renewed and strong, as it was in the beginning, and shredded down over time to the grotesque croaking. Conklin never got used to it. In fact each repetition seemed to hurt him worse, a worse shredding of his soul and sanity than before. His body revolted but there was nothing in his stomach to vomit or in his bowels to expel. No one could deserve such a punishment. It tore his heart up to see another human being treated like this. What kind of monster did this? What kind of monster played the video over and over again? What were they going to do to him?

At the moment that he thought he would die if he saw it one more time, the video screen darkened and the speakers went silent. Ten minutes of silence and darkness and the lights came on. Conklin felt cold and clammy all over as new moving air evaporated his sweat. Tears wetted his face and his chest heaved for air and his heart felt like heavy stones dropped on a steel drum.

Karolovsky came on the speakers. "Wylie, how'd you like your little pay-for-view?"

Silence held the air for a full minute. Conklin said nothing.

"Well, you viewed it. Now it is time to pay. As you may be aware, I have a camera on you and there's a microphone so I can hear you, if you choose to speak. Since you'll do more screaming than talking, I'll turn down my volume. I really don't like a man's screaming. Naked women, that's something else, ha ha!" Karolovsky's laughter sounded a little forced.

Conklin struggled to say something, wires in his mouth moving with his lips. "How da you ess-pect me to talg wif dees wirez in my mouf?"

"Oh, I don't really. You had your chance to talk and I didn't like what you said. Now is the time for persuasion. I have the same machine like they used on the woman. It's an East German design. You remember East Germany? It's called it a *Kiska Tviker*. Well, that's the Russian name for it. The Germans had another name. The Soviets improved it. They studied all the nerve places, precisely where to put the contacts and the frequency of the jolts. The Soviets blew their chances at world domination before I came on the scene but I learned it when I worked for the Russians. The FSB, the Russian Security Police. They made many videos like that. Some of those guys really get off on this stuff. They'd take them home to watch but I never understood that kind of thing. When I left Russia, I kept this disk and another one even badder than that. Would you like to see that one?"

Conklin shook his head. He couldn't imagine a worse one.

"Okay. There are seven areas of the body that we've found are really effective for electrically stimulated pain. This device randomly selects the area, intensity and duration. You see, we don't want you to anticipate where it's going to hit you. We don't want you to know what to expect. Sometimes it will go round robin, sometimes the same area over and over again. The device also selects random time limits for rest. Rest is very important. We don't want you to die but we do want you to fear dying. You see, fear is the most effective component. That's why we showed you the video. To scare you.

"Were you scared, Wylie?"

Conklin closed his eyes.

Karolovsky continued. "You may close your eyes now. They won't stay closed, of course. But you can close them for now. We'll do this first session for just twenty minutes. I'll go out and get a coffee. Like I said, I really don't like this and you don't look as good naked as that girl. The machine is completely automatic. You'll be done by the time I return.

"Wylie, are you paying attention?"

Conklin nodded and closed his eyes.

"Good. When I come back, I'm going to ask you the same question. If you're smart you'll answer 'yes' and we'll do our little giving session. Then we all go home for supper."

Conklin heard a click.

"There, I've started it. In a few minutes, the machine will start its *kiska nastroyki* although you're more of a *chlen* than a *kiska*."

The speakers went silent.

Conklin forced his muscles to relax and ordered his mind silent. He took deep drafts of air, filling his lungs, pausing and letting the breaths out slowly. He counted backwards, reciting mentally, *relax and go deeper*, like a chant. He eased the tension out of his body and let the fear in his mind melt like a ball of ice seeping through a sieve.

A minute passed and another.

It hit him in his legs, first. He arched his back and tried to roll away from the pain, like the strike of a snake, reflexive and retaliatory. The straps across his chest held his body to the mattress. He struggled to put down the pain, and scolded himself for such a show of weakness. The next blast charged like a fearsome beast roaring through a long tunnel but he was already far ahead, entering the cooling, soothing darkness. Before him he saw a light. He was almost there.

He emerged on the road to Sharbot Lake at a point where rounding a curve showed the first glimpse at the lake, shining sun glinting off water. As a boy, it was the most exciting point of the journey. In just a few miles he could run down the hill to the dock which reached out over the quiet blue waters. He could look down into the lake and see small fish. He could hear bullfrogs groan, the haunting cry of the loons across the lake. His knees buckled and his legs jerked and pain shot from his ankles like a giant machine was tearing off his feet. He clenched his teeth and put the pain away. And most of it went away, all but an oscillating tingle, manageable but annoying.

He skipped ahead to the rutted dirt road that led to the cabin. Around the bend the red shingled roof came into view and he saw a white wisp of smoke drifting lazily out of the stovepipe. Another skip and he saw Fletcher sitting on the porch with a double barreled shotgun across his lap.

Fletcher's deep brown eyes pierced his own. He nodded and shifted the shotgun slightly.

"Got plenty of double-ought. And your dad's inside with his old

Browning."

"Thanks, Fletcher. I don't think they'll come here."

"Well, if they do, they'll regret it."

He went inside and saw his dad at the table poking shells into a worn looking Browning shotgun. Dad looked up and smiled a wicked grin.

"Wylie, you really poked the wasp's nest this time, didn't you boy."

"Dad, I don't think you'll need the Browning."

"Remember when the porcupines were chewing on the posts?" His dad's smile cheered him.

Wylie nodded. The incident happened when Wylie was ten years old. They were on a "men-only" fishing trip. One quiet night they woke up with a startling noise vibrating the cabin. It sounded like freight trains chugging up a hill, except the sound made the cabin shake. They both ran outside with flashlights and saw several porcupines gnawing away at the thick vertical pine logs that supported the cabin on the hillside. His dad had run inside and returned with the Browning. The porcupines had not shown the least alarm at being discovered by the humans, whose house they were destroying.

That turned out to be a huge error for the porcupines.

Bam! Bam! Bam! Three dead porcupines. The remaining prickle-pig stopped gnawing long enough to catch the forth blast of the Browning.

Bam!

The next day, Fletcher had collected the porcupines and skinned them. And ate them. Fletcher offered Wylie and his dad a pot of the stew which they politely declined.

"Did you ever ask Fletcher how he skinned those porcupines?" Wylie asked. They both chuckled.

Wylie clutched his groin and doubled over in pain. The shriek of the transformer broke in from the other place, grinding like a locomotive's brakes. Electro-shock sawed through his genitals. His scream drowned out all sound.

Except his dad's gentle voice persisted after the transformer hum subsided. "Put it away, son. You can do it. It's mostly fear, anyway."

Gasping for breath, Wylie said, "That's easy... uh, uh, ...for you to say, Dad. It's not your balls in the sling."

His dad put the shotgun down on the table. He put a gentle arm around Wylie's shoulders and guided him over to the leather recliner in front of the fireplace. He lay Wylie down in the soft, worn leather like he was a ten year boy again. His father reclined the recliner and laid a cotton blanket over him.

"Close your eyes, son. Nothing can harm you now."

Chapter 39

From the journal of Brendan Macbean:

Dr. Bauerle and I searched all over the hospital without finding Daniel Conklin. Bauerle knew nothing of Daniel Conklin's history, the surveillance he was under or of the competition between US federal agents and Russian mobsters for him and she knew nothing about the money. But she knew where he might be inside the clinic. We searched and didn't find him.

At that point it was hard to avoid the conclusion he had finally been abducted by Karolovsky. It was time to call out the troops.

I walked down the driveway and out the gate of the grounds of St. Agatha's. I pulled out Conklin's smart phone and glanced at the screen. To my right a Volkswagen Caddy was parked on the side of the road. Two men sat in the front seat. To my left was another similar vehicle with two more men. Conklin's phone showed these two cars as green numbers on the screen. Green for the federal agents. Green for safe.

I headed toward the nearest one on my right. The driver noted my approach and turned his head to talk to his passenger. They exchanged comments. The driver started the car and looked like he was about to pull away from the curb. I walked to the front and positioned myself with my shins against the bumper.

The driver made an angry, "Get away!" motion with his hands.

I pointed to the driver window and circled my hand, like "Roll it down." The driver gave me a look of pure annoyance but he did roll down the window. I went over to the driver's side. The engine was still running. He could have pulled away but didn't.

"They snatched Daniel Conklin." I said.

"Kein Englisch!" the driver said angrily.

"Bullshit. You and your asshole buddies in that other car..." I pointed up the street. "You let Karolovsky take Daniel Conklin. He's gone. That DSL truck that left thirty minutes ago... Karolovsky and Conklin were in that truck."

He gave me a look of complete surprise. In perfect American English he said, "What? Are you sure?"

"Yes. He's gone. Put out a dragnet or whatever you guys do and go get that DSL truck. Here's the GPS fleet tracking number." I gave them the number.

"And have your boss, Bentley, call me."

"I don't know any Bentley," he said.

I leaned my head into the window and got right in his face. "Look you idiot. You have to do a better job in the next five minutes than you did in the last hour. You get this very clear. I want Bentley. Now!"

I'm not a very intimidating person but the man jerked back when I yelled a few inches from his face. "You tell your boss to have Bentley call me and if he doesn't get it, tell him to tell his boss. If I don't hear from Bentley in fifteen minutes, I'm calling the Schaffhausen police. After that your career won't be worth last week's strudel."

I turned and sprinted back to St. Agatha's. I waited in the library a full thirty minutes. Neither my cell nor Conklin's rang. I wasn't sure how much the feds knew about Conklin's gambit of new phone versus old phone. I knew they could track his whereabouts on his phone, but I had his new phone.

I took Conklin's phone from my pants pocket. The GPS program was lit up. The green lights of the federal cars had vanished. An occasional red number scrolled across the screen as an unidentified GPS tracked vehicle crossed through the area depicted on the screen. I figured out how to expand the view, kind of like panning in and out, but I was afraid to do too much exploration on this phone. Conklin may have rigged it with a password and I didn't want the phone to become unusable.

I went back to the black Mercedes and drove it to Haus Von Muller. Not being a person of their interest, the federal agents did not provide an escort.

But they had already been there. Gert was sitting in the foyer with his head in his hands. His body slumped.

"Gert. What's wrong?"

His head moved slowly. When he faced me I could see he had been crying.

"They came in here like Nazis. No respect for my house. They tore up his room. Took everything."

"Who did this?"

"Americans. Your people. They came back. Last month. Dr. Friedkin asked me to let these people in. I know they installed listening devices and cameras. Herr Conklin was a very special person. I agree as a favor to Dr. Friedkin. Then, an hour ago they came back like Nazis. Two of them held me down while others destroyed my house."

"Did you call the police?"

He shook his head. "They acted like they were the police. They were gone before I knew it. Left me on the floor."

"Have you seen Mr. Conklin?"

"No. I wish I had never seen him. Or you. He's involved in something. I should have known. I was suspicious. People following him and someone breaks into your room. The peace of my house is gone. They can do anything to my house and I can do nothing about it."

I left him sitting in the chair and ran upstairs. Down and feathers drifted out of Conklin's room like snowflakes. I stood in the doorway and surveyed the damage.

Conklin's room had been totally trashed. Everything seemed to have been turned over, torn up and strewn about. The mattress had been pulled off the bed and apparently a down comforter had been slashed and searched. Every drawer had been taken out of every chest, the contents strewn and left lying on the floor. The antique desk had been overturned. The closet was empty. Even the art had been taken off the wall and left scattered on the floor like twigs and leaves.

If Conklin had a computer, it was gone.

I ran to my room. The door was open, but apparently the goon squad left my stuff untouched. My suitcase was still sitting on the bed table and looked like it had not been opened. My leather briefcase was on the desk and the laptop was still resting on the leather bound blotter.

That's when my cell phone rang. It was Bentley

"I thought I told you to go home." His voice was casual, like before.

"I don't do well with orders. Where's Conklin?"

"We don't know."

"You haven't tracked down the DHL number I gave your boys?"

"DHL says that truck is at their maintenance facility. It hasn't moved in a week."

"Are you sure?"

"Maybe you got the number wrong. What, did you see it leaving?"

"Bentley, I got the number right. It was at St. Agatha's a couple of hours ago."

"Not so, Macbean. DHL says it's been in the shop for a week. You got the number wrong."

"It's the right number. Maybe they don't track the trucks when they're in the shop."

Silence for a moment while he pondered that.

"Look, Bentley, I know about Karolovsky."

Bentley took a deep breath. "You know way too much. Are you smart enough to stay clear? That man is a monster. He'll shred you like a cotton ball."

"Boll," I corrected him.

"He's Vladoseev's enforcer. He kills and tortures people for him. I guess there's no way I can send you home. You're staying for Bettye. Focus on her. Let me handle Karolovsky."

"But you don't know where he is. How are you going to handle him? Why would Karolovsky torture him?"

"Macbean, you know why. You and Conklin buddied up. I told you not to get involved but you did anyway. You dug it out of Conklin, who he is and what he's got. Big story in that isn't there?"

"There's no story, Bentley. Daniel Conklin is all there is. Denise is getting worse and he needs to be at her side. That's all there is."

"I can't really trust you, Macbean," Bentley said.

"That means nothing to me, Bentley. But now you got to find him before Karolovsky kills him."

"He won't kill him, but what Karolovsky does is worse."

"Bentley, we have to rescue him."

"I keep telling you, Macbean, we don't know where he is."

Chapter 40

"Are you are doing it right?" Vladoseev's voice notched up in timber, a sure sign his stress level was surging. "It's been a long time since you used the *Kiska Tviker*."

Karolovsky sighed. "I can do this in my sleep. I've never seen anyone who can take it."

"You watched him?"

"No. I went out for coffee. No need to stay here while it's operating. They jerk and scream and scream and jerk. I start asking questions when it's over. Twenty minutes most people are eager to talk by then. I let them calm down a little. I wait until the shakes are gone. So I come back from Starbucks and he's sleeping like a baby."

"He's sleeping?" Vladoseev voice rose even higher. "How can he sleep?"

"He was sleeping, Boss. Like he never got tweaked. But he did. He was covered in sweat and his muscles were jerking. Yeah, he slept through the whole thing. I even watched the video and he jerked with each jolt. But there was no screaming. It was weird like he moaned a little. I've never seen anything like this."

Vladoseev was silent for a full minute. "And he's still sleeping?"

"No, but I had a hell of a time waking him up. I slapped him, punched him. I even thought of pouring my coffee on him, but the damn Starbucks is so hot, it would scald him. I always get a little ice so I can cool it down."

"I don't give *der'mo* about your fucking coffee!" Vladoseev shouted.

"Please, Boss. Don't have a stroke. I used the ice to wake him. He came to just like he was trying out one of those sleep number beds. The fucker actually yawned at me with wires in his mouth. He bit his tongue during the session so he spit out some blood."

"Please, Koyla. When do I get my money? Do you have to go through it like you're blogging?"

"Boss, he told me to go fuck myself."

"What?"

"His voice was still sleepy. I asked him if he was ready to do some fund transfers now and he told me, 'No, I don't think so.' Like he's got nothing to worry about, 'No, you don't think so?' I ask him. And he looked at me right in the eye and said, 'No, like in, go fuck yourself, Comrade Red, you big fucking bully.'

"I'm so pissed I slap the shit out of his grinning face."

"He's grinning at you after the *Kiska Tviker?* How can he do this?"

Karolovsky shook his head but knew his boss couldn't see him. "Never have I seen anyone do this. It's not like his body isn't jerking with pain. I saw the video. He was hurting and moaning but when it stopped, he slept. And snored. It's like..." Karolovsky fumbled for the right word. "It's like he wasn't there inside his body. It hurt him, but he did not feel it. I don't know."

Vladoseev was silent for another minute. "So, what do we do, Kolya?"

"Well, we got to do it again but I can't just yet. If you tweak them too much it kills them. They can have a seizure. His body needs to rest for an hour or so. The monitor will tell me when I can tweak him again."

"Is he awake now?" Vladoseev asked.

"Maybe. He's in the room. Let me look. No, the camera shows him sleeping. Hang on a second."

Karolovsky turned on the microphone in front of him. "Wylie, are you awake?"

There was no reaction. "Wylie, I can turn the volume up a little if you're having trouble hearing me. He cranked the amplifier a notch.

"ARE YOU AWAKE, MOTHER FUCKER!"

Conklin recoiled. He opened his eyes and looked around for the camera.

"I'm awake. What do you want?"

Karolovsky sighed and turned off the mike. "Boss, he's awake."

"Can you put me on the speaker?"

"Yes, Boss." Karolovsky flipped a switch.

Vladoseev spoke like he was addressing a child. "Wylie, can you hear me?"

"Yes, I can hear. Will you please turn down the volume? I'm not deaf but I will be if you don't turn it down."

Karolovsky turned it down.

"Is that better?" Vladoseev's voice was almost soothing. "Wylie, we don't like to use these methods."

"That makes two of us."

"But we will not stop just because you seem to have put up with it the first time. We could do this for days. The toughest people in the world don't last that long. Most are eager to tell us anything we wanted."

Conklin seemed to consider this. "Okay, Vladoseev... Or do I call you Boss Red?"

"No names. I know who you are and that's all that counts. In a little while I will ask my friend to give you another session with the pussy tweaker. A longer and more intense session. If you give us what we want we will stop."

"Good. That's what I want. Stop it."

"When we get what we want."

"You won't get it."

"I have been gentle with you so far. We'll go to Denise. That place doesn't look too difficult to get into. We got you, didn't we? We'll bring her here. Make her watch. Maybe she'd like to try out the tweaker herself? She actually has a *kiska* to tweak and I hear it's much more effective on a woman. Would you like to watch her *kiska* being *prisposoblennymi*?"

Conklin took a deep breath. "Vladoseev, you really are a stupid bastard."

Vladoseev's voice spat back. "Now you are being stupid. And disrespectful."

"I won't give you what you want. Denise is going to die, and you are not going to touch her. But I will give you something?"

"What? What will you give?"

"Some advice. You can torture me all you want. I can't stop you. We're all going to die, but of all the people in this little drama, you have the most to lose, because..." Conklin smiled. "...you have the most to live for.

"Bentley is looking for me and it won't be long before he finds me. He wants the same thing you want. Bentley would do a lot of shitty things to get results, but Bentley is bound by a code. Bentley would die for his country if it came to that. Not you. Not for a second. You got money and power but no code. There's nothing you'd die for.

"I knew Karolovsky was out there watching me, waiting for me. I didn't waste my time. I found you. I know you live in the Barclays hotel in Manhattan. You hardly ever leave the place. I found where you keep most of your loot. Bank accounts. Brokers. Securities. Lots of accounts. I've hacked into some of these accounts and made a few changes on your behalf. And donations. You have been very generous lately, giving to charities, especially breast cancer research. But you can be even more generous. And this can go on until you can't afford to live in the Barclays anymore. Until you can't even afford to pay this red-headed goon. Five minutes after this call, you'll be logging onto your accounts to see if I'm bluffing. And you will see how generous you've been. And guess what? It's all automatic. I don't have to do a thing. You're going to lose about a hundred thousand a day until I get to a computer and stop it." Daniel Conklin's head movement was restricted but his eyes stared directly into the video camera. "Until you beg me to stop it. So don't talk about bringing Denise here."

Conklin closed his eyes and appeared to go to sleep.

"Turn off the speaker!" Vladoseev screamed.

"Okay, boss. It's off."

The phone line hissed while Vladoseev fumed. Karolovsky knew his boss's moods and said nothing. "Kolya, do him again. Longer and harder. Don't wait. Give him all the juice you can. Nobody talks to me like that. The little *mudak*!"

"Boss, I got to wait until his vitals calm down a little."

"Don't wait. Do him him now. I don't care if it kills him."

Chapter 41

From the journal of Brendan Macbean:

We didn't know where he was. The feds might be tracking his old cell phone, but Bentley said he didn't know where Conklin was. I had his iPhone. I wondered if they had picked up and were tracking Karolovsky's cell phone, but if they could track it they probably would. I concluded the raid on Daniel Conklin's room was a stupid attempt to find evidence where the billions were. The feds would fail.

Bentley must have thought I was small potatoes, unimportant in his big operation. He hadn't tossed my room like he did Conklin's or taken anything.

I booted up my laptop on the desk in my room and waited for the hourglass to go away. The wireless network in Haus Von Muller had been removed, by the feds, presumably. So I had no access to the internet. I did a quick search for nearby available wireless networks through Microsoft's "Connect To" command and found nothing in range.

I packed up and headed for the Mercedes. I slowly drove around Schaffhausen Old Towne, my laptop open on the seat beside me, stopping at likely places, refreshing the "Connect To" screen until I found a link. Bibliothek Agnesenschutte gave off a strong signal but was protected by a password. I made a wild-ass guess and typed in "12345678" and it worked. Funny, this was also the wireless network password at the library in Smyrna, Georgia. Okay, this was my lucky night.

According to the clock on the Mercedes dash it was one minute past midnight. I signed on to my Gmail account and saw something that raised the hair on the back of my neck. A few minutes ago I received an email from dconk231@gmail.com. I opened it and read.

"Brendan, you are receiving this email because I'm gone. For some time now I knew that my capture by Karolovsky was highly likely so I set up some precautions. I figured they would take me somewhere and interrogate me. I need you to find me and bring the cavalry.

"Last month I took some precautions and purchased several new iPhones. The feds might be tracking my old cell phone so I left it at Von Muller Hause on the charger. I've been using the new iPhones one at a time for a few days. Then I drop them in a trash container. The trash gets picked up and hauled somewhere and I fire up a new one. This is a precaution in the event the feds work out the puzzle that I'm using a new phone. All the new iPhones have the app to track the feds you've seen me use from time to time in the Mercedes.

"I've installed an app that uses Google Maps to track GPS signals on my cell phone. I've attached the program to this email. Save it and it will show the location where Karolovsky is keeping me, or at least where my current iPhone is.

"Thank you, good friend. Please hurry."

My heart sank when I read this. His iPhone was on the passenger seat beside me. His foresight in preparing this program would do no good. Still I saved and executed his little program.

The screen connected to Google Maps and showed the location of his cell phone, Munsterplatz 1, 8200 Schaffhausen, which I guessed was the address of the library I parked outside of.

I brooded for a few minutes. I was convinced that Karolovsky had gotten past the federal agents by posing as a DHL delivery man. It was most likely he stole one of their trucks.

The DHL truck had GPS fleet tracking. Its number came up red on Conklin's cell phone program. Bentley said DHL declared the truck had been out of service at their maintenance facility. What if DHL stopped tracking the truck while it was in the shop? The truck's transponder or whatever they used kept sending out signals, but the owner's didn't care where it went when they assumed it wasn't going anywhere. Like when it was in the shop.

A rare flash of brilliance illuminated my brain and I might have smiled if I wasn't so stressed. There was no way Karolovsky could have penetrated a DHL freight depot, a place surrounded by chain-link fences, where all employees had to badge in and out. But would they have the same security at their maintenance facility? Only if they considered stealing an empty DHL truck a likely prospect. Since DHL could easily locate the truck why would anyone do that? Well, one man considered it worth the risk, to use it for a few hours to get past some sleepy and bored US federal agents. Karolovsky could steal the truck and get it back before the DHL mechanics knew it was missing.

So, I had a workable theory how Karolovsky got past the feds, but, where did that leave me?

I looked at my laptop screen. Google Maps indicated I was at Bibliothek Agnesenschutte Munsterplatz 1, 8200 Schaffhausen, the Agnes Schutte Library where I hacked their wireless internet.

I opened a tab and Googled "DHL GPS Fleet Tracking" and received an article about DHL driving down the cost of fuel by installing GPS tracking devices in their trucks, but after scanning the article, I was no closer to finding Conklin.

I killed the tab and went back to studying the program Daniel Conklin had sent me. Like most computer programs, there were menu options on the bar at the top of the screen. I hit the one called "Tools." A drop down menu appeared. One of the selections was called, "Where have they been?"

I clicked on the option and it asked me to enter a tracking number. I fumbled through my pockets to find the paper where I had written down the DHL truck GPS tracking number. Then the program asked me for a range of dates and I selected the last week.

In a second, the program showed a Google Maps screen with a tracery of lines crisscrossing the Cantons of Schaffhausen and Zurich and a list of dozens of addresses. I reran the program with just yesterday's date and, Eureka! The extra lines vanished leaving just four destinations. One was apparently the maintenance facility, which was the first and last entries on the list, presumably where the truck was stolen from and returned. The second was the address to St. Agatha's and the third address was probably where Karolovsky had taken Daniel Conklin.

I clicked on Google Maps for the third destination and asked for driving directions from the library. It was about six kilometers away.

I thought about contacting Bentley but the only phone number was the one Pam Stratton, the FBI agent gave me a lifetime ago. When he had called me the first time, it was on my land line in Atlanta. The last call came from an unknown number. Apparently Bentley had blocked the caller ID information. Big surprise there!

I looked at the driving directions and started the Mercedes. I could do this although my brain was telling me to wait for the cavalry like Daniel Conklin said. But I had no way of contacting them. Maybe they were tracking me, the Mercedes and Conklin's phone. If so, they could follow me in and I half expected them to.

It wouldn't hurt to go check the place out, but to my more reasonable self, that sounded like the most ultra-foolish thing I could do. In a strange city. At night. With a mad Russian who would shred me like a cotton ball, the term used by Bentley since he didn't know the difference between a ball and a boll.

I pulled up to the address on Bahnsteigstrasse a little before one in the morning. It was an abandoned and lonely part of town. Dark and empty buildings, signs saying, "Zu Vermeiten" and numbers to call. The place was ultra quiet. A dark warehouse stood before me, with sectioned windows painted over and covered with metal grates. A single steel door looked like the only entrance to the place. There was absolutely no traffic. So, heart pounding, I left the Mercedes parked at the curb and tried the door, fully expecting the red headed Russian to come bolting out with cotton boll shredders in both hands.

Locked. The door's handle wouldn't even move. I heard a humming sound coming from inside.

Dark as it was, I made my way around to the back. I found a weedy parking lot, empty except for a car, a sort of minivan.

Dim light spilled from warehouse windows. A back door cracked slightly emitted a shaft of yellow light. The deep-throated buzz grew as I approached. I peered in through the crack in the door.

Like peeking into a Hieronymus Bosch painting, what I saw chilled me. The scene was frozen, dim yellow light filtering through a smoky haze, coming from a lighted instrument panel, the horrible, piercing sound of an electric buzz at crazy random intervals, a man reposing in a folding chair, arms across his chest, large headphones clapped to his ears, his head back, face tilted to the ceiling, one foot making tiny taps on the concrete floor like he listened to his favorite rock band while some horrible event went on within the giant box next to him.

The box... large, rectangular, maybe twelve by sixteen feet, eight feet high, covered with quilts like movers use to wrap furniture. An array of cables snaked from the instrument panel, along the floor into the box. Moaning came from the box in conjunction with the hideous electric buzz. Outside the box, scattered about the floor of the warehouse, construction material lay: two by fours, plywood scraps, sawdust, tools, soda cans, cardboard boxes and plastic bottles.

It felt like a full minute before I could move. At any second I expected the man to leap up from his chair and charge me. The man was Karolovsky, I was pretty sure although all I could see of him was the back of his head.

I put my hand on the handle of the door and eased the crack wider. The hinges made a tiny protest but the buzz and the music kept the Russian from taking notice. The door opened a little wider. I slipped inside and stopped. No plan. No idea what I would do or could do against this man who was much larger than me and powerful, well trained and determined. And ruthless.

A step toward him and another. He sat twenty feet away. Another step. My foot collided with something on the floor. I looked down. A piece of two by four about three feet long. I stooped and picked it up, hefted it. Another step. I inched toward him across the debris strewn concrete floor.

I played baseball when I was a kid. Second base. I didn't have enough arm for the outfield or the gun needed for shortstop. I was never a long ball hitter, no doubles to the opposite field, no homeruns. My coach, Mike Florence, once said, if I could keep my glasses on straight, I could be the consummate contact hitter. I could always be counted on to tap one over an infielder or roll a bunt along either base line.

That night I knocked one out of the park.

I stopped about three feet behind the man who was listening to something very compelling on his headphones. I swung, extended my arms and rolled my wrists. The two by four struck the base of his skull and he flew forward, out of the folding chair. His face struck the instrument panel and scraped against the panel's switches, dials and gages. He slithered down to the floor where his body lay inert in a semicircular heap.

I stood there posed like an Albert Pujols baseball card except I was looking down instead of over the fence. Then I remembered to breathe and took several deep ones.

The device in front of me was completely foreign. I couldn't read anything on the dials or riveted placards, but there was a large switch on the left side of the box, orange with obvious implications. I hit the switch and the awful buzzing stopped. The darkened instrument panel took away some of the light but there was still enough to see around the warehouse.

Daniel Conklin was inside the box, and I was going to get him out.

I looked at Karolovsky. He appeared to be out cold but I wasn't counting on him staying that way. I looked around and found the most useful object of modern culture, a roll of duct tape. I also found a bag of cable ties. I used both the duct tape and cable ties to bind his feet. Then I rolled him on his stomach, bent his arms behind his back and secured his wrists. For good measure I wrapped tape across his mouth.

If he came to, I could bean him again with the two by four.

Now the box. I circled it twice. Since I'm not a spy and had no way to determine if it was bobby trapped, but there was no point in being careless. There appeared to be no entrance. Like a mime, I pushed my hands against the sides of the box and worked my way around the perimeter again. It appeared to be a framework of two by fours covered in plywood and wrapped in the mover's quilts.

As I completed the circuit for the third time, I found a place where the quilts gave a little. I pealed them back and found that the plywood was only secured on by a couple of screws. In the dim light I found a power drill with a screwdriver bit in it and removed the screws. I pulled back the plywood sheet.

Inside the box was the ultimate horror. Daniel Conklin lay naked on what looked like a hospital gurney with wires running all over him. It seemed no part of his body was spared of wiring, including his feet, crotch, mouth and nostrils. I could see the gentle rise and fall of his chest, so thankfully he was still alive. His eyes were closed and he lay still.

I put a gentle hand on his shoulder and shook him.

"Daniel. Daniel." No response.

"Daniel, it's me, Brendan. It's okay. I'm here. I didn't bring the cavalry so we need to go as soon as possible."

I could see his breathing deepen. His eyelids fluttered. I started removing his restraints, his hands, legs, torso, head.

His eyes opened. He rolled his head. "Ack... bean." An attempt at a smile but the wires in his mouth and his wretched condition obviously inhibited smiling.

I wasn't sure how to remove the contacts taped to his body, but apparently Conklin did.

His hand shook as he reached into his mouth and pulled out several wires with blood covered silver clamps attached to them. I watched him remove the alligator clips pinching his nipples and the wires attached to his genitals.

Male bonding has its limits.

Once free, he struggled to sit up. I helped him climb down from the bed and he took a couple of staggering steps. Together we made it through the hole in the plywood and emerged into the interior of the warehouse. Conklin looked around like a man leaving prison. His eyes stopped roving when he saw Karolovsky.

"Daniel, I have the Mercedes out front but I have no idea where the front door is or if it's locked. You wait by the back door and I'll go get the car. Is that okay?"

He nodded. I ran out the back door and around the building like a sprinter and pulled the car around back near the rear door. I went back into the warehouse. Conklin was bent over Karolovsky's body. There was something in his hand. As I got closer, I saw it was a syringe.

"Daniel, what are you doing?"

He froze. Slowly he looked at me. His voice was raspy like he had sore throat. "This man is a monster. He won't stop. He won't ever stop.

He's got a whole box of these. Sodium Thiopental. One or two of these will stop him."

I went over and put a hand on his arm. "No. That's not the way. Let Bentley take care of him. We'll tell him where to find this guy."

"Bentley let you come here alone."

We both thought about that.

"Daniel, we're not killers."

Daniel Conklin stared at Karolovsky for a long time. The faint sound of Abba's "Dancing Queen" buzzed from the fallen headphones a few feet away. Conklin nodded and struggled to his feet. With my arm around his shoulders, we made our way to the Mercedes.

Chapter 42

From the journal of Brendan Macbean:

Dark night. Dark, sleepy Swiss town. I did not know the way to St. Agatha's but I knew that's where I had to take Conklin. I knew his phone might give me directions but I'd have to slow down first and figure out how to use it.

He was very weak and obviously dehydrated. He had asked if I had any water and I had nothing to give him. There were no open convenient stores or markets and, naked and battered as he was, there weren't too many places I could take him. No traffic, no police cruisers, no delivery trucks and no escorting federal agents. Streetlights glowed and traffic lights flashed their familiar sequence. After driving around for twenty minutes with the semi-conscious Conklin rolling on the passenger seat, it was obvious Schaffhausen was closed for the night.

And I was lost.

Gradually the circle of blocks I had repeatedly driven through became frighteningly familiar. Now and then signs pointed the way to Zurich or other towns, but I didn't want Zurich and somehow, Old Towne Schaffhausen, where St. Agatha's was located completely eluded me.

I pulled to a now familiar traffic light and sat there through several cycles. Maybe I could rouse him enough for him to recognize where we were.

"Daniel, I'm lost. Can you wake up a little and help me find the clinic?"

Conklin moaned and tossed. He took a deep breath. "Yeah. Give me a minute."

He opened his eyes in barely a squint, moved his head a little. "Geez, Macbean. I wonder what was taking you so long."

You're welcome.

"Turn right here and go about three or four blocks. Turn right again on Clabenstrasse. It has that old shop with the big stained glass windows. Lots of stonework. That's Clabenstrasse. Go about a mile and turn left. That's the road that goes between Von Muller and St. Agatha's."

With that he seemed to have run out of juice and passed out again.

I followed his instructions until I came to Le Marche Rossignol Antique, a building on the corner made of magnificent stone work and windows of sparkling colorful glass.

A movement caught my eye. In the rear view mirror, I saw something.

After driving around and seeing nothing for so long it seemed different and peculiar. I peered into the mirror and saw it again. It was a car or truck moving with no lights on. It now sat on the road motionless about two blocks back. I moved forward about three car lengths and it moved and stopped.

I did not turn onto Clabenstrasse. I floored the accelerator. The Mercedes shot forward like a cannonball. Great. Maybe I can get a speeding ticket. Behind me, the van did not turn on his lights but it too bolted forward. I came to an intersection and went straight through regardless of the light. If I could make a turn, I turned, totally without knowing where I was going. It was a desperate battle to keep the car on the road at such terrific speed and not hit anything. Tires screeched around corners, I accelerated and braked on instinct. Occasional glances in the review mirror showed Karolovsky was gaining on me.

But I did eventually wander into an area of town I recognized. I swerved onto Weisengrundstrasse and stomped on the gas. The Mercedes seemed to do anything I wanted it to do but Karolovsky still gained on me. It was obvious that he had been trained in high speed pursuit and I hadn't, the difference between a pro and an amateur.

We plunged into the tunnel under the railroad tracks. Karolovsky's van was on my bumper. I slammed on the brakes and he slammed into the rear of the Mercedes. I hit the gas and spun the wheel left onto Flurlingerweg. The Benz's engine roared under full throttle. Our digital speedometer barely kept up with the acceleration. We were going over a hundred kilometers per hour when a right hand turn loomed ahead. I jerked the wheel and the close-following van came around on my left. For a brief second I saw the determined look on Karolovsky's face as he gripped the steering wheel and fought to keep four tires on the pavement. We both flew side by side onto the bridge across the river. The van pulled slightly ahead. With a violent motion Karolovsky swung hard right and pinned us against the bridge girders. Car steel screeching against bridge steel and fireworks of flying sparks, both cars ground to a halt with just enough deceleration to prevent the air bags from blowing.

We were enveloped in a deadly silence.

I don't remember breathing but my heart pounded violently. Conklin lay in the passenger seat restrained by his seat belt, head lolling to the side. A second later I heard the grind of a car door hinge and realized the Russian, probably as dazed as I was but recovering faster because he was a pro and I was a desk-riding amateur.

I had to get out of the Mercedes. I had to stop him from getting Conklin.

The bridge was surprisingly narrow, barely wide enough for two cars. Steel grid-work flanked the road with pedestrian walkways outside the girders and high chain-link fences to keep foot traffic from falling into the swirling Rhine below. When I opened the door I felt cool air from the river and heard the roar of the waterfall just a short way downstream.

Karolovsky came charging around the SUV's rear bumper. Instinctively I went into Tae Kwon Do position one. His arms came up and he reached for my neck. I batted his hands away and punched him in the chin. Punching up goes against gravity so I remembered Master Kim's dictate, right, left, right to the chest, spin and low right again toward the groin. Karolovsky didn't seem impressed by Master Kim's dictate. He took the right and blocked the left and knocked me down on the spin. Over two hundred pounds of Russian landed on my chest, knees first. The wind went out of my lungs and a massive fist exploded on my cheek like a grenade.

I looked up as his other fist poised for next punch. But a wraith appeared over Karolovsky's shoulder. I felt I was losing consciousness and didn't recognize the wraith. It was about time my long absent guardian angel showed up. My angel stuck a hypodermic needle into Karolovsky's neck and depressed the plunger.

Karolovsky's head turned toward Daniel Conklin, now standing over him. He struggled to rise but the syringe's contents entered the bloodstream too close to the brain. Karolovsky could only manage a half rise.

My head was clearing. The pain might come later, but for the moment adrenalin made me strong. I rolled over just in time to miss the big Russian falling on top of me.

I stood and saw the naked Daniel Conklin holding onto the Mercedes for dear life. He was shaking and cold and exhausted.

"No arguments, Brendan," he gasped.

I nodded. I bent over and took Karolovsky's wrists. They were still sticky with duct tape glue. Conklin grabbed his ankles. For two weaklings to get the large man's body through the steel girder onto the pedestrian walkway required an enormous struggle, and an even larger one to get him over the chain link fence. But it took only a second for him to plunge into the dark Rhine River and a few more for his bobbing head to disappear below the surging water.

Chapter 43

From the journal of Brendan Macbean:
Conklin and I lay in the reclined leather seats of the Mercedes. We parked in front of St. Agatha's waiting for them to open up. We left the engine running for warmth. The novelty of sitting in a parked car with a naked man prevented neither me nor the naked man from falling asleep. Dr. Bauerle arrived at dawn and summoned a host of orderlies. I woke long enough to stumble into the clinic but remembered little after that.

It was close to noon when I woke in one of clinic's hospital beds. I felt better although the right side of my face was swollen and numb. Gone was the sweat and grime of last night's adventure so I guessed that someone had washed me and dressed me in an open backed hospital gown.

Bauerle stood in the doorway looking like a Vogue cover model, and for the thousandth time I wondered how anyone took her seriously when she looked that good.

"Good morning, Mr. Macbean. First I must thank you for saving Mr. Conklin. I don't know what St. Agatha's would do without him. I would offer you some breakfast but Bentley is on the phone."

I smiled and stretched languorously. "Dr. Bauerle, Bentley can go to hell. I've got a couple of questions to ask you."

She smiled the dimple-smile that by itself was worth two billion. "Yes, Mr. Macbean."

"I've obviously received medical treatment and I've been cleaned up. My clothes are gone and I find myself dressed in this incredibly compromising hospital gown."

"What is your question, Mr. Macbean?" Her dimples deepened and her deep brown eyes twinkled like a Dalmatian puppy.

"Did you bathe me? Did you take my clothes off?"

Her smile vanished. She gave me an expression that was very unlike a Vogue cover model and I immediately understood why everyone took her seriously. I fully expected and deserved a severe tongue-lashing, and I didn't care what language it came in.

"You have it entirely wrong, Mr. Macbean."

"I do?"

"I would have to take your clothes off first, of course," she said with Marilyn Monroe breathiness. She flashed the dimples again and scooted from the doorway.

Before I had a chance to engage in what promised to be the fantasy of my life, the phone rang, that weird European klaxon-like buzzing Americans will never get used to.

To my right was the standard hospital bedside table with three drawers and barely enough room for a tray and a telephone. I picked up the phone.

"So now you're the big hero. Macbean, maybe I'm glad you didn't go home." Bentley's voice had a trace of irony in it.

"Bentley, you are on my very short shit list."

"Really, why?"

"I'm not good at this cloak and dagger stuff, or locating someone taxpayers pay you to protect. I'm not good at fighting Russian agents. Have you put your guys back on the job?"

"Yeah, they're out there. Look, you went out and did what you had to do. We couldn't locate him. I told you that." He let that sink in a second. "I knew you had his phone. His new phone."

I let that sink in for another minute.

"And, Macbean, you wouldn't leave it alone no matter what I said."

I said nothing.

"What did you want me to do? Grab his iPhone. What good would that do? You had it and he didn't. Besides we couldn't track him anymore. He did something to the Mercedes which sent us all over the place looking for him. He kept ditching his phones. How many trips did we make to the city dump before we figured out he was using a string of them. Each time he threw one away, it took us several days to figure out his new phone ID. Macbean, I was out of ideas. You're the one who likes to find things. You're good at it. I'm better at hiding them."

Another minute of silence.

"Macbean, are you going to say something?"

"No Bentley. What's the point? You are the all-powerful government official. You'll find a way to do whatever you want. To whomever you want. I'm just one of those millions living a life of quiet desperation. What do you want from me?"

Bentley's voice grew sterner, his sentences clipped. "Listen, Macbean. It's time you assume the role you came here for. Conklin's mine. He's not yours anymore. I don't like to threaten but I'm responsible for certain outcomes and I don't have much leeway. So I'll give you your last warning. Do I have your attention?"

"I'm listening, Bentley and if you ask me again if I'm paying attention, I'll hang up."

"You came here for Bettye. She'll be coming out of treatment soon. You can spend some time with her. Take that time. Cherish that time. Cherish her. On the other hand, Denise is in decline. I want Conklin to support her as best he can without you. Without your help, assistance or meddling. Are you pay... uh, following me?"

"Right here, Bentley."

"I want you out of his life and back into your own. After Denise passes..." Bentley paused as if he found that part difficult to say. "Afterward, I'm taking Conklin away. There will be... no more... Daniel Conklin."

It chilled me the way he phrased it. He made Daniel Conklin. He can take him away.

"He'll be gone, vanished. And I'm going to repeat myself. I don't have any options except to do what I have to do. I don't want to hurt him or Denise. Or you or Bettye."

"Are you threatening me, Bentley?"

I heard him exhale through the phone, almost like a short, fierce wind but blunted by the buffer of electronics. "You're goddamn right, I'm threatening you. Will you please not be the rat terrier, persistent son of a bitch you are? You have no idea what we can do to you. Imagine the worst and that's child's play. Terrorists in Guantanamo will have it better than you. But it'll be subtle. Maybe a car wreck that'll take your leg off, put you in a wheelchair. Maybe that's all you need to convince you. Maybe it will be losing all your money or your house burns down or you'll catch that flesh-eating bacteria. Maybe the police raid your house and find child pornography on your computer and you get a jail cell next to Jerry Sandusky. It won't point to me, but you'll know why it happened. I don't know what it will take to get you to back off. So I hope to hell a little 'threatening' will do the trick. Is it going to work this time, Macbean?"

I said nothing.

"I'm going to take that as a yes."

The phone line went dead, but it took a long time for the chill to leave my body. Then my stupid anger kicked in. I wanted to fight him. Who did this Bentley think he was?

I got out of bed, slipped on some white cotton sandals and left the room, green gown flapping, ass cooling in the breeze. I went to Denise's room because I knew he would be there.

Denise's room was a happier scene. Conklin's bed was pulled next to hers and they held hands across the gap which was barely wider than a nurse's hips. Denise smiled thinly at me but she did not look good. Her eyes were sunken and surrounded by dark circles. Her graying skin seemed to hang from her bones. Conklin looked better. There was color in his face and although he had bruises and Band-Aids everywhere, he looked like his old self. New self? Confusing, huh?

Conklin noticed my expression. He tried to lighten the mood.

"Brendan, look. We're on the news."

I went to the back of the room, next to Denise's bed, turned around and saw what they were watching. The TV suspended from the ceiling showed a local news program. English subtitles flowed across the screen while a female voice recited in German.

"The body of an unidentified man was pulled from the Rhine this morning, near Rhineuferweg, after apparently going over Rhinefalls. A police spokesman said there was duct tape residue around his wrists and a hypodermic syringe inserted in his neck."

Daniel Conklin muted the TV. For a second silence hung in the room

In my broadcaster's voice I said, "'Police suspect foul play.'"

They both burst out laughing.

"Oh, God! Brendan, you're so funny." She looked at me. "Thank you from the bottom of my heart, Brendan. You are a very brave man."

It humbled me to hear this from her. I shook my head. "No, Denise. You're the brave one."

She reached out to me. I touched her bed to discharge the static electricity and then took her hand. Her fingers felt like hot-house flowers.

"Brendan, I have few choices left, but you have your life and Bettye's. She will need your bravery too." She looked at Daniel. "I know you will give her your best like my Wylie."

I nodded. I didn't know what to say.

"Denise, if there's anything I can do…"

Her hand squeezed mine and she looked straight into my eyes.

"Be Wylie's friend."

Her head lay back on the pillow and she closed her eyes. A tiny vein in her neck throbbed.

I walked around the bed to speak to Conklin.

"Is she asleep?"

He nodded. I pointed to random places in the room, moved closer to him and whispered.

"You never know. Bugs?"

He shook his head. "St. Agatha's is not bugged. It messes up their equipment."

"Okay, then. How did Karolovsky find us?"

He gave me a questioning look.

"I was lost. I drove around for half an hour."

Conklin shrugged. "GPS? Fleet tracker?"

"I don't think so. The feds had something on the Mercedes, but Bentley said you did something to it."

Conklin smirked. "They had a tracking device on it. Wasn't hard to jimmy up."

"Then I assume Karolovsky couldn't track us either. Not that way. Bentley also said he was aware you were switching phones. Couldn't track you that way either. Besides, I had your phone."

He seemed to consider this. "The feds wouldn't listen when you gave them the DHL truck."

"Bentley told me it was a false lead. Told me I got the number wrong. But that's how I found you. They should have been following me and shown up at the warehouse. There was nobody around. Nobody. I didn't even hear another vehicle."

We were both silent for a moment.

Conklin asked, "They didn't follow you?"

"Nope."

"Why wouldn't Bentley try to rescue me? It was irresponsible to leave it to you. They had all the resources. They didn't help, even after you found me."

"Bentley let Karolovsky get you, maybe even helped him. You have the money. He wanted to see if Vladoseev could get what out of you what he couldn't get out of you."

Conklin let that simmer for a second. "Son of a bitch. That bastard... I wonder how he'd take the *Kiska Tviker*."

"Daniel, we got away. How did Karolovsky know where we were?"

"I don't know," Conklin said, his eyes staring straight ahead.

"I was lost, Daniel. I drove around for at least thirty minutes while you were semi-conscious. Somehow he found us. I wish I knew surveillance. Spy craft is not my thing."

Conklin nodded. I saw a change of expression in his eyes.

"Zinsser."

"What?"

"You're going to go see Zinsser."

Chapter 44

From the journal of Brendan Macbean:
Paranoia makes for a good spy.

When I returned to my room, my clothes were sitting on the hospital bed. They had been cleaned and pressed and were waiting for me. My laptop was also there, retrieved from the Mercedes. Someone, presumably Dr. Bauerle, had taped a note to my laptop identifying the passcode to their wireless internet. What a sweetheart!

I dressed and headed for the Mercedes. It broke my heart to see the crumpled and dented bodywork. Our flawless car had been turned into a beater by running it into a bridge. But it was drivable, so I headed for Haus Von Muller.

Here comes the good spy part. I parked the Mercedes in front of Von Muller and walked several blocks until I caught a tram. I had a specific destination and really didn't care where the tram took me as long as I could catch a cab and be fairly sure I wasn't tracked by crooks or feds.

In thirty minutes I was seated at a table in another coffee shop in Thayengen. There I waited and sipped some excellent coffee. Conklin warned me the guy would be late and why. He also gave me a detailed review of their first and only meeting. Twenty minutes went by. I was the only person in the place.

Another ten minutes and finally a man walked in. He ordered a coffee and sat down at my table. He did not offer to shake hands but looked me straight in the eye. He was only an inch or two taller than me and did not impress me as a spy. His face was ordinary, except for the heavy beard which looked as if he hadn't shaven in a day or two. The backs of his hands were covered by coarse black hair. He could have been from anywhere. Finally he spoke.

"Macbean, I presume," a deep baritone intoned with a trace of accent.

"That's me." I said.

"An American."

"Is that what you expected?"

He nodded. "I received an email from Mr. Conklin. I can assure you there is no surveillance here and I checked to see if you are being followed. There is no one. They'd have to be very good to elude me."

"Mr. Zinsser, what expertise do you have?"

"Twenty-five years as an agent with Shin Bet. Another five as a reservist studying electronic surveillance and cyber security."

"What is Shin Bet?"

"Israeli Internal Security Service."

"Okay. Conklin thinks you have the credentials. He's at St. Agatha's being treated for wounds he suffered in the last few days."

Zinsser raised black eyebrows. "What happened?"

"Karolovsky got him. Tortured him for two days."

"But he's safe now?"

"Yes. I found him and got him to St. Agatha's where he's safe."

Zinsser looked at me with obvious incredulity.

"You overpowered Karolovsky?"

"No, a two by four did."

"Two by four?"

"A piece of lumber." I told him the story. His incredulity turned to admiration. I tried to skip over what happened on the bridge, but Zinsser didn't like skipping. He got the rest of the story out of me.

"Karolovsky's dead?"

"Yes."

"You killed him?"

"I guess, we did. Otherwise we'd be the ones they pulled out of the Rhine."

"You were very lucky."

"Agreed."

"Yes. Well, Mr. Macbean. How can I help?"

"I need to know how he tracked me. We drove away from the warehouse and thirty minutes later he found us. He knew we'd go to the clinic or to the house where we were staying. He could have driven to either place but he didn't. He came after us in his car."

"Your car, the Mercedes? He tracked your car. He had a homing device planted in the Mercedes."

"I don't think so. It was bugged by the federals and under their watch the whole time. According to Conklin, you told him how to rig the device the feds planted and send out false signals. They knew he had done that and had lost the ability to locate him with his phone. Besides, I had Conklin's phone, and I'm pretty certain the federal agents helped the Russians. My rescue was very much a seat of the pants operation. Karolovsky chased us as soon as he got free. He knew where to find us."

Zinsser nodded. He seemed to take it in stride what had shocked me, that Bentley had colluded with Vladoseev.

"Perhaps. But if that is so, the car and the phone are no longer the target."

I thought about that. "But Daniel is."

"Yes. Daniel shows initiative. If he can get phones, he can get cars. His secret, what both the feds and the Russian want, is in Daniel's head. Not a phone or a Merceedes. Bentley might partner up with the Russians, allow them to take Daniel and wring it out of him. Then Vladoseev has the money. Bentley knows Vladoseev is not so clever as Conklin, but they have to control Daniel. As long as he is alive, there is more to wring out of him."

I thought about what Zinsser said. When he was Wylie Schram, he had transferred the billions into hundreds of accounts. Only Conklin knew where all the money was. If he gave it all up, there would be no reason to keep him alive. Conklin was doomed to be chased, hunted and harried for the rest of his life.

"But Karolovsky tracked us. How did he do it?"

Zinsser thought for a while.

"The Americans have a microchip that can be tracked by the cellular network. It is implantable in humans, similar to an RFID tag used to identify pets and livestock. However it is more like a cell phone, except all it does is radio location data, which when cross-checked from cell towers. It can provide precise location superimposed on a GPS map. Anyone with a smart phone can find you if they have the app. But Conklin would know he had the chip. It's surgically implanted."

"Could they insert the chip without the patient knowing?"

"Possibly."

We both sat there sniffing the steam coming off our coffees. I think I spoke the thought forming in both our heads.

"Karolovsky had him for over forty-eight hours. He was unconscious for most of that time."

"And injured. Cuts, bruises, some requiring stitches?"

"Sure. All that and more. They stuck electrodes on him. All over. Even his balls, mouth and nose." I shuddered just thinking about it.

"The Soviets called it the *kiska tviker*. Pussy Tweaker. The KGB stole the device from the GDR, East Germany and perfected it. The machine uses electro-shock on sensitive areas to cause pain, but it also monitors the victim's vital signs so they don't kill him. Publically the use of this machine has been banned. But the Russians still use it. They are not worried the world will think them inhumane. When properly used, the victim is not too seriously injured but the machine can produce burns, nerve damage and long term psychological effects."

"He had bruises and cuts," I offered.

"Cuts you say?"

"Lots of cuts."

"The device could be inserted one of his cuts. But there would be stitches. Did he have stitches?"

I shook my head. "Karolovsky didn't stitch him. His cuts didn't seem deep, just a little bleeding. The doctors stitched him up when we got him back to St. Agatha's."

"Karolovsky could have used a pocket knife, made an incision, inserted the chip and closed it up with super-glue. On the surface such a cut would appear superficial."

"Jesus! You guys are unbelievable."

Zinsser shrugged. "In this business, nobody stays a virgin for long."

"Wait a minute. You are saying that the Americans have this technology. That's my government. Who else has it?"

"The technology isn't too secret. All intelligent services are all working on something like this. But the technology to make it small enough... not everyone has it. And the battery life is short, a few weeks. You have to recharge the battery with a magnet, which would require the victim's knowledge. Nobody but the Americans have a practical prototype. As far as we know."

"As far as we know. The important question is how would Vladoseev get it? Or Karolovsky. How skilled would you have to be to insert it?"

"Not skilled. Five minutes of training or even instructions in an email. You make a cut, you slip it in. The chip is four millimeters or smaller. Range is around two kilometers."

"Zinsser, I don't do metric."

Zinsser held up his fingers like he held an invisible grain of rice.

"Within an urban area where there are many cellular zones, it would be easy to track a person carrying this chip."

Chapter 45

From the journal of Brendan Macbean:
I drove the Mercedes back to St. Agatha's. As I approached I pulled up next to one of the federal agent's cars and stopped. I rolled down the scraped and scratched window and marveled that the engineers of Mercedes-Benz could design a window that would still work after the collision we took. The federal agent was the same one who I had spoken to on that fateful night. He looked bored but reluctantly rolled down his window.

I smiled and said, "Agent Maxwell Smart? Are you working for CONTROL today? Or KAOS?"

Okay, the guy was too young to get it but the look on his face made my day.

I drove up the driveway to St. Agatha's.

Dr. Bauerle was in her office. I walked in and shut the door.

"Mr. Macbean," was all she said. Maybe she saw the look on my face.

"Dr. Bauerle. I need to ask you some questions. It's very important for all of us, specifically Daniel."

"I'm bound by doctor-patient privilege," she said with dead-pan seriousness.

"I know. You don't have to answer me. It's possible the men who kidnapped Daniel planted a microchip in his body. He had cuts and bruises all over. One of the cuts may have been deep enough to implant a small chip, about this size." I held up my fingers grain-of-rice wide. "And closed the incision with super-glue."

"Cyanoacrylate." Her eyes shifted as if she was mentally going over Daniel Conklin's naked body. I felt a pang of jealousy and suppressed it.

"Do you remember any incisions like that? Your medical people probably stitched him up in some places."

"We closed some of his cuts with butterfly plasters. Some required stitches. However, none life threatening."

"I'd like you to run Daniel through the MRI. You have one don't you?"

She looked surprised.

"The MRI? Why?"

"Doctor Bauerle, you're pretty enough to be a movie star, but neither one of us will make a good spy. Her smile was perfunctory.

"The MRI is to help us locate the chip. Or we could x-ray him all over until we found it. But we have to remove it. It helps the bad guys track him. Like you said before, we'd be lost without Daniel."

Thank God Dr. Bauerle was a no-nonsense, do-it-now kind of person. She rose from her chair and said, "I'll prepare the MRI room. If you would be so kind, please speak to Mr. Conklin."

Two hours later the three of us were in Bauerle's office looking at MRI pictures on her computer. Bauerle was still in her scrubs. Another fantasy…beautiful female doctor in hospital scrubs. "I'm here to give you an examination…"

"There it is. A very likely place. Under his left scapula."

The screen showed Conklin's back in colorful multi-dimension. A tiny white rectangle glowed under his shoulder blade.

"Dr. Bauerle, why is that a likely place?" I asked.

"Well, if you are suggesting that it was inserted by a person without surgical training, you want to make sure they don't cut tendons or muscle. They want the victim unaware of the insertion. There is quite a range of movement under the scapula. His left shoulder might be sore for a few days, but he was sore anyway from his… ordeal."

Bauerle stood and came toward me. She spun me around with surprising strength. Then she grabbed my left arm pulled it behind my back in the classic wrestling move. She pushed my arm close the point of causing pain.

Then through my shirt she inserted her strong fingers under my shoulder blade, into a gap formed by her wrestling maneuver.

"You see? Daniel was on his stomach unconscious. The man pulled his arm up so and a gap forms under the scapula. He makes a short incision, inserts the chip and closes the incision with super-glue."

Maybe Daniel could see it, but all I felt was her long arms around me. She let go suddenly. I gasped. Unwanted, erotic thoughts came to my brain. I pushed them away. Maybe they weren't unwanted.

Dr. Bauerle returned to her desk. I found it difficult not to stare at her. She caught my eyes and blushed.

"Are you okay, Brendan?"

"Yes, of course. You're an expert." I turned to Conklin. "You don't feel anything?"

He shook his head. "Well I feel something just about everywhere. Lots of little aches and pains."

He moved his left arm around trying several positions.

"I feel something, but it feels pretty minor. I never would have noticed it.

Bauerle added, "Medical technology has many devices that are put into the body. Sometimes they cover them with a polypropylene sleeve, which encourages connective tissue to grow into it. This keeps the device from moving around."

Conklin asked, "Well, Brendan. What now?"

"Take it out, please, Dr. Bauerle. As gently as possible. Place it in a plastic bag and give it to me."

Conklin said, "Interesting. What are we going to do with it, might I ask?"

I smiled. "We have an edge. They think we don't know about it, but we do."

An hour later, I had the chip in my pocket.

Chapter 46

From the journal of Brendan Macbean:
Denise died a few days later.

Conklin marked the days from his rescue to her death by taking on more of her pain. She lay in a morphine dream, and every heartbeat moved her a second closer to the finish line. What could I do but offer weak and inadequate support?

He spent most of the time in her room. I spent most of the time in the library, knowing the silent drama that played out down the hall. Sometimes I would see him. He would drift in and sit down on the leather couch where together we had watched the Ray Suffield interview. So much had changed since that night, in so little time. Mostly he would just stare and think his thoughts.

Denise's life slipped from our grasp and the poignancy of that allusion pierced our hearts in a cruel way. We lived and she died. We, the living, felt the guilt of having a future.

He spent every moment with her except for those times when he couldn't, when the enigma of living became too great. He loved someone who was dying. He knew his love would go on without the warm and living person to give it to.

Sometimes he would come to the library and we'd talk of everything but her. We'd talk of our past. I told him everything I could remember about Bettye and me with an intimacy I never felt with another human. We marveled about the collision of our lives, the miracle that brought us together. Daniel needed me, I knew, as Denise slipped away from him. She had told me to be Wylie's friend and her command lived on in my soul. He had no one else, and indeed no one could share what we shared. We were just two men who were blind to our own futures, if we could conceive a future without the others. We were condemned like the women we loved, our days beyond theirs a blank. No inspiration could guide us into that inky mystery and we avoided discussing it.

While Bauerle cheerfully gave me daily updates on Bettye's progress, somehow I knew I would face that reunion alone. Conklin would go. We didn't discuss that either but I knew and he knew... after Denise, he wouldn't stay here.

For now we both held the responsibility of keeping our secret. We guarded the chip while it constantly told the feds he was here. We made certain it never left the vicinity of Conklin. We had to keep the secret of its discovery from them. While he stayed at the clinic, he kept it. I could come and go and the federal agents would take no notice. If we had thoughts about what to do with the chip, we didn't discuss them. But we both knew, after Denise, the feds would follow the signal and scoop Conklin up.

The day before Denise died, Conklin came to the library. I was at the computer dallying on the internet. He sat on the couch. I left the keyboard and took the chair near him.

I didn't ask him how things are going. He stared at a vision I didn't try to see. Finally he looked up at me.

"It won't be long now. She's had an oxygen mask on to help her breathe but she's asleep all the time. Sometimes she opens her eyes but she hasn't said anything in a while. Sometimes I think she's smiling at me. Or trying to smile. I'm not sure."

"She's smiling, Daniel even if she can't smile. She loves you." Empty words. I never felt so inadequate.

"I know, Brendan. I think she's trying to thank me. The last few weeks. Thanks for being in her life. She wants me to go on with my life. She thinks I'm a good man, that I have an important reason to live. I don't know how she figures that, but I guess she's always thought that. She has good reasons to be angry at me, the way things worked out. I took away the best part of her life. What I did separated us for years. I told her the biggest lie in the world. Told her I was dead and that she was alone. And she thinks I'm a good man."

It was a one sided conversation, a soliloquy, of sorts. I could add nothing to it but my own empty thoughts.

"But I'm not a good man, am I? I stole billions from millions. You go to jail for what I did. Criminals are my peers, my partners. I'd like to give it all back but I can't."

"Why not?" Another stupid question.

"Who to? Bentley? Vladoseev? They're just two more thieves. Could I look up the millions of people who lost money and start writing checks? Is that even possible?"

He looked at me, his eyes dry for now. "'Payment Differed', a novel by C.S. Forester. Whatever your crime, it always leads to your demise."

We sat silent in the gloom of the library while the mantle clock clicked a hundred times.

Conklin took a deep breath.

"Brendan, can you help me?"

A cold wind blew up my backside. Muted warning bells clanked in my head. Just a friend asking for help.

"Of course, Daniel," I said because I'm an idiot.

He looked around, but there were no federal agents sneaking up on us. Then he shook his head. "I don't know why I'm so paranoid."

Conklin reached into his pocket and pulled out a tiny square of plastic. It looked like an SD memory card, Secure Digital Storage Device, something you plugged into your computer, tablet, camera or printer. He reached his hand out to me with the square inch of memory between his thumb and forefinger.

I didn't take it.

"What is it?"

"The money. Brendan, it's the money."

A moment passed and another before I decoded his simple words. The implications ran through my brain like a freight train. I shook and couldn't stop. Greed and lust and gluttony, pride, wrath and envy made my muscles twitch and cast a wave of nausea across my guts. Six deadly sins out of seven ain't bad for a few seconds of contemplation, is it? If Bauerle had walked in at that moment we would have all seven.

"Account numbers, passwords, banks, routing numbers, instructions. It's all here."

"I… I don't want the money." Did I just say that?

"Take it, Brendan. You're the only one I can trust. And it's not for you."

"It's not?"

He shook his head. "The only thing that makes sense. It's not for us. Not for Ray Suffield to begin InCorps again. Not for Bentley for his own agenda. Or Vladoseev. What would he do with it? They don't get it. Not a penny."

He looked around the room like a condemned man might take a last look before they put the hood over his head.

"It's for this."

"This? You mean St. Agatha's?"

"St. Agatha's and others. Think about it, Brendan. What could Dr. Friedkin do if he had better funding? Or the Institute for Cancer Research, or Emory University, or the Mayo Clinic? This disease is the worst. Cancer kills millions of people. But breast cancer attacks women. It's worse than a disease. It attacks a woman's identity, her femininity. Women all over the world fear this deadly killer for more than just their lives. Women are fighters. Women have had to fight for themselves. We, guys can sympathize but we don't really understand what this disease does to a woman. It's worse than anything.

"Brendan, it's hard to explain, but I need to give it back. We give it back, to places where there's some leverage, some promise of a breakthrough. Maybe it will help us get to a cure sooner."

I sat there like a dumbass while my mind churned.

"Why me? Why can't you do this?"

"I'm vulnerable. I'm just one man. They take me out and it's over."

"I'm vulnerable too. Jesus, Daniel. I can't do this."

"Sure you can. You and me together. Two is better than one. You and me, buddy… just two guys doling out a couple of billion dollars."

"That's really funny, Daniel." But neither of us was able to laugh about it.

He was still holding his hand out with the memory chip in his fingers. He shook his hand once like he was saying, here, take it. I'm getting tired holding it.

I took it.

It burned like a hot rivet. The fire came up my arm to my brain. I had the universe between my thumb and forefinger. Everything I wanted. Right here. Everything. What did I want?

Conklin looked relived. "It is quite a burden, but I feel so much better sharing it with you."

I could barely hear him. I realized I wasn't getting everything I ever wanted. I had just been enslaved by the most massive responsibility a man could have. And I was sharing it with a man I didn't know very well and with whom I was entrusting my life.

"Brendan, we can do this. After Denise's funeral…" He said it as the inevitability it was, almost dispassionately. Where did he find the strength? "I'm going away. Zinsser's going to help me. We need to keep your part secret. If Bentley or Vladoseev find out you've got that SD card…" He didn't finish that sentence. I was a billionaire but I had to stay poor if I wanted to stay alive. Well maybe some new clothes and I kind of liked the way that Mercedes handled.

Conklin babbled on. "We'll keep regular communication and work out a protocol. I'll pick the places where we can help and you can make suggestions. We'll talk it over. We'll talk but you won't know where I am.

"This is our secret. Nobody can know."

****

We went back to the bridge for Denise's funeral. Not the one over which we threw Karolovsky but one further downstream, closer to Rhinefalls on Rhinefallweg.

The three of us faced the falls and unceremoniously threw Denise's ashes into the Rhine. Thankfully the wind cooperated and her earthly powder blew in a cloud toward the torrent of water crashing around the boulder in the middle of the river. Conklin, Bauerle and I held hands and watched until Denise's ashes disappear into the vapor. And we watched a long time after that. Somehow we all knew the right moment and turned and headed to the Schaffhausen side of the river.

I had my hands in my pocket. My right hand felt the plastic bag with the microchip in it. For a moment I thought about flinging it into the river to follow Denise's ashes. I decided that wasn't the right move... not yet.

Once on the riverbank Bauerle and I headed for the car but Conklin hung back. We both turned and faced him.

"I think I'll take a walk," he said.

We watched him go. Bauerle grabbed my hand and squeezed. I looked around for federal agents but they had left us alone.

Bauerle and I drove back to St. Agatha's without words. She went straight to her office and closed the door. I went to the library.

I've been to funerals before but never one like this. Usually there are people around, friends and family to talk about memories and the one who passed. Now I was alone. I felt like doing nothing and that's what I did. For hours.

The late afternoon sun cast lowering shadows in the tall windows of the library when Dr. Bauerle came in. She sat next to me on the couch, close like a friend, touching her hip against mine, her leg against mine. She had been crying, I could tell by the redness in her eyes, but she had made an attempt to put her face together. Her makeup was perfect and her eyes, although red, were dry. Also for once, she had left her signature designer glasses behind.

She laid her head on my shoulder and picked up my hand. Her hand was warm and soft. I don't know what I expected but the warmth and softness delivered an unexpected intimacy. I think I responded with the right amount of pressure but who can tell? I guess I had always known there was a real person inside the stern and reserved Dr. Bauerle. From the first day I met her, I had thought her the most beautiful woman I had ever known, but I knew there was a vulnerable woman inside who suffered from the toughest job in the world.

We sat there while the mantle clock clicked a thousand times. Dusk fell outside and we had the place to ourselves. From time to time I heard her breathing and occasionally felt her gentle squeeze on my hand but no more than a tremor.

Then a deeper breath.

"Brendan?" Her voice was softer than a whisper.

"Yes?"

"He's gone, isn't he?" Her question nestled into my ear, breathy, soft and feminine.

The clock ticked a dozen times more before I answered.

"Yes."

"What will we do now?" she asked.

The question was about as loaded as any I have ever heard in my life. For some reason I recalled Shelby's remark about the engraver and her indistinct command to 'Love Shelby.'

Several lifetimes ago.

"We will love him, Birgit."

I had never used her first name before. Saying it now made me feel like I had breached a barrier of intimacy.

More ticks and the world moved a little further away from us.

"Birgit," she said more fluidly.

She raised her head and looked me directly in the eye. The heat coming off her face was so intense I thought I'd burn. I could feel her breath and that powerful sensation your skin will generate when someone is about to touch you. Her lips touched mine and I felt the lubrication of new lipstick. Her scent filled my nostrils. My arms wrapped around her and she pulled me tight and strong, whooshing out my breath.

I couldn't call it a kiss... it was more of a mutual assault of our lips. Her lips on mine. Her tongue found mine, her cheeks flattened against my cheeks. When neither of us could breathe I pulled back and pushed forward again and peppered the tight warm skin of her neck. I heard her breath surge like the hot drafts of a race horse. I could feel her magnificent chest heaving against mine, her hips grinding against mine.

Our lips came together again, teeth against teeth, temperatures rising like the collision of two suns. Her energy burned me, her taste flooded my mouth, the amalgam of desire and need.

Then her tears came again and our train derailed. Falling against my shoulder Dr. Bauerle wept.

Birgit.

She sobbed as if seized by the deepest tragedy, as if the one hundred and twenty five patients of St. Agatha's had all passed on this day, as if their ashes were all crashing down Rhinefalls in a torrent of bereavement.

As if it was her fault.

She wept for Daniel. Her Daniel, for I knew she loved him. One hundred and twenty five husbands had come to St. Agatha's and she had grown to love only Daniel Conklin, without even knowing his real name. Perhaps it was his sincere devotion to Denise, or his helping St. Agatha's, but there is no rationalizing love or its reasons.

But I could hold Birgit Bauerle forever and we fell asleep like that on the leather couch in the library of St. Agatha's Clinic, a place where women come to die with their final wish, to spend just a little more time with the man they love.

Chapter 47

From the journal of Brendan Macbean:
  The next day I saw Bettye.
  I arrived at St. Agatha's at the usual time. Dr. Bauerle met me at the door dressed in a black suit and white blouse and looking better than two billion dollars. We telepathically agreed on a silence about our recent episode, chalking it up to acceptable grieving behavior. But I was never going to forget it. Never.
  Bauerle's smile was wide and she looked about as happy as I'd ever seen her.
  "Mr. Macbean, Bettye wants to see you."
  The news hit me with a blow harder than Karolovsky's punch... replaced instantly with a tidal wave of mixed emotions. Bauerle read me like a book. She gave me a smart-ass smirk. Her hands gripped my shoulders. She spun me around and sort of kicked my ass down the hall to the last open door on the right.
  I paused a moment to gather myself and finally concluded that gathering one's self was impossible in this situation. Bettye needed my support but my life recently had been a maelstrom of inescapable, bizarre paradoxes and I guess anyone might feel a little queasy under the circumstances.
  I guess.
  Bettye had endured weeks of recovery and endured it for the sole purpose of seeing me walk through the door, smiling, glad to see her, full of life and happy. She expected me to have spent those weeks totally focused on her recovery and goddamn it, that's what I was going to give her.
  I tried to recall my favorite term of endearment for her, mined from my memory of two years ago. I plastered my face in a smile and entered.
  She was not the Bettye I remembered. She had lost twenty pounds and it had a drastic effect on her petite frame. Her once beautiful face was drawn and wrinkled. Some color had returned to her face, the face that had shocked me at our meeting in the Silver Skillet... half a lifetime ago.
  And then I saw her smile. And her eyes. The eyes were the same although a little red and the smile just as wide and soul-mending.
  "Bettye Baby," I said. I rushed to her bed and her skinny arms went around me.
  "*Mon Brendan.*" My Brendan. Two years of non-history disappeared.

She could always raise goosebumps pronouncing my name. It sounded like "Brawn Dah" and I loved it. "Moan Brawn Dah." That is who I am. I'm Bettye's Brawn Dah.

She felt tiny and small and vital all at once. With dry lips she planted miniature kisses on my neck. I wanted to crawl into bed with her and cover her with my body as if I could protect her from the battle waging inside her. Like a turtle without its shell, her heart beat heavily near the surface and I could feel its vibrant pounding.

I know Daniel Conklin must have felt this, to be vital and alive near someone you loved and desperately wanted them to also be vital and alive. And they could only partially fulfill your wish. I wanted to give her half my life force but knew it was a fantasy. At that moment I felt had to pull back and I'm not sure if it was to protect me or her. I felt her clinging to me, not ready to give up the embrace.

I smiled at her and she smiled back. And it was okay. We could work out the protocol later. Right now we'd focus on our reunion.

"Bettye, my love. You look so much better."

"Ach, je ressemble à une expérience scientifique. Mais je vous remercie pour le dire. My Brendan, how could I ever live without you?"

In all my years with Bettye, I managed to avoid learning a lick of French. Bettye spoke English better than me, but lapsed into her native tongue when it suited her. And back to English without warning.

We chatted like we hadn't seen each other for a while. Thirty minutes later Bauerle came in and bum-rushed me out.

"We must let Bettye rest for now. You can come back."

"Come on, Bauerle. Just another minute."

Bauerle gave me that stern look of hers but it didn't move me. Leaving Bettye felt like pulling magnets apart.

"Just a minute, then. Please come by my office, Mr. Macbean when you have finished."

Bauerle abruptly left and I turned to Bettye.

There was an angry look on her face. *"Cette salope a un énorme béguin pour vous. La sorcière!"*

I didn't need a translation. I had forgotten about her jealous streak.

I arrived at Bauerle's office. She stood behind her desk.

"Bentley will call in a few minutes. You can take the call here at my desk."

A sense of dread filled me. "Dr. Bauerle, you haven't told him anything, have you?"

She gave me an unreadable look.

"Are you sane, Brendan? What would I tell him?"

"Nothing. He can't know anything."

"I have nothing to tell him. He speaks only to Dr. Friedkin. We haven't passed more than a few words. Ever."

"Okay. Sorry. I should have known."

Dr. Bauerle left. I sat at her desk and waited for the phone to ring.

It rang.

"How's our boy doing, Macbean?"

"He's hurting, Bentley. What did you expect?"

"Why hasn't he gone back to the Muller house? You know, to get some rest?"

My dissembling wasn't particularly nimble today. I had to think.

"I don't know, Bentley. Maybe he doesn't like his room anymore since you trashed it. Anyway, why are you asking me?"

"Dr. Bauerle said he wouldn't talk to me."

Score one for Bauerle!

"What did you expect, Bentley?"

"Maybe a little gratitude."

"For what? That daring rescue you pulled off? Look, Bentley, I'm trying to do what you told me. I'm staying out of his life. But you're asking me questions like I'm still involved. How many ways do you want to have it?"

Bentley was silent for a moment.

"Macbean, I'm trying to find out what's going on with Conklin. He hasn't left the clinic since the funeral. You went to Von Muller but apparently he stayed there."

"Nice to know you federal agents are still looking out for us. Not sure we need it with Karolovsky gone."

Bentley was silent for a few more seconds.

"Macbean, would you do me a favor?"

"Not interested, Bentley."

"Tell Conklin to take my call next time."

"I can't. I won't."

"Macbean, you're beginning to annoy me."

"Good. Anything else?"

"Can you ask Bauerle to ask Conklin to take my call?"

"No. You told me to get out of his life. Or you'd give me a flesh eating bacteria. Or something worse." I took a deep breath. "You know Bentley, you're way past annoying me."

"You don't know the tightrope I have to walk."

"Your bed. You sleep in it."

"You think I enjoy busting peoples' chops? I do what I have to do. You could show a little respect, Macbean."

"No, Bentley. You have enormous power. You wanted to be on that wall and now you're there. You hate asking for people's cooperation. You'd rather force it out of them."

"Well, it's necessary in my experience. Your sudden recalcitrance for example."

"Gee, that's a big word for a government employee. I don't cooperate with thugs, racketeers... people who threaten me."

"I warned you."

"Threaten. What kind of deal did you make with Vladoseev?"

"What are you talking about?"

"You know what I'm talking about." The truth was, I wasn't sure I knew what I was talking about."

"You let Vladoseev have Conklin. Your boys turned their backs when Karolovsky drove up in the DHL truck. You rejected my suggestion of the DHL truck being involved. When I rescued Conklin, you helped Karolovsky find us. He couldn't track the Mercedes. You helped Karolovsky find us. I'm not good at figuring you out, but you gave up on manipulating Conklin. So you partnered with Vladoseev to see if he could get out of him."

I expected hot denial, but Bentley sounded relieved instead.

"Macbean, you Irish are great storytellers. That's the biggest crock I've heard all week."

"Scot, you idiot. You know a crock better than anyone I know. "

"Look, there's no deal between me and Vladoseev. I've never met the man. And it wouldn't make sense for me to work with him. He's a gangster and I'm a..."

"A bigger bull-shitter than me. Vladoseev thinks Conklin stole his money. You also want the money. You let Vladoseev use methods you won't use because you are a schemer not a torturer. That's so like you, Bentley."

"You got it wrong, Macbean. Four years ago we raided InCorps and recovered more than ninety-seven percent of the assets. People got paid back. Ninety-seven percent. That's a huge win for Uncle Sam. We were heroes and Americans couldn't be happier. One man died and the other went to prison. Big success for the good guys and people got re-elected and bureaucrats kept their jobs. I'm sure Vladoseev's pissed but he's a criminal. Who cares?"

"Bentley, you bureaucrats are the real storytellers. That's how you keep your jobs. I know full well why you want the money."

"Really?"

"Your wife died of breast cancer. She was a patient at St. Agatha's, just like Denise and Bettye. You went through what Daniel did and what I'm going through. Your wife got better. You spent a couple of weeks enjoying life with her. God, how wonderful that must have been after all she went through. The treatments, chemo and radiation, the misery and the fear of losing the love of your life.

"God Bentley! You think I don't know what that's like? Daniel sure did. I saw him go through it. For weeks you're filled with the hope that Dr. Friedkin's going to come up the solution. In time to save her. Maybe his new treatment will help defeat the eighth prototype. And maybe it put her death off for a day. That was a day of hope, the hope you could save her. But despite all your power, you couldn't save her. You had to watch her die."

Bentley didn't say anything but I could hear him breathing.

"Maybe you spent a night of grief and anger. Not sleeping. Walking the floor. Maybe you put your fists through some walls, knowing you."

I heard him quietly grunt when I said that.

"And you came up this idea. You decided you'd help Dr. Friedkin. You were going to help St. Agatha's clinic. He didn't have many patients. The treatments were very expensive. Dr. Friedkin didn't have enough money. You believed a cure was a month away or a year. God, if you could only get him what he needed to put him on a faster pace.

"You set out to find people who could afford it. There weren't many who had the money and you had to turn people down. That must have been your own personal hell. To turn down people who wanted it but couldn't afford it. Bentley, you may be a big jerk, but you've got a heart.

"And Conklin pops up. You knew he was holding out on you. What was it, eleven lie detector tests he beat? But you knew he had it. One and a half billion dollars with a 'B'. If money was the answer, you had the answer. But bringing Conklin out of witness protection kicked over a big can of worms because Vladoseev got wind of it. And it was more than you could handle. Denise wasn't going to live and it pinched you for time. Big government types like you have to make decisions. Sometimes people have to be sacrificed… even people you like. You figured out a way to let Vladoseev get after him and not place the blame on yourself. "

For a long while neither of us spoke. I heard Bentley take a deep breath.

"That's quite a theory, Macbean. I don't suppose it really makes a difference."

"But it does, Bentley. You bet your ass it does."

"Why?"

"You are the consummate control freak, Bentley. You're suspicious of everyone's motives but your own. And you're a controller and manipulator. You use manipulation like Vladoseev uses threats. You want the money for yourself."

"It's not for me, dammit!"

"You're right, dammit. But suppose we're all on the same team? Well, except for Vladoseev. He still wants the money for himself."

"What do you mean?"

"Do you think we wouldn't want Dr. Friedkin to find a successful treatment for SP-8 or anything else breast cancer throws at us? It's too late for Denise or your wife, but what about Bettye or the next poor woman? Or all the women. Millions of women?

"Bentley, isn't it worth keeping the Golden Goose alive?

Silence.

"Why won't he talk to me? I'm a reasonable man."

"Because you made a deal with Vladoseev. They tortured him, Bentley. Conklin will never trust you. And neither will I… flesh eating bacteria? I mean, really, Bentley?"

Bentley was silent for a long time.

"Macbean, tell me the truth. He's gone, isn't he?"

"Bentley. Try to understand. You made him into a newer, better version of yourself. He's a man on a mission. He'll never be gone."

Chapter 48

Karolovsky never called.

After days of not hearing from him, Vladoseev concluded his friend had died or been taken into custody. He had few resources in Europe and after contacting Arnie all he could learn was that he gave Karolovsky the supplies he requested and even helped with the abduction of the man at the clinic by driving the truck and posing as a DHL delivery man. After that Karolovsky had dropped him off and he saw no more of him, however the body of a man matching his description washed up near Rhineuferweg. Police were still investigating.

Losing his friend was a disaster that overshadowed his failure with Wylie Schram.

It took days to sort all the cyber mischief Schram had done to his bank accounts and financial holdings. The pain of losing millions of dollars still hurt and it was a bloody nuisance to have to watch his money like a *yastreb*, to keep it from happening again.

Repeated calls to Bentley went unanswered.

His doorbell rang.

Living in the Barclay Hotel had its privileges, one of which was not having to answer the door to his penthouse.

His butler announced, "Sir, your dinner is here." He pushed an ornate cart into the room.

Vladoseev sat down and sipped from a crystal flute of champagne. He spooned caviar from an iced silver dish onto a piece of toast. Even the champagne and caviar could not dispel the gloom he felt over losing his best friend. Vladoseev took another bite and a sip.

He felt a slight constriction to his throat and wiped his mouth with a napkin. He sneezed. His depression repressed his appetite but he took another sip of champagne and another bite of caviar. He could smell the aroma of roasted meat coming from his cart.

He sneezed again. He tried to take a deep breath. His lungs shook with minor tremors. Now he had difficulty breathing. He tried to breathe again but his chest wouldn't expand. His first thought was get a sip of water. He tried to sip from the glass of iced water. It sputtered in his mouth. He couldn't swallow. Another sip followed by a fit of coughing. Air came out of his lungs but wouldn't go in.

He clutched at his now hammering heart.

The butler came in and saw immediately the distress he was in. Vladoseev grabbed at his collar and spilled sideways out of his chair onto the floor. The butler tried CPR. He pounded Vladoseev's chest and applied mouth to mouth resuscitation.

He dialed 911 and called for an ambulance.

The paramedics arrived in less than five minutes. The butler marveled at their efficiency. The lead paramedic team appeared to be highly competent. In just a few minutes they had Vladoseev loaded on a stretcher and out the door.

On the bottom floor of the Barclay Hotel, a few onlookers watched them load the stretcher into the ambulance. Headlights came on, whirling red and white flashing lights and the sound of a siren spit the night.

A light drizzle fell as the ambulance sped away on East 48th street.

After a mile, the ambulance driver turned off the siren and the flashing lights and slowed his pace. In the passenger seat, Zinsser turned and looked back at the man on the stretcher. There was no movement. No breathing. Nothing but a shape.

He took out his cell phone and sent a text message.

"Done."

Chapter 49

From the journal of Brendan Macbean:
Bettye lasted eighteen days at St. Agatha's before SP-8 arrived.

For several days after our reunion, she remained in bed gathering her strength. Every day I'd arrive in her room as early as the hospital staff would let me. We'd drink coffee together and sometimes I'd bring pastries from a French bakery I found between St Agatha's and Haus Von Muller. Her French jingoism made her wrinkle her nose at the Swiss version of French pastries, but I loved her anyway.

That first week she divided her time between Dr. Friedkin's magic and working out in the health spa. She exercised to get her muscle tone back and build her strength. Finally the day came when we celebrated her recovery by going out to dinner. Afterward, against strict orders to return her promptly to St. Agatha's I snuck her into Von Muller Haus and we made glorious love, just like people in love and happy to be alive.

As incredible as it may seem, we ignored the fact that Bettye had cancer.

We went on picnics and tours of the region, including a river trip to Kreuzlingen.

Each day it seemed like Bettye improved. Her hollowed cheeks filled out. She gained strength at an astonishing rate. At the end of two weeks, she was almost as I remembered her... except her lustrous auburn hair remained a short, peppered gray.

On day nineteen, Dr. Bauerle summoned us to her office. Bettye and I sat in front of her desk and held hands between our chairs. I cautioned myself about the possibility of bad news, but Bauerle smiled with excitement.

"Bettye, Brendan, I have bad news and good news. We have run tests all night and we are astonished by the results."

Bettye would never warm up to Dr. Bauerle. She was convinced the beautiful doctor had a crush on me and all my denials did nothing but more firmly entrench her conviction. So I was one who had to do the talking.

"Yes, Dr. Bauerle?"

"Well, the bad news is that Bettye has progressed through all the eight types of semaphorin. Our tests confirm that she is definitely expressing SP-8. Bettye should be showing signs of tumor growth, but we're unable to detect any tumors at all. We have been experimenting... a new form of nucleic-synapse manipulation."

Dr. Bauerle took a deep breath. "And it appears to be working."

Dr. Bauerle suddenly shed her iron reserve. She leapt up behind her desk and clapped her hands together making a noise like a firecracker. Bettye sat like a rock but I jumped.

What Dr. Bauerle just told us was too monumental to react to.

I sat like a dumbass and said nothing. Bettye gripped my hand with painful strength.

She leaned forward and asked in a whisper. "Dr. Bauerle. Does this mean I will not die?"

Bauerle frowned but it was a frown of concern, not sadness.

"Bettye, we can't be certain. We need to run more tests, of course."

"Of course," Bettye and I said together. We both laughed nervously.

"Dr. Bauerle, are there more prototypes?"

"We don't know. We have entered a new phase. We must run more tests."

Smiles bloomed on our faces like time lapse images of flowers.

"Dr. Bauerle, I think Bettye will agree to all the tests you want to run, but we're going to make some procedural changes.

"Yes, Mr. Macbean?"

"First thing, I'm moving Bettye into Von Muller for a while. We're through with hospitals unless 'you have to run some tests.' In the near future, we might even take the train to Paris if it's okay with you."

"Yes, Mr. Macbean."

I stood up, turned and looked at Bettye.

"Bettye Baby, forgive me but I'm going to do something that will embarrass us all and probably piss you off."

Bettye gave me concerned look.

I went around Bauerle's desk and gave her a hug. She returned the hug and kissed me full on the lips. We were soon joined by Bettye who draped her newly muscled arms around us both. Bauerle and I broke and wrapped Bettye into our three-way and we all held each other for a long time.

It struck me while in this marvelous embrace that the three of us had elevated ourselves to the level of happiness one senses in kittens, puppies and babies. The specter of death lifts for a moment and you can see possibilities and a future. With an adult's caution I knew before us lay the possibility for both pain and joy and I didn't know which came next. A dragon had been slain but more dragons still lurked out there.

Bettye and Bauerle began chatting it up in French. Apparently Bettye's antagonism toward the beautiful doctor had receded.

I didn't follow their conversation at all, but I started wondering.

Could I be this lucky? Could this be happening?

Was I smart enough to accept what was coming?

I didn't know if we had another week or a month or even if, miraculously, we had a cure. But for now Bettye was going to live.

I still had a mission but at this moment I needed to give my new life everything I had.

For as long as it lasted, such a life would be too full to think much about Daniel Conklin.

Or Bentley.

Or the money.

Now I could start making plans.

END

Author's Note and Acknowledgements

Breast cancer is a horrible, tragic disease that affects millions of women worldwide. The courageous women who battle this disease on a daily basis deserve our admiration. The valiant efforts of the medical and scientific community who tirelessly search for a cure deserve our gratitude and support.

I found it extremely difficult to write this novel. The idea for the story formed in my head years ago. It seemed hardly a month went by without hearing of another friend or family member battling the disease. We all know someone who has been through the fight. Cancer and its many forms strike everywhere.

My older brother William died on January 21, 2011 of another form of cancer. When I began the writing of Next to Life Itself, I did not have the overwhelming experience of standing by my brother's hospital bed while all powerful medical science could do nothing but make him comfortable until the sands of his hourglass drained out. His last words to me were, "Nobody's perfect." And I knew he meant those words for himself and for me.

The nature of this deadly disease seems to make the other villains in the story less evil. Even villains have to face their own mortality. Cancer victims and their families endure the exhausting battle to live, while facing all the other exigencies of life. The prospect of death makes what would otherwise be compelling problems less urgent, like loneliness, kidnapping, torture and all powerful government agents.

It is difficult for anyone who is healthy and alive to stand next to someone who is headed into the tunnel of the afterlife. We are not made to die. Rather, we are made to live and want to live. Most of us will cling to life with our last shred of hope and energy and strength. And yet if life has taught us anything, we know we will all face this deeply personal experience.

Alas, medical science has no treatment like the one described in this book. Science has studied all of the techniques described here but has not produced anything like what Dr. Friedkin came up with. Lacking the expertise to write a medical thriller or a scientific paper, I tried to add just enough realism for a novel. I am extremely indebted to many who have shared their knowledge. I would like to thank Dr. Charles Taylor, Dr. Salaam Seeman, Dr. Ross Grumet, Dr. Amy Holland and many others. Their help has made this a more believable story. Any technical errors are all mine.

I am indebted to Jose Silva, the developer of Silva Mind Control. His methods provide much more than a clever way for the protagonist to work out a problem. Silva has shown the way for anyone to improve their life. I urge you to read about Silva's work.

I have to mention the wonderful people at WXIA, the NBC affiliate in Atlanta, specifically Ted Hall, a terrific news anchor and Brenda Wood, who could easily stand in for Shelby. WXIA's highly professional news crew generously gave of their valuable time and helped an unknown writer make his novel more believable.

I want to thank my family, specifically my daughter Kira and my son Luke.

Kira is an inspiration to everyone who knows her. Kira is an award winning teacher who has taught thousands of children the joys of reading and the value of exercise. Additionally Kira has helped thousands of adults achieve their goals of long distance running. Kira is always the first to read my drafts and her red pen is relentless.

Son Luke is my trusted advisor. Not only has he guided me through the vicissitudes of popular culture, he is a ready wall to bounce story lines off of and an erudite philosopher. His insight helps me mold my crazy ideas into better novels.

Last and by no means least my dear wife Jean. Her faith in me substantially exceeds my own. I'd be lost without her energizing encouragement.

I am inspired by those who have stared into the tunnel of the afterlife, and have gone through or battled back, to stand next to life itself for a while longer. Priscilla Jones Harris, Susan Stickley, Elaine Dominy, Ellen McMullan, Paulette Mathews, Sidney Blanchard Smith, Sheryl Hall Wittig, Jane Gardner Preston and many, indeed too many more.

Next to Life Itself

CPSIA information can be obtained
at www.ICGtesting.com
Printed in the USA
FSHW021714211220
76897FS